# SOMEWHERE IN THE STARS

ESSENTIAL PROSE SERIES 141

# SOMEWHERE IN THE STARS

Frank Polizzi

GUERNICA
TORONTO—BUFFALO—LANCASTER (U.K.)
2017

Michael Mirolla, editor
Interior layout: Jill Ronsley, Sun Editing & Book Design
Cover design: Allen Jomoc Jr.

Guernica Editions Inc.
1569 Heritage Way, Oakville, (ON), Canada L6M 2Z7
2250 Military Road, Tonawanda, N.Y. 14150-6000 U.S.A.
www.guernicaeditions.com

Distributors:
University of Toronto Press Distribution,
5201 Dufferin Street, Toronto (ON), Canada M3H 5T8
Gazelle Book Services, White Cross Mills
High Town, Lancaster LA1 4XS U.K.

First edition.
Printed in Canada.

Legal Deposit—Third Quarter
Library of Congress Catalog Card Number: 2017938078
Library and Archives Canada Cataloguing in Publication
Polizzi, Frank, author
Somewhere in the stars / Frank Polizzi. -- 1st edition.

(Essential prose series ; 141)
Issued in print and electronic formats.
ISBN 978-1-77183-233-5 (softcover).--
ISBN 978-1-77183-234-2 (EPUB).--
ISBN 978-1-77183-235-9 (Kindle)

I. Title. II. Series: Essential prose series ; 141

PS3616.O42S66 2017 813'.6 C2017-902333-0
C2017-902334-9

*This novel is a tribute to my uncle, Nicholas Sparta, who was wounded while serving in a tank squadron during the Italian Campaign of World War II.*

# I

Nick could see the Coit Tower spiraling its way out of the fog, as he leaned on the railing at the epicenter of the Golden Gate Bridge, his eyes blinking then closing, a salty brine massaging his face, finding himself adrift like so many sloops on the sea or barges on a river. As a child he remembered when *Papà* would take him sailing in the San Francisco Harbor, the city rising in blue-green sea water, flanked by its bridges linking all the Bay Area, everything in motion, ships coming in and fishing boats going out, an occasional Navy boat patrolling, people walking along the shore and matchbox-size cars chasing each other across the bridges. *Papà*'s face was brown and wrinkled, his hands swollen and chapped from netting fish, contrasted by his jet-black hair, slicked back with pomade, and his light blue eyes that shined with kindness, even when he scolded his son for being a *muschitta*.

By the time Nick was a teenager, *Papà* stationed him on the rudder. His father relied on the sea, negotiating the high and low of tides and the tidal forces of nature, saying these things would help Nick navigate life. He trusted his son so much at the helm that he could shut his eyes, feel the warmth of the sun, the smell of a saline sea, something he could never do on his purse seiner searching for the mother lode of sardines. He would recount many tales of his voyages, at an age for Nick when stories could be repeated. One time, after they left the safety of the bay, on a calm and blue sky afternoon, *Papà* ordered his son to turn the sailboat around, to Nick's objections on the way back home, and when they first saw the international orange towers of the bridge, the waves began to swell above their heads, the winds howling as they slid into the bay water. *Papà* taught Nick about other things like the stars and how they were more than astrological signs, these pointed lights showing the right direction if one knew how to read them. Everything natural mattered to a fisherman and, like his father, if Nick couldn't be on the water, he liked to be near the sea or above it, riding his bike on the walkway of any bridge.

Nick's eyes opened wide at the edge of his country, high above the smokestacks of a Cunard ocean liner entering the bay, and slowly hummed the melody of Woody Guthrie's "This Land Is Your Land," a song often played on the radio he loved to listen to at home in North Beach. It was as if the words were on a ball undulating on nature's grey screen, before disappearing precipitant into the sea. Nick loved the tune but didn't believe it was about him—an American-born guy, but still having that foreign look, that Mediterranean look—*una faccia, una razza,* an old Italo-Greek saying, "one face, one race."

Only nine days before, a cataract of black smoke had zigzagged in funnels across the sky of Pearl Harbor and Nick was stunned just like everyone else across America. Though over two thousand miles away from the Hawaii Territory, he knew that things in his life were never going to be the same and temporarily lost the ability to form lucid words about what was happening. He stammered sounds that echoed scant meaning, while his thoughts turned murky as the fog that encircled him, the remaining lyrics of that folk song opaque.

There was a sudden clearing on the water underneath him and within a short while a US Naval destroyer cruised through the channel of the bay. Before it reached Fisherman's Wharf, Nick pulled out his mother's opera glasses to get a closer look. As the destroyer slowed down, it looked as if all the purse seiners were chugging away from the dock, one after the other, following the warship like ducklings to Treasure Island, his father's being the last one, judging by its height and wide frame. When Nick could no longer see his father's boat, he became anxious, as if the scene were some blurry mirage right out of a Hollywood movie. Surely it was a sleight of hand, a magician's fingers sprinkling over a puff of smoke and all is vanished. But he could not mistake *Papà*'s boat. Five minutes later, Nick hopped on his maroon cruiser, designed to look like a motorcycle, and cycled as fast as his legs could pump, hitting his first hill near

Fisherman's Wharf. He dodged a trolley clanging him out of the way, made it to Columbus Avenue, turning left on Filbert Street, passing Saints Peter and Paul Church as he crossed himself and made it back home several blocks away.

He carried his bike up the stairs and leaned it in the corner, then ran into their Victorian style house, calling out: "*Mamma*!"

His mother, Lucia, came out of the kitchen, wiping her hands on her apron. "*Nicolo, chi cosa*? Why you no in *scuola*?"

"It's a Reading Day before exams," he said, rushing the words in between breaths.

"Then, why you no study?"

"Forget it, *Mamma*. You know I get high grades. For Christ's sake, it's about *Papà*! I saw him sailing away from the dock. All the fishing boats left."

"*Allura*," she said, glancing at the wooden clock on the mantle. "Maybe they have to go to some place special to fixa them."

"It's too early for something like that. Aren't they supposed to sell off all the fish first?"

Lucia averted her eyes from Nick. "*Chi sacciu*?" His mother had always relished life in the neighborhood, but suspicious things were happening all around her now and she didn't seem to grasp it, or maybe it was her inbred, Sicilian survival skill when overwhelmed. She appeared smaller in her five foot two frame, streaks of gray suddenly poking through her black hair. His mother looked scared but wasn't saying anything, always trying to protect her son.

That afternoon the door creaked opened and his barrel-chested father walked in and, before he took his first step up the stairs, Lucia called out, while Nick stood behind her: "Gaetano, what happened to your boat?"

"I saw you from the bridge, *Papà*," Nick interrupted, as he watched his father speak with his eyes to Lucia, warning it was not the right time.

"Somethin' bad happened!" Lucia said, her hands on her hips.

Gaetano plunked on the first step. "*Nenti*."

"*Papà*, I saw the destroyer."

"Since when does stranger tella you what to do with your boat?" Lucia insisted. "Who is this *scanusciutu* anyway?"

"An officer from the Coast Guard spoke to me privately at the dock." He looked at the wall. "The word spread around."

Her eyes widened. "You never have trouble with them before."

"*Basta*!" He flicked his fingers under his chin.

"So when you get your boat back then?"

"I'll figure somethin' out."

"You always saya that."

"*Papà*, were they looking for Japs?"

"You read too many newspapers, *figghiu miu*." His father grinned but Nick could see through his feigned expression, while Lucia placed her palm on her cheek as if she were holding up her face. "*Allura*, why don't help your *Mamma* get ready for your birthday party tonight?" he said before climbing the stairs to wash away the reek of fish.

Lucia turned towards Nick, looking even more fearful than before. "I didn't want to tella your father to upset him, but Giuseppina next door told me that her husband was fired from his job on Montgomery Street. Somethin' about his being Italian and the war. She only told me because I saw her cryin' in the backyard."

"That's *pazzu*, *Mamma*. When is the next shoe going to drop?" It pleased Nick that she shared her secret with him, something she would not have done before. His mother's face looked flushed with grief, making his stomach feel weak, as if he might puke any minute. He tried to fathom his parents' past life, bounced around like cargo poorly fastened to the deck, leaving the fishing village, Sciacca, in Western Sicily for the port of Palermo, then Naples, the ocean liner hub for the Americas, dropped off like baggage in Brooklyn, the gateway to the United States, and eventually third class by rail to the San Francisco Bay Area with plenty of fish filling his nets, now more quicksilver than all the silver that had come their way after such a long journey.

"I shouldn't have brought it up." She smiled. "I don't need your help. It's your special day—I can't believe you're eighteen. My handsome son." She patted him on the face. "How did you ever get to be six feet, *Madonna*?" She left him standing alone in the living room. He turned on the radio, hoping to catch some big band jazz, anything to lighten up his 'special day.'

In the evening Gaetano instructed Nick to open the shed house. His crew had just arrived and he ordered his mates to step lively into the backyard, as if he were still on his purse seiner. His father twisted his bushy moustache, while the men brought in a makeshift table of long boards to be placed together over wooden horses, since the dining room table would not be long enough. Nick grabbed some of the heavier pieces under the watchful eye of his father.

*Zia* Concetta had joined her sister in the kitchen but Lucia ruled her domain without a cookbook on the shelf. Everyone in the family, even the neighbors, agreed that Lucia's sardine sauce was the best. Maria, *Zia* Concetta's dark-haired daughter, maneuvered around the kitchen, rinsing, peeling and chopping. Nick peeked into the kitchen to assess the assembly line of ingredients for a menu of varied *antipasti*, the *primo*, *pasta alla Norma* for the children and *pasta cu li sardi* for the adults, to be followed by the *secondo*, featuring platters of both veal and swordfish *spiedini* with *spinaci* and *patate alla siciliana* as *contorni*, rounded off with *espresso*, fruits, nuts and *gelato* for the children. *Ziu* Francesco had made his own red wine from *Primitivo* grapes. Nick's uncle carried a wooden crate of jugs from his cellar into their house, placing it on the floor of the kitchen, his *bambini*, little Francesco and his sister, Vincenza, in tow, gawking at the piles of food.

As the guests settled around a table that now extended all the way into the living room, a parade of food followed. Nick felt it could have been a celebration for the feast of *Santa Rosalia*, judging by the excitement over the colorful display of food. He made it a point to be solicitous to the old Sicilian men, who reminded him of his father. He knew the fishermen did not want to mention aloud that their livelihood had just been abducted. That would be bad manners or worse, *sfortuna*—bad luck. No need for any *malocchio*, the evil eye, to ogle at Nick on his birthday. Instead, the fishermen spun tales and gestured their way through the past for Nick, tales of the *Mediterraneo* and the Pacific coast and how they were finally able to make good money in America, netting schools of sardines spotted in the dead of night by their telltale, phosphorescent glow.

Nick devoured their stories, suspecting they might be the last he would ever hear, eyeing his father at the head of the table as he sat in silence. He was amazed that his father's expression revealed no anxiety, but then who wanted to lose face in front of guests? Nick kept up with their wine consumption and prayed nothing embarrassing would spill out from all the banter. He swore he heard whispers in *Sicilianu* about the missing fishing boats, when all of sudden everyone raised their glasses to joyful cries of *Buon compleanu*! *Cent'anni*! *Nicolo—sicilianu-americanu*! He felt self-conscious everyone was celebrating in his honor, just because he happened to have been born. Nick panned the faces of his parents, relatives and *paesani*. Narcissism got the better of him. He wanted to freeze this friggin' Frank Capra moment for what it was worth.

After the *espresso* and Sambuca Manzi, Nick worked the table, lavishing attention on his uncle's family, making the children, Francesco and Vincenza, giggle with light teasing. *Cuginu* Paul joined up with Nick when he went over to Maria. Nick held her hand. "Maria, you are a *bella donna*. I cannot believe my eyes. You have been sent from heaven to make the boys go wild."

Maria poked him. "*Pregu*, *Nicolo*, you are embarrassing me in front of everyone. You and my brother have been drinking too much of *Papà*'s wine."

"Come on, sis. Don't be so snooty," Paul interjected as he tugged her hair.

"Leave her alone, *cuginu*. I started it."

"Why don't we scram from here and hang one on?" Nick's eyes brightened as Paul added in a low voice: "Maybe we'll pick up a couple of broads for your birthday." Maria got up in disgust and sat near her mother. "Let's act like we're looking for some more food in the kitchen and we'll give everyone the slip. Whaddaya say, *cuginu*?" Paul blessed Nick's forehead with wine like a priest spreading holy water in church.

"Sure, why not?"

The *cugini* hopped a bus on Columbus Avenue and zigzagged their way to Jack's Tavern in the Lower Haight section, which was one of the few places in town that catered to Negroes. Nick looked around the crowded place dotted with cabaret tables lit by small table lamps, a cloud of smoke hanging over the customers' heads and wafting its smell of nicotine mixed with a more pungent odor. It was cheaper to sit at the bar, so they plunked onto the bar stools, placing some cash on the counter. The Negro bartender gave

Nick and Paul the once over but didn't bother to proof them. The music set was just ending with a looser version of swing, not arranged like the big bands. Nick preferred swing any way it was played.

"What'll you all have tonight?"

"A boiler maker," Paul quipped as Nick frowned. "Ah, make that two for us." Paul poked Nick in the ribs.

"You want it mixed, young man, or a shot and a beer."

"Don't mix it."

"We already had a lot of *vinu*, Paul," Nick exclaimed as the bartender stepped away to pull the lever on the tap beer.

"It's your birthday, pal. We got a lot to celebrate." They stared at each other in the oversized mirror hanging on the wall. The bartender placed the beers down and poured the whiskey. They clinked shot glasses and drank some. "Feels nice and warm inside, Nick. It's been awhile since we spent some time together."

Nick drank his beer watching his cousin and he thought about growing up without siblings, one of the many things that made him feel different in North Beach, filled with large families of Italian immigrants, first coming from Genoa and Tuscany, followed by Sicily and Calabria. Emotional ties between Paul and him went way back. His *cuginu* was more like a brother, replete with all the ribbing, but once out of grammar school, Nick wound up in Saint Ignatius High School run by the Jesuits and Paul, Samuel Gompers Trade School, and that's when things changed.

Paul motioned to the bartender for another round, tapping his glass. As soon as the bartender set the drinks on the counter, they gulped them down.

"Enlisted in the Army the other day." Paul punched the palm of his hand. "Set the date." The bartender wiped down the bar and pretended he wasn't listening. The next set began and Paul bobbed his head to rhythm of R&B, leaning on the bar with his short, wiry frame.

"You joined up!" Nick raised his voice over the music. "I thought you were going to wait till you got drafted."

"I was gonna surprise you with the news at the party, but didn't wanna rain on your parade."

"Weren't you supposed to help your father expand the business? Be a partner someday."

"Look, I wanna show everyone I'm a real American, not some guinea kid who thought Mussolini was a big deal."

"When you going in?"

"June! Right after I graduate."

"You're not going on some school trip, you know." Paul looked away and Nick wondered how carefully his cousin thought this through. "I'll buy the next round, *cuginu*."

"A double for me. So what are you gonna do?"

"What?"

"You know, Uncle Sam," Paul shouted.

Nick shrugged and lit up a Lucky Strike, as his cousin downed his double. Paul ordered several more shots for himself, but Nick waved off the bartender, nursing his second shot. About midway through the set, Paul staggered over to the side of the stage so he could get a better view of the drummer. A halo of smoke began to form above Nick's head, while he pondered Paul's declaration. Nick had mixed feelings about going to war against Italians. He really couldn't figure out what he should do. He could hear Negroes in the audience slipping in calls of 'play it' to the musicians who added their own riffs. He welcomed the distraction until it wore off and ruminated some more—just wait to be called up and then sort things out. Though Nick admired Paul's moxie, he wasn't convinced he should follow him, in anything for that matter. He watched the Negro bartender cheerfully serving drinks, a face that revealed he must have been doing this a long time. When the band was finishing its last number, the bartender came over and asked Nick if he wanted another drink, but he shook his head no.

"What's the matter, son?" Nick acted like he didn't hear him. "Worried about your sidekick?"

"Yeah, you know, the war." Nick took one last drag and rubbed it out in a crowded ashtray. "Could I have a glass of water?"

The bartender poured the water and placed a few ice cubes in it. "Where you from, son?" Nick sipped the water.

"From North Beach."

"That's where all the eye-talians live. Where your folks from?"

"Sicily."

"I'll bet you have some of those big family dinners every Sunday."

"How did you know that?"

"I used to live in New Orleans. Plenty of Sicilians there."

"To tell the truth, I don't know much about Negroes, except for jazz." Nick finished off the water. "Do you have family get togethers?"

"Sometimes we have reunions in Louisiana."

"What do you eat?"

The bartender smiled. "We have some helluva fine parties, let me tell you, with all that great food, that makes your mouth water just thinking about it. You know, one of those southern Bar B Qs."

"What's that?"

The bartender laughed. "You sure haven't been around much, have you, son? It's when you set a big grill with wood chips or charcoal, smoking and slow-cooking pork. And some special, secret sauces to go with it."

"Oh, I get it but I never had that kind of food."

"You'll have to get some real soon."

"You ever have *caponata*?"

"Capo what?"

"It is very good. You can trust me. Eggplant, onions, celery, tomatoes, capers, olives." The bartender scratched his head. "My *Mamma* makes it."

"Well, son, if you say your mama cooks it, then I'll have to try it some time."

"It's special—a secret family recipe."

"I get it." The bartender smiled broadly. Nick stood up on his toes to see what his cousin was up to. "Son!" Nick glanced back. "You said before that your folks were Sicilian." He nodded. "I saw some terrible things down south when I was a child." The bartender swiped the bar with a towel. "Let me tell you, lynching is not a pretty sight." Nick winced. "But I'm not talkin' about my people. They went after yours, too. Whether you is black or white, dangling from some danged lamppost is not something you ever want to come across. Watch out for yourself. That's all I'm sayin'."

A customer called the bartender away, leaving Nick to sort things out, and when he came back, the bartender poured Nick a shot on the house, something he needed after the warning he just received. He drank it right down.

"The set's over. You'd better go help your friend. Looks like he's soused."

Nick moved a few feet away, turned and called out: "I'll bring a jar of *caponata* next time I come here."

The bartender shook his head. "Go take care of that boy."

As soon as they stepped outside, a cloudburst soaked their clothes, so now Paul was doubly soused without any awareness of either. The bus was out of the question and Nick got lucky, hailing a lone cab passing by on Sutter Street. The cabbie gave Paul the once-over but let them in because Nick acted halfway normal. They got back late so Nick figured he'd stash his cousin on the floor of his bedroom, so as not to burn up *Ziu* Francesco, an uncle he admired since he was a kid for turning a fruit stand into a bustling *alimentari* in the heart of North Beach. Paul leaned on his cousin's shoulder the whole ride and sleepwalked out of the cab. Nick managed to lug him up the stairs, making it into the room without waking his parents. With many contorted moves, he coaxed Paul into dry boxer shorts and a white sleeveless undershirt and did the same for himself without his usual dexterity. Pellets of rain continued to hit Nick's window, the sound pinging in his subconscious. It took time for him to relax and fall asleep.

The pounding on the front door sounded so deafening in the dead of night that Nick thought that the San Andreas Fault was splitting. The door hadn't opened fast enough, so down it crashed as men surged into the house, white profiles in sharp relief to their black fedoras and dark suits. Gaetano had grabbed his son's old baseball bat from under the bed and raced downstairs, eyes bulging, nostrils flaring.

Nick heard his father yelling, "Get the hella out of here," while the ornate porcelain lamp smashed into slivers all over the floor. Nick and his mother now stood at the top of the stairs. *Madonna!*" Lucia screamed. "What are you doin' to my husband?" His mother crossed herself, while one of the intruders wrestled with Gaetano, both knocking over a table. Nick flung himself down several steps at a time to the bottom but two burly men snagged him. He saw that it was hopeless as a six-foot-four agent flashed his FBI badge and hollered: "We have a Federal Warrant for the arrest of Gaetano Spataro!" Nick couldn't grasp why his father was being arrested.

Paul spilled out of the bedroom, still groggy from all the alcohol and squinted from the banister. He sidestepped around his aunt, gripping the banister all the way down. "What the hell you doin'?" he slurred to the head agent.

"Get a hold of yourself, young man. We need to take Mr. Spataro in for questioning."

"What's my father being charged with?" Nick demanded over the shoulders of the men blocking him.

"Your father's an enemy alien." The head agent motioned to several other agents, who ransacked the house for radios, flashlights, cameras and binoculars. His mother looked on in horror, while Paul gaped in confusion. Nick wondered what the hell these men were thinking his family might do with these everyday items. After the search was complete, not one piece of furniture stood in its rightful place. The family trailed the posse out of the house and down the stoop, the rain a filmy mist on their faces as they watched an agent push Gaetano's head under the roof of the black, Ford sedan.

Nick stood on the sidewalk barefoot in his underwear, while Paul leaned against his cousin, Lucia kneeling alone on the sidewalk, her hands raised to the predawn sky. Their neighbors peeked through the blinds and saw what had only been rumored in North Beach. At that moment Nick realized why his family home had been invaded—the contrast in their olive complexions was all the reason they needed. As the unmarked cars sped away, the wind chilled the air in the San Francisco Bay and they retreated inside, as the fog spread its cover around the town.

Lucia went into the kitchen to brew some coffee, while Nick and Paul straightened up the dining room. It wasn't long before they sat at the table, sipping some *caffè Americanu.*

"*Chi facemu ora, Nicolo*?"

"I don't know *Mamma*."

"It's a damn shame, them haulin' *Ziu* Gaetano away like that," Paul said.

"Just because we're at war don't mean the FBI got a right to arrest him."

"You don't think I'm angry, too. I'm never gonna forget this!"

"We will be *mischinu* in North Beach," Lucia cried out.

"*Mamma*, we have nothing to be ashamed of."

"People will talka."

"We'll get a lawyer. He'll fix everything. *Va beni*?"

"*Figghiu miu*!" Lucia kissed Nick and wiped her tears away with her palm.

"Yeah, *cuginu*, get a good mouthpiece."

Nick knew things were not going to be that simple freeing his father. It would be difficult finding a lawyer who knew had to handle a case like this, and besides, there wouldn't be much money to go around, since the fishing boat disappeared, just like his father. Nick felt that things didn't add up—there was a hysteria building up with the Japs. Not that anyone didn't have a right to be scared after all those sailors were killed in Pearl Harbor, but why pick on his father? He was an honest, hard working *Sicilianu,* someone who loved his family, even America, despite its *stranu* ways. And *Mamma* was so ashamed that the Feds arrested *Papà*, muttering 'Not to say nothin' to nobody' and 'Not a word outside *nostra casa*'.

The more Nick thought about his father's arrest though, the angrier he got, recalling all the 'just kidding' slights and actual skirmishes he had with the so-called real Americans while growing up. His job was to get his father out, and then he would deal with the war. A few days later, his mother received a brief call from her husband, letting her know that *Papà* would be held indefinitely but he didn't understand why.

* * *

Several weeks had passed when Nick came back from his after-school job at his uncle's *alimentari* and found his mother rocking back and forth in her chair.

"*Mamma*, what's the matter?"

"*Papà* no comin' back. Twenty years we been married!" She clasped her hands, her eyes red and wet. He saw a letter in her lap.

"Let me read the letter. You must be mixing up the English." She handed it to Nick, who studied the writing for any key words of condemnation for his father.

"*Papà* has been moved to another Immigration Service facility on Angel Island." Nick looked up from the letter. "Sounds like a detention center to me." Lucia let out a cry. "*Mi dispiaci, Mamma*." Nick ran his eyes over the letter again. "Says that Gaetano Spataro is on a list to be relocated to Fort Missoula, Montana, until further notice. It's got the seal of the Immigration and Naturalization Service. Geez, they're going to lock him up in a military prison."

"My poor husband." Lucia crossed herself. "Why they doa this thing to him?" she shouted as she rose from the chair. Nick grabbed his mother who was about to faint. He placed her on the couch, while he paced in front of her.

"Wacky things happening in this town," Nick said. But his mother was far away now, gazing at the rose medallion on the ceiling. Nick eyes watered up as he looked at a family picture on the wall above his mother's head. All three of them were smiling, as they posed in front of Gaetano's new purse seiner docked at Fisherman's Wharf. Nick knelt down next to his mother. "We'll see *Papà* before you know it. Don't you worry, *Mamma.*"

* * *

Arcuri's office looked like a mess but Nick didn't have much of a choice. The lawyer motioned for Nick to sit and jotted down the details of the arrest on a yellow legal pad. After ascertaining important biographical details of Gaetano Spataro, he peered over his reading glasses.

"Kid, I have worked on many immigration cases and none of them are ever easy, but this is in another ball park." He took off his glasses and rubbed his eyes.

"What does …"

"This war is making the government short on reason. The Defense Department is sure that Tojo is going to hit the coast of California with everything they got, sooner or later."

"But what does this have to do with my father? He's no enemy alien. He loves this country."

"That doesn't make him a legal citizen. It doesn't look good for your pop."

"Why not?"

"He won't be facing a judge in civilian court. It's called an Enemy Alien Hearing. Heard about it from a judge friend of mine. Two military officers and two professional citizens. No counsel will be allowed in at these Justice Department Detention Camps." The lawyer stood up and looked out the window at the swift, dark gray clouds. "All I can do is send in a testimonial to his trustworthiness"—Arcuri turned to Nick—"and hope it persuades the hearing board to release your father."

"Once you do that, everything will be fine, right?" Nick jutted his chin out. "My father is well-respected in North Beach, you know."

"I get the picture, Nick, but the folks deciding your father's fate have heads as hard as a Louisville slugger."

Nick gazed down at his hands, squeezing them, when a hard rain began to fall outside the wide office window, streaking the gold letters of Arcuri's name.

"*Ascolta*! Your father belonged to the *Ex-Combattenti*, the Federation of Italian War Veterans in America, according to what you told me. That's the tip of the bat and I am afraid Gaetano is going to get hit in the head with it during the hearing."

Nick shot up. "Why is my father the fall guy?"

"I'll do my best, kid." Arcuri shook Nick's hand and walked him out the door. The door cracked shut, its sound bouncing off the terrazzo floor of the hallway. When he stepped onto the pavement, an abrupt burst of rain flowed into the street gutters, forcing the flotsam of North Beach down the hill all the way to the wharf like a line drive, the detritus floating with the current under the Golden Gate Bridge.

# II

Nick met his first Jewish friend at the Legion of Honor Museum in Lincoln Park, after his longest bike ride from North Beach. He wanted to distance himself from the spot where the Feds snatched his father away. Gaetano's absence changed the family conversation, pitching from melancholy to cacophony. He felt like Giufà the fool from the Sicilian folk tales his mother used to read to him. Just as the Spataros started to live well in America, now all he wanted to do was run away from home and not face his mother crying, not deal with having *Papà* gone as if Gaetano *era mortu*—not even a stone marker in a cemetery for his family to pay their respects on a Sunday. His father disappeared on a night Nick would never forget. After skipping mass, he pedaled with a sea breeze pressing against his face, which brought him to a new place where he could lose himself.

The building was solid with a horizontal line of fluted columns in the style of Beaux Arts that Nick had read about, but to him it didn't appear to be a French palace set in California but rather a faraway Egyptian temple waiting for him to climb his way up. He wandered around the European paintings for awhile with no specific artist in mind, then sat on a bench and looked up in surprise at Fra Angelico's *The Meeting of Saint Francis and Saint Dominic*, a painter whom his Jesuit English teacher raved about in class. Nick was pleased that an Italian did the work and no one was about to take it away. From the corner of his eye he saw that there was another guy sitting at the other end, sketching profiles with a graphic pencil. Nick slid over about half way to get a better look and liked what he saw but didn't comment. Someone might be watching them and he didn't want to be taken for a queer. He could hear his friends from North Beach razzing him for being a *finocchio*. Nick thought *chi minchia*, what the fuck, and spoke up.

"You some kind of artist?"

"Nah, just copying from the experts," the young man said without looking up.

"Anyway, you're good at it." The young man kept working. "I bet you could do comic strips, like *The Phantom* or *Prince Valiant*."

Nathan jerked his head up, eyes sparkling. "I'd sure get my kicks out of that. On the up and up, I'd love to be good enough to do woodcuts someday. Even better, a wordless novel like Lynd Ward's."

"Never heard of him!"

"You're missing out on something. Get a copy of *God's Man* from the library. Each page comes alive without a single word, telling this swell story."

"Sounds hep."

"You a hep cat?"

"Love jazz—swing style."

The young man continued sketching, while Nick scrutinized the painting. A few minutes later, the young man turned to Nick. "What's your name anyway?"

"Nicolo Spataro, but you can call me Nick."

They shook hands. "I'm Nathan Fein. Nate for short. So what are you doing here, Nick? Homework assignment?"

"Art's in my blood—I'm Italian."

Nathan chuckled.

"You laughing at me? Got enough problems with my friends ragging me for coming here."

"I'm not laughing because you're Italian. Come on, I'm Jewish." He shaded in some background and then looked up again. "My pop's from Germany. Warned me about talking to strangers."

Nick laughed. "Just like my mom. They worry a lot about that stuff."

"They mean well but we're not kiddos anymore. You got any brothers or sisters?"

"Nah, only child."

"An Italian family!"

"That's why my friends think I'm a little *pazzu*." Nathan had a blank look. "Crazy. What about you?"

"*Pazzu*!" Nathan laughed and Nick joined in.

"You're a bit of joker. Like my cousin Paul, but smarter." Nick's eyes widened. "But don't tell him I said that."

"Mums the word."

"So, any brothers, sisters?"

"Got a kid sister, Deborah. She's sixteen and cute but a pain in the butt." Nathan closed his pad. "You know, I've been sketching all morning. Wanna get a Coke in the cafeteria?"

"Sure."

As they moved along the line, they picked up a bunch of cupcakes and some soda, paid and bolted to eat outside since the weather was mild for January. Nathan placed the tray on the table and they wolfed down the food. Nick thought what a great park to be in—grass and trees all around contrasted by the city skyline. He recalled all those views coming in on his bike—the green sea that changes to blue or gray depending on the day, Sausalito's wooded hillside, evergreen and deciduous, and the Golden Gate Bridge not gold at all but that distinctive orange. Like all the evolving colors he rode by, Nick discovered a new friend who was different, yet seemed much like him. Maybe it was their Mediterranean looks or just two *Americani* in some random moment.

"I think we made a mistake mixing coke with cupcakes. Should have been milk, Nate."

"It wouldn't look good." They finished the few pieces left. "My father always reminds me we have to make sacrifices in life." He noticed that Nick winced when he mentioned the word "father".

"Everything okay?"

"Nothing!"

"Your eyes drooped when I mentioned my father."

"Nah, it's nothing to do with your pop."

"I didn't mean to monkey into your business."

"Not a problem, Nate. It's just . . ."

"What?"

"I really shouldn't be spilling my guts out."

"I'm all ears."

"It's my *Papà*." Nick's eyes reddened. "The G-men took him away in the middle of the night."

"What the hell for?"

"I don't know. He's Italian born, *Sicilianu*. Didn't get his papers straightened out, or something like that." Nick squeezed his napkin into a ball.

"My neighborhood is right next to Japantown." Nick wiped his eyes with the napkin. "Just the other day, I saw with my own eyes, a long line of confused Japanese Americans standing next to a building on Bush Street. It didn't look like they were going on any holiday trip." Nick recalled Giuseppina's secret, while Nathan stacked the plates and glasses on the tray.

"I guess everybody's just jumpy," Nick said. "They arrest people who never hurt a fly. My pop's *bonu come il pane*." Nathan raised his eyebrows in a quick flash. "It means as a good as bread."

"Good as gold."

"I suppose that's close enough for around here. But I'm talking about a staple of life."

"You Christians would say, 'the salt of the earth,' Gospel According to Matthew."

"New Testament and you're Jewish. And I thought I was so smart going to a Jesuit school." Nathan laughed aloud. "How'd you get here anyway, Nate?"

"By bike."

"That's swell. We can ride back part of the way. But we'll have to go fast. I'm already late for Sunday dinner."

* * *

Nathan entered his family home acting like a rabbi contemplating a passage from the *Torah*. He wanted to fool his mother, so she wouldn't *kvetch* about where he had been all Sunday, not attending to his chores around the house.

"You're late! Put the paper away and eat your dinner before it gets cold," his mother, Rebecca, said shaking her head.

"Where's Father?"

"He had to work overtime today. Insisted I shouldn't hold up supper for him. He should only know that you weren't here either. Wash your hands first. Your sister's still playing with her food at the dining room table. Waiting for you, of course."

Nathan sat opposite Deborah who studied his expression.

"Where were you, Nate?"

"It's none of your business."

"Come on, don't be like that. Betcha you were in the museum again."

Nathan nodded yes. "Don't tell Mom!"

"I'm not going to squeal on you. Anything interesting happen?"

"Met a new friend." Nathan put his head down and ate the baked chicken leg with his fingers.

"Is he good looking?"

"How do I know, Deb?" He finished off the leg and scooped the mashed potatoes into his mouth.

"Well, didn't you spend time with him?" Nathan continued eating, thinking that his sister was more nosy than his parents, but he couldn't imagine not having her around, even though she was a girl. He felt sorry that Nick didn't have any siblings. "I mean, since you must've been with him awhile."

"Yeah, I guess you would say he's handsome. He's Italian. No, actually Nick would say Sicilian."

"How old is he?"

"He must be my age. What's with all the questions?"

Deborah's deep, blue eyes widened. "Nothing." She moved her mashed potatoes in a circle until her brother got up with his empty plate and she followed him into the kitchen.

They each washed their plates in turn. When the front door lock sprung open, Rebecca met her husband as he rushed into the apartment.

"What's wrong, Ernst? You don't look so hot."

"I didn't want to miss the President's broadcast." He kissed Rebecca on the cheek and plopped into his chair without taking off his jacket.

"Aren't you going to eat something?"

"I'll eat later. I must tell you something." He composed himself. "I picked up the *San Francisco Examiner* before I ate my lunch. There was this article about Peter Bergson. Ever heard of him?"

"Can't say I have? Should I know him?"

"He's a Zionist! Anyway, he gives these speeches in Union Square." Rebecca looked distracted when her children ambled into the room. "In New York City. He's been dishing out the truth about Hitler and what the Nazis have in store for us Jews." Ernst raised his voice. "Thinks we should form our own Jewish army."

"Ernst, please try to stay calm." Her eyes motioned towards their children.

Nathan's eyes were open with curiosity, while he noticed his sister was looking at the floor. His father didn't usually get animated about things, except when it came to workers' rights.

Rebecca raised both arms upward. "The whole world is going *meshugganah*! It's not good for your system to have supper so late. Besides, I waited for you to eat."

Nathan and Deborah had already stretched out on the floor in the living room near the radio listening to a swing band. After a quick meal in the dining room, their parents sat on two matching easy chairs in time for the *Fireside Chat* of President Roosevelt.

Nathan enjoyed his family tradition of gathering around their most valued possession, a mahogany, Capehart radio cabinet as big as a jukebox. They listened to the *Fireside Chats* on intermittent Sunday evenings ever since he was ten. They never missed one and hung on the President's every word, especially his father who was one of the lucky Jews to get out of Germany. After graduating Fredrich Wilhelm University in Berlin, he had married Rebecca Moretto.

Hyperinflation continued throughout 1923, so the Feins left on a ship from Bremen to New York City to meet up with a second cousin. They found their way to San Francisco where Ernst was offered a good job at a printer's shop.

Father maintained a measure of German pride when it came to science and music but fretted about the value of a dollar wherever he lived. His concern about money disappeared overnight with the onset of *Kristallnach,* shattering all his delusions about missing Berlin. Even though the Feins were safe in America, Nathan worried what would happen to his parents' relatives and friends in Germany and Italy. Just thinking about this rotten treatment unnerved Nathan and he couldn't imagine what it was like for his parents, who could picture everything in their heads better than a movie.

When President Roosevelt concluded his talk, Ernst shouted at the radio: "President Roosevelt, you should bomb the railroad tracks leading out of Germany." He shut the radio off. "The Nazis must be sending Jews and Socialists to hidden camps. I feel it in my bones."

Nathan asked: "What can be done, Father?"

"Their only hope is to get to Italy."

"What! That's crazy—Mussolini is waiting there for them. You always carry on about the damn Fascists, too."

"When I was at the University of Berlin, I spent a year at the *Università di Bologna* as an exchange student. That's where I met your mother." Rebecca smiled. "Experience tells me that the average Italian is not going to turn anybody in to the authorities, not even the Jews, especially if they're Italian." He turned to his wife. "Is that not true, Rebecca?"

"Yes, Italians don't trust the government."

"But how can you two be so sure?"

"Your mother's cousins from Venice have been dropping Ladino clues in their letters to avoid detection from the censors."

"What's going to happen to our family over there?" asked Deborah.

"Nothing good, Deborah," Ernst answered. "That you can be sure of." Ernst looked at Nathan. "What do they teach you anyway in school these days?" Deborah sat up. "When things get bad, everyone always blames the Jews, and we Germans were too stupid to realize that." Ernst stood up. "What's going to happen to my mother? My brother, his wife and children?" Deborah started crying and Nathan hugged his sister.

"You're making me have second thoughts about my family in Venice," Rebecca added. "Maybe the Nazis will be too strong in Italy. Ernst, didn't one of my cousins warn that a *Shoah* was coming? Or was it what's his name?"

"Peter Bergson. He's the one who said it. And Roosevelt's got to do something now, before it's too late." Ernst slumped into his chair.

"Maybe we should listen to some music," Nathan offered. He stepped over to the Capehart and turned the dial like he was cracking a safe to look for something that he knew his parents would love—a rebroadcast from the San Francisco Opera. "Father, listen! It's *The Barber of Seville*." It was one opera that could cheer Nathan up, even if he found it corny compared to jazz.

* * *

One day on a late Sunday afternoon in early March, Nathan and Nick met in Golden Gate Park to play a game of catch. Paul was supposed to meet up with them. The two had become fast friends and were at it for an hour, when they noticed a bunch of high school kids approaching. Nick thought they looked like a gang of Irish kids who could have been stand-in actors in the film series, *Dead End Kids*—several with cocked hats, others with mops of tousled hair, cigarettes dangling on their lips, all moving in a shifty pack. Nate had caught sight of them when he turned to see what Nick was staring at. He nonchalantly tossed the ball to Nick as if the approaching pack were looking for a picnic spot. He figured they came from the Sunset District but wasn't going to let them intimidate him. Everything was going fine as the pack passed and continued on their way, until the ball went over Nick's head and rolled near the ringleader who picked it up.

Nick turned his head and called out. "Throw it here, will ya!"

The ringleader laughed. "Thanks." He threw the ball to one of his stooges.

"Hey, that's my friend's ball. Come on, stop playing around."

"Who axed you anyway?"

The ringleader sent several of his boys over. The one with the ball walked up to Nathan. "Take it from me."

"Look, we're not looking for any trouble. Just give up the ball." Nick went to Nathan's side as the boys circled them.

"Yeah, just be a sport and return the ball," Nick said.

The boy with the ball shouted to the ringleader: "Hey Paddy, I think one of them is a kike." He pointed at Nick. "And this one here is definitely a dago." As soon as the boy turned around, Nathan pummeled his face, while Nick tackled another one to the ground. The big mouth was bleeding from his lips, lying dazed on the ground. Nick had a lock hold around the guy's neck, his legs twitching. In the meantime, the third guy began punching Nick in the back. Nathan pulled the guy away from Nick and when the kid turned around, Nathan left-jabbed him in the solar plexus and a right to the face. Down he went with the wind knocked out of him. The ringleader came running with his remaining friend. Nick released the guy who was gasping for breath and stood up to face the last two with Nathan.

Paul had taken in the action as he hiked out of an overgrown trail. He flew over to the scene, curve punched the ringleader on the side of his head and watched him tumble to the ground. His sidekick picked up the ringleader and they both ran away, the rest of the gang following, while the trio watched their every move as they fled. When they all caught up with the ringleader, he yelled from a safe distance: "Youse guys are goin' to get it later." They trotted back in the direction they came from. Nathan grabbed his glove and ball off the ground, tossed the ball up high and held his glove out until it popped in.

Nick shook his head. "Where the hell did you learn to box like that, Nate?"

"Right in the kisser!" Paul added, as he mimicked a crouched boxer.

"My track coach taught me after I took a licking from some punks. You guys weren't so bad either."

"Oh, this is my *cuginu*, Paul," Nick said, as they shook hands.

"Heard all about you."

"Hope it was somethin' good."

"Nick said you're a sharp guy." Paul eyed his cousin.

"What you say we scram," Nick advised. "I've seen these mugs before. Better believe they'll be back like a *vendetta*."

"My *cuginu*'s right," Paul said. "We were lucky this time."

"I know a fast way out of the park. We can hop a bus there before those palookas find us," Nathan said.

When they got on the bus, they stood in the back hanging onto the leather straps and remained quiet along the circuitous route until Nathan said: "Want to listen to some jazz at my house? We're almost there."

"I'm headin' back to the guys on the corner," Paul answered.

"What about you, Nick?"

"I don't know."

"My mom is a great baker."

"Okay, you won me over."

When they got to the house, Nathan's parents had already gone out for a walk. They sat around the kitchen table munching hunks of chocolate, blackout cake with glasses of milk. Deborah joined them but sat quietly. Nathan noticed his sister staring at Nick, who was busy eating.

"This cake is really good."

"I told you she could bake."

"It's true what my brother says."

"Oh Nick, this is my kid sister, Deborah." Nick stopped eating to look at her.

"I told my mom she should open a store. But she just laughs. Says working as a dressmaker suits her fine."

"Let's listen to my favorite jazz records before my parents get home. They get annoyed when I play the music loud." Nathan brought Nick into his room to show his collection, while Deborah leaned against the door.

"Wow, you have a lot of 78s!"

"Can I stay and listen, too?"

"Sure, Sis, but don't be a pest?" Deborah wrinkled her face at Nathan.

"Nick, how about Benny Goodman's 'Sing, Sing, Sing'?"

"Swing away, Nate."

At dusk the door lock snapped open and Nathan lowered the volume before his parents entered.

"Father! Mother! Meet my friend Nick. You know, the one I told you about from the museum." His parents shook hands with him.

"Would you like to stay for supper, young man?"

"No thanks, Mrs. Fein, my mother is expecting me home. I'm not allowed to miss meals with my family, unless it's some kind of emergency."

"Another time."

"Yes, ma'am."

When the door closed, Ernst said: "Nice Italian boy. It's good for you to have friends who are not Jewish. But never drop your guard, Nathan."

"Father, he's my friend."

"Yes and he's a dreamboat." Ernst stared at his daughter but said nothing.

* * *

In the beginning Deborah tagged along with Nick and her brother on the days when they weren't playing baseball with Paul. For Nick it started with her strawberry blond hair, curly and long. He sensed she was interested in him by the way her eyes followed his movement. This was a distraction that he needed, so he wouldn't have to think about what was going to happen next to his father, and then it turned into an attraction that Nick wasn't able to resist. Deborah was a girl Nick wanted to embrace and much more, after each tryst they managed to pull off.

Nathan had suspected all along and felt that Nick counted on 'mum's the word' from his buddy, but he was concerned about the consequences—losing his friend was not an option no matter what his father said. Nathan questioned his own Jewishness because he wanted to be a mainstream American, and Nick wished he were born Jewish, better yet an Italian Jew, when he considered what Mr. Fein would think if he knew his daughter was dating him, an Italian American and definitely not Jewish.

Nick and Deborah's favorite place was the San Francisco Botanical Garden in Golden Gate Park. One time after school, in early spring, they bypassed the Great Meadow while holding hands and followed a trail of various types of magnolia trees, the petals forming cumulus shapes, some pink, others white. They worked their way back to the Great Meadow and crossed through to a garden where the azaleas were changing from red to pink dots. When she let go of his hand to get a closer look, it reminded Nick of an impressionist painting with Deborah in the foreground. These images were stored in his memory bank to fall back on when he worried about his father.

"Deb, there are more private benches by the rhododendrons. Why don't we go there?" Deborah nodded yes. They sat behind a red-pink one, taller than Nick who hushed Deborah. "*Sa-wee, sa-sew*. Did you hear that song?"

"No, where is it?"

"Over there." He pointed to a branch of a nearby tree but the bird wasn't visible. "Do you hear it now?"

"*Sa-wee, sa-sew*."

"There's another somewhere behind us."

"Oh, yes. It's so beautiful. What type of bird is it?"

"A black phoebe. Look, he flew over our heads."

"*Sa-wee, sa-sew. Sa-wee, sa-sew.*"

"I think he found his mate, Deb."

"When did you become such a bird lover?"

"Rainy days at the library. I used to page through the colored plates of Audubon. Been tracking birds since grade school."

They shared some of her mother's *rugelach*. When they finished off the last piece, Deborah stroked the hair on Nick's forearm.

"Are you sure everything's okay with your father?" he asked.

"Don't worry about him. He used to be a socialist, you know." She patted his face. "You really are special, Nicky. I knew it from the moment I first saw you."

"You're like a *principessa* to me." He looked down at his shoes. "I think I'm stuck on you."

Deborah put her hands through his wavy hair and pulled his face close to hers and kissed him. Nick noticed there was no one around, so he placed her in his lap, the only sound coming from the black phoebe, whose song intensified for his partner, as they perched high in the rhododendron. They continued in a lovemaking trance, oblivious to the fact they were in a public garden. Nick never felt like this before and wasn't sure what to make of it. He squeezed Deborah in his arms and her warm body conveyed a willingness to linger there. He worried what Nathan really thought about their secret dating and felt uneasy about Mr. Fein. Deb couldn't be telling the truth about her father, so why spoil things now, as he felt her breasts rubbing against his chest. Things were getting hotter but a family strolled by with two children chasing each other and shouting. Deborah detached herself from Nick, as the male black phoebe vented an alarm call, *tsip*, to his mate and they soared away. They both looked straight ahead and Nick said: "Why don't we take a walk through the Redwood Grove? Maybe we'll spot a red breasted sapsucker."

They stood up and Deborah kissed him and while they closed their eyes for a few seconds, Nick lost sense of his surroundings. They were like Adam and Eve in a garden, but he feared that he might lose more than an earthly paradise. This feeling of anxiousness would appear all of sudden and then it would disappear. He never liked eating by himself, yet there were times he felt destined he might wind up all alone when it was time to leave his parents.

While they walked through the grove of giants, the light was diminished by their height and width. His mood worsened.

"Nicky, what's the matter? You look like a ghost." She let go of his hand. "Have I done something wrong?"

"No, not all. It's something I can't forget." Nick's head drooped like a sunflower in intense heat, as if he were contrapose to his wooded environment.

"What is it?"

"My father is being held by the G-men somewhere in Montana."

"You never told me!" Deborah looked frightened. "He's not mixed up with a racket is he?"

"My father is totally clean. They think he's working for Mussolini or the Japs because he's an enemy alien."

"I never heard that term, except for aliens from outer space."

"Believe me, this is not the comics. It's more complicated. I'm scared he'll be locked up for the whole war."

"I'm sorry, Nicky. You should have told me sooner."

"I suppose so."

Deborah hugged him and they found their way out of the grove. For some crazy reason he felt his afternoon in the park might someday haunt him, but he wasn't sure how this could happen. He didn't have a crystal ball to gaze in, didn't have a magic wand, couldn't conjure up a friendly spirit or be saved by a superhero, stuff for the comics that he was so fond of reading when he had nothing better to do.

* * *

One evening after supper, Ernst suggested to Nathan that they stroll around the neighborhood. Nathan thought it was odd, considering there was work the next day. His father claimed he needed to lose some weight, so Nate decided not to pull the homework trick. His mother was content to rest in an armchair after cutting the patterns of the latest dresses all day. They set a quick pace for the first two blocks and ambled the rest of the way.

"Aren't you tired setting type?" Nathan turned towards father.

"It's a living." His father appeared morose.

"No, I haven't decided what I want to be."

"You can read my mind," his father answered looking straight ahead.

"I might as well tell you now, Father." They stopped. "I'm planning to join the army. Not waiting to be called up. Something's got to be done about the Nazis."

"You'll be a target!" His father's brow furrowed.

"No more than any other American."

"You don't understand, Nathan," Ernst said, raising his voice. "It will be doubly dangerous for you."

"You're just exaggerating to scare me."

"Listen to me! You will always be considered a Jew first, even if you married a *shiksa*."

"I've made up my mind, Father."

"I can see that. Have you discussed this with your mother?"

"No, Father. Not even my best buddy, Nick, knows the plan."

"You must understand that I'm very proud you will fight the Nazis, but …"

Nathan could see his father was upset and cajoled him. "But what, Father?"

"I don't want to lose my only son."

"I'll be fighting for America. Haven't you always said that America is a wonderful place?"

"Yes, that's true. On the other hand, you are still a Jew, no matter how great this country is."

"I don't think you'll ever let me forget that."

"You have a special heritage, Nathan. But I can see you and your sister are already assimilated." He look into Nathan's eyes. "And what good did it do for us good Germans who gave everything to the fatherland?"

"Father, this is not Germany."

"I know, I know." Ernst bobbed his head. "Remember. You will find anti-Semitism wherever you go."

"I understand, Father. I'm not a knucklehead."

"Haven't I always said you were a smart boy from when you were very little sitting on my lap?" He gripped his son's hand. "Do your father one favor? If you're ever captured, ditch your dog tags. Those animals will kill you if they find out you're Jewish, Geneva Convention or no." His father rubbed his chin. "And what about your friend, Nick?"

"He said he wasn't in any rush to join. But his cousin Paul already enlisted."

They continued walking. "There's something else I need to talk to you about." He hesitated a moment. "Your sister."

"Deborah?" Nathan acted surprised but knew exactly where his father was going.

Ernst picked up the pace, turning his head sideways every so often. "Don't play coy with me. Something is going on with your friend and Deborah."

"Oh, you mean Nick." Nathan laughed nervously. "It's nothing."

"Don't lie to me," Ernst shouted.

Nathan felt cornered. "He's my best friend," he pleaded with his father.

"I like your Italian friend. He seems intelligent," his father murmured, then stopped. "Don't get me wrong. I want you to have friends outside our circle. Didn't I tell you about my exploits as a socialist in Berlin?"

"Yes Father, many times," Nathan groaned. "So why does this matter so much to you here?"

"Because we're Jews and will always be Jews, even if you deny your heritage."

"I haven't denied anything."

"Son, I'd fight for Nick's rights any day. When you were a child, I demonstrated in Boston against the execution of Sacco and Vanzetti. I just can't accept Deborah being romantically involved with Nick—maybe friends, but nothing more."

"You don't make sense, Pop."

"You'll understand one day, mark my words. The first day you brought the boy home, I knew there would be trouble with your sister."

"I'm not giving up my friend over Deborah."

"Do me a favor and talk sense to your sister and the boy. I don't want to turn this into a Romeo and Juliet scene. Be a good son and help your father."

"I've got a lot of homework to do. Let's head back."

They walked in tandem on the way home. Nathan understood his father's concerns about Deborah and himself. He knew that his father wanted the best for his children, but it didn't all add up. His father made some sense about the war but was off base with Nick.

But maybe Nate had lost touch with his Jewish roots. He was determined to follow through with his enlisting but didn't know what to do about Deborah and Nick. He loved his kid sister to death. And it would kill him to have to tell his buddy that he's just not good enough for his sister, which he didn't believe anyway but things have a way of steamrolling out of control when least expected.

* * *

The following Saturday afternoon Nathan agreed to meet Nick at the St. Francis Fountain in the Mission District. Nick claimed it would be an adventure seeing who would get there first by 4 pm and was already sitting at the counter awhile and drinking a black and white ice cream soda.

Nathan tapped Nick's back and he turned his head with a tall, bell soda glass in his hand. "Nate, you finally made it." Nick slurped the foamy bottom.

Nathan sat on a stool and ordered a root beer float.

"Looks like you're all in a sweat."

"I got lost along the way." Nick looked at him askance. Nathan had lied because he was in no hurry to get there. It was time to bring up this business with his sister. His biggest fear was losing a good friend all because of his father. The soda jerk placed the float on the counter but Nathan ate only a few spoonfuls. He spotted a group of girls in full skirts sauntering by in a flirtatious manner. Nick turned around but didn't seem that interested, which made Nathan even more anxious. Not that he thought his buddy was turning queer or anything.

"So Nick, what do ya think? Yankees or Cardinals for the World Series?"

"What's it to us? *Merda*, we don't have one major team on the west coast. But if you ask me, I'd just as soon as go with the Dodgers. Brooklyn's where my folks first started out in America."

"I'll go with the Cardinals. St. Louis is as close as you can get to home." Nathan twirled the long spoon in his glass, then pushed the half-eaten remains across the table. "It's getting too noisy. Why don't we go somewhere else?"

They walked to Mission Park and Nathan continued chatting about baseball most of the way, recounting endless statistics of the Cardinals and Yankees.

"You could be an ace sports announcer, Nate," Nick said as they finally reached the park. "Let's sit on the grass slope over there." Nick pointed to a palm tree and Nathan followed.

Nick noted the children playing hide-and-go-seek with their intermittent cries of 'Ollie Ollie oxen free,' as parents watched while sharing some fruit on the grass. Nathan wasn't sure what to say without offending his buddy, but he didn't have a choice. He didn't want to face his father if things went wrong since he promised to settle things with Nick. After all, it was his fault, according to Father, for bringing Nick into the house when they weren't around.

"It's got to end, Nick."

"What are you talking about, Nate?"

"You know, my kid sister."

Nick's eyes widened. "Deb!"

Nathan shook his head yes, as he averted his eyes.

"You must have known all along what was going on between Deb and me. Never a word from you."

"It kills me to be the person to tell you, but ..."

"But what?"

"You can't see Deborah anymore!"

Nick heard the words clearly but for the moment he was dumbfounded that his best buddy told him to end it with Deb. His felt a pain in his chest, as if he were on a rack and Nathan turned the screws. He didn't want to break up with his girl.

"I thought you were my friend, Nate."

"You're the best pal a guy could have. It's my father!" Nathan felt he was getting a bum rap and was getting annoyed that Nick didn't realize it. He doubted that Nick could handle the situation and would just burn up right in front of him. "Couldn't you figure that out for yourself?"

"I'm not good enough for your sister, that's it."

"Never said that."

"Just some worthless dago?" Nick's lips pressed, while his chin pushed up.

"It's in your head, not mine. Let me explain, will ya!"

Nick stood up and turned his back on Nathan. He had dreams about being with Deb forever but *sfortuna* dogged him wherever he turned.

Nathan got up and placed his hand on his friend's right shoulder. He wanted to rephrase things. When Nick felt the weight of Nathan's hand, he imagined it as an aggressive move. He was in no mood to be touched. He swerved around and took a swing at Nathan who blocked it and then held his friend's arms back.

"Calm down, will ya. It's not me, you fat-head."

"Let go of me." Nathan dropped his grip. Nick marched off, then stopped short, turning around. "I'm stuck on your sister!"

"My father thinks you should find someone else. It's not so much about religion. More about Jewish tradition. What can I say, Nick?"

"I thought your family wouldn't mind since we're friends. Do you think mine would be filled with joy, knowing I'm dating a Jewish girl? My father never steps foot in a church except for Christmas and Palm Sunday, but I can tell you he would still want me to marry a Catholic, even an Irish girl, though he might add 'God forbid' to that."

"It's a screwed up world."

"So, I'm supposed to turn off my feelings because your father says so."

"Why don't you just cool down? Who knows, maybe I'll be able to persuade him otherwise."

"Whatever you say, Nate."

"Believe me, I don't care you're not Jewish. We're supposed to be buddies right?"

"I gotta go home now. My mother's by herself."

"Sure, let's catch the J Church streetcar. It runs by the park."

As the streetcar clanged its bell past the Mission Park, Nick leaned on the edge of an open window, while Nathan looked straight ahead, sitting next to his friend. Nathan felt bad about the whole mess and hoped that Nick would get over it and not take it out on him. He was just the knucklehead messenger. They sat for a while listening to the confluence of steel wheels against steel rails.

"Tell your sister, I'm never going to forget her."

"Why don't you tell her yourself? Just one last time, I mean."

"I don't know if I can look at her and say goodbye. There is one thing I know for sure you can do for your ol' buddy." Nick dug down into his T-shirt and pulled a gold cross and chain over his head and held it up. "Give this to Deborah. I know your kid sister can't wear this, but she can hold onto it as a keepsake. It's the only thing I own that's worth something." Nathan placed the cross around his neck and hid it under his shirt, so as not to lose it. "Tell her no matter where I go, I'll always remember our time in the Botanical Garden."

"Sure Nick, whatever you say!"

Nathan got off at Duboce Avenue and Nick continued on to the Columbus Avenue stop. Nick gaped through the bus window at folks window shopping, women pushing baby carriages and a few young couples walking arm in arm or holding hands, but that's what got to him the most, eating his heart out, as the old fashioned saying goes. When he got off the streetcar, he took the long way home, shouting out to his mother when he closed the door behind him. He found her sitting at the kitchen table, mesmerized by a piece of paper lying there.

"*Mamma*!" She handed the telegram over without looking at him.

Nick raced his eyes over the message from the War Relocation Authority at Fort Missoula. The final hearing on the status of Gaetano Spataro had been completed and he was officially declared an enemy alien to be held at the camp until further notice.

His mother looked at Nick and cried out: "*Iddu è innucenti*!"

"I know *Mamma*, he's innocent as they come." Nick put his arms around his mother's shoulders while she wept. When Lucia stopped, he stepped into the backyard to breathe some fresh air, which had the faint smell of the salty sea. He collapsed into a wooden lawn chair. The superstition, 'Bad news comes in threes,' popped right into head—*Papà*, now Deborah. He was angry with Nate but didn't want his friend to be number three. "*Chi sacciu*?" he asked aloud. "What do I know? *Nenti*!" Nick was Giufa the fool all over again, but the situations with his father and first girlfriend were true, not tales from long ago.

# III

On a Good Friday morning, Nick drove the 1,000 miles to Missoula, Montana, in a Studebaker President that Mike the Barber lent him. He could still hear Mike swearing at him not to get a scratch on his year-old, light blue sedan. Mamma and Paul rode with him not saying much. Nick tightened his grip on the steering wheel, wondering how his father was faring in the Alien Detention Center, War Relocation Camp—or whatever else they wanted to call it. Sounded more like a prison to him, but he would have to see for himself. Instead of going on a joy ride with his *cuginu*, picking up two beautiful dames and heading for the wine country of Sonoma Valley, an antidote for his blues over Deborah, it felt like he was chauffeuring a hearse and all he needed was a shiny brimmed hat.

The roads were slow and on the third day they approached Fort Missoula, facing the Bitterroot mountain range caked with snow at the top, to celebrate Easter with *Papà*. A chain link fence topped with barbed wire enclosed the internment camp that had guard towers moored to it. A black iron searchlight tower rose from the interior. Nick parked the car outside the camp. He glanced at his mother whose eyes welled up with tears, while Paul's mouth dropped, which set the tone for what was to come. It was clear to him that no matter how they treated *Papà* inside, the outside showed the determination of the feds, blessings of the U.S. Army included, to keep Gaetano Spataro locked away from the west coast of America, his livelihood, and most of all, his *famigghia*, all swapped for barbed wire, armed guards and giant flashlights, providing a new meaning to a summer camp for Sicilians who fled their country for a better life.

The internees were huddled in groups around the yard. Gaetano and a few *paesani* from his neighborhood were looking through the chain link fence. Lucia saw Gaetano first and ran over to him.

"*Cara mia*," Gaetano called.

"Gaetano, Gaetano! You look like you lost weight."

"Lucia, I'm all right." He kissed her fingertips that gripped the fence. "I'll see you inside."

Gaetano waved the boys towards the visitors' gate. The guards asked for identification, questioned their reason for the visit and examined the bags they carried. Two were allowed in, so Paul waited outside. An effusive din greeted them as they met Gaetano in a cramped visitors' room. Lucia ran to her husband, embracing and kissing him. After Nick kissed Gaetano on both cheeks, they squeezed around a table shared with other families.

"It's been a long time, Lucia," Gaetano said. "I missed you."

"*Si, anch'io*. I pray for you every night." A tear dripped down her face.

"*Chi cosa, Lucia*?" She forced a smile and he placed his hand on hers.

Gaetano turned towards his son. "Eh, how is my young man?"

"We've been very concerned about you, *Papà*," Nick said. "*Cuginu* Paul is outside."

"I can't complain." Gaetano looked at his son. "*Petra disprizzata, cantunera di muro. Capisci, Nicolo*?"

"The rejected stone will become the cornerstone of the wall."

"*Beni, figghiu miu*. You remember everything."

"I saw a few of your *paesani* behind the fence."

"They manage like me. But I hear things are worse in camps run by the Army."

"How so, *Papà*?"

"*Paesani* say they get very angry if you use the enemy language near them."

Nick lowered his voice. "What happened to your case? *Signuri* Arcuri *l'avvucatu* sent letters in your defense."

"*Si*, there was this special meeting. *Comu si dici*?"

"Hearing panel."

"*Si*, they ignore *tuttu*. They saya, Mr. Spataro, we are sorry your past history leaves us no choice but declare you enemy alien. They no sorry!"

"How is this possible, *Papà*?"

Gaetano glanced sideways.

"You looka pale, Gaetano. *Mancia*!" Lucia untied a package of sandwiches, a stack of breaded veal cutlets on crusty peasant bread. She gave one to her husband and watched as he ate.

"*È bonu*, Lucia!"

Nick grabbed one for Paul and put it in his jacket pocket, then took another for himself. "*Mamma*, eat something." He held a sandwich up for his mother to see.

"I am no hungry."

Nick devoured the sandwich and Lucia turned to him. "Go see what you and Paul find out. *Avanti*!"

"I'll try to talk sense to them, *Papà*," Nick said.

"*Figghiu miu*!" Gaetano boasted as he bolted away. Lucia took a small bite of her sandwich and swallowed it.

"How you liva with all these strangers?" Lucia asked.

"It not so bad. I even made some new friends."

"*Sicilianu*?"

"*Si*! *E altri regioni*."

When Nick stepped outside, he found his cousin leaning on the wall. He took the sandwich out of his coat pocket.

"Catch, Paul." His *cuginu* ripped half the paper off, eating in wide bites. While Nick waited for Paul to finish, he realized that he had forgotten something. "I'll be back in a sec. Forgot my cigarettes."

Making his way through the cramped quarters, he held back behind some visitors after he heard his mother blurt out: "I told you million times, getta your papers. You no listen to me. *Madonna*!"

"*Mannaggia*, already you start in. What, you have a crystal ball that you know so much? You no tella me what to do." He showed his palms to Lucia. "Look at my hands from pulling nets."

"But we have to paya the bills. What about the mortgage on the house? We stilla owe for the boat too."

"Forget about the boat! Navy took it. Then, they tell me later it'll be converted to a minesweeper. For the war effort, they saya."

"*Chi sacciu*? You never tella me."

Her husband's eyes reddened and he shouted: "I no want to be cooped up here *come un'animale*!"

"No raisa your voice," Lucia pleaded, as she inspected the room, but hadn't noticed Nick in the crowded room. "You don't know what they'll do." She wiped her tears away with a white hanky.

"*Nicolo* will take care of everything. No worry, *cara mia*."

"Gaetano, you are a good man. No matta what America say, *ti amu*!"

Nick moved around a few visitors and interrupted. "*Scusi*, I forgot my cigarettes." He picked them up and trotted back to his cousin, rubbing his tears away. He couldn't bear to see his parents arguing like this.

"What took you so long, *cuginu*?"

"I got lost."

Paul laughed at Nick. "Like lost in those books you always got your nose in."

"Cut the crap, will ya!"

"Don't get so sore. Just jokin' with you."

"Let's find the headquarters."

Nick and Paul found a guard who directed them to the Post Headquarters of the Immigration and Naturalization Service for the camp. The office was filled with tall file cabinets containing dossiers on all the internees. The INS supervisor, who wore wire-rimmed glasses, sat dead center at his desk, surrounded by his subordinates. After being frisked at the entrance, the two cousins entered.

"How can I help you gentlemen?" the supervisor asked.

"My father, Gaetano Spataro, is being held here. It's gotta be some kind of mistake." An assistant pulled out his father's file and the supervisor glanced at it.

"Sorry, but this is not a case of mistaken identity. Your father is still a citizen of Italy and never renounced his allegiance to that country, now our enemy. That's what it means to be an enemy alien."

"That's my uncle. He ain't no alien!" The supervisor curled his lip.

"My father is just a fisherman."

"His fate has been determined by Presidential Order, Proclamation 2527, signed by the Commander-in-Chief of the Armed Forces." He peeped over his glasses and stated: "That's President Franklin Delano Roosevelt."

"I know that. All I'm saying is that my father's an honest family man."

"He's already had a hearing here. I was present. Your father belonged to the Federation of Italian War Veterans. It was duly noted in his record."

"He's no Fascist."

The supervisor began straightening out the papers on his desk.

Paul reached into his jacket. "Look! My enlistment papers for the Army. I'm willing to fight, even against Italians!"

"That's very patriotic, young man, but there's nothing I can do for your uncle."

"It's not right!" Nick shouted.

"Lieutenant General John DeWitt is running the show. Complain to the War Department. They placed the general in charge of the Western Military Command. We're just following his guidelines."

The supervisor placed his glasses into a black case and eyed the guard at the door. "I have already said more than I'm obliged to. You'll have to leave now or I'll have you two shown the camp gates."

Paul grabbed his cousin's arm. "Let's get out of here, Nick."

When they got outside, they went back to the visitors' reception area. They stopped for another smoke. Paul struck a match and lit his cousin's cigarette first and then his.

"It's a rotten deal, Nick." Nick turned away from his cousin as he dragged on a cigarette. "Is there anything I can do, *cuginu*?"

"I'm thinking." From a distance, Nick stared at the rows of identical buildings, neat enough but foreboding in their battleship gray stain. He failed to convince the administrator to reconsider his father's internment. "*Cuginu*, go inside, you haven't seen your uncle. Tell my parents that I'm going to scout around this joint to see what else I can find out."

"*Beni*."

The camp maintained a casual attitude, but Nick sensed there were different stories behind every face, all of them caught up in the war and thrown together. No one stopped him from walking down a treeless, dusty road where he encountered a group of Japanese Americans tending a garden. They were busy in their teamwork, grooming the soil and planting with a definite design in mind. On the surface, it would make a good photo for the newspaper, but Nick saw something else. They were isolated by their race, even though the English he overheard was better than his father's *paesani*. Some of them glanced in his direction and their eyes revealed sadness so poignant that Nick turned away for a moment. His curiosity overcame his diffidence, so he approached the man who had continued to follow him with his eyes.

"I don't mean to bother you … but can I ask you a question?" The man, old enough to be his father, remained silent and dug his spade in the ground. "My father's Gaetano Spataro. Um, he's penned up here like you. Well, I was just wondering… how the guards act towards everybody in this place." The man handed his spade to another gardener and walked away from the group then pivoted, waving him over.

"I prefer speaking privately," he said, averting his

gaze from Nick who looked directly into the man's eyes. "You have to be careful what you say."

"I understand. So what's it like here?"

"The guards treat us okay. I supposed you could say that you can get used to anything. They even let us grow our own vegetables and prepare our food."

"I can see. That's why I was curious."

"This is not a life I ever imagined. My wife and children are American. Born and reared in California. But the U.S. government wouldn't give me citizenship. Even after 40 years living in the same state."

"That's a crummy situation."

"I put on my stoic mask as if I am in a *Kabuki*. I try to meditate but that doesn't help. I drink a lot of homemade *sake* but that does not help. I want my family back. I want my farm back. I am dying here even though they're not torturing me to confess something I am not, something I didn't do, something I don't believe in."

"I don't know what to say."

"Even though your father is a prisoner like me, it will always be worse for us. We don't look like you."

"Something like Negroes."

"Yes." The man looked into Nick's eyes for the first time.

"I have seen your father at soccer games. Everyone seems to like him, so I see that the apple does not fall far from the tree. I have a son who's 21. He's joined the 442nd Infantry Regiment. It was his idea. Made up of all *Nisei*—Japanese Americans second generation, born in this country. They'll release Akio soon from

Camp Manzanar in eastern California. A so-called Relocation War Center. That is where he is held with the rest of my family." He looked off in the distance. "But my son will restore the honor of our clan, the Minamoto." He raised his right fist as a boxer. "He has the blood of the *samurai*. My great-great grandfather was the last of the noble warrior class in Japan." He lowered his arm. "They will show America what Japanese Americans are made of."

"Do you think the authorities will set your family free?"

"I have no reason to think so, but who can predict anything now? So, in the meantime, I rot like vegetables that are not properly taken care of. Your father travels in the same boat with me, for now. You might say Noah's ark." He let out a quick laugh. "Go to your father. He must be wondering why you are missing."

As Nick shook the man's hand, he thought that their encounter layered another dimension to this internment business. He was ignorant about many things it seemed or maybe just naive. Even so, *Papà* was still trapped in Missoula and there was nothing he could do about it, which made him anxious to stand in front of his father without a sliver of hope.

Nick walked past the rows of barracks reserved for alien enemies, traipsing through the middle of them. Up close, the washed out buildings squatted on a hardened ground that could have been an outpost on Mars. Nothing green growing between these buildings. Nick came across a group of young Italian men who were chatting in standard Italian on the three-stepped entrance to one of these battle gray structures. From their vantage point, they could view of the mountains fronted by the Bitterroot River which curved around Stevens Island.

One guy with a full head of dirty blond hair called out to Nick as he passed by: "*Bella vista*! Camp *Bella Vista*!" The others laughed. Nick nodded and approached him, speaking in the Italian he learned at the Italian government's sponsored *Dopo Scuola*, an after school program shut down at the start of the war. When he mixed in some Sicilian phrases, they looked puzzled, so he switched back to the language of Dante. They had worked on a luxury cruise liner that had been seized in the Panama Canal at the onset of the war. Judging by their carefree attitude, they didn't seem to mind being there, since they wouldn't have to fight for Mussolini. Nick thought these Italians were lucky, but they weren't interested discussing Italian politics in any language—they weren't taking any chances, which was a sign for Nick to move on.

As Nick passed by the Post Headquarters, he stopped for a moment. He had been in such a rush the first time that he hadn't notice the Courtroom, so he squinted through a pair of double hung windows. So this is where they had held the 'Enemy Alien Hearings.' He winced at the sight of the place where *Papà* had been denounced, a peculiar sense of self-reproach caught in his gut. Nick argued with himself as if he were a poet composing verse. But he had nothing to do with his father's incarceration. He even got the lawyer to intercede on his father's behalf, but it kicked right back at Nick. He had failed his father, at least that's how he saw it. Gaetano would never have left him to rot here. He had delayed long enough, knowing it would be very difficult to face *Papà* with no good news.

On the way back to the Visitor Center, Nick recalled his conversation with the young Italian who jested about "Camp Bella Vista." The view was beautiful but Italians love to joke around. He guessed they were laughing at this crazy world. But for Nick he saw it as a cruel joke on his father, marooned in this miserable place looking out on this free, quintessential American landscape, a daily reminder of what he had been cut off from, the freedom to be with his family taking in the sight of San Francisco Bay and its world famous bridge, setting out on the majestic Pacific ocean and netting the silver-glittering fish that fed the city and his way of life in North Beach *con tutta famigghia*.

* * *

Lucia got out of the car in front of their home without saying a word and the cousins stared out the windshield. It was raining and damp, so they rolled their collars up in the front seat, the compartment filled with smoke and the dank smell of nicotine.

"You want another smoke, Paul?" Nick popped one out half way from the pack. They both lit up again and sat motionless.

"I told you it wouldn't work, Nick. They don't care about breakin' up families." He took a drag. "Why don't you come with me to meet my recruiting sergeant? Sez I have some more papers to fill out. Maybe we could stick together through this war, like when we were kids playing on the same baseball team."

"You know I have a problem fighting Italians."

"I know. We'll fight somewhere else."

"It's not just that. What about *Papà*? Am I supposed to run off and leave him in that place? What about my mother? Look at the way she reacted after leaving *Papà* sealed in with his *paesani* like anchovies in a tin. One way or another, he's still in the can to me, no matter how decent they may treat him."

"Geez, *cuginu*. I feel real bad for *Ziu* Gaetano too. But sooner or later you're goin' to have to make a decision." Paul looked out the window. "You know what I'm getting at." He took a long drag on the fag. "I thought we'd stick together through this big mess. You know, watch out for each other like we was brothers."

"Right now, all I can think about is my father. I can't erase that look on his face when we left him there in Montana."

"I feel it in my bones. They'll let *Ziu* Gaetano out before I get to boot camp."

Nick didn't believe the crap Paul was peddling but he would always be *famigghia*. "*Minchia*, you'd better drive 'black beauty' back to Mike's shop, or he'll come looking for us with that thick leather strap from his barber chair." Nick smiled thinly as he drove away.

That night Nick sat in the backyard near his father's fig tree, still protected with its galvanized, bucket hat, wrapped in tarpaper crisscrossed with twine. He turned his head when a light switched on and saw his mother gazing from her bedroom window. When she realized that Nick noticed her, she closed the wooden, venetian blinds. He imagined that he had interrupted an astral projection of his mother, while lighting up a Lucky Strike, and then through rings of smoke Nick began to see faces.

The first one was Paul, their last conversation still in his thoughts. His emotional ties to his *cuginu* went as far back as he could remember. He spent more time with his cousin than kids from the neighborhood. From the very beginning Nick would win all the academic awards, while Paul just got by in school. Even in baseball, Nick could hold his own in competition with Paul. But when it came to street fighting, it was the other way around. Many times Paul interceded for his cousin. Though his feelings never cooled for Nick, he sensed Paul could not accept his Jesuit school ways. They had two divergent mindsets that intensified throughout their high school days. They had this symbiotic relationship but Nick reflected whether they could maintain any relationship at all, if he refused to go off to war with his cousin, which brought Nick to a second face in the smoke when he lit up again. It was Deborah's but her soft looks disappeared before his eyes as if in the trail of a magician's vapor.

And then there was the visage of his father, more like a death mask. Nick could not comprehend how they could have imprisoned *Papà* who was *bonu come lu pane*, an accolade fit for Sicily or America. His own nephew volunteered to fight for America but that did nothing for his father. Maybe if he joined up, the Feds would let his father go. Nick didn't know what to think, but felt it was his only shot at freeing his father. Then he remembered an old Sicilian proverb his mother used to repeat: "*'U Signùri rùna 'u viscuottù a cu nun' avi rienti*'—'God gives biscuits to those with no teeth.' He didn't know where to go with all of this, like he was in a constant state of confusion at a time in his life when all he wanted to do was to have some fun. Maybe all his *cuginu* wanted was for them to be inseparable again, like when they were kids, except this time they would be playing a deadly game they couldn't possibly conceive of.

Nick had a premonition that other things would come chugging after them from nowhere, like the nightmare he had after his father was abducted, the two cousins wildly pumping a hand cart on a deserted spur with a black locomotive steaming right behind them. They came to a switch track and a grinning, bespectacled trainman diverted them onto another track, while the locomotive raced passed them by, its violent airwaves almost sucking them in. They pumped their way through a dark forest and came out the other side, which gave them a sensation of safety. They rambled along until they spotted a tunnel bored through a hill. Nick noticed the headlight of another black locomotive curving into the same hole. He yelled at Paul to jump before they entered the tunnel, but his *cuginu* didn't listen to him. Nick's voice turned faint and no matter how wide he opened his mouth, no sound came out. He tried to drag Paul off but his cousin resisted, and right before the entrance Nick jumped into a river, whose current bashed him around the rocks jutting before a precipice. He woke up screaming so loud, Lucia came running in, crossing herself over and over. '*Figghiu miu, figghiu miu.*'

# IV

Fort Hood, Texas, a flat endless place of raw heat with little or no shade, was not on anyone's list of favorite sights to visit. It had the perfect terrain for an unexpected tornado to toss someone closer to the sun. But it was wartime and this was one of the best places to get tank training. They came from boot camps all over America to form the tank battalions waiting to be assigned to the divisions that would battle the German war machine, which had already trammeled most of the European continent. Tank Destroyer crews would train here till they got things one hundred percent right. The only thing saving America for the moment was the Atlantic Ocean.

On a Monday in August just as dawn broke, the GIs piled off the buses to be sorted out into armored troops. Nick, drowsy and disoriented, could hardly make out the recruits who swarmed around him, but as fate would have it, Nick and Nathan fresh from boot camp at Camp Roberts, California, ran into Paul just arrived from Fort Ord, California.

"*Madonna, miu cuginu!*"

"Nick!" They kissed each other on both cheeks and hugged.

"The Army screwed up. Swore up and down we'd be together from the start."

"It's *nostru destinu*, Nick."

"What did I tell you, Paul? Push for tank training. Oh, you know Nate."

They shook hands. "We will be the three *moschet-tieri*," Paul boasted as they laughed and remembered their meeting.

"What's so funny, you dickheads? Get in line!" a master sergeant barked, one of many sergeants screaming that day, as they tried to untangle the mass of humanity lining up. The trio marched along with hundreds of other new arrivals in a neat column.

Having been separated for basic training, they weren't taking any chances and managed to finagle their way into the same barracks set aside for tankers. Nick and Paul were catching up on family stories while Nathan listened with interest, when a sergeant barged into the barracks. He straightened out the brim of his Brown Round, an old campaign hat that he always wore. Everyone dropped what they were doing and stood at attention. Sergeant Ackers swaggered around eyeballing anyone caught staring at him.

"What really gets to me is the army is so desperate for bodies, we are inducting any male specimen that can breathe." Sergeant Ackers stopped abruptly, brandishing his barrel chest like Roman armor, his bare forearms tanned leather. "Now look at what we have here, not one but two Eye-talians, Spataro and Burgio, and their pal here, Fein. Now let me guess. German name, right Fein?"

"Yes, Sergeant."

"And I'll bet you're a New York Jew too."

"San Francisco, Sergeant."

"Great." The sergeant grinned. "We've got three guys who have ties to the Axis armies." He tapped Nathan's face. "Just kidding. I reckon you fellows were born here, so I'll let it go at that." The sergeant strode over the polished wood floor to the center of the room. "What are the rest of you losers looking at? You are not going to disgrace me, are you?"

"No, sergeant!" they all bellowed.

"That's what I like to hear. I don't want any lame tank crews. My reputation is on the line. I need one more stripe to make Master Sergeant, so don't screw up." He glared at Nick, Paul and Nathan. "Especially you three guys." The sergeant guffawed. "I'm not mixing you with the others. You deserve each other." He strode over to the front door and turned around. "Anyone of you jokers here want to join their crew?" After a silent pause, the sergeant added: "Can't say as I blame you, but at least one of you, sure as shit, will have to team up with this sorry trio. A full crew would be five. But a whole company won't help them none anyways." He slapped his leg laughing. "What are y'all staring at? Fix up this pigsty before I come back. At ease!"

The tank training was comprehensive, including classroom and practical runs on the field. They were expected to know everything about the vehicle they would be living in for a long time, how to drive, navigate, load, shoot and maintain their iron hulk. Nick was the designated driver, Paul the gunner and Nathan the commander, but they still needed at least one other member who would be the loader, or the sergeant would send them packing to the infantry, claiming they weren't fit for a mobile unit. Their break came when Alastar Smith agreed to join their crew, just before 'lights out' in the barracks as they stood around his bunk bed.

Nick asked: "So why do you want to go along with us, when you know the sergeant hates our guts?"

"I couldn't stand his picking on you guys and nobody said nothin'. Anyway, my mom is Italian, so I felt he could have been hassling me too if he only knew. Besides, you guys coming from Frisco must be cool." He lowered his eyes. "I grew up in a small town. You probably never heard of it." His eyes beamed. "Roseto, PA. It means rose garden in Italian, my Mom says."

"Well, wherever you're from, we're glad you had the balls to join us," Nathan added.

"Yeah, welcome aboard Al, you'll be my loader," Paul said.

"So how old are you anyway, Al?" Nick inquired.

"Me." Al fidgeted on the bunk. "Seventeen! Says so right on my baptismal certificate." His eyes twitched.

"You're bit taller than me anyway," Nick said, as he slapped him on the shoulder.

Before hitting the sack, Nick whispered to Nathan: "Do you think that Al's all wet about his age?"

"Just peach fuzz on his upper lip," Nathan answered.

Sergeant Acker's harassment never wavered. He said their crew did not perform at the same level as the others, which made them more determined to prove him wrong. One day, about two weeks after they had arrived, the entire squadron returned to the compound after their first coordinated exercise. Sergeant Ackers pulled alongside their tank and shouted over the windshield of his jeep. "You four are the most harebrained, sorry asses I have ever come across. You're taking our whole company down. Captain Monroe was shaking his head." His jeep cut in front of them and sped away. After Nick parked the tank in the shed, they went behind the building for a private smoke.

After a few drags Paul spoke up. "I have had enough of that red-necked sonofabitch."

"Me too," Al chimed in.

"Look guys, don't you see what this is all about?" Nathan stomped his cigarette out. "Our crew can be as good as the others, maybe even better. Ackers wants to prove his superiority over our kind, even though he is as Southern white trash as they come."

"So we're supposed to take all this crap from him?" Nick asked.

"There's only one thing we should do—perfect our skills as a tank crew and train when everybody else is off. At night. On weekends. We got six weeks left and if we work together, we'll be the best tankers. And Ackers will look like a fool. Are you guys with me or not?" The crew surrounded Nathan and patted him on the back.

Paul spent a lot of his time with Al practicing his moves for firing off fast rounds, while Nick and Nathan choreographed their techniques so the tank acted more like a sports car than an oversized truck. Nick already understood that there was nothing as bad as getting stuck where you couldn't maneuver, or worse yet, not being able to move at all from a direct hit. Their bunk buddies thought they were crazy for working so hard, but Nick realized it wasn't just about Sergeant Ackers—it was also about their survival on the war front.

One evening they skipped their own private training to write letters, as they sat on the edge of their bunks.

Nick wrote to his mother:

> *Cara Mamma,*
>
> *You're still not mad at me anymore, are you,* Mamma? *Like I said, I'm sending everything home, except for some cigarette and beer money. How's* Papà? *I think about the both of you every day, but mostly* Papà. Credo di no *that he is still locked up. I wish Avvucatu Arcuri could do something for* Papà *now that I'm in the army. Nobody knows where we're going for sure, and I can't tell you anything, even if I did know …*

Al wrote to his large family:

*Dear Mom, Dad & Kids,*

*So how are things in Roseto these days, Mom? I don't like to gripe in my letters, but let me get this off my chest. I can't stand this lousy army chow. You know Mom, I miss your cooking bad and sometimes I dream about playing baseball in the cleared field outside of town with my kid brothers. So how's everybody ...*

Nathan wrote:

*Dear Mother, Father & Sis,*

*I hope everyone is well in the family and that you're not worrying too much, especially you, Mom. Just wanted to let you know, Father, that there are some people out here that don't like us, like our southern sergeant, you know what I mean, but I don't let that bother me because we all have a job to do. Anyway, I couldn't be with a better team—me, Nick and his cousin Paul and Al from Pennsylvania ...*

*Send my love to Sis.*

Nick sealed his letter to Lucia and then wrote to Nathan's sister:

*Cara Debbie,*

*I am sorry about what happened between the two of us. I sent you a bunch of letters during boot camp and didn't hear from you. I know your father only wants the best for you and I'm not taking it too personal. Mr. Fein is something like my pop, so I know what you're going through. Anyway, you're so pretty, the guys will be lining up. That's not what I really want though. I mean I do love you, sweetheart, but what are we supposed to do, run away from our families? I promised that I would always write to you till you said enough—we would say basta in Italian. Here I am, stuck in a tank! Maybe a miracolo will happen for the both of us. Have a black and white ice cream soda for me and make sure you keep this letter out of sight ...*

*Love always, Nick.*

A week later during one of their daily mail calls, a corporal shouted their last names and handed out the letters. At moments like this Nathan's crew split up into their own private spots to read their lifeline letters.

Paul's sister, Maria, had written for his mother:

*Caru Paolo,*

Figghiu miu, *we miss you here. I tell your father it feels strange without you* nella casa. *I hope you are not getting skinny because you will get sick and die. I pray every night to* Santa *Rosalia on my knees that you will come home safe... Maria added her own comments.*

*I feel so proud that my big brother is fighting to protect our country. The kids at school look at me differently now. But don't do anything foolish. You know how you can get. Maybe you won't tease me anymore when you come home …*

*Con amuri, la famigghia*

Al's mother wrote:

*Dear Al,*

*The whole family misses you so much. Little Pete has been oiling your leather glove so that it doesn't dry up. He wants you to teach him how to play as soon as you get back. I think your Irish father is turning Italian the way he is so worried about your not getting proper Italian food …*

Nathan's father wrote:

*My Dear Son,*

*I hope that things have not been too harsh for you. Remember that Hitler wants to destroy our people and anyone else who is not Aryan, so you're doing a righteous thing. Do not let the bigots get the best of you. Watch out for your sergeant, as he will try to provoke you until you're thrown into the guardhouse. He will get his comeuppance some day …*

*With love from everyone*

Nick moved much further away from the barracks where brush trees clustered and black-capped vireos nested. While he meandered, Nick first read the letter from his father out of respect, then skimmed his mother's note so he could get to Deborah's. He sat down and leaned his back on the tallest tree, smelling the paper a moment, and gingerly opened the letter.

Deborah wrote:

> *Dear Nicky,*
>
> *I already feel like it's years since we first saw each other. I was wondering why I hadn't heard from you. Nathan says he's staying out of this, so he hasn't been much help. I try to respect my parents who have sacrificed so much for me, but sometimes it's very hard. I am graduating early and plan to go to San Francisco State College in the spring to keep my mind off things. No matter what my parents say, I will never forget you. I just want you to come back alive ...*
>
> *Take care,* mi amor.

Nick leaned his head on a tree trunk to take in everything he had read. The line about Deborah not hearing from him was disturbing, but he shrugged it off as an army screw up. Beat from all the training, he dozed off and at first Nick thought he was dreaming but soon heard a vireo singing *zhrrree* right above his head. The memory of Deborah and him at the San Francisco Botanical Garden burst alive and he imagined hearing the black phoebe again and seeing all those bright colors right in front of him. He put the letter in his lap and the hues around him transitioned from green to brown to black after the vireo flew away.

The next day Nick remained in a sour mood, as he shifted his thoughts to his father's predicament. He reread his father's letters, some of which dated as far back as the winter, the ones he had saved from North Beach. Nick poured through the bundle filled with censored lines that had been deemed suspicious and forwarded to the intelligence unit at Camp McAlester. If his father used any Italian words or made any reference to Italy, even negative comments about his native country, they would be blackened or scissored out. When Nick was a child, his father would draw cartoons about Giufà, the village fool, in the tales his mother read to him. His father included some new ones in his letters, so his son would think things were normal. Every cartoon was deleted, as there was a strict ban on all drawings, no matter what the content. Nick tried to decipher the reasons for Gaetano's internment and struggled to imagine what was missing in all those deletions and what was really meant in his father's own words.

* * *

Nick's father spent many cold evenings in primitive barracks, battered by high winds and snowstorms in a remote part of Montana. Fort Missoula had been painted on one of the buildings over a slant of the roof in big white letters, as if they needed to be reminded of the camp's name. *Papà* would lie on his cot staring at the ceiling and, when he couldn't sleep, he would get up and look through the dust-coated window at the mountains. He had met an old fisherman friend from North Beach, who like himself had been a member of the *Ex-Combattenti*, the Federation of Italian War Veterans in America. Marco Randazzo and Gaetano fought during World War I, when America and Italy were allies. Now they were reunited against their will in an internment camp, even though they had no use for the fascists.

In the evening after supper, the two detainees played *briscula* or *scopa* because it was a link to their *italianitá*, now feeling so far removed from the extended families and their neighborhood with all its wonderful food shops, operated by *paesani* who used to speak their language openly.

"Gaetano, I have trumped you again." Marco, who always wore a white cap, slapped an ace down on the hard wood table. "You keep on losing in *Briscula*. *Come vai*?"

"*Mi dispiace*! I can't concentrate. All I do is worry like an old woman in a black dress."

"You must stay *calma*."

"But what about *mia famigghia*? What I have done to deserve such a fate? I have been humiliated in front of my family, the whole neighborhood. They call us enemy aliens!"

"So what are we to the *Amerigani*? I have behaved myself from the first day I stepped off the boat. We fought together with the *Amerigani* in World War I. Now I am a traitor. Has the FBI ever read my newspaper articles attacking Mussolini? No! *Nenti*! Even the great American magazine, *Time*, had Mussolini on the cover. *Quella fascista buffa*!"

"What can we do, Marco?"

He shuffled the cards. "Have you heard from your son?"

"*Si*, I got a letter yesterday. Nick joined the Army. He's going in right after graduation in early June. He's in a hurry to ride in a tank."

"Well, at least he won't march for miles in the mud. Remember stumbling up the slippery edges in mountains on the Isonzo Front." Marco stacked the deck on the table.

"How could anyone forget the fear of being blown up or frozen to death? So *Nicolo* tella me all the time, 'No worry, *Papà*.' I'll send money to Mamma every month. She okay, Pop. That's what he say to me."

"He's a good son, Gaetano."

"Before I go to sleep each night, I wonder what will happen to all of us."

"Some people pray to their favorite saints, but as for me, it does no good. Our fate is all in the cards." Marco tapped the deck. "It is like the lifeline across your palm." He showed his palm and lined his index finger across it. Gaetano's crossed himself, while Marco chuckled. "Don't listen to me. I am an old fool. Do you want to play some *scopa*?"

"No, *grazie*. I want to turn in now. *Bona notte*, Marco."

"*Bona notte, miu amicu.*"

*Papà* sat on the side of his Army steel cot with an Army brown blanket dangling at the edge. He pulled on the string of his reading lamp, just a bare bulb hanging overhead. He had collected a stack of letters, one from Lucia and a separate pile for Nick, which he placed next to a statue of St. Thomas the Apostle, his patron saint. He took his scuffed brown work boots off and put black leather slippers on, a new pair that his wife had sent after her first visit. He got up to look out the window and could see the tower lights shining off the barbed wire that encircled the camp. The guards had their weapons on the ready so no aliens considered escaping. Gaetano could make out the outline of magnificent mountains in the distance, but he was trapped in this camp, over a thousand miles from his entire family.

The next morning he ate breakfast in the large mess hall. The internees sat together on wooden benches at long tables lined up in rows. The food was edible but never *bonu*, and for lunch and dinner, never a drop of red wine, a drink that always accompanied dinner at home. Gaetano thought of the Sicilian proverb, '*Bonu vinu fa bonu sangu*'—'Good wine makes good blood.' There was something missing to wash down what passed for three square meals. As usual Gaetano sat next to his friend, Marco, both complaining about the food. The white bread was puffy, the oatmeal mush thick like cement, the vegetables canned and the coffee so bitter, no amount of sugar or milk could mute its aftertaste, not even lemon. Gaetano never craved a second cup of java. They usually ate in silence and only spoke Sicilian in private because they never knew who might be listening, and they did not want to be interrogated, having no information the FBI would be interested in anyway.

To kill time, the detainees were allowed to form soccer teams, the players typically chosen from the Italian ship crew members. Gaetano and Marco stood by a short fence that separated the players on the field from the spectators. The crowd was noisy, so they could speak the enemy's language freely and no one would shout at them to speak American. They could mention anything they wanted about Italy even in English and not be concerned about how it would be taken by the guards.

"They're shutting down a lot of Italian publications in California and New York," Marco said.

"Lucia mentioned that in her last letter. I am surprised the censors didn't cut it out."

"Ah, don't you see. A good way to demoralize Italians. Keep us off balance. Maybe if the government left the publications alone, they might see that Italians have turned against Mussolini and his Blackshirts."

"Our sons risk their lives fighting for America. And where does this get us?" The spectators shouted with enthusiasm. "*Allura*, we just missed the first goal."

"This game is not the same as going to a real stadium. People are free to walk off the field and go home, if they get mad enough."

"We're going nowhere, Marco. Just marking time like a referee."

"I don't want to play this game anymore."

"What are you talking about, Marco?" The crowd roared.

"You know I have other friends here from the *Ex-Combattenti*. We are sick of being here and we know how to fight." He paused a moment. "We also know how to escape."

"*Mannaggia*! What are you talkin' about? They'll catch you and then what."

"We have it all planned."

"You never told me about this."

"I knew you would never go along with us."

"*Nun capisciu*."

"We volunteered to work for the Forest Service to cut wood to support the war effort, they say. It's not a lot of money, but that's not the point." Marco winked.

"Are you *pazzu*? The FBI has your fingerprints and photograph."

"*Aspitta*! The forest is deep and dark. When the guards are busy eating their lunch, we will disappear before their eyes like Houdini." Marco laughed, as the whistle blew for a time out.

"The FBI will hunt you down to set an example. The newspapers will put your photographs on the front pages."

Marco shrugged and kissed Gaetano on both cheeks. "*Addio, miu amicu*." Marco squeezed his way through groups of men to meet with his former comrades in arms.

That night Marco did not meet Gaetano in the dimly lit room set for game playing. Gaetano decided to go back to his bed and lie down. The only thing that gave him any solace in this limbo was his friend, Marco. Now he had one more person to add to his worry list. He thought his friend might go off the deep end, to a place not even Dante had imagined.

In the morning Gaetano saw Marco leaving the mess hall and arched his right eyebrow before getting his breakfast. He complained loud enough about the institutional bread that he got permission to work in the kitchen so he could bake bread for himself and his *paesani*, using his mother's recipe for peasant bread, *pani rusticu*. It was all about the hands and how you worked the dough, but it was simple enough, some white flour, water 90 °F, salt and some yeast. Two of the galley crewmen from the Italian liner noticed Gaetano baking and were allowed to pitch in, making a different batch of dough to twist into rolls of various shapes, shaking their heads when they couldn't find any sea salt. They soon became known as the three bakers as they glided around each other from the larder to the table to the oven.

A few evenings later, right before supper, Gaetano heard a commotion outside his window and saw some vehicles with armed guards and hounds barking, as they passed by. He stepped outside noting that there still were mounds of snow all around, for the winters were long and hard in Montana. He followed the trucks to the Post Headquarters and saw Marco and his comrades shackled and being led into the Hearing Room.

By the time Gaetano got back to his barracks, the gossip had moved from one group to the next. Escapees were being shipped out to the worst internment camps, the ones run by the U.S. Army. Gaetano later learned that Marco had gotten influenza after hiding for two nights in a cave with his comrades, so he was taken to the second floor of the hospital, while the others were locked up. Gaetano visited his *amicu* in the evening. The guard on duty was sympathetic to Gaetano and let him spend some time with Marco.

"You no listen to me, Marco."

"*Cui nun spera, nun dispera.*"

"If you don't hope, you won't be crushed," Gaetano translated.

Marco coughed while he chuckled. "Your English is getting better. Maybe they set you free."

"*Allura*, where will they send you?"

"I overheard Fort Sam Houston. I think Texas. A military base. They will be more strict there."

"I feel bad they caught you."

Marco snapped his fingers under his chin. The guard had not appeared, so his friend embellished the escape story and then they sat in silence for a while until a shadow appeared in the doorway.

"*Pregu*, take care of yourself." Gaetano kissed Marco's hand.

"*Arriverdeci Gaetano, miu amicu.*"

* * *

Their eight weeks were up and the final field exam was about to commence with all of the tank groups of the squadron lined up to run through the rigorous course. They had finished their written exams the evening before. It was all about their performance and, if they failed this test, the four of them would be marching in the infantry the rest of the war. Sergeant Ackers, hoping they boloed, engineered it so they would go last to provide a good laugh for the whole squadron after a long day in the field.

When their turn came, they shook hands, jumped into the tank and Sergeant Ackers, watching from a viewing stand, pumped his arm up and down. Off they streaked at the highest speed, the left and right steering laterals firmly within Nick's grip, turning, slowing down, and speeding up, going backwards and forwards, all the while the crew listening to Nathan's commands on their headsets. Their crew fired at the first target, obliterating it with two shots, repeating the same routine three more times, returning to their original spot in record time.

Sergeant Ackers drove the CO of the squadron to their tank. Lieutenant Colonel Jones got out of the jeep and climbed onto the tank, while Captain Monroe grinned from his seat. The crew snapped salutes and the Colonel returned a sharp one. "Fantastic, gentlemen." He turned to Ackers at the wheel, "I thought you said these men were inept. Looks like you could use a pair of glasses. We're going to need men like these on the battlefield, right sergeant!"

"Yes, sir!"

That evening Nathan's crew sat on the porch having a smoke. Everyone who passed on the way to the canteen gave some form of recognition. The barracks had emptied out, but they were still hanging around when Sergeant Ackers approached. They got up and stood at attention, but he never said: "At ease."

"I'll have to admit you qualified but it was just dumb luck. So don't let it go to your heads," the sergeant said.

"Is that why you came all the way from the NCO club?" Nick asked.

"No, there is one other thing—you guys may not be colored, but you're still niggras to me. Look at your swarthy Eye-talian skin—no wonder y'all called guineas. And your Jew friend—just black turned inside out. What about your mystery friend here? No doubt, he's got Injun blood or somethin'."

Nick threw a punch at Ackers that Nathan blocked. Paul put his face right up to the sergeant, but Al squeezed his body between the two of them. "Get out of here, sergeant," Paul yelled over Al's shoulder, "before you become the first casualty of this squadron." Ackers laughed at Paul and strutted away.

"Nathan, why the hell did you block my punch, after what he said about us?"

"That's what he wanted. If you strike someone in charge during war, you'd be court-martialed. Do you actually believe anyone would take our word over his, without any other witnesses?"

"How did you figure all of this out?" Paul asked.

"A wise old Jew warned me and I listened."

The camp cycle had been completed but no one seemed to know what was going to happen next. There were naval battles going on in the Pacific and an Allied military campaign raging in North Africa against Field Marshall General Rommel. As the men killed time, they moved about as if the war were on hold. The silence and the secretiveness of things unnerved them. Nick and his friends had seen the newsreels in the camp movie house that showed the fire, destruction and human carnage taking place all over Europe, horrified by the *Blitzkrieg* against Britain.

One evening the Colonel entered their barracks with Captain Monroe. "At ease, gentlemen. Before you know it, we'll be shipping out from the port of Galveston. The troop ships will be heading in many directions, and you won't know for sure where we're actually going until we are on the open sea. Remember, the Central Command Headquarters can change orders, so don't speculate too much. Just stick together and we'll get through this. You're well trained now and you're fighting for your country. In the meantime, we will be participating in joint maneuvers with engineer, artillery and infantry units. Any questions?" Everyone remained silent.

The Lieutenant Colonel left the barracks to continue his rounds, allowing Captain Monroe to linger awhile. While the other GIs chatted away, the captain asked Nathan's crew to step outside. The young men fidgeted while they waited for the crisp-tailored captain to speak. “You can light up if you want, gentlemen. I just have something private that needs to be aired out.”

“It’s not about Sergeant Ackers, is it, sir?” Nick asked.

“Don’t worry about him, Private Spataro. I just want to say that we’ll be heading to places that might provide a less than comfortable zone for you fellows as compared to the other recruits. I happen to think your tank crew is one of the best I have ever seen and would not want to lose you. But in all fairness to the whole squadron, I have to be sure of your commitment.” All four were intent on his every word. “It might be wise to pick another corridor of warfare, if anyone of you feels he may not be able to discharge his duties to the fullest.” He stared at them. “I mean unwavering.”

Paul responded: “Don’t worry about me, sir. I’ll do whatever I’m told. I’ll be shooting at the uniforms of the Axis countries and that includes Italy, sir.”

“Ditto for me, sir,” Al blurted out.

“What about you two?”

“Captain, I have a few cousins in Venice whom I’ve never met, but I’m thinking about all the families trapped by the Nazis. I’m ready to go to Italy.”

“And you, Nick?” The captain put his hand on Nick’s shoulder.

“To be honest, I’m not sure, sir.” The captain moved his hand down.

“That’s not an acceptable answer, Private Spataro.”

“Can you give me a little time, sir?”

"You don't have a lot of it. Talk it over with your buddies, if you like, but get back to me real quick. I've got to catch up with the colonel now." The captain jogged several yards, stopped and spun around as if he forgot something. "I'm meeting up with some old friends at the Officer's Club later, if anyone needs to talk with me." He stared at Nick.

Nick waved off his crew and went off to the wooded area to think things out. He lit up a cigarette and watched the big circles of smoke dissipate into the cool night air. The important pivotal scenes in his life popped into his head while the blinking stars faded in the black sky. Things had a way of working out badly, as if he were *disgraziatu*. He had warned Paul that he had issues about killing Italians but didn't want to desert this crew of best friends. It would be a piece of cake to argue that he would be killing Fascists and helping the resistance restore the republic. But he began doubting his motives and maybe there was too much fear in him, using this Italian obstacle as an excuse. Then again, what young man wanted to die before ever having a life?

It was twenty-three hundred hours, but Nick couldn't think any more—it was too painful. Maybe the only real happiness he ever had was at those big holiday celebrations that were shared by the family clan. What had all his Italian ancestors learned from all the wars and humiliations that traversed the Italian peninsula and the islands of Sicily and Sardinia—to survive, there was just the family. Only the Romans held real power but that civilization was ancient history now. Mussolini thought he had recreated that empire—what a cruel joke to play on the Italian people. Nick picked himself up and inched over to the Officer's Club. He could hear the loud conversation, groups of men singing along with the piano player and the ever-clinking glasses. He couldn't make up his mind, even as Captain Monroe stepped outside. And anyway, how many stones did he have in his head to think that tankers would be going anywhere else but the European front, not the islands of the Pacific.

He asked point blank: "Private Spataro, do you have a problem killing Italian combatants?"

"No, sir!"

"Glad to have you on board." The captain shook his hand and returned to the club.

The lights were out in his barracks and everyone was asleep. Nick quietly packed his gear and rested it next to his crew's bags. He had lied to the captain but his bond to the trio was unbreakable and as *pazzu* as it sounded, fighting Italians would prove his loyalty to America like nothing else, the vehicle to spring *Papà* from the internment camp. Nick was learning that everything was complicated in life, whether it was his girlfriend, family or the damn war. He would just have to live with the pain of it all, so he slunk into bed without a word to his friends, the night shadows revealing themselves like so many floaters in his eyes, until his nerves wore him down into a shallow sleep.

The next weekend Nick thought it was odd that there was still no news about shipping out, so it became a case of 'Hurry Up and Wait,' leaving him anxious about everything. *Papà* and he were living in Army camps, one in Montana, the other Texas, about as far from North Beach as they ever wanted, not even a view of the sea, both of them adrift in a sailboat with no idea where the winds would take them.

# V

After months of maneuvers, an outbreak of measles and a change in orders, their squadron finally shipped out in a convoy from the port of New Orleans. They made the crossing towards North Africa at the end of April 1943. During the voyage, the troops slept in hammocks on the tank deck below, suspended from steel bars in tiers of three and when they weren't cleaning equipment, they ate or killed time, playing hours of poker and gin rummy for big stakes and little. Nick wondered how many excuses the GIs could come up with to gamble the night away. Two weeks later, under a crescent moon, the American troopships approached the French Moroccan coast, while the Royal Naval frigates from Gibraltar scared off an attack by a wolf pack of U-boats. Nathan's crew couldn't sleep, so they went up on the main deck for some fresh air, as their LST, a Landing Ship, Tank, steamed closer to the port of Casablanca, liberated by British and American forces during Operation Torch.

"There's no turning back now," Nick said after a protracted silence, while the long stern wake marked their speed. "My father once said you can see the shoreline of Tunisia from Sicily. In the hills of the *Baglio,* north of Sciacca.

"*È veru,*" Paul confirmed.

"I wonder if my Venetian ancestors ever ran into yours on Sicily," Nathan added. "Some of them were navigators, you know. Wouldn't it be something if we could travel in a time machine and find out?"

"How about using it to find a peaceful island now?" Nick asked.

"Don't we all wish," Al said, shaking his head.

"I heard a lot of Brits got killed fighting the Desert Fox's Panzers in Libya," Paul said.

"Let's not talk about it, *cuginu.*"

"Yeah, Paul. The worst thing is the fear of the unknown," Nathan added. "Who knows what the battle front will be like by the time we get there?"

After several weeks of training exercises in Morocco with new, M10 Wolverine tank destroyers, their squadron moved east to Oudja, where they spent weeks in preparation for an amphibious assault on terrain that resembled the Sicilian coast. The port of Algiers was chosen as the point of embarkation for their convoy designated Dime Force, whose target was the Gela beach, one of four staging areas in southeastern Sicily. Their squadron would be part of General Paton's Seventh Army Landing.

Though not time for mail call, a soldier came by and told Nick to go to the mail station since there was a stack of letters waiting for him. When he grabbed the bundle, he flipped through them and opened one of the envelopes from his father. He found a second one within that had a cancellation stamped October 15, 1942. He wondered why these letters were delayed for so many months. He examined the flap of that second envelope, which appeared jagged as if it had been tampered with. He shrugged and slid out a one paragraph note, which he read to himself and then aloud:

> *Caru Nicolo,*
>
> *I can hardly believe that it is* verità, figghiu miu. *I am a free man, so* lu capu *says. I say to myself,* Gaetano, nun è possibile. *There must be some mistake. Ma no! È veru.* Doppu *Columbus Day, this year 1942, I will be paroled. No explanation.* Chi sacciu? *I must carry an enemy alien card wherever I go. They give me bus money and say go home. I am already in North Beach. Your mother make me a special dish,* zuppa di pesci. *I must find some work. I will ask around. No worry about your father no more.* Allura, *the only thing missing is you. As God is my judge, I will pray for you in my own house. Your mother will go to church for you.*
>
> *Con affettu, Papà*

Nick was so relieved that his father was a free man and back with his mother. There were plenty of other issues for *Papà*, his mental state and the loss of his fishing boat; even so *Papà* was home again. As his excitement abated he wondered why it had taken so long to get the news he had been hoping for and what was in the other letters. He hadn't let on to his buddies his concern about not receiving letters from his family but in retrospect, he thought it was dumb of him not to express his feelings, instead making up phony stories about the competence of the army mail handlers. He had considered that something bad happened to *Papà* and that no one wanted to write anything to him, having to leave out the crucial part. Nick rubbed his chin. Then again, no news was supposed to mean good news, but he couldn't deny to himself that the letters had been missing. And it couldn't be the censors at Fort Missoula because his father had already been released, and then it hit him—that sonofabitch Sergeant Ackers.

After loading up their LST, the Dime Force convoy set out, first cruising by Bizerta, Tunisia and then sharply turning north, passing the small island of Gozo near Malta, before executing the attack, codenamed Operation Husky. There was still some time left, so Nathan, Paul and Al tried to get some sleep before the beach assault, but Nick was restless so he went topside. He wanted to see Sicily in a different light before the attack, so he squeezed himself between a loaded truck and the deck railing. As the LST got closer, the only night sounds were an incessant engine hum and the waves sluicing the hull. Nick swore he saw a ghostly outline of the cliffs of Sicily in the distance, but whether it was his imagination or not, the sensation was as magnetic and mysterious as all the stories he had heard from his parents and *Ziu* Francesco. He had had a premonition he would find his way back to his ancestral home, but never envisioned he might cross the island in a tank.

The first-quarter moon had set shortly after midnight, the time when paratroopers of the 82nd Airborne were dropped in the hills behind the Axis batteries. From the ship's deck Nick could see flares set off before they hit the ground. He thought they had plenty of *coglioni* not just for jumping out of transport planes, vulnerable to enemy ack-ack, but attempting it in the nighttime.

During those dark early hours of July 10, 1943, Nick spied several submarines functioning as light lampposts marking their landing points. The first to hit the beach was a Ranger battalion, followed by the "Fighting First" of the Seventh Army. As they surged in their LCIs, officially called Landing Craft Infantry, the waves crashed over their heads, leaving them drenched and no doubt seasick from its churning ride. Nick saw them jumping out when the ramp lowered as they began to establish a beachhead at Gela without any naval or air support, and as far as Nick could make out, he guessed a tactical surprise. The troops met limited resistance from Sicilian reservists who manned the coastal batteries. Next to follow the infantry was a flotilla of LSTs, amphibious vessels loaded with Patton's tanks, heavy vehicles and countless DUKWs, that everyone called ducks because they could float in water and wobble on land, a silly image that amused Nick for a brief moment, pacifying the tension that affected all his senses.

Nick squeezed his way back to his tank and lowered himself into the driver's position while Nathan's crew sat in the tank waiting for the steel trap door to open it jaws. He was scared of things that you couldn't see, like running over invisible mines. As Nick looked at the faces of the crew team, he noticed their eyes were empty and bloodshot. No one said a word as the first vehicles, ducks and bulldozers were blown up by land mines.

It was already light out when Nathan's crew disembarked. Nick heard the chaotic sounds of officers and sergeants screaming instructions, drivers shouting at other drivers, all trying to get the trucks and jeeps out of the way of the next unloading LSTs, their wheels spinning in the sand. During this FUBAR, army slang for 'fucked up beyond all recognition,' there were exploding rounds from batteries in the hills reaching them near the Gela pier, as well as shelling from Italian and German tanks camouflaged in the distance. Nathan's crew was part of the first batch of tanks. By this point, the beach had been cleared of any remaining mines, but their tank destroyer still got stuck. Everyone except Nick jumped out of the tank, their boots sinking into the ground.

"*Minchia,* the tank is in some marshy crap!" Paul hollered over the din of noise and confusion that surrounded them, while Al paced around the perimeter of the tank. "Damn, rock that baby, Nick! You know, backwards, forwards!" He mimicked with his body.

"It don't look like it's goin' to move, Paul," Al added. "Looks like it's cemented in."

"Ah go on, Al. You don't know what you're yakkin' about!"

Nathan barked: "Will you two stop it! Let's see if we can get some help,"

"We'll figure it out ourselves. We're not stupid," Paul shot back. "*Nicolo*!"

As they argued how to best move their beached tank, Nick remained in the driver's position and looked beyond his tank team. His eyes locked onto an infantryman who had reddened bandages wrapped around what remained of his leg. They had been warned about land mines buried in the sand. The soldier stared out to sea, probably drugged up with morphine, waiting to be removed to a sick bay of a transport ship. Other casualties washed up onto the shore from LCIs that breached on false beaches and had come under enemy fire.

Tired of sparring with Paul, Nathan yelled up to Nick: "Try to use the momentum of the tank. Without burning the tranny!" Paul grimaced with arms akimbo. After many attempts, he called out: "Shut it down, Nick. Now!"

Some Seabees came by and rolled steel matting across the soft part of the beach, allowing their tank destroyer and a half dozen more to reach solid ground. Nathan heard over the radio that Italian light tanks, a Niscemi mobile group from the Livorno division, had just arrived. The message seeped in for

Nick when those tanks took turns firing at them on the beach.

Nathan shouted down to the gun crew, "We got a bunch of Italian tanks up ahead. Fire when I give the order." Paul and Al hopped to it.

Nathan returned hand signals to some of the other tank commanders, while he listened on his headphones, as Captain Monroe gave instructions over the radio. Nick eyed Nathan as his friend peered above the open turret, a horizontal rotating device that enabled them to shoot 360 degrees, which impressed Nick as a great improvement over the older tank destroyers they had trained with.

"Nick, move right, full speed. Don't stop till I tell you." As Nick sped diagonally across the battlefield, Nathan yelled: "Fire at will!" Paul kept changing the position of the gun as quickly as Nathan ordered. One of the Italian tanks wandered too close and Nathan's crew scored their first knockout. At that moment naval gunfire opened up and the Italian tanks that weren't destroyed reversed their engines all the way to the Gela plain. The ammunition ran out for the tank destroyers, so Nick shut the engine down, his thoughts racing as to what was going to happen next, his crewmates silent and mentally spent.

The smoke billowed across the entire sky with intermittent orange flashes. The accuracy of naval gunners so incredible, they had knocked out every artillery battery on high ground. The Sicilian reservists, overwhelmed by the bombardment and the onslaught of Allied soldiers, became the first to surrender, while all the Axis tanks retreated. Nick had read about ancient Sicily and understood once again that these island people were under siege by another overpowering armada. He puzzled over what he was doing here anyhow, a willing participant in yet another invasion of the land of his ancestors and wondered whether his tank hit any drafted Sicilian soldiers, maybe even civilians foolish enough to be in the area where they blew up their first kill. He recalled that Niscemi was the name of a Sicilian town. *Gesù Cristo*, he knew they were fighting the guys in black hats like in the movies—combatants who were real life fascists and Nazis out there who wanted to kill Nick and his friends. The stories had been leaking out as to what these bastards were capable of. But he couldn't get it out of his head—did he kill any Sicilians? All the coastal forces surrendered after the first day of this assault. Later on in Rome, Nick would learn from an intelligence report that these Sicilian reservists were not political for the most part, the fascists and Germans never meaning much to them, or even Italians in general for that matter. He also uncovered something else he could never have imagined.

On the second day of the invasion the Hermann Goring *Panzer* Division counterattacked against the port of Gela from the northeast by way of the Biscari airfield. Their Tiger I tanks came in from the east and inflicted a lot of casualties, while the rest of the American Armored Division tanks waited to be de-waterproofed, the ammunition still scarce. When Nick first caught sight of the Tiger tanks, he realized that the Germans had upped the ante. They were trapped and were about to be buried, and no one would even know where his body was, six feet under the sand or beneath the sea. Like a *miraculu*, Nick crossed himself when he heard the Navy big guns obliterating the counterattack, starting with a barrage from the light cruiser, *Savannah*. The German tanks could not withstand the firepower from the destroyers and cruisers, so the enemy fled.

"Look at those Krauts scrammin'," Paul gloated.

"Yeah, we sure gave them hell," Al added.

"They'll come a time when we're out of range of big naval guns," Nathan cautioned.

"Ah, don't go on and spoil it Nathan," Paul rejoined.

"You don't know what you're talking about. You never listen to anybody," Nick said.

"Just drive us around, Nick. We'll do all the shootin'."

"You don't know *buona fortuna* when you see it, *cuginu*." Paul snapped his hand dismissively at Nick, while Nathan's eyes revealed he agreed with Nick. That same morning Nathan's crew were part of a small detachment of Sherman tanks that headed north on the Niscemi road to assist groups of infantrymen, who had been cut off into many pockets and pin-downed, separated from their regiment.

"Nick, we need to get to the side flank of those Panthers."

"Are you sure this is going to work, Nate?"

Nathan directed their M10, its light armor giving them a maneuverability edge, knocking out two enemy tanks in their first run. The M4 Sherman, the workhorse tank, with the help of anti-tank guns from the regiment, was able to destroy thirteen other German Mark III and Panther tanks, after a repeated exchange of hell fire. At the end of the tank battle, the 6-inch guns of the light cruiser, USS *Boise*, commenced firing, blowing up many of the remaining enemy tanks in retreat. Nick mused how long their luck would last through the nerve center of Sicily and on the spinal cord of Italy.

Throughout the invasion German bombers tried to destroy the armada and Nick checked his watch when a Ju–88 bomber off of Licata, mid-afternoon on July 11th, hit the American transport, the S.S. Robert Rowan. It was 1540. Nathan had Nick guide the tank onto the side of the road to adjust the rotation of the treads, just as that ship exploded into a blackish gray plume of smoke. The surrealistic image reminded Nick of the Greek mythology of Sicily he had studied, Mount Etna being the gateway to Hades, the smoking Rowan a harbinger of more tragedies to come.

That evening Axis planes attacked the naval ships offshore for an hour. After the enemy flew away, air transports appeared overhead, carrying paratroopers from Colonel Tucker's 504th Combat Team, who had missed their Drop Zones. Nick cringed and cried out '*Madonna, Madonna*,' while Nathan and Al gaped in horror, Paul crossing himself several times, as they witnessed the second wave being shot down under 'friendly fire' by AA guns from Allied ships and the beachhead. Nick thought how in hell could anyone come up with the term, 'friendly fire,' an oxymoron if ever there was one, a literary term he learned in his senior Honors class. On second thought, this was no time for him to intellectualize things—to call anything 'friendly fire' was simply moronic.

By the third day of Operation Husky, Captain Jones selected Nathan's crew as the point tank to lead their squadron further inland. By this time the fighting had subsided, so the squadron encamped in a secluded location off the coastal road to Agrigento. After they set up a tent next to the tank, Nick cuffed his Zippo lighter, lit up and passed his cigarette around, so everyone could light up. They squatted in a circle and didn't speak until half their cigarettes burnt.

"You know what was as scary as the beach landing?" Nick asked, as the crew fidgeted with their gear. "Sitting in that stinking LST tomb on the sea."

"You're right, *cuginu*."

"Just like a duck in water under the bead of a hunter's rifle," Nick continued.

"I can picture a black duck from my home town," Al put in.

"And then without …"

"Bang!" Paul interrupted Nick, as he mimicked shooting a rifle.

"Without any warning, the damn duck winds up dead, ass sticking out of the water."

"Yeah, drowning to death like those bodies bobbing near the beachhead." Paul took another drag.

"Face down in the black sea," Al continued.

"Don't dwell on this stuff. We all made it in one piece, didn't we?" Nathan inhaled the smoke through his nose. "But I have to admit." He took another drag. "It gives me the willies thinking about it."

"I heard having Patton as commander is our best chance to get out alive," Al said.

"Yeah, but didn't he say in one of his pep talks, 'We will get the name of killers and killers are immortal'?" Nathan asked. "It scares the shit out of me when our own officers start talking about warriors who won't die in battle."

"Yeah, like we're the Persian Ten Thousand Immortals," Nick concluded.

They buried the cigarette butts into the dirt, unrolled their sleeping bags and squirreled in. While his partners slept, Nick left the crew tent to gaze at the stars. He could see flashes on the northeast horizon, which marked the front lines where the British allies fought the German and Italian troops. He ruminated about the young GIs dead on the beach and wondered if many Italians or Sicilian *paesani* died. He thought about the flaming Italian tank they blew up, realizing he could have been in that tank had his family not emigrated to America. Perhaps they could be distant cousins. He would have to push these thoughts into the back of his mind. The pressure was already building inside and he prayed that he wouldn't crack up. He closed his eyes and thought about his mother and father reunited, the money scarce. Soon after Nick's musings detoured to Deborah and what she was doing now and if there was another guy. What he wouldn't do to be with her one more time. He looked for a shooting star but the sky offered up the usual patterns. He gave up and scrunched into the tent.

The next day Colonel Jones briefed the captains of each tank company in his squadron, the news filtering down to the tank crews. The Allied Powers' main objective was to take Messina, barely two miles from the Italian mainland. From Sicilian stories he heard in North Beach, Nick knew the island had some rugged terrain, which rose in the north with the Nebrodi mountain range, linking all the way eastward with the fiery volcano, Mt. Etna. He speculated which direction their squadron would go since their unit had been attached to Lieutenant General Patton's Armored division. Would it be taking the most direct and dangerous route, heading northeast or storming Palermo first in the west and then heading east to Messina? While the brass argued battle tactics, the tanks sat idle.

After supper Nathan played poker with Al and Paul, while Nick sat under the tent opening and smoked a cigarette. He calculated that their camp was an hour and half drive by jeep to the *paese natale* of his father. He was very curious about his *Nannu* and the family hometown, having heard so many anecdotes from his *Papà*. The next morning he checked with Captain Monroe.

"I've never seen my grandfather. He lives in a fishing village not far from here. With your permission, Sir, may I visit him?"

"We have orders from General Patton, but I'm not at liberty to give details yet." The captain rubbed his chin. "Stay right here while I pass this by the Colonel." He returned within five minutes. "Private Spataro, the Colonel likes you boys so much, he going to let you use his own jeep. But I want you back by nineteen hundred, not a minute later. You can bring one of your buddies but the rest have to stay with the tank. Is that understood?"

"Yes, Sir! Thank you, Captain."

"Before you go, there's something that's been troubling me." The captain looked straight into Nick's eyes. "I grew up in Virginia and never cottoned to folks like Ackers. The South deserves a better image." The captain smiled. "Anyway, have a great time with your granddaddy, but watch out for yourself on the main road." As Nick jogged away he added: "And make sure you don't run into Sergeant Ackers."

# VI

Nick had chosen Nathan to accompany him to find his grandfather because his friend wanted to eat an Italian dinner in the countryside. Paul had agreed to stay with Al since the grandfather was on Nick's paternal side. The pair didn't talk much while riding on the main road because they had to be vigilant for sudden strafing. When Nick turned off onto a narrow dirt road, the jeep jostled them and Nathan teased him about his driving. Midway on the journey they passed by an orchard of almond trees that had turned deep green, later on rows of olive trees full of grayish-green ovals and then groves of lemon trees, the scent of citrus lingering in the air, patches of golden-yellow brooms popping up along the way to Sciacca. They eventually descended down to the port of the town, passing rows of idle fishing boats in the *Porta San Salvatore*. Nick managed to find *Corso Vittorio Emanuele* that led to the main *Piazza Angelo Scandaliato*, overlooking the sea. A group of elderly men chatted on the stone bench, while a fruit vendor poked his head outside the window of his truck, calling out, "*pesche, meloni, arancini, limone*!"

They got out of the jeep and walked over to a half-filled fountain and splashed water on their faces. Nick surveyed the scene and chose the café as a good place to inquire about his grandfather. They entered the place and Nick noticed the customers stopped talking and silently observed them. He questioned a skinny man in his seventies who had just finished steaming the milk for a *cappuccino* and placed the cup on the bar, giving them a distrustful look. A large poster of *il Duce* hung on the wall behind him. The *barista* grudgingly gave Nick the directions to his grandfather's place—*Vincinu lu Baglio, vai*!

Nick got lost, which made them hotter and hungrier until they came across a dusty, roadside *alimentari*. It had a fruit stand outside, packed with blood oranges. The roof looked like it was ready to collapse from neglect. They stopped to buy a bag of the oranges, when an elderly woman in a black dress cajoled them into sitting outside under a large cedar tree at the side of the building. She promised to cook an *autenticu* Sicilian meal. Her grandson carried out a table and chairs, set up everything under the shade of that lone tree, putting a white tablecloth on top of the table. She produced a four course dinner with *vinu dâ casa*, everything home grown, from an *antipasto* of roasted red peppers and fried eggplant, a *pasta* with a creamy, tomato sauce, grilled lamb with herbs, finishing off with figs and *espresso*. Afterwards, they lit up *Toscano* cigars.

"Feels like our last supper before an execution," Nick commented.

"Don't go morbid on me, will ya!" Nathan tapped the ashes onto the ground. "The *Signora* gave you good directions. I'll just stay here and finish my cigar, so you can have some private time with your grandfather. Maybe even take a little nap, Sicilian style." Nathan laughed.

"See you later, Nate."

After almost driving past his grandfather's place, Nick hit the brakes. He could barely notice the farm cottage at the far end of an overgrown footpath. The sound of cicadas intensified, as he approached his *nannu*'s home. He heard the sound of metal screeching over a stone wheel. A man with a shock of white hair and a bushy moustache sharpened a long knife, using his foot to propel the mechanism. Nick could see through the open door that the octogenarian busied himself at his task and didn't even bother to raise his head when Nick's shadow fell on him.

He called out: "*Nannu*?"

The old man stopped pedaling and turned around, but still held the knife in his hand.

"*Cu è stu scanusciutu Americanu*?

"*Sugnu Nicolo Spataro*."

*Nannu* plunged the knife into a wood block. He looked the young man up and down and shouted: "*Vai, vai*, American stranger!" Nick stood his ground but felt anxious that he had found the wrong person. "Speak in English, if you wish. I know many languages."

"I am Nick Spataro. I'm looking ..."

"You want to take my land away! *Vai*!"

"I'm not interested in your land."

"So why do you call me *Nannu*?"

"I'm your grandson with the same name. Gaetano and Lucia's son from San Francisco!"

"*Si*. Come closer, so I can see you better." He touched Nick's face with his calloused hand. The old man's blue eyes glowed and Nick kissed him on both cheeks.

"How did you find me, *Nicolo*?"

"The *barista* in town. He wasn't too friendly."

"*Quella fascista*! He spreads rumors about me. That I am a spy for the enemy. He is like the fool Giufà, but not likeable at all." He leaned back to get a better look at Nick. "You looka like my son when he left with me for America. The same nose, the same eyes." *Nannu* laughed with joy. He got up from his bench and went over to table that had rows of unlabeled bottles of red wine and some short water glasses. "Come and sit here with me and drink my wine." He poured two glasses. "It has been many years since I left *figghiu miu* after your *Nanna* died." He raised his arms to the ceiling. "My sons and daughter wanted to stay in America. Make their fortune." All of a sudden, *Nannu*'s face darkened with a frown. "*Sicilia* has had so many invaders over the centuries, everyone has lost count. Why do you wear the uniform of an invader?"

"I was born in America. I am an American."

"You speaka with your head, but not from the heart. Why you fighting against the Italians?" *Nannu* pressed his fingertips together as if in prayer and rocked them, as if to say: 'Why in God's name did you do it?'

"I'm fighting Fascists, not Italians," he responded, a mantra he had to keep repeating to himself.

"Fascists, communists, socialists, liberals, conservatives. They all the same to me. All you need is country air, fresh food and a woman to share it with, maybe some children to help you with the harvesting and passing on our name. What does it matter what kind of government we have?" He stuck his chin out. "*Minchia*! The greedy always find a way to keep everything for themselves, throwing breadcrumbs to everyone who can't sense how the world works." *Nannu*'s eyes became fiery and he waved his fist. "*Allura*, Sicily will endure, despite all the invasions, the Greeks and Phoenicians, Romans, Saracens and Normans, Angevins, Spanish Bourbons, even this one." *Nannu*'s eyes gleamed then chuckled. "*Ma è veru*, I am happy the Americans and British have come to kick the Germans and the *fasciste* out. *Ma i mafiosi di cosa nostra* … these so-called men of honor," he spit on the ground, "will soon be let loose from prisons and their towns of exile, all over *Sicilia* …" Nick read the exasperation in *Nannu*'s face as he paused to catch his breath. "Lika packs of rats running down a rope dock line at every port." *Nannu*'s eyes widened and he tapped his grandson's face. "*Me niputi bellu*! You are a good boy, I can tell." He held the bottle of wine up in celebration and refilled the glasses to the brim.

"Tell me some stories about my father. When he was a child."

"Do you like my homemade wine?"

"*Si, moltu bonu*!"

"*Bravu*. I will stop telling them only when you must go back to your war." He gulped some wine down and wiped his lips with a palm. "When your father was ten years old, we left the life of a *cuntadinu* in *lu Baglio* to become fishers of the sea, *piscaturi*. At first *mi figgli* were unhappy to leave the countryside, but your father, Gaetano, took to the water like a dolphin to the sea. His older brothers made fun of him, but one day when we set out to lay out our nets, Gaetano cried and cried to come with us, while his brothers laughed. He jumped into the water and followed our boat all the way out of the port. Then I yelled, *Basta! Basta!* And my oldest son, Rodolfo, turned the boat around. *Pocu* Gaetano waded into one of our nets that we had flung out when we were near enough and pulled him aboard. From that day on, we allowed your father to act as our cabin boy."

"*Bravu Nannu*, tell me more."

"One day I heard about our *paisani* from Sciacca who went to a place in America. North End, Boston! *Chi sacciu*? What do I know of such a place? What about Brooklyn? *Alluru*, we saved our money to land where money grows on trees."

"*Nannu*, did you really believe that?"

*Nannu* laughed and filled the glasses once more. "When you are poor, *miu carinu* Nicolo, you will believe anything, no matter how *pazzu*. *Bivi lu vinu di*

*Nannu!*" They drank the red wine in two gulps and *Nannu* refilled the glasses, as he continued his family narrative.

"*Alluru*, in *Ameriga* we found a home on Elizabetha Street. *Ancora* we save our money, worka in the tunnels of New Yorka, where there is no sun and *Nanna* does piece work in the apartment. Dig and sweat all day long. We had dreams of fishing again in our own boats. *Ma*, things happened in *Ameriga*, and *la famigghia* split up. My two oldest boys, Rodolfo and Rocco, they fisha out of Boston. All the *Sciaccese* are there, they say to me, *cosi* why be among *scanusciuti*? My daughter, Antonina, she marry a barber and stay in Brooklyn. At least he was a *Sicilianu* and not a *Calabrese* or even a *Napolitana*."

"I never met my uncles and aunts in Boston and Brooklyn. Mamma says it's too expensive to travel so far."

"We are scattered like *l'ebbraiica genti*."

"Like the Jews from *The Holy Bible*, *Nannu*?"

"*Si. Cosi*, that's is why I returned to our homeland after *Nanna* died. There must be some trace of the Spatoro in *Sicilia*."

"So how did *Papà* and you wind up in San Francisco? North Beach instead of North End."

"You ask questions, *bravu*. You are like *miu* Gaetano, always questions, questions, while his brothers are silent and looka like *Fata Morgana* will casta a spell on them at any moment." *Nannu* laughed at his own joke. "Everyone in the world wanted to go to California to strike it rich. *Cosi*, I take my youngest son with me. When I left him and Lucia, they started to change sardines into gold. *Ma* without *Nanna*, I could not stay and did not want to be a burden to *figghiu miu*. It was too bad that you had not been born." *Nannu* rubbed his hands across Nick's cheeks and kissed him on the forehead.

"*Why Nannu? Pirichi?*"

"*Pirichi*—I would not have left after seeing you. *E la verità. Iu sugnu felici e tristu a chistu momentu.* At this moment, my grandson—*comu* the two masks of drama that we learned from our Greek ancestors—one happy, the other sad. *Chista è nostra vita*, Nicolo, this is our life, Nicky."

# VII

N*annu*'s tales punctuated Nick's thoughts on his drive back to retrieve Nathan. The jeep swirled in the gravel and awoke his friend. Nathan had saved the stubs of the cigars and when he jumped into the jeep, Nick lit them up.

"So how did it go with your grandfather?"

"Like listening to an epicurean and stoic at the same time."

"I like the epicurean better."

"He told me wonderful stories about my father. Things I never knew about him."

"Making up for lost time, Nick." Nathan slid the cigar to the side of his mouth. "We'd better hit the road."

The old lady waved and her grandson ran over to the jeep and tossed a few blood oranges into Nathan's lap. Nick flipped a Hershey's chocolate bar to the boy and sped away.

They got back just in time, but Sergeant Ackers pounced on them from out of nowhere. "Who gave you permission to leave? You're both AWOL." Two

MPs stood behind him. "Arrest these guys! They stole the colonel's jeep."

"What are you talking about, Sergeant? The colonel gave us permission," Nathan protested, as the MPs put them in irons.

"What are you nuts? We're not AWOL! I just spent the afternoon with my grandfather. Talk to Captain Monroe, if you don't believe me, for Christ's sake."

The sergeant motioned to the MPs. "Take them away."

"When I get out of these cuffs, we're going to settle this once and for all," Nick spat out.

"Listen to the thieving dago," the sergeant snickered.

"Release those men immediately," the captain ordered as he came from behind a supply truck. "As for you, sergeant, you're lucky we're in a war zone. Now do something productive!" The captain went around the truck to finish his conversation with the supply sergeant.

"Some day you guys aren't gonna have your little savior around. Just watch out someone don't toss a grenade into your turret while you're star gaping." Nathan and Nick glared at the sergeant as he strutted away.

"Why do I think that man is a Nazi in an American uniform?" Nathan asked.

In the evening Nathan's crew sat on the ground near their tent and passed around K-rations, the highlight being canned chicken paté and two ounce chocolate bars that they nibbled on while they wrote letters. When it got dark, Nathan, Paul and Al turned in and Nick sat on the fender of the tank. There were no stars out, just clouds that cut across the full moon. The more he stared at the sky, the more he recognized images in the vapors. One of them turned into the shape of *Nannu*'s hair. Nick remembered the touch of his grandfather's rough hand on his face and the gleam of recognition in his light blue eyes. Nick wished *Papà* had been there to share the moment. Someday he would return with *Papà* to see *Nannu* before he expired over the grinding wheel.

At dawn the armored division fired up their vehicles. The colonel gathered all the officers and tank commanders in his squadron and briefed them. "Since we're the swiftest, our tank destroyers will lead the division. We're heading northwest to Palermo, not, I repeat, not northeast to Messina. These orders are straight from General Patton himself. If there are no questions, mount your tanks!" As Nick steered onto the new course, he questioned Nathan on the logic of this move. His crew commander shrugged it off.

Nick kept the tank destroyer at full throttle, 32 miles per hour, while the rest of his squadron was stretched out along the main road in a column, followed by another squadron of heavier Sherman tanks and infantry battalions. They first followed the coastal road west to Agrigento and then headed north on the route to Palermo. As they proceeded north and began to climb higher, the spinning tracks of the tanks ricocheted off the short, stone walls on the sides of the road, giving off an eerie Martian-like sound, reminding Nick of the book, *War of the Worlds*, that he had read after listening to the chilling rendition by Orson Welles on the radio. They continued several days over dilapidated roads of serrated stones through high mountains with scary hairpin turns, as if the column following was one elongated coil of a thick-skinned serpent. They reached the extended stretch of the valley, as Nick grinded the tank tracks by farmlands that ran up hills, rectangles of once yellow harvested wheat fields now scorched brown by the Sicilian sun, the only sign of life, clusters of hard green grapes in scattered vineyards shielded by mountains. Nathan took note of a huge mountain to the left, signaling they were getting closer to the sea, later on moving west along the north coastal road to Palermo.

Nathan's crew had been cruising so fast they lost sight of their tank column in the rear. The road ahead was littered with rusted farm machinery and Nathan ordered Nick to veer off onto a nearby secondary road. They had gone a half-mile when Nathan ordered him to stop the tank.

"What's up Nate?"

"I have a feeling this is a setup." Nathan aimed the 50-caliber Browning, secured on the front of the turret, and shot off a volley that detonated land mines 50 yards away.

"Holly shit!" Nick called out to Nathan. Several minutes later, stray mortar rounds from a faraway position whammed right in front of them.

"Nick, back out! Double time!"

By the time they got back to the fork, their squadron had caught up with them with Captain Monroe's company in the lead. The captain radioed Nathan to join them '*toute suite*'!"

"The krauts must have mined the roads," Nathan shouted out as they approached the captain's tank.

The captain ordered his tank crews to clear away the blockade, and then a Sherman 'Crab' mine-sweeper was brought up from the rear to detonate any anti-tank mines on the road. When the Seventh Army made it to the Tyrrhenian Sea, it was a flat run to Palermo. The monotony of the road broke for Nick when he spotted the blue-green waters that met the jagged rocks along the coast. When the sun went down, they halted to eat and rest up. They were surprised by the lack of resistance from the Axis troops.

Nathan's crew sat on the ground in a circle near their tank and had just finished their K-ration supper. They were already looking like a bunch of unshaven hobos in uniform, their fatigues filthy and bodies reeking, not having a shower since the invasion began. They unraveled their sleeping bags to get some rest before they mounted the assault on Palermo.

By oh five the next morning their squadron was moving along the coastal road. As the tank destroyers approached the edge of the foothills, the city of Palermo stretched across the plain all the way to the blue bay. They could see the dome of the Cathedral of Palermo with its Gothic *campanile* and, not far away, at the highest point, the crenellated wall of *Palazzo dei Normanni*, grand enough for General Patton to pick as his headquarters. *Monte Pellegrino* rose to the west of the city.

The rapid advance on Palermo made some sense to Nick after Nathan explained to his crew that the Germans had already fled to Messina, leaving the Italians alone to defend the city and its important harbor. Some advance patrols had already captured key officers. On the evening of July 22nd, Nick witnessed the surrender of the capital of Sicily by *Generale di Brigata* Giuseppe Molinaro with the Junker-like scar across his left cheek. General Patton had got what he craved—the liberation of the first city of Europe.

The next morning the U.S. Seventh Army rolled into the center of the old city, clouds of dust hovering over the road all the way back to the hills. As Nathan's crew followed the column of tanks, they passed under welcome banners, the crowds waving American and Italian flags. Some of the *Palermitani* cheered from the balconies of their apartment buildings, their bodies appearing to undulate from the rumble of the tanks. As the parade clogged up the long stretch of *Via Vittorio Emanuele*, their tank crunched the hard surface of the street pavement.

Nathan, Paul and Al, standing in the wide-open turret, beamed at the crowds. Paul gave the victory sign, while his *cuginu* steered with his head sticking out of the hatch. Nick surveyed the side streets and saw devastated buildings along the entire stretch. He had read in a newspaper that the bombing of Palermo started in May of '43, when the B-17 Flying Fortresses dropped their payloads. By the time they reached the viewing stands, a Sicilian band played while the Cardinal watched from the Cathedral steps. Though the Sicilians may have been happy that the war was over for them after Palermo had been liberated, Nick wondered what family tragedies hid behind those smiling faces.

When the festivities were over, Colonel Jones positioned his squadron near the *Kalsa* section of Palermo, the old Arab quarter that fronted onto the harbor. Nathan's crew began routine maintenance on their tank while waiting for orders. As they were working, a long ragged line of Italian soldiers was being marched over to a prisoner's compound outside the city limits. Nick handed a wrench to his cousin and watched them go by along the road. All four of them had stopped what they were doing till the POWs passed. In disheveled and dusty uniforms, they dragged themselves along in uneven lines surrounded by armed guards. Nick thought many of the Italian soldiers seemed relieved and some even smiling. He was tempted to go over to speak with some of them but then he remembered the flaming Italian tank near Gela beach. Nathan handed out some cigarettes but Nick held back with the crew.

Sergeant Ackers came up from behind the crew and yelled: "Stop your gawking and get working on that tank." They all turned towards the sergeant who moved sharply to the next tank and managed to smash into Nathan's shoulder with his massive biceps, knocking him off balance. Paul picked up Nathan and

Nick got into the sergeant's face. "What the hell to do you think you're doing?"

"Mind your business, corporal," the sergeant barked, while towering over Nick, his chest pumped out. "Your friend can't even stand straight."

Nathan ran towards the sergeant and halted when he heard the colonel yell from a distance, "Don't move, Sergeant Fein!" The colonel strode over to Ackers with Captain Monroe right behind him, as a bunch of tankers circled around. All the soldiers stood at attention and saluted but the colonel didn't return the salute, bellowing, "At ease!" He glared at Ackers for a moment, and then turned to the group. "Okay, the troops need a little entertainment tonight, so you guys are going to settle this once and for all. A boxing match between Sergeant Fein and Sergeant First Class Ackers."

"It's my fight, colonel," Nick volunteered.

"Wait a minute. This is between the sergeant and me," Nathan protested. "I'm the one that hit the ground."

"Captain Monroe, you settle this. I have to see to the rest of my rounds with the troops." The colonel moved through the parting crowd.

"It's you two," as the captain pointed to Nathan and Ackers. "The Colonel has to meet with General Patton this evening at the *Palazzo Normanni*. I'll referee this fight to make sure it stays clean." The captain checked his watch. "Nineteen hundred oh fifteen, right in this spot."

The troops dispersed to their tents and Nick and Nathan sat on the fender of the tank, while Paul and Al crouched under its shade and had a smoke. "Why didn't you let me handle Ackers, Nate?"

"Remember what happened in Lincoln Park?"

"Yeah." Nick laughed.

"What's goin' on up there, guys?" Paul stood up, squinting his eyes from the sun. "You're pissin' me off. Like you two are speakin' another language or somethin'." I was there too. Maybe youse guys got a case of amnesia?"

They jumped off and dragged Paul to the ground in a playful manner, then let him go. The three of them told their versions of the story to a wide-eyed Al, exaggerating the details and interrupting each other at will.

In the evening the whole squadron turned out, waiting for the captain's arrival. Some of the soldiers were mock fighting, while others made jokes about each other. The bulk of them were placing bets with the company bookie and his two partners, who reminded Nick of the Three Stooges, except these mugs were real operators who always had plenty of dough to lend. Large groups of GIs gathered around, even ones from other companies, playing the odds in a frenzy. As soon as the officers showed up, the troopers calmed down. Nick managed to place the last bet for their crew without the captain seeing him, knowing that he disapproved of gambling.

"Listen up, gents," the captain shouted, while a lieutenant gave a shrill whistle. "Our boxers are here now, so let's form a circle. But give them plenty of room."

Sergeant Ackers broke through the crowd, bare-chested to show off his massive pectoral muscles, a gut exposed over his shorts. Nathan wore a tight, once white undershirt, which outlined his wiry frame and loose fitting fatigue pants. They approached the captain who handed them the gloves. "A clean fight and you break the second I tell you. We're following the Queensberry rules for 12 rounds. Is that understood?"

"Yes, sir," the two fighters said in unison.

The first six rounds were a standoff with neither opponent attaining an advantage over the other in points scored. After the midway point, Sergeant Ackers used the same techniques as before, but the blows had a more damaging effect on Nathan's face and torso, which panicked Nick as he tried to stop the blood from flowing when Nathan hobbled to his corner. It looked like a TKO might be declared in Acker's favor.

During a minute break into the tenth round, the captain went over to the sergeant and whispered into his ear: "If you don't take out whatever you have in your left glove, not only will I disqualify you, you'll never make Master Sergeant."

"Something's not kosher," Nick said in Nathan's ear. "Stay focused and show that sonofabitch."

"Cover that puffed eye and get that *testa di merda*," Paul advised, as Al jabbed the air with his fists several times.

The captain signaled for the next round. Nathan's agility and adrenalin came back like a sudden crack of lightning and he overwhelmed Sergeant Ackers, who was knocked down as the gong sounded the end of the eleventh. The 12th round Ackers went on the defensive and dropped his guard for a split second, enabling Nathan to knock him flat out on the ground. Ackers sat up, shaking his head and the captain declared Nathan the winner. The crowd roared while Nick, Paul and Al ran over to Nathan. The foursome jumped up and down, linked arms and strutted back towards their tank. Later, hot showers were set up for the squadron and Nathan and his crew were ushered to the front of the line.

By noon the next day, they had completed their maintenance checklist, so Nick and Paul decided to explore the *Kalsa* neighborhood. They came upon abandoned, baronial *palazzi* in a maze of narrow streets reminiscent of a medieval medina. They lost themselves for a while, then followed the smell of Arab-Sicilian cooking that came from a tiny kiosk with a twisted corrugated roof. A woman with a wrinkled face and a desperate look coaxed the American GIs into buying fish *couscous*, redolent with spices. They sat on the dusty ground to avoid the streaming sun and picked the bones clean. Paul purchased a half dozen blood oranges from her and stuffed them into his shirt.

As they continued deeper into the neighborhood, what had been a glancing view during the parade became a stark reality for Nick—cratered out buildings multiplied, some houses crumbling down in the heat and dust. The rescue workers were pulling out corpses from previous bombings. Nick got teary-eyed when he saw a tiny shrouded body being placed on an open truck, a family wailing as they followed the body in a procession as the vehicle inched its way through the rubble. Paul shook his head in disgust. Nick figured some children had missed the evacuation, their families too poor and illiterate to escape the city. They had died hiding in buildings that collapsed. He agonized over how many more *paesani disgraziati* perished and recognized that, if he wanted to get through this with any sanity left, he would have to shelve these thoughts in the back of his memory stacks.

On their way out, they became disoriented by the maze-like alleys and streets, the sun searing their brows, the sweat breaking through the back of their shirts.

"I feel dizzy, Paul. Let's stop awhile."

"You look pale as a ghost. Sit over here in the doorway. There's some shade." Nick plopped down and Paul slid next to him. He took out an orange and cut it half with his pocketknife. "Here, suck the juice out." When Nick finished, he gave him the second half. "Maybe the Sicilian sun's gettin' to you, Nick."

"You're right." Nick took out a handkerchief and wiped his brow.

"Hope I wasn't a jerk for puttin' pressure on you to team up with me."

"I wanted to spring *Papà*, so I figured I'd volunteer for this."

"I was goin' anyways, with or without you. I came here to kill the enemy, all of them. That's what we trained for. Your problem is you think too much. I ain't gonna lose any sleep over this. Just want to get the job over, so we can get the hell out of here in one piece. I'll tell you another thing *cuginu*, when we go back home, we will be 100% bonafide Americans." Paul stood up. "Grab my arm and I'll pull you up." Nick worked his way up and wiped his brow again. "I got one question for you." Paul looked down the street.

"*Chi*?"

"Why else did you agree to come here?"

"I wanted to stick with you guys. Figured maybe it wouldn't be so bad after all. A pipe dream of mine that the Italians would say *minchia*, we had enough of this Mussolini *merda*. They'd side with us before we landed on the first beach."

"Like I've said before. You think too much. Remember *cuginu*—we always played on the same baseball team." Paul smiled and tapped Nick's cheek.

Nick and Paul eyed each other that it was time to go and they stumbled over crushed building stones, somehow finding the way back through the portal gate of *Kalsa* that led to their tank. Paul delighted in Nathan's just finished artwork—a painting of a Fiat 3000 tank and two Panther tanks on the driver's side of the steel armored turret. Nick had recognized Nathan's talent right away but had nothing to say this time, the silence broken by a dog yelping as its skeletal frame foraged through the rubble. It straggled over to them but kept a safe distance. Paul took a blood orange out of his shirt and threw it near the gate. The dog dragged itself to the fruit, clamped it into his mouth and moved furtively through the gate. Nick and Paul recounted what they had seen to Nathan and Al, who smoked cigarettes in silence. After crushing the butts into the pavement, they hopped onto the tank and sat around the edge of the rear engine, facing the Mediterranean. As dusk approached and the sea darkened, Nick's buddies had already found other things to do but he remained on top.

Nick felt as if he were soldered to the steel, mulling over the bodies he had seen being dragged out of the razed homes. But his crew was lucky they weren't dead like all those young GIs on the beach, who would be buried here, never to go back home to their families and his thoughts then segued to the dead Italians from their first tank kill. Who were those men? Where did they come from? The north or south of Italy? And what about their parents, wives, children? Yes, he was only killing fascists but Nick would never know if they were real *fasciste* or just young men drafted to fight Mussolini's war.

It was not that Nick wasn't grateful they survived their first amphibious assault, but as he sat at the edge of his ancient, ancestral island, he knew, *è veru*, it was just the beginning of their odyssey, but this wasn't going to be a mythological journey. There was no mistaking that he got to Palermo in a tank and not on a passenger liner. If he could ever get himself to return someday, maybe he would see things differently, talk himself out of all the things he had seen, all the things he had done. It already felt years since Nick left home, the voyage murky and unfathomable ahead.

He didn't want to turn in for the night because he sensed a nightmare was coming on and he didn't want to embarrass himself near his buddies. He conjured up the Laestroygonians, Scylla and Charybdis, the Sirens, Cyclops and Circe, monsters that the Jesuits filled his head with, the whole damn bunch of them ganging up on him tonight, but he was not as wily and strong as Odysseus who had a wife waiting for his return. Nick went down to the sea and crawled into his sleeping bag, close enough to hear the surf. He would either meet these demons head on near their natural habitat or be swallowed up by a titan wave. Think of all the stories that would be spun about the missing Nick, lost somewhere in the *Mediterraneo*.

# VIII

After intense combat in the northwest corner of Sicily, the Allies liberated the island. Lieutenant General Clark led the new Fifth Army in an amphibious invasion of mainland Salerno, codenamed Operation Avalanche, on September 9th, 1943. An Italian armistice had been declared the day before the landing. Colonel Jones' tank destroyer squadron had been reassigned to participate in this mission. While the British forces invaded the Salerno beaches, the American troops hit the shores of Paestum.

From the deck of a transport, Nick checked his watch and precisely at 0330 the faint light spread in the sky, revealing the outline of Mount Soprano that loomed in the background. At that moment a division of infantrymen charged onto the shore, not far from the ruins of Greek temples, a counterpoint to the looming mountain.

Nick's crewmates gathered around him to observe what they would soon be up against as the visibility improved.

"They're clobbering those infantrymen with everything they got—88mm shells, mortars, you name it," Nick announced.

"They're taking all this heat for us, so we can drive onto the beach," Nathan commented.

Paul extended his neck. "Those dirty, sneakin' krauts! Why don't they show their faces?"

"Oh my God, our guys are being picked off in the water." Al pointed. "Nazi machine gunners there! In those towers."

"*Madonna*, the bodies are piling up before they even reach the sand," Nick added. "See those flashes. Must be tanks hidden in those buildings."

"They're big cannons all right. What did I tell ya, they're sneakin' bastards," Paul interjected.

"Luftwaffe! Over there! They're strafing our guys in the water, on the sand. Slaughtering them!" Nathan cried out.

Even after the defending Germans in the beach area were killed or captured, the U.S. troops still had to contend with the pandemonium of people, vehicles and supplies landing throughout the day. Further inland Nick could hear shots from the foot soldiers fighting off a squadron of *Panzer* IV tanks. Judging from his map, the Krauts must have been using the ancient Greek fortification walls. Later on, Captain Monroe revealed how the bazookas, 105 howitzers and the big Navy guns had knocked out the German defenses, their remaining Panzers retreating inland.

By late afternoon of D-Day, two companies of American tanks, the medium size Sherman M4s and the M10 tank destroyers, rolled onto the Paestum beach. Nick placed their tank in a defensive position, waiting for orders to move out. He scrutinized the area, realizing that this was far worse than the Gela beaches of Sicily. His eyes squinted at the dead bodies strewn everywhere in murky water and on the beach. The blood was already changing color in the water and he could hear the unmistakable sounds of German 88mm cannon fire booming in the distance. Nick felt the muscles in his calves tighten at the mere sound of it. He was glad that he didn't have to drive at that moment. Nathan looked aghast, his eyes welling up at the sight of body parts strung along the beach. He took the canteen from his belt and gulped the water in big mouthfuls.

Paul and Al turned their heads from the beach scene and busied themselves, Paul checking the operating system of the gun and Al positioning the ammo. Paul's eyes twitched while he examined the equipment and Al's hands shook as he moved some of the shells, as the sound of the Acht-achts, a term everyone used for the feared eight-eight shells, were getting closer and closer, pounding every minute. A piss stain spread on Al's groin area, which caught the eye of Nathan who was checking to see if they were ready for action.

Within seconds Nathan spilled water from his canteen. "Sorry I got you all wet, Al." While Al pried the wet pants from his legs, Nathan fumbled with the aluminum flask before managing to attach it to his belt. He screamed over the booming rounds: "Guess we're all jumpy."

The medics were still taking care of countless wounded, while a detail of men removed the bodies or what was left of them for burial. Nick crossed himself and muttered: "Mother of God." Things were degenerating the further they moved up the boot of Italy and he was anxious about the ensuing combat along this path.

Over the next ten days the Fifth Army would experience what was later called some of the fiercest fighting in the war. After a tactical group of tanks assembled on the beach, Nathan's crew was sent out in advance to scout the position of the Acht-achts. Just before they left, a report came in from the shifting front, describing how an 88mm gun cut a hole through two sides of a Sherman M4 tank and obliterated wide clusters of infantrymen.

On the second day of the operation, Nick drove their tank destroyer beyond Paestum to find where the Acht-achts were hidden. As they proceeded north up highway 18, Nathan directed Nick to cruise east at a fork on a country road. He had him stop on the side of the road to study his terrain map, when he spotted the telltale, smoke puffs from a battery of Acht-achts camouflaged in a small forest behind Persano.

Nathan panned the area with his field glasses. "Massive column of *Panzer* IV tanks heading south," he shouted. "On auxiliary road from Eboli. Can't believe it's General Herr's 16th Panzers in counterattack." The field glasses slipped from his fingers, dangling from the neck. "We're in deep shit, Nick! Let's get the hell out of here!"

When Nathan came across the first signal corps outpost, an air strike was called in to knock out the 88mm guns in the forest near Persano. By the time Nathan's crew reached the midpoint of their return, several companies of Sherman M4 tanks passed them up, speeding straight for the Eboli road. Their tank destroyer squadron must have taken another route, so Nathan ordered Nick to turn around and follow the medium tank column. The *Panzer* IV tanks had already spread across the valley and Sherman M4s met the enemy in a deafening tank battle.

"Nick, I can see orange flashes," Nathan called out over the headsets. "We're going to run behind the M4s parallel to the battle line. So we can reconnoiter before our company gets here."

"Got it, Nate," Nick responded.

"Paul and Al, ready the gun for rapid fire."

They followed the sound of the pounding guns in the distance and, when they were in the right position, they crossed the field of fire at the rear of the battlefield. What started out as a reconnaissance mission turned into a terrifying exchange of firepower. They could see that the M4s were taking a lot of hits. Shells were exploding all over the place but their tank had the advantage of not being pinned down at the forward position. This would be their opportunity for a swift decisive action, while waiting for the tank destroyer reinforcements.

"Nick, we're going to run the other way, only we'll be firing instead of looking, right behind the M10s. Paul and Al, are you listening?"

"We hear you," they said.

"We have to be extremely careful before we shoot. Don't want to knock out one of our own. We've seen enough casualties from friendly fire. Nick, move at full speed, then stop dead every time when you see a gap wide enough between the M4s. Paul and Al make each shot count."

With incredible precision Nathan's crew made the last run, pacing the tank, and kept rapidly firing rounds at turrets, a weak spot for the German tanks. They set aflame three of the *Panzer* IV tanks, encouraging the Sherman M4s to move forward aggressively with the oncoming tank destroyers suddenly filling in from behind with Captain Monroe in the lead and Nathan's crew rejoining the company. More *Panzer* IVs replaced the ones out of commission, so it was a critical time for naval gun support, which Captain Monroe called in over the radio. Within a short while, a pair of P-51s were overhead spotting for the cruisers, *Philadelphia* and *Savannah*, which drove 6-inch shells into the armor of the German tanks, eventually forcing them to retreat all the way back to Eboli. At the end of the day, Captain Monroe commended Nathan's crew for their courage and initiative. "Gentlemen, I only heard of one other tank crew having so many enemy tank kills in one battle. Total of Five Panzers destroyed in my field report. Outstanding!"

It took ten days for Operation Avalanche to be successful in driving the Nazis past Naples, not the two days that General Clark expected. Nick's squadron was being held back in reserve, rather than continuing north in the mountains towards the Gustav Line. During this time neither Nick and his buddies nor anyone else, not even the brass, could ever have predicted the ferocity of the fighting north in the Battle for Rome. It was one German defensive line after another, reminiscent of trench warfare during World War I. The Allies battled every day for slivers of wet, lice-infested, treacherous terrain, changing sides so many times that it was difficult to know who and where the combatants were in hills of fog and gun smoke, the bilious smell of decaying bodies everywhere. The casualty roster expanded every day on both sides within the death trap of Cassino.

There were vivid accounts in the newspapers and no shortage of rumors among Nick's tank squadron. While waiting for new orders, Nathan and the crew busied themselves maintaining their tank and writing letters. Nick grasped that they had been lucky to be held back, but what would happen next to them was anybody's guess. At the beginning of the New Year, they knew something was up when they got notice of a new, amphibious exercise.

"Not another goddamned, amphibious assault!" Nick blurted out.

"Sure as hell looks that way," Nathan said, as the four of them, without another word, retreated to their tent to lose themselves in letters from home, old and new.

The Battle of Anzio, Operation Shingle, began on January 22, 1944. Nick's tank destroyer squadron was attached to the 1st U.S. Armored Division, commanded by Major General Harmon. Their squadron was held in reserve, so the tension magnified for Nathan's crew. Nick tried not to dwell on bad things, but he saw it in his comrades' faces and felt it himself as they waited in their tank—the imminent risks stark, right before their eyes, while the amphibious landing of the U.S. and British infantry took place on the beaches at 0200.

Right before the first landing, a barrage of 5-inch rockets from the Landing Craft Tanks called LCTs eradicated the land mines hidden in the sand, the explosions reverberating in Nick's ears. By the third wave of infantrymen, the Germans sprayed the beaches with machine gun bullets causing some casualties, the first light bringing a Messerschmitt formation that blew up many supply-laden trucks. Nick saw fires fanning all over the beach and later heard the dreadful drone of Focke-Wulf fighter-bombers that swooped down and blew up an LCI nearby. By midnight of D-day, Operation Shingle was a complete success, an unexpected surprise for Field Marshall Kesselring and a welcome relief to Nick and his buddies.

Nathan's crew was part of a unit attached to Combat Command B of the 1st U.S. Armored Division, when Nick drove onto the beach towards the end of January with the rest of the division following. Even though all the tanks were assembled on the beachhead, General Lucas still had not ordered a breakout from the Anzio beaches to drive a wedge through the German defenses blocking the way to Rome.

"Nick, I got a call over the radio from Captain Monroe." Nick straightened his headset. "The infantry is bogged down near Campoleone, taking on a lot of casualties. They're still waiting for armor support. Get ready to move out of this bitchhead."

"Gotcha, Nate!"

Their unit of tank destroyers moved at maximum speed in a column followed by medium tanks and half-tracks on the road north to Cisterna. The ground began to shake, as the machines spit up globs of earth with their treads whipping around the wheels, the smell of diesel exhaust in the air. The unforgiving terrain slowed down the tanks and, when Nathan's crew got closer, they could see what amounted to a killing field for the British infantrymen who had been desperately waiting for relief. Without a warning, German anti-tank guns, camouflaged on Vallelata Ridge, began to destroy tank after tank, as if in a fairground shooting gallery. In all this chaos, four tank destroyers got mired in an irrigation ditch, one of which was theirs.

"Great! We're all FUBAR now, Nick," Nathan screamed.

"We need a dang wrecker to drag us out," Nick yelled back. When it got dark, tracers were flying over their heads, followed by a deafening cocktail of rapid firing MG 42 machine guns, the never-ending rounds of mortars and 88mm guns. Through the din Nick could hear wounded men crying out from the battlefield, the acrid odor of cordite from British weapons so strong he could taste the bitterness. He thought that they might have to abandon the tank, climb out of the ditch and make a desperate run for it, until he heard his cousin call out: "Here comes Captain America!" The wrecker dragged each tank destroyer out. Nick's crewmates were relieved to get out of there, but Nick divined that they were running out of luck. When they got back to their encampment, Captain Monroe briefed Nathan who returned to his crew, opening the flap of their tent and stepping in.

"Fellas, more bad news. I'm sick to my stomach. We lost six times as many tanks trying to repel the German bombardment, after saving four tank destroyers. We're not breaking through to Rome anytime soon. No matter what General Clark wants, no matter how hard ole bulldog Churchill pushes."

One evening before mail call, the four GIs sat on the sand in front of their tent, longing for letters from home, Paul and Al puffing on cigarettes. Nick observed Nathan finishing replicas of five Panzers destroyed during the Salerno battle. They were done in fine detail, paint strokes, added to the others on the turret.

A postal clerk who handed out packages said he would return soon with the letters for their company. While they milled around by a burnt olive tree, Nathan opened up a package from his father and squeezed out a newspaper from the manila envelope. After glancing at the paper, he held it up for his crew to see.

"Guys, look at this." Nathan stretched out the front page.

***SAN FRANCISCO CHRONICLE***
/ WEDNESDAY, FEBRUARY 16, 1944 ~ DAILY 5 CENTS.
The Associated Press report told about the destruction of the medieval, Benedictine Abbey of *Monte Cassino*, perched high on a rocky hill just 75 miles south from Rome. Two hundred and fifty bombers, including a hundred Flying Fortresses, had bombed the monastery, knocking the blue and white tower into the courtyard, the abbey roof collapsing into its core and by nightfall, only the surrounding, massive walls at the base still stood, pockmarked with king-size holes, leaving all the buildings inside a mass of rubble.

"It used to be such a beauty." Nathan said, shaking his head. "What a shame!" He described to his friends what it once looked like, having studied the art and architecture of this renowned treasure. Nathan explained that there was a lower fortress wall with a massive stone façade on top. The abbey stood palatial, punctuated with myriad cell windows. When the sunlight shifted, the stone would change hues. The blue dome of the basilica rose in the rear. The frescoes and mosaics inside were exquisite.

"Nick, did you think they'd blow up the abbey?" Nathan asked.

"Nah, it's such an historic place. Where St. Benedict started his order in 529. Not even the krauts would touch it."

"It's just a building with a bunch of monks running around the place," Paul said. "You ask me, those Nazis were hiding up there, just watching our every move, calling in all those artillery shells on our guys."

"You're my cousin, but there are some things you don't get."

"Get outta here. We're here to blow things up, to destroy the enemy."

"Aren't we supposed to be a killer squadron like General Patton says?" Al asked.

"Yeah, I got his 'Blood and Guts' speech—your blood, his guts. But I'm not talking about the danged war," Nick responded. "What about all those irreplaceable frescos and rare leather books? In the oldest monastery! So how did we know bombing the monastery was going to help the troops in the long run? Does anybody have the answer?"

"See, there you go, *cuginu*. Acting like a wise guy with all your trick questions. We're all stuck in this *merda*. We'll be lucky if any of us get out alive." Paul flung his cigarette and walked away with Al following.

"All I did was admire a *goyim* shrine and a war breaks out between you Christians."

"I love Paul like a brother, but you don't know what it was like going to grammar school with him. Anytime my teachers praised me in class, he used to giggle and not satisfied, tease me after school. It used to get on my nerves. The only time we got along was doing something physical, like riding our bikes to the Golden Gate Bridge or playing baseball."

"It's tough when you start to outgrow some of the people you love. But Paul is still a *mensch* and that's something everyone can appreciate. He's just blowing off steam. Give him a hug when he cools off."

Nick grinned, thinking how Nathan could piss him off just because he might be smarter.

"What's with the smiley mug?"

"*Nenti*!"

An hour later there was another mail call and Nathan's crew picked up their letters. Nick separated himself from the group, going behind the tank to read his.

*Papà* wrote:

> Caru Nicolo,
>
> *It has been a long while,* figghiu miu, *since we last heard from you. You say, all the time, everything is okay pop. Don't worry you say but tell that to* Momma. Allura. *I read many things about Italy in newspapers, many deaths, much suffering. I am not a holy man but I pray for one thing. That you will sit with me by our fig tree in the backyard, pick the fruit when it's sweet and eat together. I tell* Mamma *that little, old Italian women in black dresses cook* la cena *for GIs like you when you are not fighting Germans. Basta! Writing in* l'inglese *gives me a* mal di testa.
>
> Con amuri, vostru patri.

Over the next few months the fighting continued to be brutal on the ground throughout the Cassino area. It wasn't until May 18th that a Polish unit toppled the Nazi flag at the monastery and placed the 12th Podolski Lancers Regiment pennant on a branch, signaling the start of the break through over the Gustav Line.

On May 23rd at zero hour, 0545, over a thousand mortars, artillery pieces and tanks pounded the town of Cisterna di Latina. The tracers from countless machine guns lit up the enemy targets. Overhead Nick spotted a shrieking squadron of fighters and light bombers flying over Cisterna adding to the devastation. The blasting noise was so incredible, it was as if Vesuvius had erupted once again just like it had two months earlier. Nick recollected from a newspaper article how the volcano had bellowed and heaved black smoke, orange-red fire, lava and cinders, smothering and crushing every living thing in its path. He reckoned it was all the past Allied bombardments. At this very moment, Nick felt he was imploding as he confronted everything right in front of him, palpable for unseen miles, burnt into his memory to be brewed in nightmares to come.

Their medium tanks and tank destroyers had become invisible to the enemy, either hidden inside farmhouses, sunk in maneuverable gullies, covered with mounds of a straw or camouflaged in vineyards. The tanks rushed out after the barrage, searching for targets to protect the infantrymen, who had to break through the German defenses of barbed wire, minefields and the constant shelling from enemy machine guns, mortars and artillery, then hand to hand combat, using everything they had, rifles, bayonets and grenades.

With his binoculars, Captain Monroe spotted German Panther tanks that were causing a lot of damage on the right flank of the battlefield. He ordered Nathan's crew to lead a group of tank destroyers, fanning out through a wooded area northeast of the town. Nathan instructed Nick to stop periodically, so Paul could climb a tree and locate the exact position of the lethal Panthers. On the third try, the object of their mission was in their sights. Nathan had Nick speed to a clearing that put them to the side of the Panthers that had been firing nonstop from their position. He also radioed to the other crew commanders to find their own strategic spots. Moving away from the trees, their tank destroyer blasted several hits at the thinner side armor of the first Panther, which burst into flames. When the other Panther turned its turreted cannon on them, Nick reversed at full speed into the woods, as the German gunner fired and hit the trees instead. Minutes later, Nick zipped out of the woods, traversing the direction of that same tank. Paul and Al got off a volley of shots on Nathan's command, taking out the second Panther in the same weak spot. The other scout tank destroyers had already joined Captain Monroe's company, charging forward and continuing the destruction of the invincible Panthers in the battlefield.

Nathan's crew were so close to the enemy, he could hear the German Field Marshall screaming at his officers: "*Idioten! Zerstoren der Amerikaner Panzer! Sie verichten*!" Suddenly, all the big German guns, from tanks to artillery to rocket launchers, barraged their tank and the other charging tank destroyers. Captain Monroe radioed his tank crew commanders to pull back immediately into the woods and regroup with the main attack force.

"Nick, get the hell out of here! Stand on it!"

Nick maneuvered the tank, heading for the cover of the woods. Unexpectedly, a Tiger I tank drove through the front façade of a barn and fired several blasts from its big 88mm gun, one shot hitting their front end, the other traveling through two sides of its armor. Their tank destroyer spun around but Nick managed to sputter its way into the tree grove before smacking into a large tree.

Nick cried out in pain from his smashed right leg that looked like hanging meat in a North Beach *macelleria*. He inched his way out of the driver's hatch, groaning all the time and crawled over to the edge of the smoking turret, while flames burst from the engine in the rear. Nick yelled down: "Nathan! Paul! Al!" No one responded. "For Christ's sake, somebody say something." This time he heard a moan and Nathan's voice: "My head's bleeding. I can't see too well." Nick stretched his neck over the turret opening and saw Nathan starting to black out.

"Nate, stay awake. Nathan!" Nick screamed with such force it caused Nathan to crack his eyes open and recover his senses.

"Paul and Al are on the floor," Nathan cried out. "I'm still a little dizzy. I'll try to lift them up. Get a grip as soon as you see shoulders." Nick winced in pain as he leaned into the turret and grabbed the back of Paul's shirt, dragging him over the top as Nathan heaved him up. They repeated the same routine with Al. Nathan climbed out, while Nick pulled Paul to the edge of the tank. Nathan jumped off and fell to the ground. He slowly pushed himself up and opened his arms, as Nick slid Paul down followed by Al. Nathan hopped onto the tank and got Nick off, then leaned him against one of the wheels. He carried Paul on his shoulders and placed him behind a tree and did the same for Al. Nathan made his way back to Nick who put his arm around Nathan. He limped along with his friend's help and was placed next to his cousin. The wide berth of the tree protected the four of them, when within minutes the tank blew, billowing up clouds of black smoke.

"Paul, wake up. *Cuginu*! Please, it's me, Nick. *Madonna*!" He loosened Paul's fatigues and saw a red soaked t-shirt. As the tears welled up in his eyes, he crossed himself and hugged his cousin.

"Nick, Paul's gone," Nathan said, as he put his hand on Nick's shoulder.

"What about Al?"

"Al's dead too." Nick looked at Al's body lying on the ground. He saw his brain exposed from the left side, as Nathan stared at Nick who vomited. Nathan went over to Al, turning his head to the other side, a profile they could recognize, and moving his eyelid down.

"Poor guy didn't know what hit him," Nathan mumbled.

Nick turned towards his cousin and the glint of Paul's gold cross caught his attention, as the chain drooped from his cousin's neck. He gently pulled it over Paul's head, kissed the cross and dropped it into his shirt pocket. Nathan closed Paul's eyes and moved him closer to Al. Nick sat impassively near his dead comrades after Nathan passed out. Hours later, the medics found what remained of Nathan's crew after their hazardous search.

Their crew was separated at the rear lines, two for the field hospital, the other two for a temporary morgue. The next morning Nick woke as the pain-killer wore off, while Nathan lay in a coma, his head still swathed in Carlisle dressing with pink stains over his right temple, his body surrounded with tentacles of life-support. He slept on Nick's left side, while another tanker from their company lay on the other side with burns on half his face. From a distance he could see a row of wooden coffins that were bound for the Sicily-Rome American Cemetery in Nettuno and recalled his last impression of their stiff faces. He took out Paul's cross and wrapped it around his right hand, squeezing the gold cross in his palm.

"Medic!" Nick called out. One of the attending medics acknowledged him by waving his hand. He came over when he finished changing a battle dressing.

"Corporal Spataro, how are you feeling today?"

"Lot of pain, but that's not why I called for you." Nick looked at his nametag and epaulet.

"What can I do for you?"

"Specialist Kelly, I need a favor."

"Sure, but call me Bill. And you're?"

"Nick."

"Do you need more morphine?"

"Yeah, Bill." Nick grabbed his shirtsleeve. "But I need something else."

"Shoot."

"You see those wooden boxes out there?"

"Yes."

"Well, my two buddies died the other day." Nick grimaced and moved onto his good side.

"Are you okay?"

"No, but let me finish. I want to go over there and say goodbye. You know what I mean."

"Your leg was smashed up real bad. I don't know if I would recommend it."

"I just need a little time, that's all. Whatdaya say, Bill?"

"I'll ask the Captain but I'm not promising anything."

"Thanks. Could you also find out what's going on with my buddy, Fein?" Nick motioned with his head in Nathan's direction.

A half hour later Bill returned. "Captain Randazzo said fifteen minutes and right back to the cot. Your buddy is being carefully monitored until we move him to a fully equipped facility. The doctor said not to worry. He's seen plenty cases of serious trauma to the head and he thinks Fein's chances are good."

"You're a pal, Bill." The wrinkles on Nick's brow flattened out.

"When I am finished making the rounds with Doc, I'll help you over there. In the meantime, let me give you some more morphine to fortify you."

Two hours later Bill came back with a crutch and got Nick up.

"Jesus Christ, easy Bill."

"I'm doing the best I can. You're not supposed to be up anyways."

"Don't remind me." Nick grinded his teeth when he was standing.

"Okay, put your weight onto my shoulder and then we're off."

The Staff Sergeant from the graves-registration unit checked the Graves Registry, found Nick's crew-members and pointed them out. Bill practically carried him over to Al's coffin and Nick patted it. He then hobbled over with Bill to Paul's wooden box and leaned on it. He rubbed the wood.

"Do you want to say a prayer, Nick? You're Catholic, right?"

"In name only, but you can say one if you like."

Bill recited the "Hail Mary" and when he finished, Nick said: "One last favor."

"Sure."

"Could we go over to the table to see if there's any personal stuff for Paul? He was my cousin, you know."

"I'm sure the sergeant won't mind if we take a look."

When they reached the table, Bill asked and the staff sergeant retrieved a small envelope. Bill eased Nick into a folding chair and unfastened the contents spreading them on the table. He reached for Paul's dog tags among the few items. He ran his fingers over the perforations, kissed the tag and dropped it back into the envelope.

"Ready, Bill."

When the specialist grabbed Nick's left hand to place over his shoulder, he commented: "Those paws of yours are filthy. I'll get them all cleaned up as soon as we get back."

After Bill adjusted him to sit upright on the cot, he returned with a basin of steaming water, brown soap and a white hand towel. Nick smiled thinly.

"I can do this myself, Bill. You go ahead and take care of the other guys. Thanks again."

Nick washed his hands in a methodical way, scrubbing gritty layers of dirt, dried blood and grease embedded in every crease of his palms and fingers. He scrubbed again, as some tears dropped into the basin, then wiped his hands with the towel now smudged gray and brown. He flung it to the ground, moved the basin to a rickety table next to him and slid himself under the sheets so that only his forehead was visible. His face rippled the sheets in short spurts, until he inched for some air, a stew of sulfa, iodine, blood and the indefinable smell of death, an odor Nick could recognize but not describe, bringing him back to North Beach for another scene of *lu mortu*—the family gatherings at wakes with the ever-present, sickly sweet odor of white lilies and the ugly floral face of death, white gladiolas.

* * *

One morning toward the end of May 1944 *Ziu* Francesco received a telegram, which he brought into the dining room, opened it, then handed it over to his daughter, Maria. *La famigghia* gathered around the table, as she read the message:

> THE DEPARTMENT OF THE ARMY REGRETS TO INFORM YOU THAT YOUR SON PAOLO BURGIO SPECIALIST IST CLASS WAS KILLED IN ACTION IN THE PERFORMANCE OF HIS DUTY AND IN SERVICE TO HIS COUNTRY …

Maria stopped reading because she couldn't see through her tears and placed the telegram on the dining room table. *Zia* Concetta grabbed the table and lowered herself to a chair and wept. The younger children cried as they looked at the faces around the table. *Ziu* Francesco remained dumbfounded near his wife. Concetta rose and wrapped her arms around Francesco and still he did not cry. He could not have heard such a thing, his mind playing tricks on him. The youngest Francesco, or Ciccio as Nick liked to call him said: "*Papà*, is it really true that I'll never see Paolo again." Then *Ziu* Francesco broke loose and screamed so loud, his voice could be heard down the block and echoed all the way to the top of the Coit Tower. He grabbed onto his wife and sobbed in her arms, a story told *in verità* to Nick by his *cugina* Maria, one that resonated more than any Sicilian tale he had ever heard from *Ziu* Francesco or his *Mamma* and *Papà*.

***

Rome had fallen on June 4th to the Allied Powers. General Clark's units of the Fifth Army were the first to reach the city, a picture of him standing by a large road sign for ROMA, printed in the newspaper. Not long after, Nick and Nathan were moved to a military hospital in the eternal city, still recuperating from their wounds. Colonel Jones had received a notice from the Counter Intelligence Corps (CIC) in Rome that they were looking for Italian and German interpreters who were getting harder to find. The colonel passed the information on to Captain Monroe. When the captain visited them at the hospital, he went over their qualifications. Nick had spent many afternoons back home picking up standard Italian, something his *Papà* encouraged him to do despite protests from his father's *paesani*, who felt his son might act superior to his parents. Nathan's father taught his son German at an early age. After reading the medical reports, the captain offered to let his men transfer out, since the severity of their wounds made it unlikely they would be able to return to his company. Nick's leg injury not only tore through the muscle tissues but also the nerve endings, while Nathan's head injury from shrapnel in the back of his cranium on the right side affected his sight and hearing.

"So what do you think about the captain's offer?" Nathan asked while lying on his hospital bed.

"Paul and Al are gone and look at us." He stretched and held up a crutch. "Look at me. And your head is still bandaged up like Frankenstein."

"What do you say?"

Nick raised his voice. "You look like Frankenstein."

"You don't look so hot yourself."

"How's your head?"

"I'm okay except for that seizure I had in the field hospital. The doctor said you never know when it might happen again."

"That's what I'm concerned about."

"Ah, don't think anything of it. Maybe, we'd be able to stick together if we get assigned to that intelligence unit."

Nick sat up and looked out the Palladian window, once a perfect example of classical symmetry, now askew in a cracked and scarred stucco wall. He looked at the sky. "I wonder what *cuginu* Paul is doing upstairs. Not that I'm such a good Catholic. More like being superstitious, when you come down to it."

"After what happened to our buddies and my relatives, I don't know if I can step foot in a *shul* again."

The next day a nurse led them to the inner courtyard that had a garden with a fountain in the center. The sun felt luxurious on Nick's face as he read a library copy of Dante's *La Vita Nuova.* Nathan had a bunch of newspapers on his lap and spread out the *International New York Times*, scanning it for any news about Northern Italy.

"There's not a damn thing in this rag about the Italian Jews. And what about my cousins in Venice? It's like we're an invisible people."

"You have to keep saying to yourself, no news is good news. I think I'll write to my father before we get the mail, this way it'll go out sooner."

Nick wrote to his father:

*Dear* Papà,

*How is* Mamma? *I am sitting in the garden of the hospital now. I'm sorry that I have not written lately but I feel mighty bent. I miss my* cuginu, *Paul, and my friend Al, the* paisanu *from Roseto. I feel guilty I survived and they didn't, but then again I also feel lucky to be alive. I don't know what to make of it, Pop. You know, many GIs feel you're lucky to be wounded, so you won't have to face the daily routine of killing or being blown up yourself. Never knowing when it would happen. My leg has been severely damaged but it's considered* bona fortuna. *I have heard of soldiers creating their own luck, if you know what I mean. I suppose I should be careful as to what I say in a letter. Papà, all I can say is that I would lie prostrate at the altar of our parish church, pray that if I had a son, he should not have to go through this. No one should. I would like to come home right now, but that is just a dream. I need to change the subject, pop. I shouldn't be talking about this stuff, so do your own censoring for* Mamma *when you read it aloud.*

Con affettu, Nicolo

By the time Nick finished writing, a hospital attendant was bringing in the mail and Nick placed his father's letter in the attendant's hand. Nathan waited for Nick to read the news aloud from his own family instead of his stumbling over the blurred words. After reading the letters for his buddy, Nick read his first letter and a short while later, he let it drop to the floor.

"What happened? You look white as a ghost." Nick didn't respond and focused on the drizzling fountain outside the window. "Okay Nick, give your old pal a clue."

"Your sister ditched me. Met someone else. Says she's sorry, but it's all over. That's just grand with me stuck on the other side of the ocean."

"Come on, Nick. You know my father well enough that this was bread that wasn't going to bake." Nathan groped his way over to Nick's hospital bed, but he turned his head away. "What are you scared of? Before I got hit in the head, I got a bunch of letters from Deb. Turn around you jerk and listen up." Nick faced Nathan. "My kid sister has nothing but good things to say about you. Deb said she worries about you and me every day. She needed something to get her mind off things. That's why she started dating this guy in college."

"I don't want to hear it."

"She wanted to let you know, so you won't think about her in the same way." Nick's eyes floated to the ceiling. "This relationship with Deborah is all in your head, spinning around like the stars you like to gaze at."

"Humph! And I thought you were my friend."

"Look, I'm sorry, Nick. We're both caught in this juggernaut and nothing will ever be the same. Just forget my sister. I know it'll be hard, but you've got no choice now."

"You always have an answer for everything, don't you?"

"Slow down when you speak, Nick." Nathan pointed to his ear. "You're making a tragedy out of this. You knew where this was going with Deb."

"Whatever you say."

"Buddy, let's just try to get through this war in one piece. That's all we can do. I am really sorry about this mess."

Nick left the other letters unread, inching his way on crutches to the garden, and sat on a ledge surrounding the fountain. He fixated on a distorted reflection. Nathan shrugged and went back to his bed, skimming the words in his letters. Nick didn't acknowledge him after that, even though their beds were just four feet apart, except for the morning when Nathan woke up for breakfast and had a seizure, falling onto the white terrazzo floor, while Nick screamed for a nurse. Nathan had no recollection of what happened after he recovered. The concussion from bashing his head against the metal of the tank had left its mark. He resigned himself to waiting for Nick to work things out, checking him out from the corner of his eye as he read his newspapers with a magnifying glass the nurse had lent him.

A few days later, as if they were in the middle of a conversation, Nick blurted out: "You know, Nate, a woman would do anything to have somebody love her the way Dante loved Beatrice."

"You're in a Renaissance mood." Nathan laughed. "Certainly in the right country for it."

"Why don't we get out of this crappy room and go into the garden? You can sketch it. It would be like old times. Me watching you do magic with colored pencils, pen and black ink, pastel chalk, you name it."

"I don't know. I'm still having trouble with my vision."

"Come on. Give it a try. Something to remember this place by."

Since their condition showed signs of improvement, they were allowed to sit outside in the garden on a regular basis. One day before dusk, the light was perfect for Nathan to exhibit his chiaroscuro techniques. Nick still felt anger inside when he thought about the loss of Paul and Al, and then more gloom, when he thought about his first love, Deborah, as he muddled along in a hospital garden.

"*Minchia*."

Nathan looked up. "What did you say?"

"Nothing, Nate. Just finish what you're doing."

When Nathan completed the drawing with several crumbled attempts on the ground, he showed it to Nick. "What do you think?"

"Turn it into an oil painting."

"Guess you like it."

"Why don't you get some supper without me? I want to stay here for a while and watch the sunset."

"Sure, buddy."

Nick struggled with a cane over to the fountain. He sat on the edge and ran his hand through the scant water, barely creating a ripple. He glimpsed at the North Star blinking, the rest of the sky empty. He heard a nightingale sing in a trance-like pattern from a hidden spot. His mood muted the bird's song and he was unable to stop the sadness from creeping its way back into his thoughts. Nick remembered last drinking wine with Paul that tasted of raspberries and spice, so far away, *Zia* Concetta smothering him with kisses and *Ziu* Francesco telling tales of the old country at family parties, very far away, *Mamma* and *Papà* and the magnetic field of family charges, enduring but also invisible, now so far away, playing baseball with Paul on the grass in Lincoln Park or a story of Al playing catch with his brother in Roseto, so very far away, yet still closer in his thoughts, holding Deborah close to him in the San Francisco Botanical Garden, framed by pink azaleas, conjuring up a shower of cream-colored, magnolia petals floating around them—the magnolia part never really happening to Nick, but that's how he wanted to remember it now, like a remembrance of lyrics or melody of a favorite song of his and connecting it to her countenance. Nick wished that he could somehow write an exquisite love sonnet like Dante, for a brief time to have the fire of the poet's words, so he could let all the pain drain out of his head, but he didn't have it in him, not like Nathan anyway, instinctively a painter, Nathan more like a brother than a friend, a cliché that Nick recognized and *in verità*, Nathan was even better than any real or imagined brother. All he could do now was struggle to move along, putting pressure on the cane to ease the pain in his leg, glaring at the fading sun, not a *inamorata* or a sparkling star in sight, the North Star already gone and even the damn bird speechless.

# IX

The transfer came through before Nick and Nathan were released from the hospital and it wasn't long before they shared a room in the sprawling headquarters of the Counter Intelligence Corps in Rome. They were called upon to interrogate prisoners, translate captured documents or act as interpreters when dealing with the locals. They also spent many hours listening to intercepted Axis radio messages, which would became a monotonous duty for them but they were happy to have a private space when their work was done.

"Look at that view, Nathan," Nick said as he held the dark curtain to the side. "We can see all the way to the *Campidoglio*."

"Yeah, it's swell." Nathan sat straight up on the edge of his bed.

"Is something wrong?"

"You know. I'm worried sick about my cousins in Germany. And right here in Italy." Nick understood those emotions—worrying about family. Everybody had their stories to tell but from what he had heard, just being Jewish this time around could prove fatal.

Nathan looked out the window. "It is an amazing structure. Still around after 19 centuries." He turned towards Nick. "Where will all the Jews be after the war's over?"

Nick didn't have a good answer for his buddy. This was no time for platitudes. He better understood Nathan's determination to join up—his European *cugini* needed help right away. While Nick changed into civvies, he thought how this topic was making his buddy all nerves and not something he wanted to dwell on either. Nathan lay on his cot with his hands behind his neck like he was some kind of prisoner, so he figured he would play his best cards to keep Nathan's mind off things.

"Do you want to go for some *pasta amatriciana*?" Nathan remained in the same position. "How about that new dish, *pasta carbonara*? Maybe pick up a few broads later."

"Nah, I'll stick around here and write some letters."

"Why don't you sketch the *Campidoglio* from the window?"

"Sure, Nick."

Nathan was humoring him but Nick worried that the head injury was affecting his buddy's moods as well. "*Ci vediamo*, Nate."

Nick and Nathan had purchased motor scooters, nicknamed the Paperino, after their first month at the CIC. Though Nick still walked with a wooden cane, he managed to operate his light green scooter. He placed his right leg around the seat putting his weight on the cane from the left side, and then thumped himself on the black leather seat. He jabbed his cane in an improvised holder on the side fender, started the engine and, in a short while, crossed the Palatino Bridge over the Tiber River.

Nick searched for a *buona trattoria* in Trastevere and circled around until he found one that looked promising. The *trattoria* was cramped with long wooden tables lined up indoors and a few tables outside on a crooked sidewalk. Nick pulled up and worked his way through the crowded place. He sat next to an extended family munching on varied *antipasti.*

"*Caminiere, prego. Vorrei una pasta amatriciana.*"

"*Da bere?*"

"*Vino rosso. Un mezzo litro. E dell' acqua minerale con gassata.*"

The waiter jotted the order down, never making eye contact during the transaction. It took more time than usual and Nick felt self-conscious sitting alone in the *trattoria*, so he pulled out a copy of Vittorini's novel, *Conversazione in Sicilia*. He read a few sentences but the noise distracted him and his hunger for food brought on other desires. He knew a *buono bordello* where he could go. A young woman with long, golden brown hair approached him in a poised manner and stood by the empty chair opposite him. She motioned to it and he said: "*Prego, signorina. È libero.*" The woman sat down but did not speak to him. She ordered a *fritatta ai funghi* and a glass of *vino bianco.*

Nick pretended to be absorbed in his book but caught glimpses of her when she looked sideways at some of the commotion taking place. She was a *bella donna* all right but her eyes were icy. The waiter placed the *pasta* in front of Nick who put the book down on the table. He ate fast but tried not to eat like a *porcu*, as his mother used to scold him for at the kitchen table.

"*Un caffè, per favore*," Nick called out to the waiter flying by. The young woman observed him briefly and then forked her *frittata* in a nonchalant way. She slipped her high heels off without bending over. Nick was glad he ordered the coffee. She moved her hair back with a delicate, right hand and he noticed an anxious look on her face, not out of fear for him but something else that he couldn't discern. It was as if there were some mystery behind those green eyes but she managed to smile at him when she caught him staring at her. Her teeth were small but pearl white and symmetric.

The *espresso* came sooner than he wanted, so Nick sipped from the cup, while the young woman had eaten half her *frittata*. She placed her right foot in his crotch and then took it away. There was nothing left in the cup but Nick still held it in midair, grateful he hadn't dropped it.

"You must be far from home," the young woman said.

"*Allora, lei parla l'inglese*."

"Yes, I studied it for many years." She was unnerving him, as she finished the glass of wine. "You are American, no?"

"Yes."

"You notice lots of things."

"Even if your face might throw me off, I knew you had to be an American?"

"*Come*?"

"No Italian would be reading a book while sitting alone in a restaurant."

"I don't understand. *Non capisco*!"

"An Italian would never be self-conscious while eating his favorite food, whether alone or with friends."

"I love the food but never thought of it that way."

"Did you know Vittorini was arrested by the *fasciste* for that book you're reading?"

"*Non lo so*."

"I can hear a slight, Sicilian accent when you speak Italian." Nick shrugged. "*Allora, sua famiglia è Siciliana*!"

"*Brava*, you are a detective." The young woman smiled. "*La commissaria*, have you also deduced I need more than food?"

"A man does not live by bread alone. Nor does a woman."

"You don't strike me as the religious type."

"Neither do you." She glanced at the group next to her and noticed that some of them were eyeing her. Her cool demeanor changed to an edgy one. "We can't talk here with all these nosey people. We Romans love to gossip, you know."

"Sure, let's get out of here. This joint is stifling anyway."

She left the *trattoria* first and he held back awhile so it would not appear she had picked him up. Some of the customers cackled as she passed the cramped tables. A rotund postman sitting by the door, who had been watching them the whole time, called out *puttana* as she closed the door behind her. Laughter circulated within the place, while the young woman waited for Nick to catch up. He tied up his cane and got on the Paperino in his usual manner. She bunched up her skirt and sat behind him, placing her hands around his hips. He glanced to his side to ensure her legs were in safely and gave her first-class gams the once-over.

He revved the engine and shouted: "Don't pay any attention to those *cretini*!"

"They are invisible to me," she responded.

"Where to?"

"I'll guide you along the way."

Having crossed the *Tevere*, Nick became disoriented after a few blocks. Every turn took them in another unfamiliar direction. Her path avoided all of the usual bordellos near the *Stazione Termini* where the women with heavy makeup lured the wandering, drunken soldiers with their bulging cleavage, slit up skirts and molded round asses. While bouncing around on a confusing drive, which he suspected might have been intentional on her part, she pointed to an apartment building in an alley. She instructed Nick to shut the engine off as they turned in and they glided into the dark, stopping at a ten-foot wooden door. She hopped off, took out a large key, unlocked the door halfway and turned to him.

"*Vieni qui*!"

"Okay, whatever you say."

Nick grabbed his cane and edged off the motor scooter, not wanting to stumble, and followed at a quicker pace so as not to appear disabled, while she held the door for him. He wondered if he were walking into a dream or nightmare. She intrigued and frightened him at the same time, and this was the first time he had been sober with a Roman woman.

He was surprised to see her room had no fanciful sexual images on the wall. It was clean and exhibited style, not garish at all, just well-thought out for someone who didn't have a lot of liras. She poured some Strega into brandy glasses.

"Here, drink this. You look nervous." Nick downed his glass and she drank half of hers. "First time!" She laughed.

"Very funny. I can show you a few things."

"You already have." She pointed to his groin. "Lie down and relax."

Nick jumped on the tarnished brass bed while the young woman turned away and undressed in a deliberate way. Yet she didn't look like a woman of the night. She wasn't tarted up at all and let him initiate their contact as they lay together. He kissed her affectionately on the cheek, something he had not done before with a *puttana* from the street. He exhibited better control over his sexual appetite, spending some time stroking her firm breasts. She didn't stare at the ceiling and seemed to be enjoying her time with him, not faking an orgasm for effect. When they were satisfied, he was surprised that she sprang up from the bed and put all her clothes back on. He thought that he must have mistaken her tender touches, her brilliant eyes, making up things in his head, something that Nathan had admonished him for.

"Leave the *soldi* in the envelope on the night table." She walked over to the window and looked out towards the façade of a church, its bells clanging an erratic tone.

As he dressed, he reconstructed every moment from the serendipitous to the lascivious, from the tender to the enigmatic, but all Nick could say when fully clothed was: "How much?"

"As much as you can afford. *Prego*, don't forget to walk your scooter to the main street."

Her voice was sexy and intelligent at the same time. Nick raised his eyebrows. "*Bene*." It would make his getaway more difficult but he wasn't going to whine about it.

The next morning Nathan and Nick ate breakfast in the interim mess hall below their room. Some *partigiani* from *Firenze* came into the room, escorted by a lieutenant from their unit. The group passed their table and sat down to eat. The lieutenant returned to their table and said to Nick: "Captain Smith needs your assistance. These Italian freedom fighters have some very important information we need. They don't speak a word of English."

"I'll take care of it, lieutenant."

The officer left and Nathan leaned closer to Nick. "See what you can find out about my Jewish *paesani*, will you?"

"I'm not supposed to repeat anything. You know, the eyes and ears of the enemy."

"I don't give a damn about Uncle Sam's slogans. Just do it."

"All right, relax, will ya. I'm just kidding," Nick said, realizing that this issue ate at his friend's guts.

"*Grazie*. By the way, how did it go last night, buddy? Bet you found some cute *puttana*!"

"*Vafonculo*, Nathan!"

"Hey, can't you take a little ribbing? So what happened last night?"

"*Niente*. Forget about it."

"I think we're getting on each other's nerves."

"Whatever you say."

That afternoon, the *partigiani* sat around a conference table with Nick and several officers, including the lieutenant from the morning. After an hour of questioning, the officers left. Nick ordered some *cornetti al mandorla* and *espresso* from the café across the street, brought in by a boy who carried the porcelain cups on a silver-plated tray. The men appreciated his gesture. He waited until they were finished eating and then inquired about the Italian Jews. They related that, once the Italians surrendered and sided with the Americans, the German SS and Gestapo made no exceptions for *ebrei italiani*, not even the *bambini*. If caught, all would be deported and sent to their deaths in concentration camps. He could see that the Italians were disgusted with the Nazis' treatment of their countrymen.

That evening in their room, Nick recounted what he had heard from the *partigiani,* knowing that this would sicken his friend. Afterwards Nathan sat at a beat up desk they had picked up in the street, scribbling designs on typing paper. Nick tried to divert his friend's attention, reminiscing about Roman women and food.

"That's real swell. You and me riding around in a jazzy Paperino while my cousins get deported to an *inferno*."

"Stop beating yourself up. We're going to win this thing. Are you coming out with me, or not?"

"I'll be no fun. Maybe another time, Nick."

"You can't stay cooped up in this room."

"I think I had another seizure before, damn it."

"Did you see the Doc?"

"I woke up on the floor."

"You should at least let him know."

"Leave me alone. You're not my mother. Anyway, I need to write a letter to my father."

When Nick closed the door, Nathan massaged his head, a habit that Nick had noticed developing whenever he wrote a letter or tried to sketch something.

Nathan wrote:

*Dear Father,*

*I hope that Mother, Deb and you are well and that no one is worrying too much about me. As you know, I sometimes have to interrogate German prisoners of war. In the past I've tried not to mention the war, as I don't want to frighten anyone. But I must tell you that a few days ago I questioned an SS officer. It was very disturbing, as this arrogant Nazi had no remorse. His face revealed a loss of affect when I questioned him about the massacre of 335* partigiani *in the Ardeatine Caves just outside Rome or the deportation of Roman Jews to Auschwitz. In a moment of anger, I could have taken out my .45 pistol and blown his head off if they left me alone with him, but you would have thought less of me for not seeking justice but revenge. And yet I also felt sorrow as I questioned a regular, Germany infantryman. He seemed in a daze and scared for his life, though we clearly had no intention of taking it. I gave him a cigarette and when he relaxed, he didn't have much to offer of strategic value, but kept on fretting about his wife and children in Germany. And to think that one man, Hitler, could have started this massive fire all over Europe and Northern Africa, convincing this conscripted, German soldier that he was just fighting to protect his beloved fatherland. Sitting across this broken-down man, I wished that I could be home, but who knows how long this war will go on. Are things still the same at …*

*Love, Nathan*

Nick zoomed down the streets of Rome with no particular place to go. He couldn't eat after talking to Nathan. He pulled his motor scooter over to a wall that follows the *Tevere* meandering through the city. He could see the Bridge of Angels in the distance, and instead of delighting him, it saddened him. The world needed an army of angels to stop all this madness, but that was just fantasy thinking. Things would continue to get worse before they got better. He thought about the angels in a pamphlet from his religious instruction class in grammar school.

Nick tapped his forehead and recalled the nameless, young woman from the previous night, her shining hair sloping down her back before she put her clothes on. He had paid her plenty of dough but never said a kind word to her. She was just a hooker and what did one night with her mean? Suppose the condom was defective, this woman could have given him gonorrhea or even worse, syphilis. She could send him down the road to blindness.

He mounted his bike in the usual way and drove around for kicks before the first rays of dawn, just like he used to do with Nathan when they first were reassigned. After a short while he got tired of aimless riding. He now had a mystery to solve, a nameless woman and an unknown address. But Nick had no clue to where she lived except for one—that beautiful, diminutive church in the alley. The only trouble was that he didn't know the damn name of the *chiesa* in a city that had nine hundred of them.

# X

Nick finished reading *Zia* Concetta's letter from over 6000 miles away. He could tell that *cugina* Maria was her ghostwriter. His aunt recounted how *Ziu* Francesco had placed the Gold Star in the front window in honor of their slain son, Paolo Burgio. She asked for any mementoes of Paul's that he might have, anything to attach a story to, keeping her son's memory alive for family and friends. As for Nick, he could hardly relate to the world of North Beach that had become so remote now. He was concerned that if he stayed put in Rome long enough, he would lose all connection to a place he once called home. His eyes floated over her neighborhood gossip until he ended with an image of *Papà* and his boat. The Navy had returned his father's purse seiner so banged up, it was unseaworthy, leaving Gaetano so distraught, *Mamma* could not console him. Nick's parents had never mentioned this incident in any of their letters. *Zia* Concetta implored her nephew not to let on in his correspondence to them.

Nick placed the letter next to the cigar box on his night table and opened the lid. He put his chin under his clasped hands and reimagined *Ziu* Francesco's dining room—a wall of family photos hanging near an oblong table, shots of alfresco birthdays and holy days that evoked feasts of the past, and now the most prominent in a *gauzzabuglio* of moments, Paul dressed in uniform, the last trace of his persona, memory fading with the days, months and years. The war had brought on a new circle of hell for anyone who loved his *cuginu*.

Nick riffled through the contents of the box and found a few of Paul's letters at the bottom that his *cuginu* had shared with him. He grabbed a large envelope and wrote down their address. He took off Paul's gold cross, kissed it and draped it around his cousin's letters, sealed the contents and later mailed it to North Beach, San Francisco from the Vatican Post Office on *Piazza San Pietro*, Rome. He would have liked to shrink himself to fit inside the envelope and go home too. Nick laughed to himself that he hadn't lost the ability to fantasize yet, the one thing he had going for him against the reality of what was going on here, not some newsreel viewed in the safety of a movie house back home. He would never forget the image of Paul being sent off in that wooden box bound for a burial ground on Italian soil, his *cuginu* no longer be able to sing with him: "This land is your land, this land is my land from California to the New York Island." Nick thought about this spinning planet in its solar system, the constellations of stars and Dante's three spiritual *cantiche*. Where are you now Paul, in this *mishmash*?

* * *

It took Nick a week of drives from the train station before he spied the small church near his mystery woman's apartment early one evening after many wrong turns and dead ends on his motor scooter. It was the Santa Maria dei Monti, the eponymous name for the neighborhood that was one of the twelve original *rioni* of Rome. He waited outside the alley and planned to intercept her as she headed to the door. It wasn't long before Nick saw her approaching arm in arm with an older Italian gentleman. He hid behind a garbage dumpster before they turned into the alley and was surprised by the anger this scene caused him.

The next day, right after his duties at the CIC were completed, Nick made it back to the front door of her building. A woman in her late twenties wearing black let him in when she saw his uniform. Without a word she raised her arm in the direction of the apartment upstairs. He knocked on her door, then tried the lock. *Niente.* Nick sat on the floor and leaned against the wall, its paint chipped and flaking, figuring he would scare aware any stranger coming up the stairs. He would later find out that Caterina, for that was her name, never left the apartment key with anyone. Said it was a good business practice. She carried on how customers did not like to be discovered in the primal scene by a potential blackmailer. Caterina had learned how to earn money other ways, implying it wasn't based on her night time activities. Nick concluded she wanted to maintain some privacy in her life. She was available during these terrible times and he needed her to escape for a while. He popped up when he heard her coming up the grungy, marble stairs.

Later that evening he sat up in bed and turned to Caterina, while she smoked a Lucky Strike, compliments of Uncle Sam, blowing tiny halos of smoke that rose above her head, vanishing into the plaster medallion on the ceiling. The more he had sex with her though, the more he felt a need to get closer to her, and she, in turn, did not chase him out as fast. It was a chance-turned-convenient, business relationship morphing into something else.

Several weeks later, Nick crept into bed after midnight, while Nathan lay prone in the dark. He noticed the neck of whiskey bottle sticking out of a trash can.

"Still hanging around with that *putana*?" Nathan asked.

"She's not a whore!"

"Just joking."

"I didn't ask you to butt in about the girl, so don't piss me off."

"You can't be serious about her? Who knows how many Germans she's been with?"

"Why don't you just lay off the booze?" Nick sat on his bed and took off his shoes. "She doesn't mean anything to me, but it's better than cooping myself up in this room, when we're off duty."

"You see this?" Nathan muttered as he held out a letter. Nick unbuttoned his shirt, while his friend shot up in bed. "There's only one of my cousins left in Venice. Carlo's in hiding. The Gestapo arrested the rest of the family." Nathan wiped his eyes with the sheet. "If he doesn't escape soon, they'll cart him off to a concentration camp."

"Geez, I'm sorry, Nate." Nick limped over and sat at the edge of Nathan's bed.

"Our troops finally got past the Arno Line ..." Nathan punched the mattress. "But they're stuck at the Gothic! And Carlo is trapped above the line."

"Captain Smith says one of Germany's best field marshals is in command. Not good for your cousin. We'd have a hell of a time getting to him in Venice now."

"It eats my heart out. Carlo and I used to exchange postcards, ever since we could write. I'd send him one of the Golden Gate Bridge. He'd send me one of St. Mark's Square."

"How's he related?"

"My mother's brother. He's a Moretto."

"Maybe Caterina knows someone who could help."

"Who the hell is Caterina?"

"The girl I've been seeing. In basic Italian, *la ragazza*. Okay." Nathan shook his head yes and turned toward the wall.

The following evening Nick had arranged to meet Caterina in a café facing the *Fontana dei Monti*. She had a glass of Compari and soda in front of her.

"*Ciao*, Caterina." He sat down without kissing her on both cheeks.

"Are you embarrassed meeting me here?"

"I've got something important to discuss."

"Like a true American, business first."

Nick realized he had hurt Caterina by not kissing her in public but kept it to himself. "Nathan is very worried about his *cugino* in Venice."

"*Cugino di* Nathan *è italiano*?"

"*Si*, but he's Jewish."

"*Ma* it is no matter. *Allora*, he is still Italian, yet Nathan fears for his cousin's life, no?"

"*Si*. Can anything be done?"

"*Molto difficile*! *Ma non è impossible*!"

"What do you mean?"

"There is an underground for Italian and foreign Jews in Assisi."

"You mean there's hope. All of my buddy's family was arrested, except for Carlo."

"There are no guarantees, but I know a Franciscan monk in Assisi and ..."

Nick laughed.

"What, you think it's funny? This whore knows a priest. I thought you wanted to help your friend."

"*Mi dispiace*, Caterina." Her eyes dampened. "I am a *cretino*. *Prego*, continue."

"The monks, nuns and villagers have been hiding Jews and forging identity cards for the past year, even when the Gestapo was in Assisi. They continue to help Jews and other refugees in whatever way they can. But it's not safe at all for Jews to move around northern Italy." Nick blinked several times. "I will write to *Padre* Esposito tonight and post it tomorrow morning."

Nick paid the waiter without asking Caterina if she would like to leave. His body language was a sufficient signal to her that he wanted to bed her. She looked at him with piercing eyes but he had misunderstood her, not having realized she was probably more complex than he gave her credit for, with those brilliant, green eyes brimming with wit and passion and not the *puttana* Nathan made cracks about. He didn't want to let on that he had feelings for her, not wanting to be Dear Johned again.

As they crossed the street, Nick spotted the outline of the Colosseum, looming at the end of *Via dei Serpenti.* No matter how many times he ran across these ancient landmarks, a time travel aura set in, causing him to lose himself along the short walk to her apartment, Caterina several steps ahead. Things went along perfunctorily right up to her last words to him that evening: "Your time is up, so you can leave," as Caterina pulled a robe around her tightly.

Nick knew that Caterina was still angry with him and placed the liras under a lace runner. As he descended the wide, white marble stairs, he could hear faint sobbing emanating from her room. He had behaved badly, even if their relationship was conditioned by the war. Nick had to remind himself that Caterina had feelings. He picked up his pace by putting more pressure on the cane, wanting to get back to Nathan as fast as he could. He remembered to glide the motor scooter out of the alley and then raced away on his Paperino at full throttle, as if he were being shelled by high explosive ordinances out of nowhere, the booming sound in his head real enough that he kept shaking it, scooting over streets that had now become familiar to him.

***

A week later, Nick thudded his cane coming into their room waving a letter. Nathan threw the newspaper down on a pile that had been building up. He pulled up a chair beside his friend and gave him the lowdown.

"I just translated this from the Italian. It seems *Padre* Esposito has a plan to save Carlo but there are many risks. The Franciscan monk has a lot of contacts throughout the region, including the *partigiani*." Nick could see his friend synthesizing. "Nate, let's go to Assisi."

"I'll clear everything with Captain Smith tomorrow morning. Convince him I need R&R." Nathan tapped his head. "I'm sure Doc Bradley would back me up, considering my last seizure."

"What about me?"

"He's my cousin. I'll go it alone."

"Like hell you will."

"Suit yourself, but there's no need for the both us to wind up dead if things go wrong."

"We're supposed to stick together. Isn't that right, Nate?"

"All right. You can tag along to Assisi. Hasn't your leg been acting up lately? I hear you wincing in pain when you think I'm asleep."

Nick banged his cane on the floor. "By the way, Caterina insists that she go too."

"That dame you sneak off in the evening with? What does she have to do with this?"

"She's the one who got us the contact. Besides, it'll look better for me if we include her."

"Is there something else going on?"

"Who said it's something special. Just accommodating her, that's all."

"All right, all right. We'll bring what's her name along."

"It's Caterina." Nathan turned in for the night and fell asleep but Nick tossed around in bed. His body ached and he didn't know if it was from his wound or something else. At least Carlo was safe for now. But what about getting across the Gothic Line. Nick mused whether or not he was getting sweet on a whore. If that were the case, Nate would put his two cents in, something he could bet on.

* * *

Nathan convinced Captain Smith that he and Nick needed to go on leave, the pain of their old wounds resurfacing. The captain granted them a seven-day leave but warned them about coming back on time. They had a *cappuccino* at a dingy bar near Caterina's apartment and then sped off on their *Paperini* with Nathan in the lead and Nick with his *ragazza* wrapped around his waist. They headed north through the region of *Lazio* and followed a path of destruction left by the retreating German army, villages burnt out, planted fields despoiled and farmhouses in ruins. Nick spotted vegetables rotting, when there was a shortage of food, and the farm equipment, rusted and twisted, strewn about with no one to fix it. They witnessed long lines of refugees dragging themselves south to Rome, the expressions on their faces are what got to Nick—children whose expressions, once bright with the joy of discovery, now blank with fear, their mothers weeping silently not to make the *bambini* more jittery, and the men, young and old, with eyes bleary from their predicament. The thing that fortified Nick was his mission to save Carlo, one he hoped was not a fool's journey *come* Giufà.

They found the road that took them east through landlocked Umbria, weaving right and left around its green hills. Some of the olive groves and vineyards survived and Nick wondered what it would be like cruising around here when there wasn't a war. He felt exhilarated and disenchanted at the same time with Caterina hanging on and never easing her grip. He guessed that she might also harbor mixed emotions, a term Nick thought was phony, but for now he didn't have much choice on how things played out. He maneuvered the scooter over the dirt road in a trance, trying to unscramble why this beautiful girl had been caught up in prostitution.

They finally found the road leading up to Assisi, situated on a slope with Mount Subasio as a backdrop. As they entered the town's *Porta San Pietro* at dusk, the bells for vespers chimed from the *Basilica San Francesco d'Assisi*, echoed by the *campanile* of the other churches. A group of turtledoves on a tile roof fluttered off and, as Nick glanced up, he managed to catch sight of the distinctive, black chevron on white, under the tail of the last one in the flock. As they swerved down the streets and alleys of Assisi, the rosy tint of the stone houses was still visible. They stopped at the *Piazza Santa Chiara* to get directions for *San Damiano*, where St. Francis had his first encounter with Christ. The monastery was around 1.5 kilometers south of Assisi, going through *Porta Nuova*.

In a short time they vroomed their way past olive trees, lining the approach to the *chiesa*, where *Padre* Alessandro Esposito greeted them under an arch of the medieval stone church that had an adjoining monastery. He wore the brown robes of a Franciscan, tied with a knotted cord, and leather sandals. They followed the monk into the refectory, where a long dining table was set up for *la cena*. It was already past the designated hour for supper at the monastery, so they would be dining with *Padre* Esposito alone. As soon as they sat down, a monk came out of the kitchen and placed the food on the table.

"Ah, this is Brother Ginepro. He doesn't speak English but nevertheless he is capable of guiding you around the monastery. *È vero, Fra' Ginepro tu sei la guida*?" The brother smiled in recognition, revealing several missing teeth. The guests returned the smile before he left the room to retrieve the rest of the food. On first glance, Nick was not able to distinguish whether *Fra'* Ginepro was simple or simple-minded, but either way, he sensed that the *padre* was fond of him.

"Besides Brother Ginepro and myself, there are only two other monks left in the monastery to care for the garden and the fruit orchard. I sent all the others away on a mission to help the *disgraziati* in the city of Terni. The city, just 56 kilometers south of here, was terribly bombed. Whatever comfort the Franciscans provide for these refugees will be appreciated. Assisi has been most fortunate being designated a holy town, spared the devastation that I'm sure you have seen all over our beautiful country."

After the food had been brought out, they passed plates around that had little meat but plenty of olives, some cheese, *pane antico* and red wine. Nick noticed that the wine was watery, disappointed that it didn't measure up to Umbrian standards, but in deference to *Padre* Esposito, he bragged about wine of this region. Nathan paid no attention to the wine and ate quickly, anxious to get to point of their visit. Caterina kept her eyes lowered the whole time, picking at the olives. When they finished the meal, the *Padre* got their attention.

"Let me get to the heart of the matter, *miei amici in Cristo*. Your cousin, Carlo, is in great danger. When Mussolini was in control, it was easier to protect

Italian Jews. In reality, the Germans never trusted the Italians, who many times interceded for their own countrymen, even if they were Jewish. The Gestapo and the OVRA, the *fascista* secret police, knew there were countless Italian Jews who were never reported."

"Father Esposito, what does this mean for Carlo?" Nathan interrupted.

"Your cousin must get out of Venice as soon as possible. If the SS or Gestapo find him, no Italian in authority will be able to intercede."

"But Padre Esposito, how can we get Carlo out with the war raging up north?" Nick asked.

"I'll get to that momentarily. In the past, when it was safer for our Jewish refugees to travel, they could escape to Switzerland with forged identity cards, or as things worsened, through our own Italian underground by way of Assisi, Perugia, Florence and Genoa, sneaking them onto a neutral ship leaving the country. After the fighting intensified throughout northern Italy, we decided to hide Jewish refugees, *paesani* or foreigners, right here in town. With help from my printer friend in town, we can replicate new identity cards for Carlo and one of you."

"When do I go, *Padre*?" Nathan asked.

"Wait a minute, Nate," Nick said. "You can't go. If they find out you're an American Jew, you're a dead man, and besides, you can barely speak Italian."

"I know enough. You are only here because I said you could tag along."

"*Basta*! Let me at least go over the plan first," Padre Esposito insisted. Nick pressed his palms together as if praying, while Nathan sat rigid. "The safest way to Venice now is by sea, not by land. I have a friend, Giuliano the fisherman, who is a *partigiano* from Ancona, a city east of here, on the coast of *Le Marche*." Padre raised his hands up as if he were blessing something. "He is *un uomo di fiducia*, a man of trust." *Padre* put his hands down. "He can navigate all the way up through the inlets and coves around Venice. He's in communication with other *partigiani* there. One of you must go disguised as a Franciscan monk. Brother Ginepro will show you how to wear the robes. Next, the town printer will make a perfect identity card for one of you. No one will detect it as fake. We have never lost a Jewish refugee here. He'll duplicate another identity card for Carlo. I'll gather a monk's robe and sandals for him as well. My friend is also expert at making various city seals and official rubber stamps. All you'll have to do is trim a photo of Carlo and stamp it in the correct manner. The printer will show the proper technique when he's done."

"*Padre* Esposito, we haven't settled the problem. Who's going up north?" Caterina interjected with a wrinkled brow.

The monk remained silent, twisting his cord belt, and walked over to the hanging crucifix and prayed awhile. Then he turned and faced the table, his hands still folded.

"Nick is right. If he is caught, he has a better chance to survive. We don't need any more Jews dying." The monk unfolded his hands and extended his arm towards the oversized dark oak door.

"But Father, Nick doesn't move as fast as I can. You see he has a cane."

"Nate, you're stepping over the line," Nick snapped back.

"*Basta*, gentlemen." He motioned toward the garden. "*Prego*, let's go into the cloister and walk off the meal. I must show you our lovely roses."

As they entered the garden Caterina pleaded: "*Mi scusi, Padre.* I am not feeling well. *Buonanotte.*" Nick looked at Nathan inquisitively and the *Padre* called for Brother Ginepro who waited in the shadows.

"*Prende la signorina alla sua cella, per favore.*"

Caterina trailed the monk out of the garden and Nick's eyes followed her as she left, noting her lovely profile, lit up by a full moon, passing by each semicircle stone arch balanced on top of the columns. Brother Ginepro held a lantern and continued up the steep stone stairs with Caterina in tow. He guided her past many doors made of holm oak until they reached the cell prepared for her. The brother bowed his head before leaving.

Still lingering in the garden, Nick complimented the friar on the variety of beautiful roses, saying he preferred the more visible, white ones. The sweet fragrance of the roses reminded him of Caterina's perfume. *Padre* Esposito's eyes drooped, so Nick suggested they retire to their rooms. They walked up the stairs with Brother Ginepro lighting the way through the darkness. When they reached the top floor, *Padre* made a left turn to a nearby cell, his "*Buonanotte*" echoing off the stone walls. Brother Ginepro brought his guests to the end of the hall, stopping at the last two cells and opening each door for them. Then the brother extinguished the lantern, disappearing into the dark. Within a few minutes, Nick left his cell and knocked on Nathan's door.

Nathan cracked the door halfway. "Nick?"

"What's with the cane business in front of Caterina?"

"Forget it. I didn't want you going instead of me."

"Where's Caterina anyway?"

"Beats me. She must be in another wing."

"Yeah, that figures—monastery."

Nathan rolled his eyes. "Come on, buddy. Don't get yourself all worked up. You'll get to see her soon enough." Nathan winked and Nick let out a laugh.

"Pipe down, Nick. This isn't North Beach."

Two hooded monks suddenly appeared at the top of the stairs in a dark yellow haze, each one carrying a candle that illuminated their faces as they glided left on the corridor, chanting "*Pax et bonum*."

"Step inside for a minute." Nick entered the dimly lit cell. "I gotta say something." Nathan hesitated.

"Spit it out, Nate."

"I've been meaning to say this for quite awhile. I am sorry about what happened between you and my sister."

"Like water off a duck's back."

"You're full of crap, Nick." Nathan rubbed his chin. "Anyway, I just wanted you to know that my parents would be so grateful for what you're going to do. Not that they would change their minds about Deborah and you, but …"

"I understand. It's a family thing. I'm not happy about it, but don't go bangin' your head on a wall."

"You're a real pal. What else can I say?"

"Do me favor, will you?"

"Sure."

"Keep an eye out for Caterina. Be nice to her."

"I'll treat her like my sister." Nathan responded with a smart alec grin.

"Swell. Remember, a sister." Nick faked a jab to Nathan's stomach and left.

The next day, after a quiet breakfast of stale bread and unsweetened coffee made with chicory, sugar being rationed, Caterina took Nick along on a walk to meet an old friend at *Caffé Minerva* on *Piazza del Comune*. She told him that Isabella and she had met at the university. Her friend had returned to her hometown, Assisi, to work for the local bishop as a cook, the only job she could get during the war. Nick nodded when Caterina explained that Isabella had been stealthily passing messages for *Padre* Esposito because the OVRA had been monitoring him. *Minchia*, he mumbled to himself, these two women in their own ways knew how to survive by their wits and nerve.

They found the *piazza* without getting lost. Isabella was already sitting in the café with a good view of the *Tempio di Minerva* with its six Corinthian columns and Roman pediment that fronted a church.

Isabella vigorously waved to Caterina who ran over to her friend, while Nick admired Caterina's glimmering, brown hair bouncing on her shoulders. They kissed and hugged so much that they caught the attention of everyone sitting. Nick was amused by their flamboyant affection and got a load of the long-legged Isabella who was more buxom than Caterina.

"*Come bella appari, Caterina.*"

"*Basta, Isabella, imbarazzarmi*! *Parla l'inglese come ci abituavamo in università.*"

"*Certo.* You are still beautiful after all you have been through."

"No, the men always look at you. *Mi scusi*, I am being so rude." Caterina put her hand on Nick's forearm. "Isabella, this is Nick, an American friend of mine."

"*Piacere*," he said and shook Isabella's hand.

Isabella turned away from Nick and looked Caterina up and down. "As God is my judge, I have seen your face in several frescoes here." Caterina blushed as her friend motioned towards the wire-backed chairs. "Let's sit down and enjoy the view."

"*Signorine*, I'll leave you two school buddies alone."

"*Prego*, sit with us," Isabella protested, while Caterina tugged him down.

Isabella called the waiter over and they ordered *cappuccino.* Nick opted for *un caffè* and as the girls chatted, he could see their school bond surfacing, punctuated by the laughter of Isabella, who was prone to snapping her head backwards when something was funny, her curly, black hair floating over her shoulders. He noticed how Caterina absorbed her friend's infectious humor.

"*Ecco*, the *cappuccino* has arrived," Isabella called out to the waiter who placed the *cappuccino* in front of her with flair.

Caterina took her time scraping a teaspoon of sugar from a chipped, porcelain bowl and stirring it into the coffee. She looked into the cup as she spoke. "Nick is going to get himself killed."

Isabella looked confused, as Caterina looked away. "*Non capisco*, Caterina."

Nick raised his right palm out. "Let's not talk about it."

"*Prego*, now I must know. Speak *sotto voce*."

"Do you want me to leave you two alone?"

"*No, sta qui Nicolo*," Isabella responded. "You are too handsome to leave." Isabella laughed and bent forward to Caterina.

"He volunteered to rescue someone. And *Padre* Esposito blessed the choice of Nick over his best friend, Nathan."

"*Mi dispiace*. But what can you do about this?" She sat up straight.

"*Niente*, except worry every moment Nick's gone."

Isabella grasped Caterina's trembling hand and said to Nick: "The Goddess Minerva will protect you."

"I wish I could be as sure as you," Nick said.

Isabella let her friend's hand go. "We need to laugh when there is sadness, otherwise these dark days will consume us."

"It feels like ancient times when we studied with Rachele at the *Università di Padova*," Caterina said. "How is she doing now?"

Isabella lowered her voice. "Rachele is still hiding here in the convent of the Poor Clares, even though she doesn't have to."

"Rachele is the other reason I came to Assisi. I never told Nick about her." She looked at him as he played with the *espresso* cup. "But I worry about her." Her eyes dampened. "I wanted to see her again."

"It continues to be a sad story. *Anch'io sono molte preoccupata perla*. I try not to dwell too much on her condition. *Allora*, we need to bring sunshine into our lives." Her laugh seemed to accentuate her breasts or that's how Nick perceived it. Caterina eyed Nick who smiled back. "Let's talk about our happy times at the *università*," Isabella continued, while Caterina dug out the remains of the *crema* from her *cappuccino* and spooned it into her mouth. Nick and Caterina exchanged curious glances at each other while her friend dominated most of the conversation.

The following evening was hot, so Caterina and Nick stayed up late before retiring to separate cells. During their visit they had spent a lot of time reading to pass away the hours in the monastery. They had tired of their books and sat on a stone bench in the garden near a cluster of high growing, pink roses. There was a well in the center on the sacred ground of St. Francis. Nick appeared distracted, so Caterina put his head on her lap.

"What happened to the crown of your hair?"

"*Fra*' Ginepro was my barber." Nick snickered. "*Padre* Esposito said if I didn't have the tonsure, it would be a dead giveaway that I wasn't a monk."

"*Madonna*. What's next? Why did you volunteer to go anyway, when it's Nathan's cousin and not yours?"

"We already went over this. He's more vulnerable. Stop worrying, will ya! *Padre* Esposito said you and Nathan could stay in the monastery till I get back."

"When are you leaving?"

"Tomorrow morning. The *partigiano* from Ancona will pick me up before the breakfast hour. He'll drive us back there *subito*."

"Suppose you never come back."

Nick didn't want to discuss the danger of Carlo's rescue and took a cue from nature.

"Do you hear that hermit thrush? It's such a beautiful song."

"I can't hear or see anything." Her eyes were watery and she turned away. "Why do you talk of birds now?"

"I associate good things when I hear birds. It makes me forget bad things that ring in your head as if you're sitting next to the bells in a *campanile*."

She bit her lip. "The walls are blocking what little breeze there is tonight."

"Winds have a way of shifting unexpectedly, *Papà* used to tell me when I was a kid. My father would to take me sailing ..." Nick recalled running to Paul's house, telling him in detail about his sea adventure.

He rose up from her lap and remained silent for a while.

"Finish, your story, Nicky." He remembered that Deborah used to call him that and then he became even more distant from Caterina. "You're far away from me now, even though I feel your leg rubbing against mine."

"Like I was saying." He rubbed a tear away. "My father would borrow his friend's sloop and take me out sailing in the San Francisco Bay. He taught me how to tack the sails properly." Nick looked up. "There are no stars out tonight. I hope this fisherman friend of *Padre* Esposito can find his way without them. You never know what to expect when you're out on the sea."

Caterina twisted her hands as if she were running a Paperino and Nick grinned in recognition. They left the monastery and he retrieved his motor scooter. They rode to the outskirts of town where the trees were thickest. He leaned the scooter against a pine tree, while Caterina laid out a blanket on the ground. He left his cane in its pouch and limped a short way to her, dropping down next to her without tumbling over. As they made love, he didn't worry about the missing stars. He wanted only to be lost in her arms and body, and when all the passion was released, feel the soft warm skin of her face resting on his cheek. He was in the moment of his last night with her before he headed north, shutting out any dark thoughts.

They sat up when some stars broke through the sky, flashing little beads of light, helter skelter as the clouds passed through.

"Some stars are pulsating, Nick."

"I can see them, Caterina."

"And do you see me?"

"I didn't know about your university life. But I'm not surprised, if that's what you mean?"

"So you don't see me as a *cretina* or other things?"

"I always thought you were smart from the first moment I met you."

"You never mentioned it."

"Why did you get into this business anyway?"

"There's no point talking about it. I had a different life in another time, before the *fasciste* seized the government."

"*Papà* and his friend Marco hated them."

"*Allora*, my father was different than yours."

"I guess we don't know each that well."

"I know you better than you could ever imagine. Nicky, keeping things inside you does not help. Everything comes out in your sad eyes."

"You're a mystic now."

"I have no powers over you. I am not happy with my situation but sometimes we become trapped by circumstances. Do you see me past your sexual desires?"

"I see you as clear as the stars that just peeked through the darkness. And I'm moved that you worry so much about me." He gazed at the sky. "I see you better than any light that stars could bring." He looked at her. "Because I like being with you. But don't ask for the stars when it comes to me." His brow furrowed. "I lost my bearings when I crossed the ocean, a long time ago." Nick stood up and extended his hand.

# XI

The two mysterious monks were in the garden, one clipping with a rhythmic sound, the other countering with the thud of his spade. Nathan stopped to watch them and noticed Caterina sitting by the well. He stepped behind a stone column and had an urge to sketch Caterina as she sat there daydreaming. He imagined she thought of Nick riding with the *partigiano* on the road to the Adriatic Sea. Nathan had suspected she didn't want to sit with him in the refectory for their spartan breakfast and he couldn't blame her, considering all his unkind remarks about her, not all of them behind her back.

Nathan recalled when the three of them had been drinking too much whiskey in a Trastevere café and Nick left to pick up some cigarettes at a nearby *tabaccheria.*

"So where's your plumed hat, Caterina?"

"*Come*?"

"Ever seen any of Kirchner's paintings?"

She pursed her lips. "*Non lo so.*"

"He's a German expressionist. Nazis declared his work degenerate. Killed himself in '38."

"*Allora*, what is your point?" She moistened her lips with the whiskey.

"He loved to paint Berlin prostitutes who were fond of dressing up like birds."

"You're not funny at all, Nate. Maybe you're jealous, no?"

He drank his whiskey in one gulp. "So tell me, how many fascists and Nazis did you go to bed with before you met Nick?"

"You're drunk and disgusting. You know nothing about me yet you judge me." She finished her whiskey. "The answer to your ignorant question is none."

This scene faded out as Nathan reflected on Nick making his way to Venice. After all, he had promised to look after the *ragazza*. When Nathan moved closer to her, he noted that she cradled a cup of *cappuccino* with both hands. As she sat alone in the garden, a silhouette of brooding, the aroma perked up when he got closer.

"*Buongiorno*, Caterina." She put her cup down on the ledge and nodded. "Nick must have reached Ancona by now. I heard him leaving right after dawn." She picked the cup up and sipped the coffee that left some foam on her upper lip. "You've got a moustache." She wiped it off with her fingers, her expression blank. "Look, maybe I should learn not to butt into somebody else's business. But you've got to understand. We look out for each other."

"I know what you think of me. You call me a *puttana* to Nick's face."

"I was just teasing. You know, GI talk." He sat down next to her.

"So you were just teasing about looking like a Berlin whore?"

"I was soused and people say stupid things when they're drunk."

"You're always ready with an answer or one of your jokes."

"I'm not trying to wiggle out of this, but I got a lot of things on my mind."

"I know. That's why Nick is gone from us." Her eyes were bloodshot.

Nathan shook his head and looked away. "*Mi dispiace*!" He looked at her. "I'm really sorry."

"I am going to the *Monastero di San Quirico* to see a friend."

"I'm bored. Do you mind if I go too?" Caterina remained silent. "I'll behave myself."

"You could walk with me, if you like." She stood up. "That's if you're not embarrassed by me."

* * *

The wrought iron gate of the beige, stone wall convent dragged along the ground as one of the extern nuns, the only sisters allowed to interact with outsiders, let them in. The sister befriended Caterina, as she led her to the reception desk of the guesthouse. Nathan thought the setup was odd and sat on the stone bench, taking out his sketchpad to wile away the time. Caterina disappeared through another doorway leading to the cloister. An hour passed but Nathan stayed put. He didn't want any tales spread about him when his buddy returned, God willing. The same nun, who first greeted them, led Nathan into the dining room of the guesthouse. Caterina was already sitting at a table with another nun.

"Nathan, this is Rachele, *mia cara amica*."

"Nathan Fein. *Piacere*!" Nathan extended his hand but Rachele looked at the table, as he sat down next to Caterina, and said: "You can speak English."

Rachele kept her eyes on Caterina. "It has been very hot this summer, Caterina. *Molto caldo.*"

Caterina turned to Nathan. "Rachele was saying before that their peaches are very sweet."

"*È vero.* We try to grow all our food on the convent grounds."

Rachele glanced at Nathan with blank eyes. "Where is your uniform?"

"Oh, I ditched it in one of *Padre* Esposito's cells." Her eyes locked into his face, which made Nathan apprehensive. "And are you Jewish?"

"Yes."

"I see." Rachele turned sideways toward Caterina. "It has been a good year for the garden so far. It is a blessing."

His artist's eye noted the nun's face, which had the whitest skin, and some strands of auburn hair peeking out from the white bandeau, almost as if she were a lost movie star from a German expressionist filmmaker like Fritz Lang. As Nathan focused in closer, he thought her face turned paler as their light chatter tapered off. He was mesmerized by her presence and glad his vision had been improving since that near-fatal day. Nathan was taken aback when the friendly sister entered the room and motioned to Caterina that it was time for Rachele to return to the cloistered part of the convent. The extern nun let them out the front gate.

"So what did you think of Rachele?" Caterina asked as they walked away from the convent walls.

"I'm stunned. Such beauty and tension in her face at the same time."

"But we only spoke of harmless things together."

"Yeah, I know. But I can sense things. Guess I'm used to looking at people and things from a different perspective. Even when I'm too depressed to sketch, I do it in my head. The eyes can reveal a lot of things about someone."

"Rachele Stein is *ebrea*, Jewish."

"Not surprised, considering her name, but is she really a nun?"

"It's a complicated story. She was one of my best friends when we lived together in the dormitory at the *Università di Padova*. She is originally from Berlin."

"Hey, that's where my parents came from."

"So that's why you're so clever about Berlin."

"Are you riding me now?"

"I think you should weigh your words." Caterina pressed the tongue into her cheek.

Nathan looked nonplussed. "*Oy vey*, Caterina!"

"*Allora*, let's be serious. As you must know, bad things have been going on in Germany for a long time. My father had a lot of influential contacts, so I asked him to find out if Rachele's family was safe in Berlin, but it was already too late for them. The Gestapo had arrested them on the trumped-up grounds of her father's communist leanings. I warned Rachele not to return home. *Padre* Esposito used to visit our university and gave lectures on the frescoes of the Basilica of St. Francis of Assisi. I majored in Art History, so we started to correspond. I arranged for the *padre* to hide Rachele in Assisi."

"No wonder the poor girl is so nervous."

"There are other things, but maybe I shouldn't say." Caterina bit her lip.

"Don't stop now."

"My family comes from *Milano*."

"Wait a minute! I thought you were Roman."

"I never told anyone, not even Nick. I figured what was the point? My former life in *Milano* is gone."

"Are you pulling my leg?" Nathan gazed into her face and realized that this was one babe he couldn't second-guess. "I gotta hear this one."

"Where can I begin? I was born into *una famiglia aristocratica*. My line goes all the way back to a nephew of one the cardinals during the Renaissance."

"Are you *meshugenah*?" She looked puzzled. "*Pazzo*!"

Caterina's eyes welled up and she walked ahead of him.

"*Mi dispiace*! I didn't mean you're really crazy," he called out. He caught up with her and stood in front of her. "Tell me more." They continued walking at a slower pace.

"My father was *Baron* Ferdinando Rossetto. He got caught up in Mussolini's web, joining the *fascista* party. My mother died while horse jumping, but she never cared for politics. I was against this whole business from the start, but my father would not listen to a young, university student. That's how Rachele and I bonded over our disgust with fascism and nazism."

"I see." Nathan's eyes brightened at the sound of Rachele's name. He tripped on an upturned cobblestone but gained his balance.

"*Attenzione*, Nathan!"

"Hold up. I gotta digest all of this. So why the hell were you selling ...?" His voice trailed off, when they stopped.

Caterina glowered at him. "Go ahead. Finish what you have to say."

Nathan waved his palms up.

"My father moved down to *Roma*, so he could be closer to the central government. I left the *Univeristá di Padova* so as not to be trapped up north. The Germans were seizing more power. Many of my professors had gone into hiding with the *partigiani*. I wasn't in *Roma* too long before the *partigiani* dragged my father out to the street right before the Americans took control of Rome." Caterina winced. "They shot him, leaving him to die in the gutter. One of them set our apartment on fire. I hated his politics, but he was still my father. Anyway, I had no money or family in Roma, so I had to survive."

"And you're never mentioned any of this to Nick?"

"Swear that you'll keep this to yourself. I am not looking for his sympathy."

Nathan nodded yes.

They reached *San Damiano* and met up with *Padre* Esposito but there was no word about Nick, so they returned to their cells to meditate about things beyond their control. When Nathan opened his casement window, he could see the outline of the *campanile* of the Basilica of St. Francis rising in a sky full of puffy clouds, the cypress trees pointing up in the hills, sentinels for the orange-red tile roof farmhouses scattered about. He brooded over what was happening to Nick up north, trying to smuggle his cousin out. Nathan regretted that he hadn't been chosen instead of his buddy, but he didn't want to dwell on it. His thoughts turned to Rachele and the swatch of red-brown hair marking her brow. The clouds blew away to reveal a fresco blue sky, almost like a cabalistic signal. He left his cell and rapped on Caterina's door, coaxing her to follow him into the garden.

As they strolled around, he said: "You're a student of art history. If I taught you how to draw, you could connect better with the art world."

"I have tried to paint but I gave up. That's why I decided to major in Art History."

"That's because you didn't have me as a teacher."

"I suppose I could try again." She sat down by the well and looked up at Nathan, the sun over his head. "What do you want in return?"

"I'm not trying to make a pass. Not that you're not pretty. You could have been a model for Piero della Francesca."

Caterina blushed and laughed. "So Nathan, you now find me attractive!"

"You're my buddy's girl, you know, off limits!" Nathan smelled one of the tall, white roses. "Anyway, I'd like to see Rachele again."

"That's easy enough. Remember she's very fragile like that rose you were holding."

"Nah, don't worry about it. Just looking for some good conversation."

"It might be helpful for Rachele, but I'll have to act like a chaperone. Don't make a face." She smiled with such perfect, white teeth he studied her features. "She's living in a convent."

"I can see now why Nick is stuck on you."

"I'm not so sure about that. Do you know something I don't know?"

"Nick can be an enigma sometimes. Seems moody when you least expect it."

"What do you mean? Emotional?"

"I can't say. He can be very protective about you. There's something else."

"What?"

"Since his cousin Paul died, he gets lost in his own world. The funny thing is that's what he accuses me of. So why not ask him about it?"

"I don't think he would want me to pry. Why don't we stick with painting lessons for now?"

* * *

Nathan, Caterina and Rachele spent several mornings together in the parlor of the convent guesthouse. Caterina had arranged everything with the Mother Abbess, who spoke to Caterina through the open shutters of a double grille, behind which the cloister was situated. Caterina assured the Mother Abbess that everything would be proper. On the third visit, Caterina didn't join them and watched from the nearby kitchen window as Nathan and Rachele conversed.

"Do I speak English too fast?" Nathan asked, as her face signaled pain to him. "I can also speak German."

"I told you yesterday that I was a linguistics major and I'm fluent in many languages." She looked at the floor. "Besides, I never speak German anymore."

"I'm sorry. You're right." Nathan could see the quizzical pain in her face, as if she were repelled and drawn to him at the same time.

"Caterina, she's always trying to save me. What for, I don't know," she said at length, while Nathan listened patiently.

"You don't have to wear that habit anymore, Rachele. The Nazis are gone."

"Are they really gone? What about your cousin? The one you mentioned yesterday."

"Carlo." Nathan's face blanched.

"*Mi dispiace*! I can't help it. When I hear these stories ..."

"I shouldn't have mentioned my cousin."

"Why?" She raised her voice. "Do you feel you have to tiptoe around me like we're dancing in some kind of French ballet?" Rachele looked at her black sandals. "I'm sorry. I shouldn't be speaking this way." A tear lined her left cheek. "My whole family is gone. My two beautiful, young sisters probably raped and murdered. That's what Nazis do to young, defenseless women, you know."

"There's always some chance they might be alive."

"There's no hope now!" Her lovely white skin turned even paler than before.

Nathan thought she might be right but said, "I haven't given up on my cousin Carlo, so why should you give up? For me, I'm betting on Nick." Nathan placed his hand on hers and this time she did not push it aside.

"I'm so confused. I don't know where to turn. Why can't I get myself to leave this convent?" For the first time she broke down and sobbed. "What has become of my family? Can you answer that, Nathan?" Nothing came to him there but in the quiet of his own cell, he would mull over everyone important to him this side of the Atlantic—Rachele, Nick and Carlo, even Caterina, then segue to his family on the other side, or *al di là* as Nick might mumble in Italian when he missed his *la famigghia*, switching to Sicilian.

"I need to rest now," she said, placing her hands into her lap.

"But couldn't we stay longer? There's no rush."

She left and, though Nathan could only see the back of her black coif over the brown habit, he sensed she was crying.

As Nathan and Caterina trekked down the path to *San Damiano*, they remained quiet most of the way.

"I'll teach you some more art tricks in the garden before dusk."

"*Grazie*, that would be lovely. Keep our minds off of things, no?" Caterina gave a sideways glance at Nathan who kept looking down at the path.

"It's funny ..."

"*Continua*, Nathan."

"I have always been very comfortable with women. They always seem to like me." Caterina chuckled and he faced her, never missing a step. "I'm not a sheik like your *paesano*, Nick."

"Don't take it personally. I'm just amused by your new interest in my friend. But you are right about Nick." She giggled. "He does spend a lot of time in front of the mirror, but go ahead."

"There's something special about Rachele, despite all her fragility." Nathan shook his head. "I can't explain her appeal to me."

"You have to be able to describe it; otherwise it's just make believe."

"Her spirit speaks to me in a way like no other girl has before. She brings out my anima like Jung says is found in a man's personality. You know the female side of man."

"To be in touch with your true inner self."

"Yes, and I want to travel with her wherever she goes, even to the dark places. You see, I want her to get better even if she never likes me in the same way."

"Who can say what will happen? You might as well try and read tarot cards, Nathan."

After they entered the monastery, they went upstairs to their separate cells. When Nathan shut the door, he lay on the cot with his hands wrapped behind his skull. He felt a tightening sensation in his head and then it went away, grateful that he wasn't slipping into another seizure. He didn't want to be shut out by someone like Rachele. There was always something new about her, like a spring awakening, after each brief encounter. It was *meshuganah* or maybe the way the cards had been dealt. He didn't have magical powers that could transform things on the spot. He had his art, but she might be someone who could help him get through this war, but … but he couldn't reach her. The damn deck was stacked against the two of them.

# XII

After several days of readying Giuliano's boat in a marshy cove below the *Via del Conero*, waiting for calm seas, they edged northwest along the coast of *Ma l'Adriatico*. Nick's eyes opened wide when he witnessed all the heavy traffic on the Grand Canal of Venice, a jumble of every imaginable type of craft. The fisherman managed to pilot his boat down a narrower channel, where he throttled the engine slower making them more noticeable. Dusk slipped into darkness and they still hadn't found the right docking spot. In the distance an open door cast light on a man smoking a pipe near a zebra-striped wood piling. As they got closer, Giuliano shut the engine off and floated over to the Venetian. Nick threw a rope to the man, who promptly tied it to the piling and ushered them inside the house without a comment. They walked through the house that connected to another canal on the other side, climbed down into a gondola and glided on an even narrower channel.

Nick had ditched his cane in the monastery cell, after he had practiced faking a normal stride with insightful coaching from *Padre* Esposito. He thought it would be better for Nick not to draw any attention to himself since the Gestapo might wonder why he limped. From his work with the CIC, Nick learned that even a Roman priest was not safe. One had been killed by the SS in the Fosse Ardeatine massacre of 335 Italians of all ages—*partigiani*, random bystanders and 75 Jews from the Roman ghetto. Instead of a firing squad, SS Captain Erich Priebke organized the execution by having each victim shot in the back of the head aiming for the cerebellum, their bodies piled up and then moved to a cave sealed by explosives. This horrific story was something that lingered in Nick's mind and he figured that this mission was not going to be any Tom Sawyer adventure.

Venice was dark as pitch with all house lights turned off under German blackout orders. Nick heard the swooshing of the water as it slid off the huge oar, the sounds so distinct as if the canal water were self-referential. He worried whether they would get out alive. They reached what looked like tar-stained garage doors, which opened and closed behind them. They followed their gondolier up stone steps, wet and slippery with brown and green moss. They waited in a dining room until an older gentleman and a young man entered. Nick noticed that the young man had a dimpled chin similar to Nathan's. He lowered the brown hood of his monk garb, as their host spoke in Venetian dialect. He asked the older one if they could switch to English, Nick's native language.

"I have known Carlo's father since he was a child,"

said Don Ca Botto who stroked his white, Van Dyke-style beard. "We worked in the same import-export business. One of my workers stopped Carlo before he reached home, the day the Gestapo arrested his family. They were sent to Buchenwald. The boy has been here ever since. Very dangerous if the Gestapo gets hold of Carlo." He nodded towards the young man who remained silent.

"Your *cugino*, Nathan, has been very worried about you," Nick said. "He sends his *tanti auguri*." Carlo smiled a bit. "He was annoyed when *Padre* Esposito wouldn't let him come."

"So he sent a monk for me," Carlo responded, gazing out the window overlooking the canal illuminated by a sliver of moonlight. "My parents and younger brothers are missing." Carlo looked at Nick. "I have no delusions. There are many death camps and that's where all Jews are headed."

"I am here to bring you back behind Allied lines." Nick tugged on the neckline of his robes. "I'm not a Franciscan monk, you know. Your cousin and I were in the same tank crew, till it got blown up. You'll be safe once you're in Assisi. Put this on." Nick took the Franciscan robe out of his backpack. "I have an identity card too. I'll attach your photo to it and mark it up with a seal just like an official one." He pulled out a rubber stamp from under his robe.

"Carlo, you're like a son to me," Don Ca Botto said. "But you must leave now or risk being found and sent to your death. There's nothing you can do here for the Moretto family. It's what your father and mother would want." Carlo peered out the window again.

"I will go then, Don Ca Botto."

"*Ben*! Do what these brave gentlemen tell you."

After a supper of homemade *gnocchi* and a carafe of yellow brown Soave, Carlo led his new friends through a hallway to a huge armoire. He opened the doors, stepped in and vanished. Nick and the fisherman looked puzzled until Carlo waved his arm through the cloaks to follow him into the concealed room, where the only light source was through the skylight from the North Star. After donning the Franciscan robes, Carlo sat down to put on brown leather sandals. Giuliano approached with a barber's razor and some soapy water.

"*Mannaggia*, what do you think you're doing with that razor?" Carlo asked.

"*Calma*! You need a bald spot on the crown of your head. Otherwise you will give yourself away. *Ricorda*! *Tu sei un monaco francescano adesso*."

"Ah, it's not so bad, Carlo," Nick added. "Have a look for yourself." He took off his skullcap and bent his head down. "Stop squawkin'. It'll grow back."

"*Ben*!" Carlo stuck his chin out.

Don Ca Botto entered the concealed room within an hour. "The fog has rolled in. You must go now. Our gondolier will get the three of you to the fishing boat you came in with. From there, your fisherman friend, Giuliano, will pilot you to a safer place."

"What shall we do, Don Ca Botto?" Nick asked.

"Act like monks. Pray. Pray for your lives."

"What is the worst danger?" Carlo asked.

"Going under bridges. The German patrols frequently stop on them, when they want to have a smoke. They are bored, so they stare at the traffic below." Carlo embraced the old man, who had tears in his eyes.

"We'll make it to Ancona with Giuliano at the tiller," Nick said.

"From your mouth to God's ears," Carlo added.

Don Ca Botto's men had already stowed provisions below the deck of Giuliano's boat and moved it out of the canals, flying the flag of the winged lion and anchoring in darkness on one of the islands surrounding Venice. The three of them set out in a waiting gondola for Murano, a small but busy port known for exporting Venetian glass. Nick and Carlo sat together in the middle with Giuliano right behind them. They faced the gondolier who steered the flat-bottomed boat, shiny like a black coffin, through the fog in the narrow channels. He called out haunting whistle sounds at dangerous curves, increasing Nick and Carlo's anxiety. As they approached the last dimly lit overpass, several German soldiers aimed their strapped submachine guns at the gondola. The sergeant flashed a light on them. The gondolier in *sotto voce* warned his passengers not to move. They crept under an arched, marble bridge and the German patrol moved to the other side with their fingers on the triggers. The German sergeant yelled *Halt*! The gondolier jerked the oar out of the water, while the sergeant observed the monks praying, the fisherman fast sleep.

He changed his mind, calling out *Vershwinde*, while his patrol lowered the nozzles of their MP40 guns. The sergeant doused the light and lit up a cigarette.

Upon entering the Grand Canal, they slid into a docking area where there were many gondolas. They scurried across a narrow walkway and jumped onto a tiny motorized craft that had been idling. They continued through the dissipating fog, motoring northeast to the midpoint of the Grand Canal, then lighted through a narrower connecting canal that led them past the tiny island of San Michele. They were returned to their fishing boat, fueled up and waiting for them in the elongated harbor of the famous, glass blowing island. They switched boats for the last time and Giuliano took the helm, cruising out to sea.

"I don't like it," Giuliano shouted over the engine noise. "*Le cose sono troppo calma cosi vincino Venezia.*"

"But Don Ca Botta said the worst danger was the bridges," Carlo said.

"*Don Ca Botto sa Venezia. Mal'Adriatico è la mia area,*" Giuliano said, as he piloted the boat from his rear bench.

"Is there anything we can do besides praying?" Nick asked.

"*Si*, I stash a Beretta submachine gun *e due* Carcano rifles under a blanket *sotto il ponte*." He pointed to the hatch in the middle of the boat. "*Vai adesso*, Nick. Make sure they in good working order. Carlo, you keep a look out."

Murano was no longer visible as they headed south to Ancona, when suddenly, a German S-boot gunboat, churning up waves at 40 knots of speed, came out of the blackness in pursuit of their fishing boat.

"*Attenzione*, Giuliano!" Carlo shouted.

"*Calma*. Tell Nick grab the Beretta. Keep the hatch open *un po'*. He no come out unless I cough. Then sit on my left side and read your Bible. I will do all the talking. I have done this many times *sul largo*."

In a short while the gunboat slowed down running parallel to them and an SS officer shouted in German. Getting no reaction, he spoke in Italian. "*Come fa in Murano*?"

"*Ho preso questo padre*," Giuliano responded. "*Lo prendo al monastero in Assisi*."

Giuliano had Carlo hand his identity card over to him and he opened to the page with a photo and waved it in the air.

"*Dummkopf, non posso vedere la carta d'identita*."

Nick had his finger on the second trigger for automatic fire. As the gunboat positioned itself to board, he remained hidden in the dark and first heard the thud of the leather boots of the SS officer above his head, followed by other footsteps. He could make out what was going on through the opening. Nick got the drift of the conversation—the SS officer wearing a tin death head visor cap interrogated Carlo, and then spoke contemptuously to Giuliano about the Italians' role in the war.

Nick sweated profusely while still gripping the automatic beretta. He had to decide between busting out onto the deck and firing away or waiting for the signal as Giuliano advised. When Nick was just about to break out, inexplicably an excited plea came from one of the crewman on the gunboat. The only words that Nick understood were *partigiani*, *Venedig* and *polizei*. He heard the gunboat come close by again and then noticed the black boots missing from the deck. The SS officer and two storm troopers had jumped aboard the gunboat, which swiftly swung away from the fishing boat, causing the water to swell over its deck.

When the gunboat turned around to a north position, the SS officer ordered his machine gunner to open fire at the fishing boat and screamed: "*Homosexuell priester*." By this time Nick was standing on the deck with the Beretta. The shells from the gunboat flashed across the water hitting the hull and rear deck of the fishing boat, riddling Giuliano, who slumped over the helm, and grazing Carlo's head as he dropped to the floor. Another burst flew over Nick's head as he returned the fire. The gunboat closed in to finish the kill when, all of a sudden, it sped away leaving behind a long wake, Nick's bullets already out of range. Nick figured the SS officer must have got a second emergency call to get back *direkt* to the canals of Venice. He removed Giuliano to the deck floor, while Carlo, blood staining his brown robe, grabbed the tiller.

"Giuliano is bleeding like crazy," Nick shouted.

"The first aid kit is under the seat."

Nick ripped all the gauze from the kit and wrapped Giuliano's head and chest like a swaddled baby, applying careful pressure to the most visible red traces on Giuliano's body. "I don't want another comrade dead on my watch." Nick glanced at Carlo. "Are you all right steering?"

"I've got a good grip."

"*Managgia*! Your head's bleeding too."

"Just throw me a linen towel."

"*Va bene*." Nick found a clean one and flung it to Carlo, who quickly tied it around his head. "He's waking up, Carlo." He pleaded with the fisherman: "Giuliano, stay awake this time, for Christ's sake."

"Elevate his head with a blanket, then see if there's any grappa below," Carlo called out, as he steadied the boat through the waves that smacked the bow.

Nick found a dusty bottle of *grappa* and brought it up.

"That SS boat is way out of sight. I think we can make safely it to Ancona."

Nick poured some into Giuliano's mouth. The fisherman grasped his hand and then let it go.

"Are you sure you can steer this tub?"

"I won't get lost. *Sono veneziano*!"

Nick hoped that alcohol numbed some of Giuliano's pain, as he knelt down beside the fisherman, praying to St. Francis Assisi. Carlo mouthed a Jewish prayer for healing his father had taught him as a child. The last time Nick had ever done anything religious was when he was an altar boy, assisting the priest at mass in Saints Peter and Paul Church. He swore he could smell the incense while he continued praying over Giuliano's contorted body. He had prayed for a *miracolo*, but the blood ran from Giuliano's nostrils and mouth and his body became rigid. He made the sign of the cross and Carlo said the *Kaddish* for the dead. Nick covered Giuliano with a blanket. The chilling night air blew away all the clouds and, while Carlo piloted, Nick navigated with his eyes following the path of stars, keeping the North Star at his back, and far off on the horizon due south, on the look out for the pulsating beacon of the Ancona lighthouse.

# XIII

The morning of August 4, 1944, a radio war correspondent announced that the Allied Powers had taken Florence and were preparing to battle the German defenses at the Gothic Line further north. While the news spread around Assisi, Nathan drove a *camioncino*, a three-wheeled truck he borrowed from *Padre* Esposito, back to the convent. As the vehicle whined its way up the hill, Caterina reiterated the story of how she had convinced Mother Abbess that Rachele was strong enough to leave the cloister for the day.

While Nathan waited at the gate with the engine running, Caterina retrieved Rachele from the circle of nuns who ran the guesthouse. Rachele wore a white peasant blouse and skirt, carrying a mesh string bag over her shoulder that contained the picnic the nuns had prepared. She placed it in the back of the open truck underneath a canvas and squeezed herself into the front compartment after motioning to Caterina to get in first. As Nathan pulled away, the externs waved to Rachelle but he noticed that she didn't look back.

They stopped in front of *Caffè Minerva* and got out of the truck.

"Rachele, I want you to have fun today." She hugged Rachele's limp body and let her go. "I'm meeting Isabella here, so you two can get know each better. *Allora*, I don't like playing chaperone. It makes me feel old." Caterina laughed alone. "*Va bene*?"

"*Si*, Caterina."

"I'll take good care of your friend," Nathan added.

"It's a beautiful day, Rachele," Nathan shouted over the engine, as they chugged along. He turned sideways to look at her. "I found a lovely spot not too far away. There's a great vista of all the bell towers of Assisi." She did not speak and sat with her hands in her lap.

After a short drive with a one-way conversation, Nathan pulled into an alcove where a lone picnic table stood, rotted in parts and sunk diagonally into the ground. Rachele set up the table while Nathan pulled a bottle of *sangiovese* wine out of the leather bag.

"I was lucky to find this bottle. Hope you like red wine."

Nathan sat down at her side, while she fidgeted over the setting. "Don't fuss so much. The food looks beautiful by itself. A palette of reds, yellows and earth colors."

"I just want to get everything right, Nathan." Rachele stopped arranging. "This is my first time outside the convent walls," she confided to Nathan as she refolded the napkins.

"Take as long as you want." Nathan looked at the

view up the hill and then opened the bottle of wine. The cork broke off halfway, leaving crumb-like traces all over the table.

"You're not making things easier for me." She swept away the debris from the bottle and finished arranging the food while he got the rest of the cork out.

"Looks beautiful, Rachele. Where did you learn how to do this?"

"My parents owned a chinaware shop in Berlin. Our family name, Stein, was etched in gold lettering on the window. Setting up the displays was one of my jobs until I left for university."

"My father is a printer and my mother, a seamstress."

"Everything is changed now." She cried then wiped her eyes. "I don't know how I can go on. I'll never see my parents and sisters again."

"You just got to live in the moment. Take one day at a time." He saw that she paid no attention to what he said and thought his words were just inept clichés. "Why don't you eat something? The nuns will be very upset, after all the trouble they went through to …"

"I'm the one who's upset. Can't you see? How can I even be here having a picnic with you?"

"Isn't it good for a young woman to be with someone? You know, share things."

"I have my friend, Caterina."

"Yeah, and I have Nick, but I'm not talking about that kind of friendship."

Rachele blushed and turned away.

"Why don't you have sip of wine?" She shook her head. He filled his glass halfway, drank some and banged it down. "It's corked."

"Does that mean I don't have to have any?"

"We'll just drink the water. That's all we need." Nathan drank some and tittered. "On second thought, I think I'll drink the wine."

"You're confusing me."

"It's not so bad. After a while, you get used to it." He poured some more wine for himself and gulped it. Rachele nibbled at the food.

"You're not eating much, Nathan. You said you could eat a four-course Italian meal when we found a spot."

"Maybe it's the wine." Nathan filled up the plate and ate a small portion. He tapped his right foot to some errant bird chirps to pass the time. When the birds flew to a neighboring tree, he broke the silence. "You know, you're perfectly safe now. They can't hurt you."

"I feel safe while you're here." She put her hand on his for the first time. "But I like it better in the convent." She took her hand away.

"I understand, Rachele. But at some point, you're going to have to leave the convent for good. Not just a little outing with me." Her face looked strained. "It's not like the nuns don't care about you … but you're not one of them."

"I am too. That's what they told me to say if anyone asked."

"You don't have to make up any stories now."

"You're so sure the Nazis won't come back."

"Rachele, I don't have a crystal ball, but it's just a matter of time before we beat the Germans."

Rachele got up and ambled over to a sapling where the birds were perched. She shook the trunk and they fluttered away.

"It's like they were listening to our conversation."

"They were just talking to each other, just like we're trying to do. Why don't you have some of this peach with me? Look, the juice is oozing." He held the peach up.

"I don't believe in God."

"Who said anything about God?"

"How can I be a believer after the Nazis took away my family?" She sat down beside him. "I'm trying to tell you something."

"I'm sorry, go ahead. I'm glad you even want to talk to me."

"I don't think I'll ever leave those convent walls. The world is too dangerous. Can't trust anyone outside."

"What about me? Caterina?"

"Neither of you are going to change this world. You spoke about seeing some horrific things yourself. I don't even know what I'm talking about." Rachele wept and Nathan put her head on his shoulder.

"That's it, Rachele. Cry your eyes out." She picked her head up and composed herself.

"Are you sure you're just a friend of Caterina? Did the Mother Abbess send for you?"

"Rachele." He placed his hand on her shoulder. "What are you talking about?"

"Are you some kind of psychiatrist? What do you do in the army?"

"I work as a translator and interpreter in Rome." She looked perplexed and he removed his hand. "It's called the Counter Intelligence Corps, if that helps."

"Like I said."

"Please, Rachele. I interrogate German prisoners of war. Translate intercepted Nazi messages. Seeing you every day is making me lose track of time. So much so, I have already overextended my leave."

"Will they arrest you?"

"Nah, I always come up with a good story."

"Forget everything I've said. I can't help it." Her face turned despondent.

"Everything is okay, Rachele. I wish you would trust me. There isn't anything I wouldn't do for you." They both picked at the food in silence for a while.

"Help me clear the table. The sisters will be wondering why I've been gone so long."

Nathan cajoled Rachele to take a short hike before returning to the convent. They walked down a narrow path, past an olive grove and reached the main road. She picked a white wildflower on the side of the road and held it in her hand, as they climbed up the hill to the *camioncino*. Later, they caught up with Caterina at *Caffè Minerva*.

When the *camioncino* pulled up to the convent gate, they got out of the truck. An extern nun escorted Rachele inside the guesthouse, while Nathan and Caterina followed. When they reached the restricted area, Nathan said goodbye, but Rachele did not turn around. The cloister door slammed shut, the black, wrought iron lever clanking and sliding into locked position.

After they got back to the monastery of *San Damiano*, Caterina went into the garden, while Nathan got his art supplies for another lesson. She leaned over the well, staring down the dark hole, and was startled when Nathan came up behind her.

"Making a wish to St. Francis?" Nathan asked. Her face turned white. "I tried it myself, but it doesn't seem to work."

"How about I draw the flowers next to the well?"

"Let's sit in the shade over there, Caterina. It has a better angle." Nathan set up everything for her. "Remember, it's all about the chiaroscuro technique." She started sketching while he peeked over her head and placed his hands on her shoulders. "You're getting good at this."

She turned her head sideways and he removed his hands.

"You're just saying that to flatter me."

"I really mean it."

"*Forse*, because I've been playing, *come si chiama*?" She put the graphic pencil down and he sat next to her.

"Matchmaker."

"*Si*, that's it. So how are things going between Rachele and you?"

"It's strange. Her moods shift into very dark ones. It's like she's emotionally shut off from me. I guess I've convinced myself that she needs me around." He looked away.

"Just be very gentle with her."

"I am a man, you know. I have normal desires."

"Is that why you touched me before?"

"I'm sorry. I'm stymied by everything."

"You may be Rachele's only hope. You've got to get my friend through this."

"That's a tall order for anyone. It's not like I'm some kind of savior. I'm just a GI caught up in this whole mess."

*Padre* Esposito came running into the garden with Brother Ginepro close behind and called out: "They're back. Thanks to *San Francesco*." Caterina scurried after the monks to the front door with Nathan behind her.

"*Madonna*!" Caterina exclaimed as Nick limped towards her. She rushed over to him and wept on his shoulder, while Nathan hugged his cousin, who had a confused look on his face until he explained their relationship. Carlo's face emanated with the joy of finding a family member alive, one whom he had known only from stories and postcards.

Nathan had noticed Nick's movement over his cousin's shoulder and called out. "Your limp seems worse. Where's your cane?"

"I slipped on some steps in Venice."

"Where's the fisherman?" asked Nathan as he glanced around the room.

"Giuliano *è morto*," Nick blurted out. *Padre* Esposito made the sign of the cross and Brother Ginepro copied him.

"What happened Nick?"

"An SS kraut killed him for the thrill of it," Nick said.

"*Si*, it was awful, Nathan," Carlo added. "I feel sick to my stomach that Giuliano lost his life to save mine."

"We met some *partigiani* when we docked in Ancona," Nick said. "They took Giuliano away so he could be buried at a family plot outside the city. Carlo and I followed them there, where we met Giuliano's family. It was very sad to see the wife and children crying. Giuliano's wife insisted that we should stay overnight with them. The neighbors prepared a dinner in honor of Giuliano. We spoke about his quiet courage and consumed a lot of wine and *grappa*."

"I'm very saddened by all of this," *Padre* Esposito said, placing a hand on his brow. "I was never a worldly man. Maybe it is my peasant roots. One day, I decided to dedicate myself to the teachings of Saint Francis. My good friend, Giuliano, may not have been a member of our society, but he lived an exemplary life. Without ever donning our brown robes." Brother Ginepro nodded his head. "*Prego, Fra' Ginepro. Vai al campanile e suoni le campane sull'ora*." The brother bowed his head, folded his hands in prayer and left.

*Padre* Esposito went to change into his black vestments so he could say a mass for Giuliano in the chapel. The others paired off in the garden to talk privately, waiting for the friar to call them for the service.

"I tried to stay *tranquilla* the whole time, Nick," Caterina said as they sat near the well. "I kept everything inside, but never stopped worrying about you."

"It was scary as hell, but we made it back," he said, as Caterina put her arm around him. "Giuliano deserves all the credit."

"He was a good man. But what happened to your leg? Did those Nazis kick you?" She rubbed her hand across his leg.

"I'm fine, Caterina. I spent too much time cramped on the boat, so I guess my injury is acting up again."

"You said you slipped on steps."

"A lot of things happened. I'm just happy to be back."

"And what about me?"

Distracted by the conversation of Nathan and Carlo, Nick looked the other way. "I thought about you too, baby." She stared at him until he turned to her and smiled.

Nathan and Carlo continued their discussion sitting on the ledge of one of the arched corridors facing the garden.

"Does your head wound still hurt?"

Carlo brushed his hand along the bandage. "It's not too bad. Looks worse than it is."

"Did you hear any news about your family?"

"Those Nazi vermin came and took everyone away. They're probably all dead by now. What did we ever do to deserve this?"

Nathan's eyes moistened as he looked at the evening sky. "Just being born Jewish, nothing else." He put his arm around his cousin and suggested they walk in the garden.

As they strolled towards Nick and Caterina, Carlo said: "This place is a perfect oasis, but they might as well rip up all the flowers and pile them up for the massive funeral taking place in Italy."

"I know how you feel." Nathan ran his hand over the tops of some red roses. "You can stay with Nick and me in Rome until we figure out a better arrangement for you."

"Are you sure it will be okay with your commanding officer?"

"No sweat, Carlo. I'm in tight with all the big chiefs at headquarters." Nathan knew he was already in deep shit with his captain and Nick and he would have to deal with him as soon as they got back.

Later, as the bells tolled to alert the villagers of another funeral mass, the clanging reverberated in Nick's cell, the metallic chimes amplified to the point that he had to cover his ears, even though he was not physically in the tower. His stomach hurt and then his leg began pulsating, so he held his stomach with his left hand and massaged his leg with his right one. The bells stopped ringing but his head ached from the memory of the death at sea, Giuliano gurgling up the remains of the *grappa* mixed with blood.

When the service for Giuliano ended, they all ate a simple supper. *Padre* Esposito and his four guests withdrew to the garden and drank some homemade *limoncello* the *padre* had discovered in the cellar. They wore themselves out with conversation and drink, dragging themselves back to their individual cells.

They woke up late the next morning and Nathan left to visit Rachele, while Caterina and Nick took Carlo to the café near Minerva Temple to meet Isabella. Caterina's friend was drinking a Campari and waved the group over to her table. Isabella and Carlo hit it off right away, her laughter charming him. Caterina made up an excuse that she needed to take care of some personal business in town with Nick. They agreed that the four of them would meet at Isabella's favorite *trattoria* that night.

They headed towards the Basilica of St. Francis and, as soon as they were out of sight, they chatted about her matchmaking game.

"Maybe they'll become lovebirds, Nick."

"You're as a sly as a cat. It's no wonder your name is Caterina."

"I am so relieved you're back." She patted his face. "You can be as clever as you like." They kissed in the middle of a cobblestone sidewalk oblivious to their holy surroundings while the villagers squeezed around them.

That evening all met at *Trattoria Carlotta*, but Nathan bowed out, not wanting to be a *camioncino.* The restaurant had exposed stone walls with white tablecloths and a votive candle on each table. They were finishing *la cena* with *del caffé* and some Sambuca to make a *caffé corretto.*

"You put too much Sambuca in, Carlo," Isabella said, bobbing her head back as she laughed.

Caterina placed her hand over her cup when Nick picked up the bottle. "Too strong for you. I'll put an extra shot in my *caffé*."

"Nick, you already had too much wine to drink."

"You're not my mother."

"*Cretino*, you take my friend Caterina for your mother?"

"*Basta*, Isabella. Don't interfere."

"You can take a little joke, can't you Nick?" Isabella asked.

"Swell, babes." Nick turned to Carlo. "Are you okay?"

"*Si*! But the wine is making me sleepy. Maybe we should get some air. *Prendiamo una passeggiata*!"

"Okay. Let's get out of here," Nick concluded.

The night sky was dark blue lit with a crescent moon. They strolled in no particular direction, breaking off into couples at a distance from each other.

"You are a very attractive woman, Isabella, especially when you laugh. It feels good to hear the sound of laughter."

"I was worried that you might be withdrawn, but you held your own in the conversation. There's one thing though. You have a habit of shaking your leg when you sit." Carlo smiled for the first time since he arrived. "Are you nervous?"

"Don't mind me." Carlo exhaled. "I'm happy to share this time with you, but I go to *Roma* tomorrow morning."

"You are very sweet, Carlo."

"No, I do not feel sweet at all. I have become *il pane amaro*."

"You can put your arm around my waist, if you like." Carlo pulled her waist close to his side. "My father always held my hand as a child during *una passeggiata*. When I was older, arm in arm with my girlfriends. Walking with no one to hold would be a lonely thing."

"*È vero*."

"I barely know you, but I already feel I can talk to you. These are terrible times, but you must blend *il amaro con il dolce*. You may think, who am I to speak, but we have such little time and few choices. *Mi dispiace*. I must sound like a priest."

"No, not all. Is there some place where we can be alone?"

"*Certo,* Carlo." Isabella laughed loud enough that Nick and Caterina turned their heads. Carlo smiled as he followed Isabella leading the way down an adjacent alley towards her apartment.

"Nick!"

"What?"

"Do you remember the first time we disappeared into the night?"

"What kind of question is that?"

"You know what I mean."

"I never really thought about it that way."

"There was an unspoken attraction for each other."

"You want to go back in a time machine?"

"Don't hide behind some childish game. How about the night before you left for Venice? Wasn't that something special?"

"Too many questions, Caterina."

They returned to that same spot and made love but Nick became restless after the heat of the moment.

He drifted far away to a place that Caterina had not been. He couldn't articulate his heartache at the loss of Deborah and left Caterina to wonder about him, the two of them not finding common ground after all they had gone through. He was not able to sort things out, nor give someone else the love she deserved. Nick picked himself up from the ground and as he extended his hand to Caterina, he grabbed his leg in pain.

"Are you okay, Nick? Answer me!" He grimaced and Caterina shot up. "It was too soon to give up your cane."

He straightened himself up and caught sight of Orion, The Hunter in the Sky. "Look at that! See the blue-white shine."

"Yes Nick. I see it. But I think we both need an antidote from the bite of a scorpion."

"I thought you didn't follow the stars."

"My mother told me this Greek myth as a child one night, when we looked through my father's telescope."

"You never say much about your family."

"It is too painful to talk about it. *Prego*, lean on my shoulder on the way back. No one will see us."

The following day they climbed onto the motor scooters, Caterina behind Nick and Carlo behind Nathan, who had arranged for *Padre* Esposito to tell Rachele that he would be back on the weekends, assuming he might get a pass again. *Padre* Esposito waved, as Nick and Nathan revved away, the engine sounds echoing off the stones walls of Assisi, their passengers holding on tightly in anticipation of the myriad potholes on the road ahead with no guarantees that the four of them would land upright on *terra firma* as they jolted their way back.

# XIV

When they entered the CIC headquarters, Captain Smith chewed Nick and Nathan out for being AWOL for five days, emphasizing that it was a serious offense during wartime. The captain began detailing all sorts of punishment but stopped short when they interrupted with the rescue story of Carlo, who had been waiting in the outer office. At first the captain smiled and complimented them, then told them to get the hell out of his office. After their encounter with the CO, the three of them settled into their room but within a few days Nick packed his gear.

"Where're you going, Nick?" Nathan asked.

"To Caterina's place."

"With all that stuff?"

"You don't have to leave because of me," Carlo said.

"There's plenty of room for all of us," Nathan said. "Where do you think you're going?"

"I'm moving in with Caterina. Plain and simple."

"*Prego, Nicolo*," Carlo pleaded. "After all you've done for me, I am embarrassed you have to leave."

"I want to do it. Besides, you two will have more room. Just forget about it. It's okay with me."

"Whatever you say, Nick, but don't slam the door on the way out."

"I'm not angry, Nate. You're the one who has a problem."

Nick arrived early in the evening and untied his duffle bag and a carton from the rear of his motor scooter, slinging the bag over his left shoulder and dropping it at the front door, then retrieving the carton while balancing himself the whole time with his cane. He dug into his pocket to get the keys that Caterina had given him the night before. Nick twice climbed the marble stairs, scooped like *stracciatella gelato*, one step at a time, letting himself into the empty apartment. He dropped his belongings next to the bed and placed the cardboard box on the kitchen table. Nick hated when he had to do something twice when once would have been the norm. He flung the cane into a corner.

Nick found a note from Caterina saying she had gone food shopping and that he should make himself comfortable. He found an opened bottle of Frascati and poured some of it into a glass tumbler. It tasted like vinegar but he drank it anyway while he studied Caterina's apartment. He examined a bunch of her sketches of Assisi hanging over the bed. They were quite good. He wondered if she were self-taught or if she ever modeled in the nude for an art studio, maybe getting lessons in exchange. He had no idea she was an artist, but he realized that there were plenty of things that he didn't know about her. He heard the lock in the door click and got up to meet her.

"Ah, you're here, Nick!" She kissed him on both cheeks and he grabbed her mesh bags, putting them on the kitchen table next to his box.

"What is this?" She opened the box and placed the items on the table. "*Madonna*! You got all of this for us?" She admired the olive oil, salt, sugar, and shiny brown coffee beans, which she ran her hands through. She looked up at him and said: "Where did you find all these wonderful things?"

"Let's just say I have a good connection at Headquarters."

"*Bravo*!"

"What's for *la cena*?"

Caterina smiled. "You just got here and already you are hungry. Relax while I prepare a quick sauce."

"I'll stay nearby if you don't mind. It's something I used to do as a kid, watching my mother cook."

"Just watching." Caterina laughed.

"Well, I used to eat a few meatballs right out of the frying pan."

"No meatballs tonight, Nicky. *Sugo all'amatriciana*. You can boil the water for the *bucatini* while you're waiting."

They sat down at the kitchen table after everything was prepared and ate in silence. Nick broke off a piece of hard peasant bread to mop up the remaining sauce but pushed aside the remains of his Frascati.

"You seem very distant, Nick. Don't you find this a better arrangement, rather than sneaking off into the night *da me*." She laughed and he found her joy infectious but he preferred to keep his observations to himself. "*Allora*, not even one day and you miss your buddy, Nate."

"No, it was my idea to leave."

"*Bene*! Shall I make some *caffè*?"

"Whatever pleases you!"

Her expression bore a suspicious look, as she set about grinding some coffee beans and preparing the *espresso*. "It was very thoughtful of you to bring all those things to cook with. But why only a half-filled duffle bag?"

"I just brought some clothes. Didn't want to clutter your place with too many personal things."

She turned around as the coffee brewed. "I'd like to see some of your favorite things lying about."

"I'm sure you wouldn't mind seeing my private things." Nick grinned.

"I didn't mean it that way. You seem to have one thing on your mind." She swept her hand around the room. "*Allora*, you can store whatever you like here. Consider it our place." She looked at Nick for a facial clue but saw nothing. "I am not for sale anymore. I found a new job. It does not pay much, but I have saved some *lire* over the past year."

"So what are you doing?"

"I am working in the office of *Ospedale Fatebenefratelli*."

"I thought you said you could never find a job. Forced to do other things."

"It's a long story." The scent of coffee drifted to the table.

"Let's hear it. I'm curious."

"It was *Padre* Esposito. He had a contact at the hospital." Caterina got up and flipped the coffee pot, waiting for the liquid to drain.

"I see."

"I didn't tell you but Isabella finally got it out of me—how I was earning a living." She glanced at Nick. "She made such a fuss and told the *padre*."

"Do you like the job?" She brought the cups over and sat down.

"The work is routine but they're happy to get someone who has a degree for, what would you say, cheap?" He poured two teaspoons in, while she put in a half.

"Great." He gulped the *espresso* while she sipped it.

"You don't sound too enthusiastic. I did it for you. I can earn more money doing other things, you know."

"I'm sorry. I get in a bad mood without warning." Nick's brow furrowed. "Let's have some more of that *caffè*. I need to settle my stomach."

Caterina brought over the last two cups, then she stood behind him.

"Don't you want any, Caterina?"

"You drink it, since you enjoy it so much."

After Nick savored the java aroma and drank two in a row, Caterina rubbed her hand over his hair, then slid her fingers across his cheek. She sat down next to him and he placed his arm around her waist.

"Come to bed. You must be tired after your move."

"I'll have a smoke first by the window. Want to see if there any stars out tonight."

Caterina quickly cleaned up the kitchen and got the bed ready. She changed into a creamy, silk negligee, likely a gift from a wealthy old customer. As Nick puffed away, he searched the sky.

"Hey, Caterina. Come over here."

"What is it Nicky?"

"You can see the Big Dipper. The edge of the cup is pointing to the North Star."

"*Si*, it is lovely." She wrapped her arms around Nick's neck. "Have you always followed the stars?"

"It's not like I'm some kind of astronomist. They're out there shining pretty for everyone, no matter what's going on down here." He squished the butt out on the stone windowsill and flicked it down into the inner court.

"*Vieni*, I will be your star tonight." She led Nick to the bed and they lay still for awhile, looking at the ceiling that had the faded remains of a fresco with a light blue sky dotted with a few stars, half of an angel's wing and a vague outline of a man and a woman. He pulled Caterina close and she kissed him many times in a tight embrace, not allowing him to touch her breasts right away. She moved his hand away from her vagina, when he tried to hurry things along. Since Assisi, Nick realized the chemistry was different between them. Their bodies entwined under the stars, inside and outside the room. It became a ballet of sexual potency and emotional energy, as if she had turned from the black swan to the white one. As *cretinu* as Nick could be about women, it hit him over the head—he was no longer her john. His urges were always more immediate, but he felt that the least he could do was to accommodate her. Nick ran his fingers lightly over her breasts, down her flat, smooth belly and placed his hand between her legs, his palm on her mons rubbing back and forth slowly, then faster until she moaned with pleasure. The heat of the moment prompted them to roll around the bed, changing positions to please each other at a moment's notice, managing never to let go of each other, their dance of bodies segueing to a *tartantella*, the sweat dripping from the small of her back, his from the back of his neck until Caterina fell asleep in his arms.

As Nick looked at the ceiling, he imagined Deborah as an angel in a missing part of the ceiling fresco. He was in a semiconscious state and the recurring sounds of a nightingale echoed through the open court window. Its song brought him back to the hospital garden, where Nathan and he had recuperated. He knew that he was not dreaming and yet he lay mummified in the bed, as if participating in an ancient ritual. His spirit levitated from the bed and he traveled to the battlefield where he grasped his cousin's limp body. If Nick were dreaming, his face wouldn't be wet with tears. Then the scene shifted and he was in a San Francisco park where Paul and he had played baseball in summer. His spirit returned to the bed and above his head he swore one of the stars pulsated. The male face in the fresco, looking less faint than before, emerged into the likeness of *Ziu* Francesco, who stared at Nick with a look that unnerved him. Then the visage receded. He heard the nightingale song more clearly and he sprang up, moving to the window in time to see the bird fly away.

Caterina woke up and said: "*Nicolo*, *amore mio*, come back to bed. *Prego*!" He slid into bed without a word and Caterina fell asleep. He wrapped himself around her, so he could listen to her heartbeat to assure himself they had not died too, encased in one of those *sarcophagi* exhibited in the National Roman Museum, part of it used now as a military hospital.

The next morning Caterina rose at six and dressed trying not to wake Nick. She kissed him on the forehead before leaving but he pretended to be asleep. When the door lock snapped into place, he smoked a cigarette at the open window. He felt it was going to be a hot day in Rome. He would have a busy day interrogating a bunch of captured *fasciste* found hiding in an abandoned farmhouse. As Nick dragged on his Lucky Strike, he tried to remember everything from the previous night, to sort out what was real and what was imagined. He couldn't figure out why he had held Caterina at arm's length for so long, especially after she called him *mio amore*. Nick found himself loving and resisting her at the same time. He did not want to hurt someone who loved him more than he loved her. *È vero*, things were different now between them, but he wondered how deep his feelings were for Caterina.

Whenever he tried to sleep, he had this war draped over him, making any bed he lay on uncomfortable. Nick gazed out the window at grey clouds blocking the advance of the morning sun, and the alluring melody of that elusive bird had long expired, the light of the stars extinguished.

# XV

During the fall season, when the weather was a tangle of warm and cold days, when the colors and stripes of nature changed chameleon-like, sometimes a black *vipera* lay under damp leaves, nature's booby trap for the unsuspecting. And so Nick and Caterina decided to join Nathan and Carlo for the weekend on one of their frequent visits to Assisi. Nick wanted to see firsthand how the stories his friends told him were working out. He instinctively knew that a young guy's embellishments, 'some stretchers' as Mark Twain called them, had to be parsed from a jumble of words, at least when it came to dolls. Nick surmised his buddy was not making headway with Rachele, so he hoped to spark a reaction from this sheltered, young woman. Caterina had first suggested it and then encouraged him, since she had been successful in getting Isabella and Carlo together. Lately, Nick noticed an edgy side to Nate's cousin, no doubt from what he experienced in Venice. But this trip may have been more about his own relationship with Caterina and maybe staying so long at her place had not been the best idea, like they were married or something. Nick wanted to be with Caterina one last time in Assisi, something out of their Roman routine, but felt their relationship had been a game of shooting craps with each other, running hot and cold.

When *Padre* Esposito heard the throttle sounds from their motor scooters, he stepped outside the monastery doors to greet them.

"You are all here together. What a pleasant surprise! *Fra'* Ginepro, *Fra'* Ginepro*!* Where is he when I need him?"

"*Padre*, he's right behind you," Nick said.

"*Si, si, ma naturalmente*! *Prego, porta nostri ospiti del vino rosso.* You must stay here in the monastery." *Padre* Esposito smiled and waved then to come closer, so he could hug them all.

Later in the evening Nick and Nathan retired to their cells while Carlo went to meet Isabella at *Caffé Minerva. Padre* Esposito pulled Caterina aside before she ascended the stairs.

"Do they treat you well at the hospital?"

"Yes, *padre*. I am treated with respect by Romans."

"I told *il direttore …*"

"You don't have to explain. I never thanked you, *mi dispiace*, but I … I was ashamed." She made the sign of the cross.

"Who has not sinned in this country? I said nothing when the *facsiste* took power. Only later during the war did I agree to help our *ebrei italiani*. You, my child, are a casualty of your father's politics."

* * *

*Caffé Minerva* was the one place that stayed open late. Carlo and Isabella chatted inside over *Negroni* cocktails. They did not want anyone listening to their conversation, so they spoke in English, as if they were conspiring, Carlo and Isabella's pairing more impulsive while Nick and Caterina's situation had been complicated from the start.

"I've been lonely waiting for you."

"I missed you, Isabella."

"Did you come with Nathan?"

"*Si*. And Caterina and Nick."

"*Bravo*! I must see them tomorrow. Those two are way ahead of us." Isabella laughed snapping her head backwards.

"I love your laughter …"

"Why is the table shaking?"

"What table?"

"Look, the glass is sliding." She grabbed his thigh under the table. "*Basta*, Carlo. Why are you nervous?"

"I told you before. It is a habit I picked up as child. I can't help it."

"You were saying."

"I forgot." Carlo looked away.

"There is something wrong." Carlo clenched the glass. "You are lying, Carlo. It is written all over your face."

"It is difficult to say when, but I must leave you."

"You don't love me, Carlo!"

"It's not about love but something else."

"Please tell me. *Prego*!"

"I'm going to fight with the Jewish Brigade."

"*Perchè*?"

"It's something I must do."

"There is little chance that your family has been spared, may God forgive me for saying it. *Allora*, you may be the only survivor. And then what happens if you are killed too?"

"I have made my mind up."

"Take a *passeggiata* with me. Maybe the fresh air of Assisi will make you think more clearly."

* * *

The next morning after breakfast, Caterina discussed the strategy with Nathan. Nick would be a go-between for Nathan and Rachele, who already hankered to meet Caterina's boyfriend because he helped save Carlo in Venice. Nathan reluctantly went along with their plan, yearning for a breakthrough. Caterina got permission from the Mother Abbess to take Rachele to *Caffé Minerva* so she could meet up with Nick.

After gathering at the café, they engaged in small talk so as not to rattle Rachele. Caterina used an excuse that Nathan had wanted to show her a perfect place to sketch a panoramic view from the town. They would return in a short while.

"What would you like to drink, Rachele?" Nick asked.

"I'll drink whatever you are drinking."

"*Un cappuccino*."

"Yes, that would be fine."

When the waiter came over, Nick asked if there was a little dark chocolate on top. Rachele motioned to the waiter. "*Anch'io prende del cioccolato, per favore*."

As they drank the coffee, she peered over her cup at Nick, who thought it was odd that she was so direct, judging by the Nathan's detailed accounts of his time with Rachele.

"I wished I could have done something like you did for Carlo. You saved one of our own."

"I just got lucky, that's all. I don't want to upset you, but Giuliano the fisherman lost his life as we fled Venice."

"You are much better looking than Nathan." Nick smiled at her.

"That's not true. Rachele."

"You are being modest. Protecting your friend, no doubt."

"Nathan thinks about you all the time. Maybe a bit obsessed, but I don't mean that in a bad way."

"No, I don't think you could ever be bad."

"I'm not so sure your friend, Caterina, thinks that way."

"She adores you and I can see why." Nick squirmed in his chair. It occurred to him that this was a mistake, playing go-between. That he was making things worse for Nathan, by feeding into her fantasies about himself from the stories she heard from Caterina and Isabella. Even worse, this business about Caterina adoring him also made him uncomfortable. Nick felt they were all getting deeper and deeper into wartime love entanglements that didn't have good baseball stats for winning. Look what happened to Cio-Cio San in Puccini's *Madame Butterfly*. Not that Nick was going sentimental all of sudden, but he had to admit to himself that the opera, the first one his parents had taken him to see, was one tearjerker at the end for the mother and her child. Not a dry eye in the opera house.

Caterina and Nathan returned to the café and Nick's head popped up. "I forgot that we promised to meet up with *Padre* Esposito at the farmer's market. We'll leave you two here awhile." He grabbed Caterina's arm and ushered her away from the table, calling out, "*Ciao*," while Caterina raised her eyebrows.

"Nick, what are you *pazzo*?"

"I had to scram out of there. This idea of yours went kerflooey."

"What happened?"

"Rachele has a crush on me."

"You are so conceited, Nick."

"I'm tellin' ya, she's nuts about me."

"*Prego*, this is the first time she met you!"

"That's the whole point. It's all up here." Nick tapped his head.

"Nathan will work something out. Don't you have faith in your friend?"

"You're the one that got me into this mess."

"You make me wonder sometimes."

"About what?"

"I'll give one of your standard answers—*niente* or is it *nenti*?

"I'm going to take a walk. By myself."

"*Bene*!" Caterina watched him disappear into the darkness before she turned back to the monastery.

Before suppertime, Nick had a crazy notion and drove his Paperino to the convent. He asked the extern nun if he could see Rachele in the garden, mentioning that he was a good friend of *Padre* Esposito. The Mother Abbess agreed as long as the extern nun could watch from a distance. Rachele was surprised to see him again so soon and appeared to read more into his motives for the visit.

"I was worried that you left so abruptly. Was it anything I said?"

"No, not all." A certain smile emerged that reminded him of Deborah. "I thought I could've painted a better picture of my friend, Nate."

"As long as you're here, I don't care why." Nick found himself drawn to her in an uncanny way, yet he was supposed to be an emissary for Nate. He imagined that being close to Rachele was like being home with Deborah, both of these women imaginary for different reasons, but he relished spending a little more time with her now. Nick rationalized that he made Rachele happy, but when he had to leave, the realization set in that this get-together had been going off the tracks. They would crash into a dark forest that Rachele was trying to find her way out, derailing all Nate had been doing, while the weight of a train crushed Nick. It seemed that Nick and his buddy wound up in some roundhouse, where random engines had been assigned to drag miles of baggage in all directions over the matrix. The time had spun out for Nick and Rachele, each grasping for a star of their own, when the extern nun approached the chairs where they sat at an axis opposite to each other. Theirs was a collision that had to be avoided in the galaxy where all of Nick's friends orbited.

That evening after dinner, the *padre* had to visit an uncle who was ill and excused himself, while Nick, Nathan and Caterina strolled around the garden. Carlo had not been back to the monastery since their first meal there, choosing to spend all his time with Isabella. Caterina sat in the corner, reading a short story from a Verga collection set in Sicily. Nick and Nathan were on a stone bench closer to the well.

"That was the best meal we had here," Nathan said. "Father Esposito must have found a good source for getting the best ingredients."

"Some of the food is produced right here. That's the best sign of authentic, Italian food."

Nathan motioned his head in Caterina's direction. "What's with the isolation? She didn't seem too bubbly at dinner."

"*Nenti*!"

"That's very informative."

"I got nothing to say on the topic."

"By the way, your harebrained scheme didn't work."

"That wasn't my idea. It was Caterina's."

"Why are you so hard on her?"

"It's none of your business."

"Well, I tell you what's my business. Were you coming on to Rachele?"

"What?"

"You heard me. She talks about your wavy, black hair and hazel eyes."

"Will you stop it! I was just trying to help. Don't blame me because she's acting delusional."

"She is not delusional."

"I said acting and keep your voice down. I don't want her to hear us." Caterina slammed her book and glided her hand on the wall up the stairs. *Fra'* Ginepro met her at the top landing with a lantern and led Caterina to her cell.

"Now that she's not in earshot. Did you teach Caterina how to paint while I was away?"

"So what of it?"

"Maybe just a good excuse to get close."

"You'd better shut up," Nathan shouted as he stood up. "Why don't you use some of that emotion sewn up tight inside there?" Nathan tapped his heart. "Appreciate Caterina for who she is now and not what she's done in the past."

"Now that's a switcheroo. Caterina goes from *puttana* to *Madonna*."

"You're the one deflecting when it comes to Rachele."

"You're all wet."

"And I'll tell you another thing."

"Go ahead. You're already standing on a soapbox."

"The two of you should never have come here. You're digging yourself into a hole with Caterina, and now I'm getting deeper myself with Rachele." Nathan moved toward the stairs and *Fra'* Ginepro lit it up for him. Nick walked over to the well and sat on the ground, his back to the wall. Later, he saw a light cascading down the stairs and Caterina appeared at the bottom, the glow snuffed out above. She went over to Nick and sat next to him and they spoke without looking at each other.

"Nick, why were you fighting with Nathan? I could hear you two all the way upstairs."

"We're getting on each other's nerves."

"Nick, I thought coming to Assisi might bring back some good memories. You've hardly kissed me."

"We can go outside, if you want."

"That's not exactly romantic, but maybe I've been kidding myself all along."

"You're making up things like your friend, Rachele."

"You don't have to rub my face in this."

"We seem to be going around in circles."

"I know what's bugging you. That I've been with a lot of men."

"That's your life."

"You don't know anything. My father was shot right out in the street and by the time I came home I saw his body in the gutter. Flames shooting out of our balcony window." Caterina eyes filled up wet and reddened. "I tried to reach my father but the mob grabbed me when one of them recognized I was his daughter, another *fascista* sympathizer to them. They were enraged and knocked me to the ground. Some of the women were going to shear off my hair when several nuns came running out of a nearby church and pulled me away, rushing me off the street."

"I didn't know, Caterina."

"You want to know why I prostituted myself. No, you don't want to know. But I'll tell you anyway. I had no money, no way to getting at whatever money my family had left, and worse of all, no one would give me any job."

"I didn't know."

Caterina rose and staggered upstairs in the dark, inching the way back to her cell. Nick heard her door slam but he did not get up. He sensed pain in his leg that was traveling up his body, but it was as much emotional as it was physical. The swallows were flying high and low in erratic patterns looking to pick off some unsuspecting insects. He saw a stray cat with protruding ribs creep low in an area where some water had collected, hoping one of birds would drink after their wild chases. Nick considered throwing a stone to scare the cat off but he didn't bother. The swallows called out a sharp *siflitt* and flew out of the cat's reach. Nick had been away from home so long now, it got to the point that he didn't care about birds or even operatic characters named after a butterfly. He didn't even raise his head to see what stars were shining that night.

# XVI

A Roman winter brought in a surprise dusting of snow outside Nick's hospital window, where he had been readmitted for his leg wound, the whiteness conjuring up a vision of battle raging on the northern front, along the Gothic Line in the Apennine Mountains stretching somewhere from La Spezia to Pesaro. Sitting at the edge of the bed on his third visit since the summer, he wondered how his former captain and squadron were faring, as the weather turned their tanks into moving iceboxes. The pain in his leg had slowly intensified after Venice, but he refused to let it show in his gait. Nick also had periodic nightmares of his last day with Paul, as he held him dead in his arms, drenched in blood. He sometimes saw Alastar's bloodied face on the ground. These night pictures seemed more real than that fatal day with his tank crew. He tossed about so much that he must have been wrenching his bad leg.

Captain Monroe's recent letter mentioned that slight twists of fate brought soldiers closer to death or further removed from it. The tone of the note had a sad quality to it and, though the captain hoped the war would end soon, he continued to fear for his men. After what Nathan and Nick had gone through, he wished them well. Captain Monroe concluded that he never shook off his Virginia accent or his Methodist ways, and maybe they could say a few prayers for the boys in the unit. Nick placed the note in his shirt pocket when the doctor came in.

"Where's your cane, Corporal Spataro?" He shrugged and the doctor shook his head. "What the hell did you and your pal do with yourselves this past summer? Last month, Sergeant Fein's seizures came back with a vengeance after stabilizing at the beginning of summer. Now we've got to redo the pins in your leg." The doctor shook his head again. "You two are supposed to be recuperating with your desk jobs, not relapsing."

"It's due to complications, that's all, Captain Randazzo."

"Great, now you're doing your own diagnosis." The doctor shook Nick's hand and continued holding it. "Just take it easy will you, Nick. And sell that damn scooter."

* * *

One evening Nathan sat on his bed dressed to go out, as Carlo walked in.

"I got tickets to see the army swing band." Nathan held them up. "Made up of jazz players from different units in Rome."

"I don't know, Nathan."

"Look, I'm feeling better for the first time in a month. Anyway, didn't you tell me you were a big fan of Benny Goodman and Louis Armstrong?" Nathan got up and put his hand on Carlo's shoulder. "I don't know who feels worse. We need a little music in our lives."

"Okay, I'll get ready."

"*Bravo cugino*."

Nathan had picked a concert to put them in the right groove and when they got to a packed auditorium of GIs, he saw Carlo's eyes light up with enthusiasm for life that he had not seen in his cousin since the first day they met in Assisi. The music set lasted straight up for one hour, hitting every emotional chord in their psyche.

As they scatted to the tune of Glenn Miller's "In the Mood" on the way back to their room, they passed by a tiny shop cut into a wall that still had its yellowed lights on. There was a restored oil painting visible from the street that caught Carlo's attention and he entered the shop. The owner kept working at his bench. He noticed a painting of a young, voluptuous woman gathering olives in her apron, the Basilica of St. Francis rising on a hill in the background. Nathan couldn't resist and slipped into the shop, looking over Carlo's shoulder.

"Looks like Isabella!" Carlo commented.

"Ah, your imagination is running away with you." Nathan laughed. "Are you stuck on Caterina's friend?"

"We just like to talk together, that's all."

"Who are you kidding? I wish I was half as intimate with Rachele."

"There are other issues."

"What are you getting at?"

"I have other things on my mind."

"I know. That's why I wanted you to listen to some swing. *Andiamo, Carlo*."

The following evening Carlo challenged Nathan to find the best pizza in Trastevere. They were having a good time drinking decent, white table wine from one of the neighboring hills, until Carlo had to go the bathroom. He passed by the oven, the flames from the wood traveling across its brick ceiling, an image that lit up all the rumors about the concentration camps. By the time he got back, Nathan could see him frowning as he sat down.

"What happened? Couldn't find the *bagno*." Nathan laughed nervously.

"I found it all right. Here comes the pizza. *Mangia, cugino*."

They found the pizza to be perfect, a good corniche, slightly burnt on the edge, the right balance of mozzarella, *San Marzano* tomatoes and basil. Nathan tried to bury himself in his enjoyment of this simple preparation and hoped that Carlo would rid himself of the demons in his mind, his leg pumping the floor so hard that Nathan could feel it vibrate under his feet.

"I'm joining the Jewish Brigade."

"You ought to think this over before you take a plunge."

"I don't want to be filled with guilt anymore."

"Don't you think this stuff is on my mind too? It will eat you alive, if you're not careful."

They finished the meal quickly. On the way home, they discussed the change in the weather but there were other things on Nathan's mind. He ruminated about his cousin as they trudged through the dark, but in the end Carlo would have to find his own way. He wondered if Nick and Caterina were happy together and what was really going on between Carlo and Isabella. And he thought his cousin was just going along for the ride to Assisi keeping him company. All of a sudden a downpour drenched them, as they ran the few remaining streets to the room.

* * *

Several weeks after the concert, Carlo walked into Nathan's room with a grin on his face.

"I did it *cugino*!"

"Did what?" Nathan's mouth opened.

"I signed up with the Jewish Brigade." Carlo paced around the room. "I'm going to hitch a ride with a US army transport group heading north. I have to catch up with them, *subito*!"

"Hold your horses, will ya! You're going too fast for me."

"Last week I met Brigadier Benjamin's orderly and he told me all about this Palestine Regiment. It's part of the British army."

"I never heard of them."

"It's made up of mostly Jewish soldiers from Palestine, but Jews from other countries can also join. So there it is. We're going after those Nazi scum."

"I am glad you're all excited about this, but remember this is a bloody war. There's nothing romantic about it. It only takes a couple of seconds to do something stupid." Nathan hugged his cousin, so Carlo didn't see the anguish in his face. He had already come to the conclusion that none of Carlo's family was likely to have survived. Now he might lose the sole survivor of the Venetian branch of his family. Carlo gathered his things and, after sharing some *Sambuca* together, he marched out of the room. Nathan looked out his window and saw Carlo strutting down the *viale* and yelled out, "*Buona fortuna*, kid," but his cousin was oblivious to his call.

Nathan thought about what Rachele was doing. He visited her every weekend he was free, as the seasons passed, summer, fall and winter, but they never had much physical contact. The beginning of their relationship began with promise but now was punctuated with stray marks of Rachele's odd behavior. He never knew what to expect from her, what her mood might be. Nathan kept on going back to her until the day he got a note from the Mother Abbess that he had become a strain on Rachele's emotional stability, that she had become more afraid to leave the convent, even briefly. He crumpled the message. "I spent so much time trying to help her. Every God damn weekend pass I could get. I pitied her too much and drove her away. It's all my fault for being a *schlemiel*." He tossed around in bed all night, never finding a comfortable position.

It was another sunless Sunday morning, his cousin gone, and he called out to the empty room: 'Damn it, Nathan, she doesn't seem to fit in the outside world. You're not going to save Rachele. She's fragile as a porcelain doll.' Despite not having broken through her resistance, he was still determined to go back to Assisi and try again, even though the nuns didn't want him around anymore. If he overextended his leave, then let them throw him in the stockade. What would it matter anyway?

After hours of straining his Paperino, Nathan slid the motor scooter to a halt. He was in such a frenzy he had no recollection of the scenery he had passed. To him it was like a canvas smeared with green and brown with patches of white, shapes but no recognizable forms. He had no idea what he could say to change things around, but the nuns would not stop him from speaking to Rachele. Let them call the *carabiniere*. Nathan completed his run and banged on the cloister door with such force every nun in the convent must have crossed herself. The Mother Abbess spoke through the grille without showing fear.

"*Signor* Nathan, we already wrote to you about Rachele's worsening condition. There is nothing you can do. It is in God's hands, not yours."

"Mother Abbess, *per favore*, I beg of you. Give me a chance to see Rachele. If it doesn't work, I promise never to come back. I swear on my family's honor."

The Mother Abbess closed the grille and a few moments later opened it. "You can speak to her in our church. Remember that God is watching what you say. He does not care about your passion, only what is in your heart. Wait by the baptismal fountain inside. I will send Rachele there if she agrees to see you."

Nathan stepped outside the convent to get some fresh air but the wind blew dust into his eyes, which he rubbed, irritating them further before entering the church of *San Quirico*. The church was empty, void of sound, and dark except for groups of flicking votive candles in front of various saints. He felt that an hour passed instead of fifteen minutes, when a familiar extern nun opened the high, wooden door and brought Rachele in, whispering that he could have ten minutes with her.

The thick door slammed shut behind them as Rachele walked down the aisle. He imagined they were models for a phantasmagoric painting, the focal point of the composition, this pretty woman stretched in black distortions, his form receding in the background, his face unrecognizable. Rachele knelt at a small altar dedicated to St. Clare and counted her prayers on black rosary beads, the smell of burning wax in the air. Nathan stood behind Rachele, calling her, but she did not turn around. He came closer and she got up, crossed herself and swung around in a frightened way.

"*Prego*, sit with me in the pew." He took her by the arm and guided her to the first row and both sat sideways.

"Why do you come here to this holy place?"

"Rachele, you don't have to remain in black anymore. You're safe now."

"No one is safe. I stay awake during the night and sleep during the day. No matter how my sisters try here, they can't break this cycle. Neither prayers, nor gardening, or even baking can help me to fit into the peaceful routines of their daily lives." She grasped her knees and put her head down. "But still, I have no place to go. I belong here."

"Rachele, you're not a nun. You're Jewish. You don't have to conform to anything. All you have to do is get back to a happy place."

"I try to go to these happy places, as you call them, but everything is blurred. My dear sisters try to coax me into feeling good about myself. When their words hurt too much, I get a throbbing in my head that feels like it'll just burst through my temple and I scream."

"You're not screaming now."

"You're different but I don't know why. Are you Jewish too?"

"Rachele, I have gone over this before, from the first time we met. I wanted you to know that our people will survive despite all the horror that hounds us." He placed his hand on hers. She did not move it but showed no sign of recognition. He squeezed her hand gently but it remained limp.

"Why are you here?"

"It's you, Rachele. Can't you see in my face what I feel?"

"I see a handsome young man. Are you in the pictures?"

"No, Rachele, I'm just an American GI." She took her hand away.

"I can never leave here. This is where I will stay the rest of my life."

"You don't have to do this. You can change your life."

"You don't know what runs around my head. You can't know and why would you care?"

"I need you as much as I think you need me." Nathan faced the statue of St. Clare and looked down at her plaster feet. The chapel felt like the most silent place in the world for Nathan, until he turned and spoke emphatically. "I loved you from the moment I saw you. I don't know what you remember and how you remember, but I am alone and so are you."

"I am not alone. I have all my sister friends. They protect me from everything."

"You don't feel anything for me, is that it?"

"You treat me like a patient."

"That's not true, Rachele. *Prego*, stop placing imaginary barriers between us."

"I don't know what you're talking about. You sound like the doctor. Did he send you here because he's frustrated?" There was a thudding noise at the door. "I must go back to my cell."

"Before you go, can't you express how you feel about us? Anything." He stood up. "Some day, I'm going back to America, don't you understand?"

She got up and walked to the back of the church while the extern nun opened the door and ushered her out. Nathan felt as if the white marble would crash down on his head at any moment before he was able to exit the church. His hand started to jerk and he vomited when he reached his motor scooter. Feeling dazed, he sat on the ground until he regained his composure, and made sure he wasn't going into a full-blown seizure. When Nathan fired up his Paperino, he gazed over the walls. He could see a lone light on the top floor and swore it must be Rachele's cell. She would not be throwing him a spool of thread to grab while she held the end of it, no *filo della vita*, a lifeline that Italians held on the pier while their relatives clung to the ball, unraveling as the steamer for America slid into the dark. There were other immigrant stories that Nick had told him, and they all had sad endings like his own.

Nathan sped back to Rome and no longer cared where he would wind up. Things would be the same no matter where he was, the road kicking out from his tires, the black trees swaying in the dark sky, the only sounds in the night, the roar of his engine muffling the thumping of his heart that he felt deep within his ribcage, heavy and plodding, no lifeline.

# XVII

It was Christmas Eve and Captain Smith dismissed his staff at fifteen hundred hours, so Nick used the time to get a gift for Caterina on the *Via dei Condotti*. He wanted to buy a silk scarf even though it would be expensive, something that she would appreciate considering their time together. The shopkeeper was patient, displaying each scarf across his chest like the ceremonial sashes that Italians love to wear in public, until Nick found one he liked.

Pleased with his purchase, he looked out the shop window while his present was being hand wrapped with pizzazz. He squinted his eyes in disbelief when he saw Caterina leaving the *Antico Caffé Greco* across the street with an older Italian gentleman, the same one he saw her with at the beginning of their relationship, if that's what it was. His face turned pale noting the same moustache waxed at the tips, the ascot puffed out of his sports jacket, the assured gait. They disappeared in the direction of the *Piazza di Spagna*. The shopkeeper repeated '*Signore, Signore, prego, Signore*,' as Nick envisioned Caterina taking a *passeggiata* with the old man around the fountains, admiring Keats' house and ascending the Spanish Steps for a view before heading for his hotel room.

Nick returned to his old room and found Nathan by the light of the window finishing a painting from one of his Roman sketches. He dropped the wrapped present on the table and sat down, while Nathan gave a sidelong glance and resumed working.

"It's for Caterina," Nathan said. "Should be done for the New Year. Real sweet of her to invite me to your Christmas Eve dinner."

"Yeah, sweet all right."

Nathan put his brush down and sat next to Nick.

"It's always something, Nick."

"I saw her on *Via Condotti*."

"So she's not allowed to shop?" Nick grimaced. "Okay, tell me what's eating you."

"Caterina is back to her old tricks."

"If I get your meaning, I think you're off base, no matter what you saw."

"There you go again taking her side. If I didn't know better."

"You're going *pazzo* on me."

"I saw her with that same ritzy, Italian guy again. You remember from last time."

"No, I don't remember."

"I'm telling you she's with another guy who looks like he has a lot of dough."

"I'm sure there's a logical explanation. So don't go jumping the gun."

"Can't believe how you're always taking her side now."

"For cryin' out loud, why can't we just have a little fun tonight? You'll get over it."

"I'm not done with this yet."

"Don't do something stupid. Give her a pass. I'll get ready and we'll walk over together like nothing ever happened."

When they got to Caterina's apartment, the table had been set with some red candles. She sang the popular song, "*Oh Mia Bela Madunina*," the one dedicated to the gilded statue on top of the *Duomo* in *Milano*. While Caterina glided from stove to table, she paced all four courses of the evening, including variations on *calamari*, *vongole*, *gamberi* and *pesce spada*. They drank the two bottles of Frascati Nathan brought that were young and tasted of white peaches and apples, the way good Frascati should be. They also polished off three other bottles lying about and afterwards, *del caffé* and Sambuca. Caterina laughed at Nathan's jokes while Nick watched the two of them.

"Caterina, you have it all, looks and cooks," Nathan slurred.

"Nick, I have a secret admirer."

"Or two."

Caterina laughed. "*Certo, anche tu*!"

"I'm not talking about me."

"Oh, come on Nicky, it has to be you." Caterina giggled. "Stop being a silly goose." She patted Nick on his cheek. "Maybe you need another shot of Sambuca."

Nathan stretched over and tapped Nick on the shoulder. "Easy buddy. Don't ruin the party."

"Isn't it getting late for you, Nate?"

"I'm not leaving till I have another Sambuca for the road." Nick got up and looked out the window.

"What's with Nick?" Caterina whispered to Nathan.

"Ah, don't pay any attention to him," Nathan responded, then raised his voice. "He'll get over what's bugging him. Won't you, buddy? Oh, ignoring your old pal. You know somethin' …" He slammed the table with his palm. "You got one hell of a gal! So Nick, take out that poker you got stuck up your ass and wise up!"

"*Vafonculo*, Nate!"

Nathan pushed himself up and tripped over the chair. Caterina helped him up after struggling with him a few minutes.

"Take your friend home, Nick. He could fall and hit his head. And then what?"

"Sure, whatever you say."

Nathan leaned on Nick's good side, as he balanced the both of them with his cane. Caterina sat down and poured herself another Sambuca and swirled it around the glass, the door slamming on their way out. Several hours later, Caterina heard the key in the lock and Nick sat opposite Caterina.

"*Madonna*, have you lost your mind, Nick. And on Christmas Eve!" She squeezed the silk scarf with her left hand. "Say something. You spoiled the holiday after my slaving over the stove."

"Who was that old guy I saw you with coming out of *Caffé Greco*."

"*Signor* Giacomo Parini. He was a banker friend of my father from *Milano*."

"I thought you were originally from Rome."

"I am a *Milanese*."

"Another one of your secrets."

"You are jealous of an old man?"

"Who said anything about jealousy?"

"You obviously have made your mind up. You can take this back." She slid the scarf to Nick.

"I don't want it back."

"Is that all you don't want back?"

"You went to bed with him, didn't you?"

"And what if I said no, would you believe me?"

"That's not the first time I saw him."

"So you work in an intelligence unit and think you know everything. *Tu sei un cretino*!" She swayed her praying hands. Nick got up and threw the empty bottles into the garbage pail. "Maybe you should stick your head out the window to listen for a little bird. *Prego*, watch that a star doesn't crash on your *testa dura*."

He stomped back to the table. "You can mock me all you want, but you can't hide the truth about yourself."

"So you judge me too. I once had boyfriend, Stefano, who I met in what you would call high school. We separated after I went off to *università*. Ours was an innocent love. I would often think of him when I had sex with other men, so as not to think I was lost, *disgraziata*. And then I found you and thought only about you."

"*Non capisco*! You never mentioned this young man."

"Stefano Bonati came before you. The man you saw, *Signor* Parini, he secretly backed the *partigiani*. *Allora*, he had information I wanted. Stefano è *morto*. Killed in an American bombing raid in *Milano*. He was a *partigiano*, fighting against the *fasciste*. After *Signor* Parini wanted to give me some *lire* but I refused."

Nick sat down and slid the scarf in her direction but she brushed it aside. Caterina sobbed as she poured another glass of Sambuca. He poured a glass for himself and gulped it down. They both continued drinking until the two of them passed out, heads on the table, their hands inches away from each other, their dreams shifting faster than the flicking scenes of a classical Hollywood film, except none of this was make believe for Nick or Caterina. He would now have this scene mixed in with the other scenes of his life, all their flashbacks more negative than the film itself, too sensitive to the light of the sun, the moon and the stars.

# XVIII

Nick and Caterina had recently celebrated New Year '45, throwing a few chipped china plates out the window into the courtyard, toasting each other with chilled, crisp Prosecco, happy to be alive. Nathan's painting of the *Campidoglio* hung on the wall. A week later, the projected weather forecast for Saturday was a mild 54° F, so for fun Nick suggested that they spend that day taking a gander at sites of Rome, acting like a couple of tourists on holiday. He purposely left his cane in the room. After a *cappuccino* and chocolate-filled *cornetto* at a nearby café, Nick rode around on his Paperino for an hour with Caterina wrapped around him, weaving through the streets of the *centro storico*. Whenever he accelerated, dodging a few *camioncini* and military jeeps along the way, Caterina laughed like a schoolgirl. Except for an occasional horse-drawn carriage, they had the Colosseum to themselves, circling the massive structure several times and admiring its ivory, travertine stones, almost touching the grey clouds, and other sections of arches that had collapsed after a forgotten earthquake.

"*È bella* but you're making me dizzy, Nicky."

He glanced at Caterina and laughed. "We'll stop at *Piazza Navona*." He headed across the *Via Dei Fori Imperiali* with the Roman Forum to the left, then parallel with the Tiber River on *Vittorio Emanuele*, getting off on one of the side streets to the *piazza*. The sound of the muffler echoed through *Piazza Navona*, as he slid the bike to a halt. The water in the fountains was turned off.

"*Bravo*. Now we can walk," Caterina said as they got off the motor scooter.

"Let's get some *gelato* in Tre Scalini."

"It's too early, no?"

"It's never too early for *gelato*."

Nick grabbed her hand, leading the way with an imperceptible limp to the café. At the counter he chose his favorite, *pistacchio*, and Caterina, the classic *tartufo*. They consumed the *gelato* and continued their adventure through the old quarter, peeking into empty shops where artisans still worked with wood, marble or glass, stumbling across the Trevi Fountain, standing sad sack without a drop of water, its marble statuary hidden somewhere underground, a not so subtle reminder of the distant war. They kept walking and Caterina placed her arm around his waist, the move encouraging Nick to put his arm over her shoulder. They passed a *chiosco*, a newspaper stand plastered with war headlines in a half dozen languages, but they ignored them and ambled around until they got tired. They both agreed it was time for *pranzo* and Caterina insisted on the famous *Caffè Greco*. Nick first wanted to say 'over his dead body,' but he remembered Nathan's admonishment about not ruining the party, so why spoil it for Caterina.

They walked through the glittering café and sat at a table in the *Sala Venezia* near a wall of paintings set above the chair rail, evoking that city of canals. A short waiter in a frock coat sauntered over, took the order and returned with a carafe of red wine and *acqua minerale*.

"I read it's been here since the mid 1700's. A writer's haunt. Did you know Keats lived in a *villa* right next to the Spanish Steps before he died of consumption at 25?"

"I didn't, Nicky. Would you like to go there afterwards?" Caterina asked.

"Nah, it's all closed up now." He looked around the room admiring the artwork awhile, as if his mind was somewhere else, while Caterina watched him in silence. Nick caught the gaze of her eyes. "Caterina, when you think about all the crap that's going on, it's like we're stealing a little time from the war. Just you and me here and loving every minute of it."

She leaned over and kissed him, causing him to smile widely.

"I never noticed your dimples before."

"That's because I don't have much to smile about." He picked up his wine glass. "Now and in another place and time. You're the best, Caterina."

They clinked glasses. "*Cin cin*!"

A man with a salt and pepper, bushy mustache, in a rumpled suit came by their table. His gray hair was slicked back in the fashion of the thirties.

"*Mi scusi, Signore e Signorina. Posso prendere il vostro photo per un buon prezzo*?"

He pointed to the camera and said: "Leica." Nick turned towards Caterina and saw how beautiful she looked, sitting so near him.

"*Va bene*!" Nick responded.

The man bowed his head, took a bunch of shots and promised to bring the finished results to Nick's office '*subito*,' which turned out to be a week later. Before leaving, he jotted down their address in his black, Moleskine notebook.

The waiter carried in steaming *pasta* from the kitchen, *penne all'arrabbiata* for Caterina and *spaghetti alla carbonara* for Nick. They dug into the food, mopping up the sauce with the rustic bread.

"You know, back home I would sometimes spend a day with someone special like you. I guess life's all about time racing on, yet standing still in your memory. Like being caught in one of those movie posters with a climatic cameo of *innamorati*." Nick blinked his eyes for a minute and Caterina drank some more wine.

"Was she pretty?"

"Who?" Caterina rested her jaw on the palm of her hand and stared at him for several minutes.

"Yeah, but it's over." His face was taut as he looked over her shoulder.

"*Allora*, how can time race on and stand still? *Non capisco*!"

"You see, things are going so fast like one of those flipping calendars in a movie. Then all you have is one, maybe two, frozen frames of film left that you remember. You know, like those movie posters I was talking about."

"What's going to happen to us, Nick? Will we be in one of your imaginary posters?"

"*Non lo so*. Nothing remains the same anymore. Just look around us."

"Will this place be one of our frozen frames?"

"Sure, baby. You want some *espresso*?"

"Why don't you get *il conto*?"

"Yeah, let's keep moving. Sistine Chapel, next stop."

They tried to retrace their steps, getting lost down some of the alleys, and inexplicably found themselves back in *Piazza Navona*. Nick sped away and within a short time they crossed the *Ponte San Angelo* to *Piazza San Pietro*. He applied the scooter kickstand and they strolled out of the north side of the *piazza* to the Vatican Museum, his limp becoming more obvious. They met two guards, one in a uniform of blue, yellow and red, who stood at attention, holding a razor sharp spear and axe on a long pole and wearing a gleaming helmet with a red plume. Nick showed his U.S Counter Intelligence card to the other Swiss Guard, who wore a black beret and had a Beretta Modella 38 submachine gun strapped over a blue version of the dress uniform. He saluted Nick and Caterina as they went by.

"Things are scary, Nicky, even at the Vatican."

"Forget the Beretta. We've got better things to look at. *Va bene*!"

"*Si, andiamo.*"

They went straight to the frescoes on the ceiling of the Sistine Chapel, glancing at the *Last Judgement* and other famous paintings in the adjoining rooms. Michelangelo's depiction of the nine stories of *Genesis* would be enough for them. There wasn't a person in the room, except for a sleepy guard at the entrance of the chapel. They contemplated the mix of muted colors—green, blue, yellow, red and many others, then felt the electricity between the finger of Adam and God the Creator. Caterina must have imagined touching the nude, muscular figures of men, while Nick traced the curvaceous bodies of women through his eyes and viscera.

"Why don't we lie on our backs and take in the view of the master's work? Just like Michelangelo did."

"Are you *pazzo*, Nicky?"

"No. This is a private showing for the two of us. *Il Pape* himself gave me permission. Sent his personal courier to my headquarters."

"You are a silly boy, but if it will make you happy, why not?" She turned towards the entryway and saw that the guard was still dozing.

They lay down together on the cold, polychrome inlaid marble floor and traced the scenes with their eyes long enough that the coldness crept into their bones. Nick rose and pulled Caterina up to him, kissing her on the lips.

"Nick, this is a holy place," Caterina protested. She looked around and then kissed him on the forehead, pushing him out of the chapel.

The guard opened his eyes as they left for Caterina's place. When they entered the apartment, they shed their outer layers of clothes and lay on the bed. They were both tired but almost telepathically came to the same thought—one more frozen frame of lovemaking to carry with them wherever their film script took them. They made up a storyline aloud, as if thinking alike. But they couldn't come up with an ending. Nick didn't care and just wanted to share the passion of the moment with Caterina, so alluring on the bed—her face, her body, her spirit—and the hell with happy endings because the images playing outside this room were too bleak to think about.

Nick wanted to give Caterina one perfect day in Rome to remember him by, something to erase any trace of guilt over their time together, his lust trumping love in these times or love unrecognized by these times. He was glad Caterina had not asked him to ride over to that legendary *Bocca della Verità* outside the *Basilica di Santa Maria in Cosmedin* and have to put his damn hand in the mouth, not that he believed that stupid myth about it biting your hand if you lied. But it would be just like him to be so *sfortunato* that the stone lips would have collapsed on his fingers from a sudden domino triggering of an unexploded bomb nearby.

# XIX

The last Sunday morning of February brought in the remains of the chilling winds from the mountains that blew down Rome's streets and alleys, and the dampness found its way into the joints of Nick's body. The weather had been so bad, he left his Paperino in a garage under the CIC headquarters. He looked out the window of Caterina's apartment, lit up a cigarette, and waited for her return with some items for breakfast. Lately he had been thinking about Deborah and imagined their reunion but in his gut he knew it was a knucklehead idea, considering she sent him a 'Dear John' letter that he had been trying to erase from memory. Too much time had passed between Deborah and him. Besides, there were other issues beyond his control, and yet he would like to see his old girlfriend again. It was as if a film about Caterina and him were spliced together in a continuous spin, only to unravel off the reel.

Nick observed the flowerless oleander trees, not a bird on a limb, as he puffed smoke out into the courtyard. Caterina had quit smoking and had no patience for the smell anymore. She tried to mask the burnt aroma with the scent of lavender twigs that had long lost their potent aroma. He began smoking heavily but was reluctant to attribute it to his edginess, yet it was there wherever he moved about in Rome. Nick tried to blame his irritation on the bad weather, which could change the mood of a saint, especially in the *mezzogiorno*, where the *paesani*, no matter how poor, at least had the warmth of the sun. Gray skies muted the light through the apartment window and were spreading shadows in unexpected directions. Nick had found Nate to be withdrawn because Rachele was locked into what his friend called her convent tomb and also upset that he hadn't heard any news about cousin Carlo since he left for the front.

Bloody images of the war still rattled around in Nick's brain. Then he recalled an incident that he had never mentioned to anyone, nor was he likely to. It was just after Nathan and he had first returned from Assisi with Carlo. Captain Smith had received transfer orders and ordered Nick to straighten out his office before he left, making sure all the files and reports were organized and secured away, ready to be shipped to a different location. He came across a bound report lying flat on the bottom of a file cabinet and proceeded to hang it up on the guide bar in alphabetical order. He noticed the words, BISCARI AIRFIELD, on the cover with a 'confidential' red stamp in several places. He realized that Biscari was in Sicily, not far away from where they had landed on Gela. The temptation was too much to resist, so he blocked the front door with the same file cabinet and scanned it, going back to the salient parts.

With growing despair he read that on July 14, 1943 there had been a skirmish between infantrymen from the Seventh Army and Italian soldiers who used machine guns and sniper fire. When it was all over, 12 Americans were wounded and 36 Italians were captured. The CO ordered his infantrymen to line the Italian prisoners up by a ravine and execute them on the spot. About a mile away an NCO from the same company replicated the execution, when the sergeant had his men march another 37 Italian soldiers away from the airfield for the purpose of interrogation. The sergeant took a sub-machine gun from one of his men and killed every Italian. Captain Compton and Sergeant West were court-martialed separately, the CO's case being dismissed later, the NCO sentenced to the stockade. An addendum to the case stated that the captain was killed in action almost four months later and the sergeant released after a year, demoted to a private.

"Ah, Jesus Christ," Nick shouted out. When he realized no one had heard him, he furtively put the report away and moved the file cabinet back. He sat at the captain's desk and spun around the chair in slow motion trying to comprehend this double massacre. He realized that he had nothing to do with the slaughter of unarmed, Italian prisoners in Sicily, but at that time he also served in the Seventh Army under Patton, wearing one of the same patches on his uniform as the court-martialed soldiers. This was not something he would want to share with anyone, another bloody image for him to remember on his journey through Italy.

Everything seemed to be jumbled up in his head and that is why he still sought comfort in Caterina's arms, but he already knew he would not remain in Rome when the war ended. During the first week of March, *Marzo pazzarello* as the Romans like to call it, Nick heard at the CIC headquarters that the Allied Powers had crossed the Rhine in Germany. Captain Smith had always maintained that the German defenses would collapse on the Northern Italian Front by the end of April. Nick felt the numbness in his bones spread, and then a shooting pain ran through his injured leg, as if it were in a wooden box where a magician had slid a razor-sharp sword the wrong way, his assistant screaming in pain. He knew that he had changed from his days with his cousin in San Francisco and could hardly recall his times there with Nathan, everything blurred by his own pain and memories of death.

Nick heard the lock turn and threw his cigarette out the window. Caterina entered and put the *cornetti* and a container of *latte* down.

"You know I don't like cigarette smoke in our place."

"You didn't mind in the beginning."

"It was different then."

Nick offered to make *caffè Americano* while Caterina set the table for *prima colazione.* He had never been that helpful around the apartment but it was a good excuse to busy himself.

"Was the *pasticceria* crowded?"

"Not like it should be."

While they munched on a *cornetti al cioccolato*, Nick tasted an unusual bitterness in his pastry. He first shrugged off it as tainted cocoa seeds from Ghana, then acted peevish. "The seeds got mixed in with the leaves." He dumped sugar on the *cornetto* but it didn't help. He continued the doctoring.

"What are you doing, Nicky?" Caterina grabbed his forearm but he moved it away. "You know it's still difficult to get sugar."

"Everything has been tasting off since I got here."

"What did you expect? I do my best with what we can find." Caterina got up and stood over him. "It was you who said that we should live together. You have changed. You run hot and cold, but mostly like the water we get piped into our place during winter, only a hint of warmth."

"I don't know what you're talking about."

"Maybe I should never have told you that I went to *università* or that I was a *Milanese*." He held his right palm up. "Maybe you preferred that I was a Roman *puttana* whom you could discard at any moment." Caterina sat down and crossed her legs in a tangle. "I'll tell you another thing. My father was a *barone* and we lost everything. Do you not see what the war has done to me?"

"I never mentioned my family came from *Sicilia*. But you had to make a point of my accent when I first spoke Italian to you." He got up and poured the remains of the coffee into the sink. "You must've felt so superior coming from *Lombardia.* And now you tell me *che tu sei nobilità*!"

"Why are you bringing this up now? Like I have fallen for that North-South divide you seem to be accusing me of. You are picking a fight out of thin air." She twisted her hair into knots, a few strands hanging loose. "*Non ti capisco*? *Non ti conosco adesso*!" His eyes were blank. "I don't understand you, Nicky. I don't know you now! *Chi sei*?"

Nick knocked the chair backwards banging on the floor, as he rushed out the door. He returned much later, past the time they would have *la cena* together. He could see two dishes of *pasta amatriciana* lying in the sink basin uneaten and an empty bottle of red wine on the table. Caterina gazed at the wine glass and ignored Nick. He found an old *San Francisco Chronicle* on the dresser, which his mother has sent him weeks ago. Before Nick picked the newspaper up, he spotted a picture of the two of them, his arms around Caterina sitting at a table in *Caffè Greco*. It was wedged into the frame of the attached mirror. He removed the photo and studied it for a while, then placed it back in the same spot. He grabbed the paper and sat down at the table, pretending to read an article for a few minutes.

"*Mi dispiace*! I shouldn't have acted the way I did."

Caterina turned her head and said: "Come and watch the stars." He followed her to the window, where she traced her finger on the upper part of the glass. "One of your favorite things to look at, no?"

Nick opened the windows and they peeked out.

He placed his hands on her shoulder, lowering his head to get a better look. "That's the Pleiades up there. The Seven Sisters of Calypso."

"A good omen?"

"Yeah, Caterina. Good things are in the stars tonight." He lied knowing the myth revealed that, while mourning for a loved one, the sisters committed suicide.

She swung around and grabbed his hands. "Come to bed. You won't think so much when you lie with me." Caterina led him there but their lovemaking did not last long. Nick got up from bed, went over to the window.

"*Prego*. Shut the window. It's getting cold here."

He ignored her, took out a cigarette and lit up. She remained silent and waited for him to finish his smoke, as she pulled the covers up to her neck.

"I'm going back to my old place. There's been a lot of activity at headquarters. I need to be closer in case of an emergency."

"What are you talking about? Just because Nathan is alone, you have to run back now. He'll do fine without you there."

Nick threw the lit butt out the window, as it smoked itself out. He put his trousers and shirt on and quickly tied his shoes.

"Where are you going so late in the night?"

He grabbed his coat off a hook on the wall and swung it over his shoulder. "I think we need to be separate for awhile, so I can sort things out for myself."

"You walk out on me now, then I swear you will never see me again." She sat up in the bed. "I thought you loved me!"

"I never said it that way."

"*Allora*, you feel love in your heart not with idle talk. I thought to myself, sooner or later, the words would follow, but you leave me now as if I have just been paid." She got up and turned her back to him, her shoulders heaving up and down. "*Va*! You can sneak in here to get the rest of your things when I am at work." His footsteps echoed down the stairs.

Nick pulled his collar up, as he hiked back to his old haunt. As his feet crunched on the ground, he assessed how things were unraveling. He had reasoned for a clean break with Caterina since Nathan and he were being sent north to *Firenze* within the week, where the CIC was setting up a new unit. He hadn't told Caterina about his new assignment, but the more he thought about it, Nick convinced himself that he didn't want to be cemented to any woman, rationalizing that Deborah and now Caterina had turned into phantasms floating above him at night. And anyway he couldn't trust Caterina after the second incident with that *strunzu* from *Caffé Greco*. Maybe going to the same café with Caterina had been a lame-brained thing to do. But things were never that simple, as if anyone could redo things and erase the past like it never happened. Sure he was being hard on Caterina but a lot of his emotional guts had been spilled as soon as he landed in Sicily.

He also couldn't get it out of his head that, even if his luck held out and he returned home safe to his *famigghia*, his *cuginu* was still dead. How could he face *Ziu* Francesco, who would forever connect Paul and him going off to war together? He never should have teamed up with Paul, like he was bad luck for his cousin. Caterina, a *Milanese*, would never understand an American, especially one with Sicilian roots. She would be better off without him. He was so conflicted about everything he didn't know who he was fooling, least of all himself.

Nick gently opened the lock of the door, closed it behind him but still woke Nathan who had become a light sleeper.

"What's going on, buddy?" Nathan rubbed his eyes and sat up.

"I'm back."

"That's obvious."

"Carlo's gone and I didn't want you to be lonely."

"You left Caterina?" He scratched his forehead.

"Yeah."

"You're a dumb *schmuck*!"

"That's not what you said when I first started seeing her."

"You never let that go. When you were in Venice, I found Caterina to be a complex person, full of life. Despite everything, she's a *mensch* and I stand by my comment. You're a *schmuck*."

"I'm going to bed."

Nick didn't bother to take his clothes off and flopped on the cot, face down. Nate continued cursing his buddy in English, peppering it with Yiddish, German and Italian, for making such a poor decision. Nick covered his ears with the pillow until Nathan stopped. Before falling asleep, he mulled over his lie to Caterina about the sign from Pleiades.

# XX

By the spring of 1945 Nick and Nathan were ensconced in their new Florence location and had read the full battle report on liberation of the city during the summer of 1944. It had been declared an 'open city,' sparing *Firenze* the destruction of its Renaissance *palazzi* and *chiese*. But before the German Army retreated, the Gestapo executed many *partigiani* and political sympathizers in the streets and the *Piazza Santo Spirito*, a prominent public square across the Arno River from the headquarters of the Nazi Command and the fascist OVRA, stationed at La Villa Trieste. German soldiers set off mines, blowing up all the bridges on the Arno, except for the *Ponte Vecchio*, reducing to rubble the old neighborhoods on either side of that bridge, including sections of the *Vasari* Corridor that connected the *Palazzo Vecchio* with the *Palazzo Pitti*, the access to the bridge sealed off.

The tedium of their work wore on them, as they waited for the war to end, so when they had some free time, they explored the cultural sites that were still open, including the grandest one of all, the *Duomo*, the *Basilica di Santa Maria del Fiore*. To reach the lantern in the *cupola*, they would have to climb 463 steps. Nick considered his bad leg and Nathan's unexpected seizures and felt that the climb might be a mistake. Nick motioned to the front pew and Nathan sat down and he slid in next to him. They studied the massive core of the dome.

"That's some *fresco* in the dome, Nick. Too bad it's coated with dirt and dust."

"From what I can make out in that section …" Nick pointed to the bottom where naked bodies were dangling upside down, moments before their eternal punishment. "We're all destined for a hell one way or another—a personal one if we survive, a hot one if we die."

Nathan sighed as he rubbed his forehead. "Can't resist the dark side, can you? The damage could have been worse here. Look, the Dome is still intact, considering part of the roof caved in." Nathan tilted his head upwards again. "We'll come back some day, Nick, when it's all spruced up."

"I'm never returning."

"Why don't we keep on exploring the city? Sure to find some gems, despite everything."

"What we'll run into, Nate, are grey mounds of smashed stones lining the banks of the Arno. All those caved in church roofs from the impact of exploding mines."

"I've got eyes. Why don't you focus on a new life after the war? What do you say, Nick?"

"Let's get out of here."

"One more place, buddy. The Uffizi Gallery."

"Why not!"

Though the museum was not open to the public, Nathan, flashing his Intelligence ID, talked the security guard into letting them in for a brief visit. The hoary man waved them in but all they found were a few shrouded statues in the debris-filled hallways. Most of the rooms had the light outlines of where the pictures used to hang.

"What the hell, Nick! Everything is gone."

"That's wacky. Maybe the staff hid all the good stuff from the Nazis."

"All I wanted was to peek under the protective covering to see Caravaggio's *The Sacrifice of Abraham.*"

"If it were up to me, then Botticelli's *The Birth of Venus.*"

An official from the museum walked into the room and spoke in English when he saw the American uniforms.

"Luigi di Nofri, *il Direttore di Galleria degli Uffizi.* I am sorry to say that you have wasted your time visiting our museum."

"We had hoped to sneak a view of a few Italian masters," Nathan said.

"There is a good reason the Uffizi is closed, gentlemen. As you can see, little remains. Before the top-level Nazi officer, General Wolff, fled the city, he commandeered the collections of the Uffizi Gallery and Pitti Palace. We will have to wait until the end of the war to get our masterpieces back. The guard said you work for a U.S. Intelligence unit. Perhaps you will be able to find out where the artwork is hidden."

"We'll get it back sooner or later," Nathan said. "You can bet on it." The official led them out to the street and they shook hands.

Before they got orders for their return to the states, a report had come into their unit that General Karl Wolff had ignored orders from the highest levels of the Nazi government to transport truckloads of the stolen art north across the border into the Reich. The General later risked his life to negotiate a secret Nazi surrender with American spymaster, Allen Dulles. All the hidden masterpieces found their way back to the Uffizi and other museums, after a special team uncovered them. Nick was relieved that their promise to the Director had been carried out and that Nate would be able to visit the Uffizi some day in all its former splendor.

By early September 1945, around 15,000 troops including Nick and Nathan were packed into every available space on the Queen Mary, its exterior painted navy grey and the interior stripped of all its luxurious decorations and amenities, having been outfitted as a troop ship since May of 1940. The staterooms were converted to triple-tiered standee bunks. The ocean liner nicknamed "The Grey Ghost" for its speed and color, moved dead slow out of Southampton harbor, its three smokestacks trailing funnels of vapor when it ramped up the knots out on the open sea.

They stayed on the deck for fresh air as much as possible, walking around the circumference of the ship for exercise and avoiding the noise and card playing inside the cramped quarters. Sometimes they jogged a lap, stopping at the middle of the bow to rest if Nick's leg acted up.

"Nick, there's two deck chairs free over there. Let's sit."

"This ship really cuts those waves, Nate. Separating us from the last several years."

"Happy to be going home in one piece. Tell me something, buddy. Do you ever miss Caterina?"

"Nah, it's all in the past now."

"I don't know if it's the same for me."

"Rachele!"

"Yeah, like a part of me is still in Assisi."

"All you should be thinking about is going home. As soon as you see your family, you'll be okay."

"You're very sure about that."

"I can already hear the jazz playing at Jack's tavern."

Nick lied about everything being okay. Sure, he wanted to see his folks. Loved them to death. But he had no woman in his life, neither San Francisco nor Rome. Sure, he was happy to be alive but there were plenty of things in Italy to haunt him. It would take more than the soulful sounds of jazz to get him through his darker thoughts.

At the end of their long journey, the Queen Mary slipped into the New York Harbor and, when Nick and Nathan saw the Statue of Liberty, they burst out in a cheer, "The Grey Ghost" passing the Empire State

Building on the right before nudging its king-size hull into the Cunard dock.

If ever there would be a time for Nick to be happy, this was one of those moments. They started off with an early supper at Nick's aunt's house in South Brooklyn. *Zia* Antonina, Gaetano's sister, had a reputation as a cook only second to his mother's from what he heard, Nathan's eyes glistening with the thought of a *cena deliziosa*, his first in America. Afterwards they celebrated on 52nd Street, hopping from one jazz club to another, the bebop notes syncopating in the air, inside and outside, all night long until they crapped out in their hotel room.

There was still the long train ride home to California, starting with the New York Central's Pacemaker to Chicago and then the "City of San Francisco" to Oakland. But first, Nick and Nathan had to report to Fort Dix, New Jersey, the following morning and get their physicals, and later on the "Separated from Service" papers, a tedious process they longed for, ending life in the military with its orders, restrictions and ever-present chance of death—*il tutto*, the whole shebang, *il gran finale.* Yet some things in the past have a nasty way of lingering, extending their shelf life and for Nick there were things he could not forget, others he did not want to remember or maybe it was a combination of both.

# XXI

Stockton Street in North Beach looked the same to Nick as he sauntered down the block, a patch of green from Angel Island still rising at the end of the sloping street of attached houses with Victorian touches, though not nearly as detailed as those of Alamo Square. He made a promise to himself that he would not be seen with any sort of limp, the casual rhythm of his stride deflecting attention. A banner hung underneath the bay windows read 'Welcome Home, Nicky' and brought a smile to his face, countering a fleeting, dark memory of his father being dragged down those same steps that he was now climbing to a victory party, starting the second he opened the door.

"A toast to *figghiu miu, Nicolo*," Gaetano announced operatically over Caruso's voice, singing the *aria*, '*Vesti la giubba*' from *Pagliacci* on a 78 single, one of a collection that his father gathered over his lifetime in America. Someone turned the music down and Gaetano managed to quiet everyone for a moment. "We are proud of you and wish you *bona fortuna. Salute!*" A chorus of blessings continued, from *Cent'anni* to "Cheers."

Lucia ran up to her son and kissed him on the forehead. She turned to the crowd. "May he marry *subito*. Eh, we need some *bambini in casa mia*." Everyone toasted again and the laughter and conversation bounced off the tin ceiling, the noise carrying over to the backyards of the adjoining houses.

Streamers hung from the living room ceiling and a '*Benvinutu a Casa Nicolo*' banner stretched above the couch. The dining room table was set with a linen tablecloth and his mother's wedding china, which only left its display in a mahogany cabinet during holidays. Nick slumped onto the couch after countless *baci e abbracci* from family and neighborhood friends. The noise level rose as Nick scanned the room of familiar faces, amused by their animated expressions, but there was something bothering him throughout the festivities. His father pulled Nick up from the sofa and put his wide arm around his son, coaxing him to greet the new arrivals, everyone smiling, laughing, a few crying.

Paul's family came in later, a moment that he had been dreading, and he was relieved that *Ziu* Francesco hadn't shown up. Not that he didn't admire his uncle who ran a successful, neighborhood business, not that he didn't love his uncle, no, it was all about Paul. After an emotional greeting with the entire Burgio *famigghia*, *Zia* Concetta made no reference to *Ziu* Francesco's conspicuous absence. Nick breathed in heavily when the door opened five minutes later and

*Ziu* Francesco entered. The conversations quieted down as Nick's uncle approached him. He sized his nephew up and down, hugged him, handing over a bottle of his homemade wine. No words were exchanged and Nick preferred it that way.

The chatter and laughter took off again, mixed with the wine and beer and pitchers of Hurricane, a rum cocktail created in New Orleans during the war that Gaetano's cousin had described to him in a letter. Nick grew to hate it with each taste. It became one of those moments in a movie where all you saw were the lips of people moving but no sound. Nick became disoriented and began to sweat from traces of pain in his leg. The moment he had dreaded was over and there had been no scene at all with his uncle. He still felt empty inside, despite those many nights dreaming of riding his bicycle again along the bay, going over the red bridge and seeing his father sail under it a free man, and maybe even running into Deborah. He wanted to be as happy as all those smiling faces that greeted him like *Mamma* and *Papà*. The noise level spiked again to a high volume, just like the sound of a film rushing back to end a scene, the camera focusing in on the main character. Nick was back home.

Later in the evening, after most of the people had left the party, Nathan stopped by. Nick led his friend into the rear garden, holding an open bottle of red wine and two highball glasses.

"Let's sit on top of the picnic table. We can get a bird's-eye view of the sky."

"You haven't changed, Nick." Nathan laughed. "Stars and birds. For me, I'll take people, starting with you, buddy."

"Have some wine." Nick poured and handed him a glass, watching his friend drink. "So what do you think?"

"Smells and tastes of southern Italy. Has a homemade quality, but it's good stuff." Nathan grabbed the bottle and observed that the label had the type and year, Zinfandel 1944.

"It came all the way from San Francisco." Nick revealed a set smile. "Paul's father gave it to me."

"How's he holding up?"

"Hard to say what a person feels. Let's try and enjoy his gift of wine." Nick poured more wine in both of the glasses and drank all of his. "My cousin, Maria, is getting married next year, you know. What a looker!" Nick drank half his wine and stared at the ground. "My father gave up fishing. He just tends to his garden. My mom is still working as a seamstress." Nick rubbed his hand over the wine label. "Anyway, a little remembrance." Nick held up the bottle. "My last time with *cuginu* Paul at my house." Nick drank the glass in one gulp and poured another one for himself. "Why do I have all this dang guilt, Nate?"

"We all do. Look at how many died in our tank squadron and we're still here. Don't get me started." He finished his wine. "Hey, buddy. I thought we made a pact in Florence not to talk about the war when we came back."

"I know, but with you it's different. At least your *cugino* Carlo escaped the Nazis." Nick poured another glass of wine for Nathan and himself. "Paul never got a chance to come home again. And what about our buddy, Al from Roseto?"

"It's not our fault, Nick." Nathan took a sip of wine. "But I'll tell you what else we still have on our chest." He drank most of the wine. "Rachele and Caterina. They're alive, God knows somewhere in Italy. It must be over six months since we last saw them."

"I never think of her anymore."

"You're not going to bullshit me, Nick."

"No use cryin' over spilt milk."

"Go ahead, hide your feelings, if that's what you want. But the whole thing with Rachele still bothers me."

A shooting star trailed its white streak in a rapid sweep across the night sky. "Geez, did you see that, Nate?"

"Sure, clear as the expression on your face."

"I swear it's Paul signaling us."

"Maybe you're right, buddy." Nathan tracked the stars.

"Remember when Giuliano was gunned down by that *pezzo di merda* SS officer?"

Nate shook his head in recognition.

"You know, Nate, after all we went through, I've always wondered what did happen to Carlo."

"My father thinks he must have left for Palestine after the war with the others from the Jewish Brigade. They wanted to set up a new homeland for Jews worldwide."

"Maybe he stayed in Italy."

"The only way we would know for sure is if we went back and retraced his steps. But I don't think either of us will be going back any time soon."

Nick put his hand on Nathan's shoulder and then he looked up at the stars.

"Imagine for a minute that Paul is looking down at us from somewhere in the stars, while we're drinking his father's wine. Here's one for you *cuginu*." They clinked glasses and finished off the wine, including the dregs.

# XXII

The morning after the celebration, Gaetano found his son sitting at the redwood picnic table the family set up in the backyard, an *al fresco* version of their kitchen table. Nick drank a cup of coffee while tapping ashes into a pressed glass ashtray. Gaetano sat next to him and waited for Nick to speak, the silence louder than the festivities of yesterday.

Nick remained silent not out of disrespect, but rather cataloging in his mind all the topics that would be off-limits. He already knew that marriage was not on his agenda, though he recognized that's what his parents most wanted, and of course, grandchildren, a boy for his father and a girl for his mother. There would be nothing to stop his parents from hinting around that theme, so from day one, Nick's strategy would be a full-toothed smile followed by responses they wanted to hear. What happened in Italy during the war, a country so far away now, would not be broached at any table, inside or out, except for one topic.

"*Papà!*"

"*Come stai, Nicolo*?"

"*Beni, Papà*. I spoke to *Nannu*."

"*Nannu*? *Non possibbili*!" Gaetano's face turned white. "*Patri miu è mortu*! The *Municipio* wired me his death notice. No relatives left in Sciacca."

"You don't understand. I spoke to him when I was in Sicily. Right before our squadron headed out for Palermo."

Gaetano pinched his fingertips against the right thumb and shook his hand lightly, as if to say: 'What in God's name are you saying?'

"*Nannu* must have died sometime after I left him," Nick blurted out, wiping some tears from his cheek.

"July 24, 1943, *figghiu miu*."

"I'll always remember that afternoon with *Nannu*. He may have been very old, but the lines in his face showed strength." Nick's eyes lit up. "He charmed me with so many stories about you."

Gaetano wept and Nick hugged his father.

"Pop, he said I looked like you."

"*Si, è veru, tu si un Spataro. Bravu, Nicolo*."

* * *

By the beginning of the 1946 New Year, Nathan had enrolled at the San Francisco Art Institute in the Russian Hill district to study graphic arts, while Nick started at the San Francisco State College majoring in American Literature, the GI Bill of Rights picking up the cost. Throughout the spring semester they would meet up at the Legion of Honor Museum like before and take in the latest exhibit, followed by a game of catch in Lincoln Park, avoiding subjects that might remind them of the war years. They buried themselves in their studies and the semester moved along in an uneventful way.

Nick took a psychology course as an elective and enjoyed reading about behavior and the dynamics of family and how they related to the outside world. He didn't like it when he saw himself as someone boxed in by these ties and his North Beach enclave. The saying that 'you can take the person out of neighborhood, but you can't take the neighborhood out of the person' troubled Nick not because he was sorry about his life in North Beach, but that he might be forever stuck in time and place. So he put his textbook down and lost himself in novels from the nineteenth century, Mark Twain his favorite author since high school. He had been closed out of a British Lit course from the same time period and chose Russian literature as a good counterpoint to his major.

One spring afternoon at San Francisco State, Nick sat on a small patch of grass under a Bronze Loquat tree near the old main building with its soaring, Italianate tower. The sun shone and some red, yellow and white tulips slid out of green sheaves, a cool breeze cutting the new heat of the sun, while he read Chekhov's story, "The Lady with the Pet Dog." Nick was so engrossed by the narrative, he lost sense of his surroundings. When he finished the story, it was the first time in a long while he felt right with the world, even though he didn't have a woman to share it with. He began to sound more like his mother and tried to stop her words from echoing in his head. Nick thumbed through the pages of the short story and reread the climactic closing. When he looked up, he heard *kew* notes ending with a whistle from the tree right above him. As he searched for the exact location, a western bluebird, its head and feathers a brilliant blue over a rust body, flew away to rendezvous with his mate. He watched its flight as the male bird found refuge in a tree across the street. His eyes dropped to the students passing by and came across a familiar face that didn't belong on campus and he rose up to greet her.

"Deborah, is it really you?" Nick would have liked to rehearse what he wanted to say, but she was right in front of him, anxious about this moment since his discharge from the service.

She laughed nervously as she put the break on the carriage she was pushing. "Nicky, I can't believe it. Nathan told me all about you. You look so mature now." She laughed again. "I mean in a good way." He flashed back to their time in the San Francisco Botanical Garden, as she fixed the blanket covering the baby.

"You're still pretty as ever, Deb." Her face turned pink while he mumbled something as the baby cooed. Deborah pushed her long hair back as he asked: "Babysitting?"

"What? Oh, he's mine. Didn't Nathan tell you anything?"

Nick winced, then composed himself. "Let me have a look. Cute, very cute." It was his misfortune to run into Deborah, with a kid no less, and still beautiful. He was just a *schmuck* still going to school, while she was getting on with her life. "How old is she?"

"It's a boy. Has the good looks of his father."

"Nah, he's a dead ringer for you." He lied but continued. "I see a little of Nathan in the kid too."

"No, he's all David. Oh, that's my husband. We got married before he joined the Coast Guard. He's going nights at San Francisco Law School, thanks to the GI Bill."

Deborah may have appeared nervous but Nick's stomach tightened in pain, and then his leg began to act up causing him to wince. His eyes glazed over Deborah and the child. He wanted to end this conversation.

"Nicky, I'm really sorry. I hope that you don't hate me. The last letter I got from you was when you were still in tank training."

"That's strange. I sent you letters from Morocco and Sicily and never got anything in return."

"I never got them and figured you forgot about me. Anyway, you know how strongly my father felt about us not keeping company." Deborah pressed her palms on her cheeks. "That's why I sent the last letter, when you and Nathan were in Rome. Hope I didn't sound too awful." Nick looked off in the distance and recalled Nathan saying he didn't want to get in the middle of this. When he faced Deborah again, her eyes had turned glassy. "Forget it, Nicky. It's not your fault."

Nick wanted to get the hell out of there but held his ground to save face. He was relieved when she made up a phony excuse about having to rush home to meet her husband for lunch near his father's real estate office. It sounded like a garbled message breaking up on a walkie-talkie from the war. When Deborah was out of sight, he dropped down under the tree, pushed his books aside and leaned his head against its thin bark, shutting his eyes and returning to the San Francisco Botanical Garden. After a short while he found himself wandering the empty streets of Rome. He had coiled up in a ball on the grass and covered his head with the spring jacket he had tied around his waist and cut the rest of his classes. He daydreamed about Caterina and him living together, how she cared so much about him and tried to soothe his anguish over the lousy war, her body wrapped around him in unconditional love.

That evening after supper, Nathan came by Nick's house and they went into the backyard, sitting in the same spot on top of the picnic table. Nick lit up a cigarette and offered one to Nathan.

"I'll pass. I only smoked on breaks in the army to keep out of extra duties."

"Suit yourself."

"I heard you met up with my sister today." Nick glared at Nathan. "Okay, I acted like a *putz,* but I just couldn't bring myself to tell you. I said to myself what are the chances of the two of you running into each other in this big city? I'm sorry, buddy."

"Doesn't matter now. I'm happy for her."

"Really?"

"What do you expect me to say?"

"I was going to say something to you, believe me, but was waiting for the right moment. Anyway, I think it was crummy when my father busted up your relationship with Deborah. He threw your letters in the incinerator. Just the other day, I reminded him. 'Father, do you realize that Nick risked his life for Carlo, your own nephew.' He was speechless for a while, which is unusual for my Dad, but he admitted you're a true *mensch*. That you acted like a brother." He placed his arm around Nick. "It's just too bad my family was too blind to realize what a great guy you are. As for David, her husband, he's all right, but he'll never measure up to you."

"I'm okay, Nate. I get lost in my books."

Nathan pulled out a postcard. Nick could see an Italian stamp but didn't say anything. "This may not be the best time to show you this but I'm too excited not to. I know we made a pact about the war but you said it was different for you and me, so …"

"If you want to talk about a woman, just make sure it's not Caterina."

"It's hard to believe, but I received the postcard this morning." Nathan smacked it in his hand. "From *Padre* Esposito. Got my address from his priest friend at the Vatican. He's better than a detective."

"Spit it out, will ya!" Nathan looked nervous and happy at the same time, but Nick didn't like where this was going.

"Rachele! It's about Rachele!"

Nick flicked his cigarette onto the ground. "I thought she was a goner, lost in space."

"Stop with the glib attitude. Let me say something."

"Go ahead, I'm all ears."

"Something happened over there in a *villa*. The countryside north of Assisi. A well-known psychiatrist came up with a new theory for treating patients suffering from gross stress reaction. Takes them out of institutional settings to live on a working farm. Spends a lot of time talking to the patient in a garden setting."

"But you're back home, Nate!"

"*Padre* Esposito says she's better. Not a 100%, but …"

"Do you think she still remembers you?"

"After Rachele was there for six months, she started mentioning my name. The psychiatrist asked *Padre* Esposito: 'Who is this Nathan? It's not an Italian name.' That's when the friar decided to track me down." He looked sideways at Nick. "I'm going back."

"Are you *pazzu*?"

"Yeah, I'm *meshugganah*, but I'm going anyway."

"What about your art studies at the Institute?"

"As soon as the spring semester is over, I'm heading out."

"Chasing rainbows!" Nick felt bad after he said that but it was too late.

"No, chasing the missing chink in my heart. I'm not going be a chump like you when it comes to women."

"Thanks for the vote of confidence." Nick looked up at the night sky but didn't see anything. "*Buona fortuna*, buddy."

Nathan got off the table. "I want you to come with me."

"What for? You think I'm a loser."

"Stop it, will ya. Listen to me. If I fail with Rachele, I couldn't face this alone. I'll go out of my mind. I need you there."

"Sorry, no can do."

"You're one sorry ass."

"We're not in the army anymore, so you can't order me around, sergeant."

"You know what, Nick? You're still a *schmuck*."

"Go back in time *alla* H.G. Wells. I'm staying right here, where it's nice and safe."

"You're just as miserable as me, and you know exactly what I'm talkin' about. So why don't you wise up. I'm going to Assisi." Nick shrugged. "And I thought you were my buddy."

Nathan banged the back door shut and Nick waved his hand in disgust. He lay flat out on the picnic table and fell asleep. When he woke up, the night sky had brightened up with several constellations. He jumped off the table and ran into the house, slamming the door. His father came halfway down the stairs.

"*Nicolo, chi cosa fai*?"

"*Nenti*, Pop. Go to bed."

"*Managgia*! The door keeps banging."

"I fell asleep, *Papà*, and had a bad dream. It's *pazzu* but I saw myself flailing my arms through the Pleiades constellation. You know, the one with seven Greek sisters. A bad omen, no."

Gaetano shook his head several times before going back to bed. Nick sunk into the sofa and grabbed his copy of *Crime and Punishment.* That his assigned book somehow meshed with his own personal life made him feel like singing the blues. Nick wasn't a murderer like Raskolnikov, yet there was this thread of dead relationships for him on both sides of the Atlantic as he lay there reading, until his eyes blurred into a twisted sleep from the yellowed, artificial light, the book tumbling onto the floral, wool rug, the empty sound of night outside marked by the muffled tempo of the mahogany, Seth Thomas mantle clock.

# XXIII

The next morning after breakfast, Nick sat at the picnic table facing the fig tree framed by a wooden fence. It was still shrouded with its galvanized, bucket hat, wrapped in tarpaper zigzagged with twine. He lit up a cigarette, watching a plume of smoke float in the wind, not focused on anything in particular. He heard a tinny scratch and saw a female northern cardinal with dull colors of golden brown and olive. Within seconds the unmistakable male with his red plumed crest and sash bottom alighted next to her. Nick was thrilled to see them together. He sat motionless in his North Beach backyard, letting the cigarette ash up, in a place where he would more likely see a common house sparrow. The male bird fed the female a tiny seed. Soon after, they alternated a song, *what-cheer, what-cheer… wheet, wheet, wheet, wheet.* When they finished their melody, Nick inched his way off the bench to get a closer look at the songbirds. The female cardinal flew away, the male chasing after her without a moment's hesitation.

The image was bookmarked in his head like all those National Audubon prints in the library, the brilliant, dazzling colors stored in his youthful memory, especially when the rain pelted against the large windows of his neighborhood sanctuary. That was long ago when birds were just something to wonder at—their colors, their movement, their songs—connections to other living forms, but Nick needed to see the birds and even the stars in a new way, offering some inner meaning to patch up the tormenting thoughts he clung to—what he should have done or how he could have handled things differently. But there he was, thinking too much, reading too much, as his *cuginu* admonished him for. For now, Nick would have to put his last conversation with Nathan in a secret place, as easy as out of sight, out of mind.

* * *

As soon as Nick had returned from the service, he continued the routine of spending Sunday with his parents, eating their customary multi-course dinner. His spring semester of college recently completed, Lucia returned from an early mass and spent the rest of the morning arranging an *antipasto* of local air dried meats and imported cheese, and preparing *pasta al forno siciliana* and a *secondo* platter of pork *braciola* and meatballs, to be followed by fruits and nuts, and *caffè* e *un po di Sambuca*. Nick read the *San Francisco Chronicle* and other newspapers stacked up on the table and Gaetano listened to his Caruso records in the living room, as the sun lit up the rear kitchen. When Lucia called out, Nick got rid of the papers and Gaetano scurried in, sitting at the head of a white porcelain enamel table.

"*Nicolo*, you no look happy," Lucia said. Nick waved his mother off. "I slaved all week over my Singer and then my stove, only to seea that sad face." She smiled. "I coulda made *pasta cu sardi* for your father, but no, I made your favorite dish."

"Lucia, leave the boy alone."

"It's okay for you to say, sitting like King Tut, but your son has a sour puss on whenever he comes in the house."

"*Mi dispiace, Mamma*."

Gaetano gestured towards the *pasta* that Lucia had already ladled into their dishes. "*Mancia, Nicolo*. Your mother can't help it because you mope around the house and we worry. What are we supposed to do?"

"I got things on my mind. Let's just eat."

"*Va beni*!" Gaetano reached over and poured some red wine in everyone's glass. "*Salute*!" as they clinked glasses.

They ate with a minimum of conversation, and at the end of the meal Gaetano took out two, stubby Toscano cigars.

"Nicolo, step into the backyard and have a smoke with me. The sun's rays will do us good." He arched his right eyebrow and grinned at his son.

Nick followed his father out the back door, when Lucia blocked his way and said: "*Innuccentu*!" She pinched her son's cheek.

"I don't think so, *Mamma*." He kissed his mother's hand. "Pop is waiting outside for me."

"Good. I no want him to stink up the house."

The cool breeze coming from the Bay tempered the warmth of the sun. They sat next to each other at the picnic table. Gaetano had already lit his cigar and handed one to his son who opened his Zippo with a ping and torched the Toscano.

"*Mannagia*, you'll set yourself on fire."

"I got everything under control, Pop."

"I can see." Gaetano puffed on his cigar and blew smoke into the air, spiraling away. Nick repeated the same pattern as his father while they stared for a while at the covered tree in the corner of the yard.

"Do you want me to liberate the fig tree, Pop?"

"*Beni*."

Nick leaned the cigar in a glass ashtray and proceeded to undress the tree, starting with its bucket hat, cutting the rope and wrapping it around a stick, then unraveling the black coat and furling it, placing each item on the table.

His father clenched the cigar in his teeth while approaching the tree and gently spread the branches out.

"Do you think we'll have a lot of figs, *Papà*?"

Gaetano took the cigar out of his mouth. "Don't worry. When the figs are ripe, we can eat them with some *prosciutto* on top. *Allura*, what happened to your friend, Nathan? He don't come around no more." Gaetano stubbed the cigar out in the ashtray.

"Nothing, Pop."

"Your friend hasn't returned since he banged my back door. *Non capiscu*."

"Nate has some cockamamie idea that he should run after some woman he met in Italy."

"Does he love her?"

"*Si*."

"Then why should he not pursue her?"

"I don't know." Nick walked over to examine the fig tree. "It's none of my business anyway."

Gaetano followed his son to the tree. "*Bravu*. Eh, but why you no speaka to each other?"

"He wants me to go with him to Italy and I refused."

"Isn't Nathan your best *amicu*?"

"He used to be."

"*No, non possibbili*! There must be something else you're not telling me."

"I don't know what you're getting at."

"Tell me the truth. You always confided to me since you were a *picciriddu*."

"For Christ's sake, Pop," Nick yelled out. "Don't you know where I've come from?"

"No, I know nothing about what happened to you during the war." Gaetano raised his voice. "I guess in time you'll tell me what's bothering you."

"What's going on out there?" Lucia called out, as she stepped out the door. "The neighbors!"

"Lucia, I am just having a little talk with our son. *No problemu!*"

Lucia shook her right hand in the air and went inside.

"Nicolo, let's sit down again."

"Okay, Pop."

Gaetano sat opposite to his son. "There's something else troubling you. Besides Nathan. I heard you were once sweet on his sister. Deborah, right." Nick nodded. "A nice girl. But she is married, I understand. Anyway she was Jewish, so how was this going to work out, you being a Catholic?"

"I'm not interested in the Catholic Church anymore."

"You used to be an altar boy. When you were in the sixth grade you told your mother and me you wanted to be a priest."

"That was a long time ago, Pop."

"But thank God, you came to your senses when you discovered girls." Gaetano pointed his index finger at his son. "*Ma Nicolo*, you are still Catholic. We are not heathens."

"Pop, you only go church on Palm Sunday, so you can get free palms to weave into fancy crosses for us to wear." Nick ran his hand over one of the limbs. "Oh, I'm sorry, I forgot Christmas."

"Never mind! Your mother goes every Sunday."

"Let's get off this. I don't want to hear about it."

"Okay, so what else is bothering you? Your *cuginu*, *Paolo*?"

"I don't want to talk about the war."

"It was terrible what happened to my nephew and what it did to *Ziu* Francesco and *Zia* Concetta. *La tutta famigghia.*"

"And what about what happened to you? The government should be ashamed of themselves for throwing you and your *paesani* into one of those internment camps."

"FDR shoulda stopped the whole damn business from the beginning. And to think we Italians, loyal Democrats, helped put the President into office. And when we sent our sons to fight in the war, they still called us enemy aliens."

"The G-men stole you away in the middle of the night. Right outside."

"You should of been at the camp to witness their riddles. The interrogator, he says: 'Who do you want to win this war?' I saya just like this: 'Think of your mother as one country and your wife as another country. You love your mother and you love your wife, but not in the same way, that is if you're not *pazzu,* excuse me *signuri*, crazy.' So I thought for a moment and finished. 'I love my mother country, Italy, and equally love my new wedded country, America. Sir, would you be able to choose one over the other? I only want them not to fight against each other, just like we did in the last war.' Still I was guilty as charged, an enemy alien. *Allura, we* are a proud people and don't complain, but everything remains here." Gaetano tapped the side of his head.

"*Si papà tu sei un uomo di fiducia*, a man of trust, as *Padre* Esposito would say."

"*Padre* Esposito?"

"*Papà*, if you are a proud man, then you must find other work. You can't sit around the house while *Mamma* sews in a shop with two temperatures, steaming hot or damp cold."

"It is easy for you to say. You are young. I am too old to start a fishing business again." Gaetano became lost in his thoughts, then mumbled: "*È veru, figghiu miu ma ...*"

"But what, Pop?"

"I did not want to tell you all these things, but the U.S. Navy returned my fishing boat. It was unseaworthy, good for nothin'. Do you know what I did to that boat, which your mother and me scrimped and saved for, the fastest purse seiner in the bay? Do you want to know what I did? I set the useless junk boat afire at the dock of Fisherman's Wharf, right where it once rested gently in the water, its shiny wood gleaming in the sun."

"A lot of crazy things went on during the war, Pop, but there's nothing we can do about it now. Don't take this in the wrong way, but I have an idea. You could work in *Ziu* Francesco's *alimentaria*. Help him supervise the young busters. Maybe even set up a fresh fish counter in the back."

Gaetano put his head down. "Maybe, as you say. We'll see." Gaetano looked up and tapped Nick's cheek. "I've got it," Gaetano said with a questioning look. "Before, your *faccia* shows it. There has to be some other girl. You can no fool your father."

"After all you went through, we're back to this topic. *Minchia*!"

"I am right."

"*Beni*! Okay, okay. I was with an Italian woman in *Roma*. A *Milanese*!"

"*Minchia*! Don't get involved with the Northerners. The ones from the *Mezzogiorno* will understand you better, especially the *Siciliani*."

"I'm American, Pop. Remember, I was born here."

"*Maleducatu*! Don't get smart with me." Gaetano smiled at his son. "Continue with your story about the *Milanese*."

"I even lived with her a while."

"*Si*, of course. Go on."

"You wouldn't like what she did to get by during the war."

"Don't say anymore." Gaetano raised his palm up. "*Va beni*. The war is over and you are safe at home. You'll meet another woman."

"It's not as simple as that, Pop." Nick rubbed his hands through his hair and stared at the fig tree.

"What's her name?"

"Caterina."

"You love this woman?"

"I don't know, Pop. I don't even know where she is now."

"I don't think your mother would like *comu si chiama*?"

"Caterina." Nick's face showed exasperation.

"Your mother would want a nice Sicilian girl for you. If no, then an *Americana* who comes from a respected family."

"I don't want a nice girl, Pop."

"You are my only son and I want you to be happy." His father's eyes popped out. "I'll make a deal with you. I don't care what happened with this *Milanese* girl from *Roma*. If you like, I'll convince your mother about Caterina's purity. I am very good at telling stories."

"I appreciate everything you and *Mamma* have done." Nick embraced his father and then let go. "But it's best if you let me sort this thing out myself."

"So maybe you should go with your friend. Nathan *è bonu comu lu pane*."

"As good as bread, *Papà*."

Gaetano tweaked his cheek. "He needs you now. You can go back to school in the fall."

"I don't know, Pop."

"Maybe the trip will do you good. *Allura*, all you do is read your books and take notes." Gaetano clasped Nick's shoulders. "You need to pick yourself up. You will have an adventure!"

"As *Mamma* and you have noticed, I'm very mixed up right now."

Gaetano grabbed his son's face and turned it toward him. "Look into my eyes, *figghiu miu*." Nick stared at his father. "Do you know what I see? You left as a boy and came back as a man. Your mother and me are very proud of you. And as you are a man, you have known love, and may still be in love. Your father knows about these things." Gaetano wrapped his arm around his son. "You know there is an old Sicilian saying—*Amari e disamari nun sta a cui lu voli fari.* You don't choose whom to love and not love. *Capisci*?"

"I guess."

"*Bravu.*"

As they walked back in the house, Lucia was standing at the door, teary-eyed for things she could not hear but must have felt. He thought about his parents, and how they must have not slept one peaceful night till the day he stepped back into their home on Stockton Street. He told them he was going to take a walk and not to worry so much.

Before he left, he went into the kitchen and shouted to his mother who was whispering to Gaetano in the living room. "*Mamma*, do you have any *caponata* left?"

She stood at the entrance. "*Si,* there's a sealed one left on the top shelf."

"Can I have it?"

"*Certo*. For your girlfriend?"

"*Grazie Mamma*!"

Nick trekked for several miles until he reached the jazz joint, Jack's Tavern. The same bartender, Billy McClellan from his 18th birthday party, was still there. Nick held the jar of *caponata* in the air for the bartender to see, who smiled when he recognized Nick. He took off his apron and had his barback take over for him, motioning to Nick to follow him outside because there was a bebop set going on with its *fortissimo* brass sounds racing away.

"After all these years! It's Nick, right?" Nick smiled. "And what's this? Wait a minute, you brought me some capo ..."

"*Caponata*."

"Yeah, that's right."

"I wanted you to have the eggplant appetizer that my *Mamma* made."

"Well I do sure appreciate that. "It's been awhile, but I remember you was regulars before you guys left for the army. Glad you made it back alive. Where's your cousin?"

"My cousin Paul was killed in action when we were in Italy."

"God damn, I am sorry to hear that, son. It must hurt bad!" Nick grimaced and Billy rubbed his chin. "But I do have some good news to share. My boy, William Junior, he joined up before he finished college and came back in one piece as 1st Lieutenant. Tuskegee Airmen of 332nd Fighter Group. Only Negroes to fly in the war. Woo-eee, that boy was some pilot."

"Glad your son made it back safe."

"You look a little under the weather, Nick. Is everything okay?"

"I don't want to keep you from your job."

"I'd rather talk with you awhile. I get mo' tired these days."

"Well, there is one thing now that you mention it."

"Shoot!"

"See my other buddy, Nathan. He used to come here too."

"You mean the fella who always came in with a sketch book?"

"Yeah, that's him. Anyway, he went off to Italy to find a girl he was sweet on. But I didn't want to go with him."

"Well, I suppose he can take care of hisself. Is that all?"

"He's desperate. Needs me there and I turned him down because …"

"Because why?"

"I am afraid to go back. I left someone there too, you know, but it was a bad situation."

"That's something only you can deal with when it comes to matters of the heart, if that's what you getting' at. As for your buddy, you can't desert him."

"As soon as classes ended, he scrammed on the first train for New York City to catch an ocean liner. He should be somewhere near the port now."

"I know what you could do. Listen here! My son has a few connections with the flyboys. Maybe you could hitch a ride in one of those transport planes at Travis Air Force Base. They go to New York. I think it's Floyd Bennett Field."

"Wow, I don't know what to say?"

"Don't say nothin'. Come back tomorrow and I'll let you know if you going on one of those big mamas."

Nick returned home by midnight and tiptoed out to the backyard. He sat on top of the picnic table and gazed at the stars and tried to read them, so he might figure out how he might handle things with his buddy, Nate, and whatever else he might run into. He mulled over his father's advice and the bartender's counsel many times. Nick wondered where Caterina was at this moment, eight hours ahead in another time zone. As the rosy dawn was waking her, he wondered what she might have been dreaming about. Did she ever muse about their times together in Italy or was their Roman encounter not even worth a bad dream for her?

# XXIV

Nathan embarked on the Swedish American Line's Gripsholm from New York to Gothenburg. He held onto the rail as the ship sliced through the brown water of the harbor, the cry of seagulls circling without purpose. He wondered if he were going to cross over 3000 nautical miles just to set himself up for failure. Once out of the New York Bay, the ocean liner increased speed to 17 knots per hour, running parallel to Long Island, an endless succession of waves that separated him in due course from the solid ground of 'The End'.

Out on the open sea, the sunrays grazed the metal hull, turning into flashes of exploding shells that skimmed the ocean's surface, dredging up memories of the dead and wounded of Italy, a country he thought he would never return to. He was not the same man, though no one in his family noticed, and then there was Nick. What a damn disappointment, after all they had been through. The war had changed Nick too. Nathan could not decode what motivated his best friend anymore. And to think Nick didn't get what a great gal Caterina was. So water continued to rush and swoosh along the side of the ship, leaving a wake touching the horizon, while he steamed to Rachele. Nathan reflected on the nature of mental illness, a condition that doesn't disappear because a person wills it. Something else had to come into play and Nathan did not want to live on the "Boulevard of Broken Dreams," as the song goes, but he had to give it one last chance. He felt a hollowness that bored through him, adrift on the vast sea until someone jerked his body with a smack to his shoulder. Nathan spun around and then his jaw dropped.

"Did you think I would let you go on this *meshugganah* adventure all by yourself?"

"Nah, I was hoping you'd change your mind, buddy." Nathan grinned and shook his head. "How did you manage to catch up with me?"

"I hitched a ride on a military transport thanks to Billy, the bartender's son. You remember Willie from Jack's Tavern?"

"Sure!"

"Would you believe it? Billy flew one of those fighter planes in Italy. Broke the color barrier flying planes."

"A *mensch* if there ever was one. Nick, remember when we came back on the Queen Mary?"

"Yeah and passing the Lady in the Bay. I could've kissed her feet." Nick laughed a little. "And our ship packed like my father's favorite fish." They both laughed. "Speaking of fathers, I accidentally ran into yours before I left."

"Are you kidding me?"

"Not when it comes to Mr. Fein. See, your father apologized for all the grief he caused me. Said he never should have interfered. The funny thing was his not being pissed at you for leaving. My mom made many signs of the cross as I walked out the door."

Nathan placed his arm around Nick's shoulder as they scoured the waters for dolphins, whales or any other creature with fins, giving a cheer even though they only saw drifting debris, neither of them giving a damn what the other passengers thought.

"Like old times, Nick," Nathan said.

"Yeah, like old times, Nate."

After a week on the ocean, they arrived at Gothenburg, continuing on their journey by ferry, then a patchwork of connecting trains till they caught the last one from Rome to Assisi. *Padre* Esposito was waiting for them at the station and, after an emotional greeting, the friar drove them in a Fiat 500 to the monastery where they had stayed during the war. After they washed up, the three of them ate a supper of *salsiccia all'uva* prepared by the two mysterious monks, including asparagus, new potatoes and rosemary from their own garden, accompanied with a chilled bottle of Orvieto Classico. Afterwards, they drank *espresso* and nibbled on good chocolate from Perugia and the conversation picked up.

"I'm so happy to see you boys again. I never thought I would live to see this day."

Brother Ginepro walked in from the garden with dirt on his forehead and stopped at the dining table.

A smile stretched across his face as the two *Americani* jumped up and hugged him. Nick spoke affectionately in *l'italiano* with *Fra'* Ginepro for a while before he picked up the plates and joined the other monks in the kitchen.

"You have something else on your mind, Nathan. *È vero*."

"It's great seeing you again, *Padre*, but you're right. There's someone else."

"I hope you have not come on this journey for nothing, but Mother Abbess urged me to contact you. The nuns convinced Rachele to leave the convent, but they wanted her to be in a transitional place. So she could adjust herself to the outside world she ran away from. The psychiatrist, Antonio Russo, is well-respected in the field and took on Rachele's case."

"*Capisco, Padre*."

"The breakthrough came when she mentioned your name. Weaving it into conversation at odd times, *il dottore* could see a visible change in her. He observed his treatment in the garden setting causing a stimulus for this sudden emotional well-being or …" *Padre* grinned. "He witnessed a *miracolo*, despite his being an atheist."

"Well, *Padre*, I'm not much of a believer myself, but there must be something to Rachele repeating my name."

"Let us pray so, for it seems the two of you lost something the last time you were here." *Padre* Esposito studied their expressions, while Nathan had listened intently. "In the morning I will drive you to the *villa*.

Nicolo can amuse himself in our beautiful village or hike in the countryside. *Allora*, let's have some *limoncello*. It was made right here at our monastery."

The next morning Nathan set out from Assisi with *Padre* Esposito, driving an hour to Gubbio through the foothills of Umbria. It was early June and the heat of the sun was getting stronger, allowing the sunflowers to grow taller in the fields, while along the road, yellow pansies and lavender were sprouting and marking the route. Nathan periodically glanced at his watch, as they spoke of the weather and the growing season, and encouraged the Franciscan monk to stick with Mother Nature for conversation. Nathan was anxious about meeting Rachele and hoped that her progress was real.

They arrived in the mountain village while the weekly outdoor market was still active with wooden stands that displayed pots and pans, cheese, spices, lines of women's blouses and leather wallets. *Padre* Esposito couldn't resist and insisted they look for a bargain. Nathan indulged the monk since he wanted to delay things. As they browsed around the market, Nathan left the *Padre* for a short stroll around the 2,500-year-old Gubbio with its green mountainside as a backdrop to gray stone houses flanking a stream. It wasn't long before he looked at his watch and retraced his path to the miniature car just as a smiling *Padre* Esposito returned with some bags of red pepper flakes and oregano, their smell hovering in the air. The father drove another fifteen minutes on a circuitous road and then onto a dirt road with hairpin curves.

They got out of the *Cinque Cento* and meandered up to the *villa*, which had burnt siena stucco walls and a roof of weathered tiles that had lost most of their reddish-orange color. There were clay pots scattered around filled with geraniums that were beginning to bud.

"This is the place where Rachele has been living. What do you think, Nathan?"

"It's very lovely, *Padre*."

"*Si, molto tranquilla*! The *Padre* smiled. "I have some business to take care of with a local priest. I'll pick you up later." He gripped Nathan's hand. "*Buona fortuna*!"

Nathan waved to the *Padre* as he drove away and realized he would be better off handling this by himself. He combed his hair, took a deep breath and lifted the brass knocker, hesitating a moment before letting it bang. Within a minute a chubby woman dressed in a white apron appeared and let Nathan in, urging him to sit on a wooden bench while she called the psychiatrist. He squeezed his fingers over his eyebrows until he was called in.

"*Signor* Nathan Fein, *prego*, sit down and make yourself comfortable." The psychiatrist looked down at a thick folder and flipped to the back, reading a few lines to himself. "*Mi scusi*, I was just checking something. Rachele Stein is the lone survivor of her family, all of whom perished in Buchenwald. She still has unresolved guilt, a lingering shame. But we have made great progress with Rachele in the last two months. I have been successful before using my methods, mainly based on changing the environment of the patient into one that is totally tranquil, a bucolic garden if you will. I try to center on the individual, slowly moving Rachele out of the patient context, gaining her trust and more importantly, her confidence in herself. Am I moving too fast, *Signor* Fein?"

"No, go ahead. You can call me Nathan."

"It has been difficult to retrieve the happy moments of her childhood because they invariably lead to her immediate past. But I did make some headway. The seeds of her breakthrough, I believe, may have started during her time in the convent. She adored the nuns, who not only saved her life but also treated her like their adopted daughter. It wasn't long before your name came up. I could see in her face a warmth I had not noticed before. I thought to myself: *I must try and find this young man*. And so here you are. *Grazie* for listening patiently, Nathan." The doctor gazed at Nathan as if he were looking right through him.

"Dr. Russo, to be honest, I'm very nervous."

"There is nothing to fear, Nathan." The doctor smiled thinly.

"You don't understand. I am not worried about myself." He paused to look out the window where he could see a row of peach trees blooming. "I'm afraid she'll get worse if she sees me."

"No doubt you must have loved her; otherwise you would not have traveled so far. Instead of thinking of the two of you as a failed relationship, consider the possibility of renewal."

"Will I be able to reason with her?"

"Nathan, I am not a gypsy fortune-teller, but if you are successful in communicating with her from the beginning, in time we may liberate Rachele from her pain enough so that maybe she'll get on with her life. The only advice I have is to be *calma* and pay attention to her facial expressions, especially her eyes. Don't expect elegant words of recognition. Let me take you to her. *Andiamo*!"

Dr. Russo locked arms with Nathan and the two went out the side door to the garden, where the psychiatrist dropped him off by a curved stone bench that faced Rachele. She sat on a cushioned wicker chair facing a flowerbed of white and red azaleas. She gave a tight smile towards the doctor, flattening her black dress out over her knees, as Nathan eased his way onto his seat. There was an awkward moment of silence, broken by a warning call from a turtledove that landed on a fountain, trickling a tiny stream of water.

"Do you recognize me, Rachele?"

"Nathan?"

"So you remember me."

"*Si*. You have come far."

"Yes, but I had company. Nick. Do you remember him?"

"*Si*, the name sounds familiar but I'm not sure. *Aspetta*! The good looking one!"

Nathan looked away for a moment, tapping his foot.

"Have you seen Caterina?" Rachele smiled and Nathan fidgeted on the stone. He grasped the side of the bench with both hands. "The two of them were an item."

"*Non capisco*!"

"You know, a couple of lovebirds."

She smiled in recognition but her eyes drifted towards the turtledove that was bathing in the fountain.

"Do you recognize me, Rachele?"

"*Si*, you are that young, American soldier who visited me many times in the convent. A long time ago."

"Nathan F …"

"I know your name. I'm not crazy."

"I didn't mean to insinuate such a thing. My buddy, Nick, sometimes he thinks I'm *pazzo*."

"You must be, if you traveled all the way from wherever you came just to see me."

"San Francisco. The good old USA."

"Where is your uniform?"

"Oh, I'm out of the service. Going to college now. Graphic arts."

"Then why are you here? Shouldn't you be spending all your time learning from the *maestri*?"

"You're right, but you see, I just came here on a lark. I mean a chance. I mean I wanted to see you one more time."

"You have come a long way, so I do not want to be *brutta figura. Capisci*, a bad impression, but I am feeling tired."

"*Bene*! I'll go now. *Padre* Esposito will be wondering what happened to me." Nathan stood up. "Will I be able to visit you again? I came a long way."

"It is not like anyone wants to see me, except *Dottor* Russo. I am not in control here."

'You've more presence than you give yourself credit for." Nathan smiled at her. "*Ciao*, Rachele." He shook her hand, which was damp and limp.

"*Addio*, *Signor* Fein."

Rachelle walked deeper into the garden, turned her head towards Nathan, then continued on. Dr. Russo, smoking a cigarette by the back door of the *villa*, invited Nathan back to his study and ushered him in.

"*Prego*, Nathan." Dr. Russo motioned towards the leather chair and took out a notebook. "So, how did you find our Rachele?"

"To be honest, *Dottore*, I found her very tense but that's not going to stop me."

"You obviously have feelings for the girl and it is important that Rachele knows this." The doctor circled something in his notebook. "She needs a connection to someone other than myself or the nuns."

"Does that mean you think we should continue with these meetings?"

"This country garden setting is very helpful for the recovery of my patients. They can sometimes drag up their darkest times and reach epiphanies for themselves. And yet, they need what all so-called sane people want—companionship, even if it is just one human being." The doctor looked out the window and then turned to Nathan. "Umbria has a way of bewitching people to remain. The only Italian region untouched by the sea. *Allora*, you'll have another reason to stay here."

"As long as she agrees to it, I'll do anything you say." Nathan stood up. "It's hard to explain my feelings, Dr. Russo, but I do know I love her. It's funny …" Nathan shook his head. "But I can't articulate exactly why I do love her, so why would it be easier for Rachele to sort this thing out? But she did remember me despite all the stuff she went through during the war. Anyway, you thought it was significant enough to get in touch with me, right? So here I am."

They shook hands and Nathan met *Padre* Esposito outside. The monk drove him back to *San Damiano* where they met Nick in the garden.

"So how did it go, Nate?"

"She was acting somewhat strange but still looking beautiful."

"Give her some time to get used to you. That's all you can do."

"I don't know, Nick, but I'm going to keep trying until …" Nathan looked at his feet.

"You must have patience, young man," *Padre* Esposito added. "Remember! *Pazienza*, *pazienza*, *pazienza*. Keep chanting that to yourself."

"Easy enough for the both of you to say."

Nathan locked himself in his old cell of the monastery and refused to come out despite the repeated efforts of Nick and the friar. He felt as if his brain were about to erupt into one of its old seizures. He opened the window, knelt on a wooden chair, resting his right cheek on the cold stone, staring out at black hills and hoping the sensation would pass soon.

Nick, already disillusioned by Nathan's experience, wondered why they had bothered to make the voyage. He hiked up to the town and went to the best restaurant he could find. He ate a four-course meal by himself, savoring the smell of the food before each bite, trying to transport his body to a gastronomically safe haven. The halo effect lasted until he stepped into the monastery and acknowledged that one of things he hated most in the world was to dine by himself, recalling how Caterina first identified him to be American and not Italian, as he read and ate at the same time. Nick decided, since it was his buddy who got him in this predicament in the first place, he was prepared to break the door down and drag Nathan with him for their next meal.

In the morning, *Fra'* Ginepro slipped a note under Nathan's door. He read Dr. Russo's message, dressed and made it down to the dining room. He dunked a plain *cornetto* into his coffee, finishing both the pastry and coffee within minutes and hinted to Nick what his mission was. *Padre* Esposito was already waiting at the front door and the two of them took off in the *Cinque Cento.*

Rachele, wearing a pale yellow dress, was running her hand through the basin of the garden fountain when Nathan came into the circle. She didn't turn around but asked: "Nathan?"

"Yes, Nathan."

"Come closer. The dove left one of his feathers from yesterday's visit." She held it up to the light and turned around. She placed it into Nathan's hand and then sat in her chair. "*Prego*, sit down. You look like a butler, standing there."

Nathan relished her attempt at humor but remembered to stay *calma*. Anything could happen, he realized, so he sat and chattered about the beauty of the Umbrian landscape and how he should do some sketches. She was paying more attention to him than his discourse, or at least that's how he viewed it. It was as if Rachele were the first woman he had ever spoken to and that he had reverted to his awkward youth. Every word he uttered made him feel foolish. He gritted his teeth to block out his dark thoughts and hoped she was sweeping hers away.

The turtledove returned to the same spot and Rachele clapped.

"Persistent, nosey guy, wouldn't you say, Rachele?"

"Our little friend, nonetheless. St. Francis used to talk to the birds, and yet no one accused him of being crazy."

"You're right! It's a term that gets thrown about all the time, like curse words that have become common modifiers to every event that happens."

"You remind me of a *professore* from my university."

"Is that a compliment?"

"*Si, si*. He was very handsome, very intellectual." Nathan's cheeks flushed red. "I have gotten a reaction out of you." She laughed flippantly.

Nathan realized that he was acting more formal than Rachele, who was a young woman filled with all kinds of emotions that had been caged up like a canary for so long. During periods of silence, it seemed they transcended their positions in the garden. As he moved from one free association to the next, it hit Nathan like one of Dr. Russo's epiphanies—his feelings for Rachele were not about saving her, that would best be left for *il dottore* or the sisters. He loved her as a unique woman—the way she looked, her delicate spirit, and in some crazy way, that she was a female doppelganger for himself. Lost in thought, he imagined someone was talking to him until he realized Rachele had just repeated something to him.

"Nathan! I'm glad you have come ..." She rubbed the silk sash of her dress. "But my feelings still get jumbled."

"Nothing about you is jumbled for me." Sitting here for the second time, all his memories of them during the war flooded his mind. He had to remind himself how fragile Rachele was, just as Caterina had warned. He sat on the stone bench, more aware of its hard surface than what he should say next. Maybe she read his mind. It was funny that Rachele was content to sit near him without any words in this secluded garden. He thought it was about time he screwed up a little *mut*, after everything he had been through in Italy, show a little courage.

"I'll never leave you. Unless you insist I go home."

"What?"

"I promise to come here every day till things change."

"Too many words." She whispered: "I don't understand. *Non capisco. Ich verstehe nicht*!"

Nathan got up and dropped on his knees, holding her hands. "I love you! *Ti amo. Ich libe dich*."

She kissed his cheek and rose up. "I have to go now. Dr. Russo will be looking for me." She spun around and moved towards the French doors of the *villa*, while he stood there confounded. Rachele turned and pulled a postcard out of the pocket of her dress and extended it to him as he got closer. "Make sure you give this to Nick."

Nathan stuffed it into his shirt without looking at it. "Can I see you again, Rachele?"

"Tomorrow, Nathan."

As Nathan waited outside the *villa* for *Padre* Esposito, he prioritized his future plans—find a studio apartment in Gubbio, buy a Vespa and get an Italian tutor. He swore that he would wait forever, if he had to. He could hear the exhaust from the *Cinque Cento* approaching, and the lyrics of "It Had to Be You" from one of his 78s came to mind, which he hummed as he moved towards the car.

Late in the evening Nick took Nathan to the same *trattoria*, happy he wouldn't be dining alone. The owner of the family-run place welcomed them and they sat at a table with a view of the hills.

"Wait till you bite into the first morsel of food. *Paradiso*," Nick boasted while he twisted his index finger into the right cheek, as if to say: 'It's very good—*buonissimo*!'

"I can smell the truffles from the kitchen."

They ploughed through all the courses and two bottles of Orvieto Classico, ending with *grappa* from Bassano. They clinked glasses, bellowed "*Cent'anni*" and drank it down.

"*Dottor* Russo advised me to watch for the signs in her appearance, the way she holds onto things, the expression in her eyes."

"I gotta hand it to you. I don't think I would have the patience."

"It's our survival, Nick. I don't have to tell you our world has changed."

"That's for sure. You know, while we were eating, I noticed how you spoke about Rachele. It's like you're singing a melody from Irving Berlin, the Gershwin brothers and Cole Porter all rolled into one. I envy you, buddy."

"I've got something for you Nick." Nathan handed him a postcard.

"Great, I'll give this to my Pop. Loves collecting Italian stamps."

"*Cretino*, read who it's from."

Nick read all the way until he hit the signature, 'Caterina.' He placed the postcard on the table and pushed it over to Nathan. "I think one hunt for a missing person is enough, wouldn't you say, Nate?"

"What are you talkin' about? We know where she is now. She's on the island of Panarea."

"Never heard of it."

"Come on, Nick." He picked up the card, pointed

to the picture and placed it nearer to Nick. "It's part of the Sicilian islands, the *Isole Eolie.* You know the Aeolian Islands."

"Okay, I get it. The islands from Homer's *Odyssey.* So what?"

"Stop pulling my leg. You'd never find your old girlfriend in Rome, but now Rachele comes up with this postcard from Caterina." Nathan slapped his hand on it. "There's no return address but it's marked Panarea." He turned it over and touched the cancellation stamp. "Caterina left *Roma* for a small island."

"Good for her."

"What do I have to do, spell everything out for you, Nick?"

"Our relationship died with the war." Nick's eyes darkened. "Besides, why would she be interested in seeing me anyway?"

"For old times' sake. Isn't that good enough?"

"That's a helluva trip to go down memory lane. I'll have to pass on it."

"You know, I thought I didn't have the courage to tell Rachele how I feel about her, but when I look at you now, I think you're the one with no *coglione.*"

"I'm the Italian here, not you."

"No, you're wrong. A branch of my family is as Italian as yours, or have you forgotten?"

"Okay, you're a regular *paisan*. I'm not going anywhere. Besides, what's it to you?"

"I got to know Caterina better when you went off to get my cousin out of Venice. She's worth a journey."

He grabbed Nick's wrist. "Look, I'm indebted to you for what you did for Carlo." Nathan released his grip.

"You would have done the same for my *cuginu*."

"I got the gal all wrong. Caterina is one hell of a dame. Smart, good looking. When I was teaching her how to paint, her technique was poor at first, but she worked hard at it. She has the passion for it."

"You two seemed to hit off real well while I was gone."

"There you go again, tryin' to get out of something by cooking up *spuntini* filled with jealousy. Go where your heart is, *smuck*. Remember how I kept on cursing you out in several languages when you broke up with her."

"Couldn't hear you. Had the pillow over my head."

"Stop hiding your feelings. You can't bullshit me. Don't let her get away, will ya? If you do, you'll never forgive yourself for not trying. You were so close to something happening big in your life and you let it slip away. If she told you to go to hell, I can't say you wouldn't deserve it. But you're the best buddy a guy could have, so I'm not going to have it on my conscience that I didn't press you to go. You've got nothing to lose. Maybe you just want to sit by yourself in restaurants the rest of your life looking at the paintings on the wall or maybe just marry the first woman willing to put up with you."

"Stop getting under my skin!"

"No, you got it all wrong again. Caterina should be under your skin."

Nick felt Nate had just hit the nerve endings in his bad leg but didn't let on.

"You know something, Nick, with all the things that Rachele has gone through, she still remembered her good friend, Caterina. Maybe she can't articulate her feelings well, but I could see she was worried about Caterina when she handed me that postcard you tossed aside. And what about you, Nick? Aren't you at least curious as to what happened to her?" Nick's eyes watered up. "Don't do it for me, buddy, do it for yourself."

"*Signor, altro bicchiere di grappa per me e mio amico*," Nick called out and then turned to Nate. "Okay, okay. I'll go."

"Now you're talking, buddy. Tell the waiter to leave the bottle when he comes back. Who the hell cares if we wake up the monastery tonight?"

# XXV

The last ferry of the day from the Milazzo port docked at Panarea, the night sky aglow from the volcanic fire northeast on Stromboli. Nick wondered if he were entering *paradiso*, as other travelers liked to call the island. Or was it really a way station for that erupting island in the distance or the other one he passed, the southwesterly island of Vulcano, known for its sulfuric air marking its harbor? He headed for a brightly lit café on the southern edge of town, passing a few stores and a row of fishing boats lined up on the beach near the port of San Pietro. When he reached the place, he ascended the steps imbedded with black lava stones that led to a small *terrazzo* facing a group of tiny islands barely visible and Stromboli further up. He carried his gear in a hiker's backpack and dropped it on the floor under the outside lamp. The thud of his pack hitting the floor brought the café owner out onto the terrace. A man, who looked around fifty, observed Nick's attire before speaking.

"*Inglese, Signor*?"

"*No, Americano*."

"You have come a long way. *È veru*."

"*Si*. From San Francisco."

"I know about San Francisco." The owner smiled. "Big red bridge. I have a cousin there. Perhaps you know him?"

"It's a big place. *Come si chiama*?"

"*Giuseppe Randazzo, cuginu miu. Io sono Salvatore Randazzo*."

"Like I said, *molta genti*. Don't know any Randazzos."

Salvatore stroked his beard. "*Mancia*!"

"I'm not hungry. *Vorrei un caffé*."

"*Certu*."

The fireworks on Stromboli intensified while he waited for his *espresso*. Nick was alone on a mission that Nathan was surer of than he was. Not that he didn't want to see Caterina again, but after the way he disappeared from her life, his journey to reconnect was as perilous as bathing near the shoreline under a volcano, waiting for sizzling lava to slope down a path where it has been dropping for years, creating a whirling cauldron in the sea.

"*Ecculu, Signuri. Comu ti chiami*?"

"Nicolo Spataro."

"That name sounds *Sicilianu*."

"*Si*."

"You have returned home. It is in your blood."

"I'm not sure why I am here. I just need a place to stay."

"I have a room available upstairs. It is not expensive."

"*Grazii*, Salvatore." Nick sipped the last drop of *espresso* and followed Salvatore to his new room. He placed his backpack on a chair and settled on the bed without taking his clothes off. He couldn't sleep and got up to look through the casement windows. After opening them wide, he could still see the volcano smoldering away, leaving steamy puffs of smoke obliterating the skyline. He went back to bed and fell into a deep sleep filled with a dream that he would not choose to recall in the morning, when he awoke with a soaked undershirt. But he could not stop the flashback to the ferryman who had asked Nick for payment to get off at an unfamiliar island. He dug deep into his pockets, then rifled though his backpack and came up with nothing, while the ferryman seem to loom larger over him with each second. As the ferry moved backwards from the dock, the ferryman's mouth extended so wide while he yelled for his money, Nick thought he would be devoured at any moment. He begged the ferryman to understand his situation but was catapulted into the sea. He swam, smashing his arms and legs on the water's surface towards the sole light in the pitch-blackness, a fire at the summit of another island, while a shark's fin sliced the water in a decreasing circle around him. He changed strokes to those of a synchronized swimmer, hoping to fool his stalker while mumbling every saint's name he could think of, as well as every permutation of Mother Mary's name.

At breakfast inside the café, Nick watched some of the villagers stop by for a *caffé* and a *cornetto*, chattering in Sicilian, Italian, or a combination of both. He lost himself in the banter of the morning regulars. When the café got quiet, Salvatore sat down next to Nick.

"Did you have a good rest?"

"I slept, but not peacefully."

"Your backpack is gone and yet it seems you still have a weight on your shoulders. Another Atlas."

"I carry more than a myth but I'm not seeking solace."

"*Mi dispiaci*, my nature is to be *simpaticu*."

"Well, maybe you can help me. I'm looking for someone."

"*Una bella donna*." Salvatore laughed. "We men are always looking for one."

"Okay, if you don't want to help."

"*No Signuri Nicolo*. I was just having a little fun."

"Just call me Nick."

"Whatever you say, Mr. Nick."

"I'm searching for a Caterina. Her last name is Rossetto. She is a *Milanese*. Met her in *Roma*."

"Ah, you must be very careful how you treat such a woman."

"You don't know her."

"*Tu sì giustu ma … Allura*, she is not from here. That's all I can tell you."

"Are you sure?"

"I have lived here my whole life and know everyone and everything. And whatever I don't know, someone will gossip to me before long. There are always some *scanusciuti* here, *è veru*, looking for something, but no Caterina. Who knows, maybe she snuck in when I was away? Why don't you take a hike on the road and find a beach to walk on? You can throw your troubles to our winds." Salvatore raised his right forearm, palm open and slowly lowered it. "I'll ask around if there is *da donna mistiriusa* from *Milano, Roma, et cetera.* We can talk when you come back for *pranzu.*"

As Nick strolled east along the narrow trail, he passed by houses hidden by whitewashed walls, some with purple bougainvillea clinging to them, the sea revealing itself unexpectedly. He discovered a small church, *Chiesa San Pedro.* There was no one inside and he lit a candle in front of the saint's statue. He made the sign of the cross and stepped out the door. The sun blurred his vision, as if a sign that his search would be futile. He continued on and found a beach on the cove of *Zimmari.* Nick took off his boots and socks and carried them, as he ran through the red sand in slow motion to confirm that he belonged on *terra firma.* When he came to the end of the cove, he sat on a rock, dropping his footwear, to have a smoke and enjoy the unspoiled setting, but there was no one to share the moment with. Within minutes a shooting pain began from his right calf and wrapped around his lower leg, clamping it like an alley cat sinking its sectorial teeth into a hapless mouse. He limped to the edge of the water, rolled up his pants and waded up to his knees. The cold water shocked the heat in his leg. Before returning to his rocky seat, he scooped several handfuls of muddy sand and smeared it over the sore leg. He lowered himself onto the rock, as the throbbing subsided.

As Nick stared at the Tyrrhenian Sea, he rationalized that this business of being alone wasn't such a big deal, until Caterina morphed into this watery scene and remembrances of her floated around the undulating sea, memories that he had tried to wash away when he returned to San Francisco. When the sound of the surf brought him back to the present, Nick rubbed the caked mud off, unrolled his pants gingerly and put his socks and boots on. He returned to the café, picking up the pace in anticipation of what Salvatore might have found out. The salty air invigorated him and, as he passed the tiny church again, he wondered why he had not seen or heard the chatter of birds, a sign of bad luck as far as he was concerned.

When Nick got back to the café, he sat at the same table on the *terrazzo* and watched the movement of fishing boats and the scheduled ferries docking. Salvatore brought out an *espresso* for Nick, assuming he would need a late morning jolt. He placed the cup down and smiled, but Nick continued peering at the sea.

"*Bon giornu*, Mr. Nick. How did your hike go?"

"*Va beni.* Did you learn anything from your *paisani*?"

"*Mi dispiaci. Nenti*!" Salvatore rubbed his beard. "Perhaps something will turn up."

Nick drank his *espresso* to the bottom and walked into the rear of the café to find the *bagno*. As he approached the door, there was an *occupato* sign on the lock mechanism. To kill some time, he moseyed around the middle of the café admiring plates with a sage green, yellow and blue design displayed on a shelf. He turned one around and saw it was crafted in Caltigirone. On the opposite side he noticed a painting in an alcove that would normally have had a statue of a saint. He moved closer to get a better look. The rendering was of a fountain, which reminded him of the one in *Piazza Madonna dei Monti*. His eyes ran over the canvas and led to the right corner where he saw a name scribbled.

"Salvatore, *veni cca*," Nick shouted, while Salvatore finished rinsing a glass.

"What's all the fuss?"

"It's signed Caterina. The last name starts with an R and trails off. I thought you said there was no one on this island with that name."

Salvatore looked up to the ceiling. "*Si*, a woman who is new to Panarea gave it to me to hang on the wall." He looked back at Nick. "Said it was on loan for a while. She advised me to fill all the walls with local artists. *Ma chi sacciu*? But what do I know? She laughed at me for being *rusticu*, not knowing how to attract tourists." Nick just wanted to know who dropped the painting off. In exasperation, he extended his right hand palm down, opening and closing four fingers on his thumb, but Salvatore ignored him. "Telling me my place needed to look like the bohemian cafés in *Roma*. So to keep her happy, after all, she is very attractive, *marone*, her breasts ..."

"*Pregu*, who is she?"

"Her first name is Isabella. That is all I know."

"Caterina had a friend named Isabella." Nick tapped his forehead. "*Allura*, what else can you tell me?"

"Isabella came here six months ago and rented a *villa* beyond *Chiesa San Pedro*."

"I went by the church this morning."

"There is a small child. A boy. They hardly ever leave the *villa*. My nephew, Giovanni, sometimes runs errands for them. If you wish, I'll get him. You would need him to lead you, as the *villa* è *molto difficili* to find."

"*Pregu*, it is my only lead."

"I'll make you a light *pranzu*, *insalata di mare. Va beni*?"

"*Grazii*, Salvatore." Nick ran off to the bathroom.

The next morning Nick trailed several steps behind Salvatore's nephew who looked unhappy that he had to play guide, as the boy strode down the trail, just wide enough to fit a *camioncino*. Before they reached San Pedro, the boy deviated left on a path, motioning Nick to follow. It was a trail that one person could fit on, winding down an incline. The nephew stopped at a lookout spot and pointed to the *villa* and said, "*Dda*" and then took off leaving Nick by himself.

The path widened as Nick got closer to the *villa* and he chose a hidden vantage point behind a group of prickly pear cactuses where he could see who came in and out. He was thirsty and drank some *acqua minerale* from a thermos while he waited. A red heron landed on the outside wall of the *villa* that was covered with purple bougainvillea. The bird had lighted its long body on the top of the wall, made no sound, then flew away. He thought for sure this was a sign and decided to stay as long as it took to see the *signora* who had dropped the painting off.

Nick munched on some *biscotti* that Salvatore had stuffed in his shirt picket. He dropped the biscuit when the door opened and saw a woman who held a small boy by the hand. She looked familiar to him. The sun was in his eyes and he rubbed them, as he struggled to get a better view of her as she climbed up past him. This was the same Isabella he had met in Assisi, but her curly, black hair was cut much shorter. Perspiration lined his neck at the thought that Caterina was likely to follow, but the door remained shut. He tracked Isabella and the boy into the village, keeping back so far that he could have lost her because he feared she might recognize and interrogate him. If Nick could be unnerved by Isabella's presence, he couldn't imagine how he would react if he ran into Caterina.

That night he opened the window to his room to observe the nature show that took place each night. There were billows of smoke emanating from the cone of Stromboli and the star patterns were murky. He could hear the sound of the surf that beat on the shore below his window. He figured since he had come this far, then the least he could do was approach Isabella. There would be no harm in that. He saw the outline of a pair of birds in a channel of water, and judging by their beaks, he thought they were red herons. He wondered if one of them had been the visitor on the *villa* wall, keeping a watchful eye on him. He undressed to his boxers and white undershirt and stretched himself out on the bed, waiting for sleep to come.

The following morning, encouraged by Salvatore, he set out for the *villa* again. He reached his destination much faster than he expected and hesitated before knocking, cleaning the dust from his boots on the back of his dungarees. A middle-aged woman in a pastel housedress came to the door, opened it half way and questioned Nick's presence at the *villa*. He waited like one of those undertakers who stands at the center of the funeral home, directing mourners to the viewing room with an expression that belies emotion—mulling over how he should act if Caterina were to materialize in front of him after all this time. Or maybe he was already dead of emotion lying in the casket, and near him a faux night table with a photo of Caterina and him and some funeral holy cards of his patron saint stamped on it.

Nick overheard a woman's voice from another room, allowing him to follow the housekeeper onto the *terrazzo*, where he busied himself watching a sailboat heading south towards the island of Vulcano. A cool breeze blew under the tent-like structure that he stood under. The *signora* of the *villa* entered with a boy who hid behind her.

"*Buongiorno, signore. Mi dispiace per mia governante di casa.*"

"*Buongiorno, signora. Forse, è migliore noi parliamo in l'inglese.*" Nick tilted his head towards the child.

"*No problema*. That's my son, Nicolo." Nick's face whitened at the sound of his own name. The boy ran circles around the two of them. "Maria! Maria!"

The housekeeper appeared at the entrance to the *terrazzo*. "*Si, Signora*."

"*Maria, prenda adesso bambino mio alla spiaggia, per favore. Anche abbiamo bisogno di granita limone qui*."

"*Subito, signora*." Maria took the child by the hand and left.

"Isabella?" Nick asked.

"I'm Isabella, *Signore*," she said straight-faced. "And I remember you. News travels fast here on Panarea."

"Then you're Caterina's friend," he said, trying to read her impression of him.

"*Si*. Why are you here?"

"I'm such a *cretino*."

Isabella laughed while she responded: "No, you are not an idiot."

"I'm looking for Caterina."

"That has become a big problem for you. I can see it in your face."

Maria came in with the *granita* and set it down on the table, the child calling for her to hurry up to take him to the beach.

"Have some *granita di limone, Nicolo*. Maria made it this morning. It is very refreshing." They devoured the slushy, semi-frozen lemon ice that was both sweet and slightly sour. When they finished scooping the remains, Nick sensed Isabella was uncomfortable, assuming it was some bad news about Caterina, so he changed the discussion to what he thought was a safer topic.

"Where's Carlo?" Isabella seemed distant. "Have you heard from him since the war ended?"

"I'm happy you remembered Carlo Moretto." She looked at her sandaled feet.

"How could I forget? Helped Nathan's cousin get out of Venice."

"Then you remember that Caterina set me up with Carlo at a café in Assisi."

"*Si.*"

"So where's Carlo?"

Isabella face turned ashen. "I'm sorry to tell you *ma Carlo è morto*!"

"Oh Christ." Nick's eyes reddened. "After everything we went through."

"He promised he'd come back to me. But Carlo has never left me." She slapped a hand on her breast.

"I am very sorry to hear this, Isabella. Nathan will be devastated. You remember him, don't you?"

"*Si*, the one who was devoted to my university friend, Rachele." A tear ran black as her mascara melted on her face. "I have already shed many tears for Carlo. To tell the truth …" She stopped to wipe most of the black line away. "We never had a chance to marry. As you know, he went off to fight with the Jewish Brigade. Carlo became an infantryman for the British Army. They fought the Germans on the Northern Italian Front." Isabella rubbed her eyes and

Nick sat closer to her as she continued. "He died on April 13, 1945 at the Battle of the Argenta Gap, near the Po River." She crossed herself. "Hit by the last of the German artillery shells. When I wrote to him before he died that I was with child, he swore he would return to Assisi and marry me. He thought we should name the child, Nicolo, after you, if we had a son."

"I am honored." They both stayed quiet for a while. "So how did you wind up here of all places?"

"Carlo had instructed Don Ca Botto to leave whatever was left from his family estate to me and his child. So we would avoid the poverty so many Italians now face. All because of the *fasciste*." She mimicked spitting on the floor. "You mentioned Nathan before. Where is he now?"

"We came back to Italy together. He's staying with *Padre* Esposito and visits Rachele every day at *Dottor* Russo's *villa*. Somewhere in Gubbio."

"Is there hope for my friend?"

"It's hard to say but Nathan is determined to go all the rounds of this fight. He's the one who showed me Caterina's postcard to Rachele, postmarked from this island." He handed her the card and Isabella smiled as she looked at it. "How did you come by Caterina's painting that's hanging in Salvatore's café?"

"Caterina gave it to me as a going away present, but I felt that her work should be appreciated by others, hopefully some wealthy, foreign tourists."

"I see." Nick lowered his eyes. "So what do you do to keep yourself busy on Panarea, besides running after little Nicolo?"

"I am working on folk pottery of *Isole Eolie* or *Isuli Eoli*, as the Sicilians would say."

"*Bravo*, I am jealous of your endeavor."

"*E tu*?"

"I'm studying American Literature at San Francisco State College, not far from where I live." Nick paused and stared at Isabella. "*Ma adesso*, I am looking for Caterina."

"I know she'll be angry with me for telling, but Caterina is right under your nose, Nick. You see, two months ago, Caterina asked if she could stay with me for a while. She wanted to work on her painting and I have a little guesthouse just below my *villa* near the water. I knew it would be perfect for her. Naturally I agreed. She is there right now."

"*Mille grazie*, but I don't know what I should do."

"You men are all the same. When it comes to sex, you are very aggressive, and when it comes to love, you are always conflicted. If you love Caterina, you must fight for her just like Nathan is doing as we speak. You must face *il tuo destino*."

It was a warm, sunny day and Nick wiped the sweat off his brow with a white handkerchief and trailed Isabella down to the water. In the distance Nick could see the rocks jutting from a cluster of islets and further north the fuming Stromboli. The one-room guesthouse walls were whitewashed and two bright red bougainvillea plants climbed the stucco and crowned the top of the front door. There were patches of yellow hibiscus plants, some buds already full and waiting to open up. Isabella knocked on the door and entered the artist's studio. Nick heard Caterina yelling at Isabella, who came out of the guesthouse with her hands over her ears.

"Go around to the back where it faces the sea and find yourself a chair. If you're patient enough, she may have a few words with you. *Buona fortuna, Nicolo*!"

After an hour, Caterina, wearing a cotton dress the same hue as the bougainvillea, broke through the light blue beads that led to the terrace. She stood there for a while, her brow and lips pursed, brown hair streaked lighter from the sun and braided down her back. She sized Nick up and down. The way she glared at him reminded him that she had every right to despise him.

"Caterina, is it really you?"

"Why are you here?"

"I had to see you again."

"*Bene*, you have seen me, so now you can go back to North Beach."

Nick got out of his chair and walked up to her. Her face lacked any expression. "You don't understand, Caterina. Things have changed since our days in *Roma*."

"*Si*, you state the obvious."

"Can't we at least talk for old time's sake?"

"*Pezzo di merde*! I hate you."

"I am sorry. *Mi dispiace*!"

"Meaningless words! You walked out on me. Never even wrote me a postcard."

"I'm sorry."

"You said that already."

"We can't undo things of the past. We just have to get on with out lives. I just thought ..."

"I'm going inside now."

The beads crackled in his ears as she left. Nick trekked up to the *villa* and spoke with Isabella who tried to console him. He returned to the café and Salvatore took one look at him and gave him a glass of *grappa* and left him to sort things out on the *terrazza.* Nick could hear laughter from the café, as Salvatore spun a few stories in between serving his customers.

"Salvatore! Salvatore!" The owner came out wiping his hands on his waist apron.

"Mr. Nick, you sound upset."

"I need a sailboat. Do you have one?"

"*Certu.* I let you borrow mine. It's right over there." Salvatore pointed to its mooring. "You can sail?"

"My father taught me a long time ago. *Grazii.*"

"Good luck fishing." Salvatore laughed and went into the café.

Nick checked the seaworthiness of the sloop, examining the lines, halyards and sheets. Everything was secure, so early next morning he picked up a few provisions for the day at the *alimentari*, loaded up and set sail due south. The morning brought the salty-sweet smell of the sea, the wind billowing the sails, the Sicilian sun warming his face and the breeze tossing his hair. The cry of seagulls followed him part of the way. He never felt more alive than at this moment distancing himself from that Calypso-like island he left behind. The *canto* of the sails transformed him, while the lines hummed and the sales flapped, the water slapping the wooden sides and spraying his face. This heightened sensation suspended all memory and Nick lost himself in the exploration of the two islands that diagonally bookended Panarea.

His father had taught him well and he handled the tiller and adjusted the sails with aplomb. He laughed aloud at himself for succumbing to the gloomy clouds of his life when all he had to do was set sail alone, wherever the winds took him. *Minchia*, he was happy to be alive after all that happened. He didn't need anyone to fulfill his life as long as he could breathe the fresh air that emanated around him. Without any perception of time, these thoughts repeated themselves again and again. What shocked Nick out of his revverie was his sense of smell, his nostrils and eyes wide open to the odor of rotten eggs. He carefully tacked his sails, then switched on the inboard engine, gliding into the port of Vulcano and tying up the boat, as it bobbed in the sea.

Nick followed a road past the hissing and fuming of sulfur coming out of the ground and came across the mud baths of *Laghetto di Fanghi* where he paid the attendant a few liras to enter the natural site. There was no one there so he had no inhibition about stripping naked to bathe in the pale brown, hot mud, rich with minerals. After immersing himself, he meditated for 15 minutes. He got out and was amazed there was not even a tingle of pain in his right leg. He stepped over to the nearby beach and washed himself off in the warm, spring-fed blue sea. Later, he bought a bottle of *acqua minerale naturale* and carefully hiked up to the rim of the *Gran Catere*, clouds of sulfurous gas in the air and within an hour made it to the top for a spectacular view of the Aeolians as far as Stromboli, then returned the same way to his sailboat heading northeast for that other fiery island.

After hours on the sea, Nick went ashore on Stromboli, detecting the power of the volcano as his feet touched land. He meandered around the rocky shoreline until he saw a man in his early thirties examining rocks and placing one in a sample bag. He moved closer to him and discerned he was British, judging by his safari hat and khaki shorts with knee-high socks. He smiled thinking that no self-respecting Italian, especially a Southern one, would be caught dead wearing pants only fit for children.

"*Tu sei inglese, no*?" Nick asked.

"Right you are, English!"

"I'm American sailing around the archipelago. Nick Spataro." He offered his hand and the Englishman cranked it.

"Nigel Dickens, no relation." He grinned like a Cheshire cat. "Sailing round the Tyrrhenian sea, is it? Lovely idea. Would like to do that myself. But as you see I'm quite busy with these volcanic rocks. The magma ejects all kinds of interesting forms. So what made you stop here at the 'Lighthouse of the Mediterranean'?"

"Can't say I'm much interested in rocks and minerals. But I do find watching the eruptions exciting from Panarea, where I'm staying. You know, smoke and fire spurting. Lava spilling."

"Ah, you like the fire and brimstone," Nigel said laughing while Nick grinned.

"First time to Sicily?"

"No. I first came during the American invasion of southeastern Sicily."

"Blimey, I was there too. Engineering unit under Montgomery. And you?"

"Tank destroyer squadron, Paton. But if you don't mind, I'd rather not talk about it." Nick pursed his lips.

"Right you are. No point to it now. We have to get on with it."

"Are you doing academic research or exploring for a mining company?"

"On a grant from Oxford to study the effects of surface change over time. No doubt you Yanks might find all this boring."

"Everybody has to follow their own stars."

"I see. You like all those dreamy things. Are you a writer of sorts?"

"Nah, but I am majoring in American Lit."

"A man after my own heart. Can't get enough of your American English, as they call it. Always changing, not like our stuffy British English, but then again we do have Shakespeare. And Dickens, of course." They both laughed.

"I just met you and you're making me laugh."

"We all have to laugh at ourselves, don't you think? Can't take yourself too seriously. Life's too short, right mate?" He slapped Nick on the shoulder.

"Seize the moment."

"There you go. That good ole American can-do spirit. Well, I guess I better continue with my work. Jolly good money to play with my rocks." Nick laughed again. "Better be heading back for Panarea before it gets dark. Never can tell on the sea."

"It was fun chatting with you. Look for me at the café in Panarea, if you get bored playing with your *coglione.*"

"Ah, I knew there was some Italian in you, Nick Spataro."

"And some Dickens character in you, Nigel Dickens."

Nick smiled and Nigel chortled as they shook hands. He returned to the sailboat, floating out of the safe inlet. He headed out about a mile when all of sudden a charcoal fog swept in out of nowhere, closing in from all sides. He found himself moving much faster that he would have preferred, as if being pushed by unknown currents that crisscrossed at different times. There were eight islands as far as he knew, so if he happened to run aground on one of them, Nick hoped his body wouldn't be splintered up like the boat.

Nick realized he had drifted away from the archipelago, considering the time he was already out on the sea. Then the first bolt of lightning struck, crashing on the horizon with howling wind and a rising sea, and thunder afar cracking out booms, closer and closer, which brought him back to Salerno when he first heard the Acht-achts, those horrible eight-eight shells, pounding incessantly. Sweat was pouring out of his sulfurous smelling body, till one of those electric bolts hit dead center at the main mast, causing Nick to lose control of the boat and tossing him and everything else around. When the boom swung low and swift at his head, he was slammed on the deck like he had been thrown by a deep-chested wrestler and knocked unconscious. It was as if Nick entered an abyss where he spiraled down around an upside-down cone trapped in a dark cavern, everything locked up like Houdini in the Chinese Water Torture Cell, but no chance for Nick to squeeze his way out.

The following afternoon the sailboat had drifted back into the waters of the Aeolian archipelago. Salvatore, standing on the deck of an Italian Coast Guard craft cruising at maximum speed, spotted his sailboat. The crew members got Nick aboard the boat and a medical team revived him, as Salvatore hovered over Nick's sun burnt face and assured his friend that he would be okay, while they bandaged his skull, trying to ascertain the severity of the concussion. A coordinated team set up a bridle to tow the sloop and then the helmsman cruised to Panarea. By the time they got back, the entire village was huddled by the dock with Isabella at the front. With Salvatore in the lead, the medical team carried Nick on a stretcher to the café where the local doctor waited.

Isabella followed on the side the stretcher. "*Madonna*, thank God you are still alive. I don't think

I could take another death." Her son grabbed onto the stretcher as he walked with Isabella, while Nick winked at the boy and glanced at Isabella.

"It all started with Vulcano, the gateway to hell. Thought I was done for."

"*Basta* with these dark thoughts." She crossed herself. "You have everything to live for."

Nick squinted his eyes and said: "*Grazie Isabella. Tu sei molto gentile.*" While they were entering Salvatore's place, Isabella noticed Caterina, who watched from the top of the incline on the road leading to the *villa*. Isabella waved to her friend who turned away, walking back to her hideaway.

* * *

A week later in the early evening, Nick sat in the café having an *espresso* when a notion popped up as if he had just come out of a drowsy daydream. "Salvatore! Salvatore!"

"*Mannaggia,* Nick. I am not your *Mamma.*"

"One more request."

"No sailboat."

"I need your rowboat."

"Tsk, tsk, tsk, Nick. You are breaking my balls now. No boats for you. *Nenti*!"

"I swear I'll only take it to Isabella's *villa.*"

"You mean you want to find Caterina."

"I didn't say that exactly."

"If you want to play Rodolfo Valentino, *in bocca al lupo*. But don't wreck my boat. *Capisci*?"

"I promise."

"You are one mixed up *Sicilianu Americanu.* It's a good thing for you, Mr. Nick, that I like you. So go ahead and make a fool of yourself. I know about these things when it comes to women."

That evening Nick hugged the coastline of Panarea south past San Pedro, gliding into a small cove. He could see Caterina's guesthouse lit up and rowed near the tiny rocky beach in front and anchored the boat. The volcano on Stromboli shot out a volley of sparks on this very clear evening. The stars lit up the sky in a panorama of clusters. He played the waiting game because, on such a beautiful night, she was sure to venture outside. A half hour later, he heard the beads rustle and Caterina stepped out onto the *terrazza.* She wore a blue sarong, its color picked up off the string of lights on the perimeter. She hadn't noticed Nick as her eyes followed the fire from the volcano.

"Caterina." His voice echoed across the water. She spied him in the boat.

"Go back to your parents. You are ruining this night for me."

Nick stood up. "I'm not leaving this spot until you ask me to come ashore."

"For what? Some Romeo and Juliet scene where we both wind up dead."

"Do you want to hear the truth?"

"Talk is cheap."

"Since I left you, my feelings have been out of kilter. It's like motion sickness on a boat but time hasn't cured me. *È vero, sono un cretino.* When I returned home, there was no faithful Penelope waiting for me."

"That's your problem, not mine." The volcano was smoldering gray puffs, as the fire died down.

"See the constellations out there?"

Caterina looked at the sky. "*Allora*, I see the Pleiades very clearly. Perhaps this is a good omen for you? Didn't you tell me what a good sign it was supposed to be when we were in *Roma*? All lies, you tell me! Then like your stars you vanished without warning. I suppose you would call it a natural phenomena."

"Nature is unpredictable and I learned it the hard way."

"What were you doing out there anyway, trying to kill yourself?"

"It was just bad luck, Caterina."

"On second thought, no. You're too narcissistic. The sympathy game suits you better."

"If sympathy works with you, that's okay with me."

"You men just want to win all the time. Ride out any storm, defy the flow of lava."

"Maybe so, Caterina. I already proved to myself that you can't stop nature's power. But there's one thing you shouldn't stop ..."

"Words and more words."

"Shouldn't stop the natural power of the heart, even if it sounds corny."

Caterina retreated to her house, the beads crackling in the night air. The lights went out and Nick sat down again, stationed on a darkened sea, the volcano leaving a wind-blown ash cloud on the horizon. He turned away from the house and lay back in the middle of the boat to gaze at the stars, propping the small of his back on life jackets. The soft waves lulled him into a drowsy state where he imagined that he drank from the waters of Lethe, so he would never have to remember his own odyssey to the islands of wind.

Several hours may have passed or at least that's how Nick perceived it, when he felt the bow tip. He assumed the tide was beginning to shift and opened his eyes to stars that blinked in no special pattern. He conjured the floating stars into the shape of Caterina's face, that she was somewhere in the stars and she would always be there for him, no matter what his miserable life was like on this planet. Nick couldn't blame Caterina for rejecting him because it was the worst mistake of his life. He had no right to think that she would take his pathetic self back into her new life on an idyllic island in the *Mediterraneo*, no less. Suddenly, Nick felt chilled drops on his forehead. Caterina knelt beside him smiling, her hair hanging loose, pressed to her sarong, her breasts visible through the cotton cloth. He knew this was not a dream as she wrapped herself around him. He felt the cold sting of her wet shape for a second but soon their body heat took over, as they nested in the same wooden boat on the same cobalt blue sea under the same dazzling stars.

# Bibliography


Bettina, Elizabeth. *It Happened in Italy: Untold Stories of How the People of Italy Defied the Horrors of the Holocaust.* Nashville, Tennessee: Thomas Nelson, 2009.

Clark, Lloyd. *Anzio: Italy and the Battle for Rome—1944.* New York: Grove Press, 2006.

D'Este, Carlo. *Bitter Victory: The Battle for Sicily, 1943.* New York: Harper Perennial, 1988.

Konstam, Angus. *Salerno 1943: The Allied Invasion of Italy.* South Yorkshire, England: Pen & Sword Books, 20007.

Morison, Samuel Eliot. *Sicily—Salerno—Anzio: January 1943–June 1944.* Urbana and Chicago: University of Illinois Press, 1954, 2002.

Parker, Matthew. *Monte Cassino: The Hardest-Fought Battle of World War II.* New York: Anchor Books, 2004.

Wolff, Walter. *Bad Times, Good People: A Holocaust Survivor Recounts His Life in Italy During WW II.* Long Beach, New York: Whittier Publications, 1999.

# Acknowledgments

My gratitude to my first reader, my wife, for having faith in me during this four-year process. Thank you to Michael Mirolla, Publisher and Editor-in-Chief of Guernica Editions, for publishing this novel as part of the *Essential Prose Series*, works which deal with "the pleasurable understanding of different cultures." My hope is that this novel will lead to better understanding of the Italian American experience during World War II and the survival of Italian Jews during the Holocaust. Martha Hughes, a novelist, was most helpful with advice on the first draft through an N.Y.U. program. Editor/novelist Maxine Swann read the entire work and provided many useful suggestions. My good friends, Richard Holz and Pete Smith, carefully read and critiqued the chapter on boating and military history, respectively. Thanks also to the members of MCCA for their support of all my literary endeavors.

# About the Author

Frank Polizzi was the editor of *Feile-Festa,* a multicultural, literary arts journal (http://www.medcelt.org/feile-festa/). He worked as a Vista Volunteer in New London, CT, an English teacher on the original staff to reopen Townsend Harris HS at Queens College and the Head of Reference and Instructional Services at the Hormann Library of Wagner College. His poems and stories have appeared in *The Archer, Bitterroot, Electric Acorn* (Dublin Writers), *Mudfish, Paterson Literary Review, Wired Art* and others. The Guild of Italian Actors (GIAA) accepted his one-act play, *By the Light of a Barber Pole* for its reading series in 2009. Two years later, Finishing Line Press published *All Around Town,* his poems exploring Sicilian American roots and experiences in NYC. Several chapters/stories were published from his novel, *A Pity Beyond All Telling,* and one of them was shortlisted for the Fish Prize in Ireland. In 2015 Bordighera Press published *A New Life with Bianca,* a story of a young man's love for Bianca, told through a series of sonnets in English, Italian and Sicilian. His new novel, *Somewhere in the Stars,* made the 2014 Long list of the UK publisher, Lightship, for its "First Novel Prize" and was accepted for publication by Guernica Editions in early 2016. Frank died on August 23, 2016.

FSC
www.fsc.org
MIX
Paper from
responsible sources
FSC® C100212

Printed in January 2018
by Gauvin Press,
Gatineau, Québec